Robin Van der Kellen

1 The Dutchman 3, Three Musketeers   By Susan Eddy

Ezra August

2 The Dutchman 3, Three Musketeers   By Susan Eddy

Chapter One   Riding Up Front

"Right this way, Mr. and Mrs. Van der Kellen." The porter led them up the stairs into the train.

Robin caught him by the arm. "That's Mr. Van der Kellen and the widow of a good friend of mine, Mrs. Miller. If you would, please."

"Oh. Oh, I do beg your pardon. I made the assumption. You have two cabins, side by side. Right here. Number 1 and 2. Is there anything else I may do for you? I'm so sorry," the porter said.

"Well, you can move her things to room #1. That would be a good start," Robin said.

"Right away. Right away, sir."

Elizabeth met eyes with Robin as the porter dragged her trunk to the hall and up the first cabin of them all. "Perhaps you will permit me to sit in here while my things are moved." She sat on Robin's sofa, adjusting her skirt around her.

"Of course. Of course." Robin stood back against the small bar, keeping out of the way of the porter.

The porter returned to grab her gowns from the closet and carried them next door. "I beg your pardon again."

"I know this is terribly awkward for you. I apologize." Elizabeth looked up at Robin beside her.

"Not at all. I have been in far more awkward situations with you." Robin smiled and waited with folded arms as the porter returned for more things.

Elizabeth laughed.

The porter made two more trips and then excused himself.

Robin and Elizabeth both started to speak at the same time and then Robin bowed a bit to differ to her.

"Do I make you that uncomfortable? I should not have come," Elizabeth said.

"No. Of course not."

The train suddenly lunged as it started forward and Robin fell directly toward her. Both of his hands landed on either side of her on the back of the sofa.

Elizabeth looked up at his mouth and throat so close to her. She laughed.

Robin collected himself. "I beg your pardon. Wasn't expecting that."

"I had best get to my cabin and settle in." Elizabeth slid toward the open door and stood up.

"May I escort you to lunch when they ring?" Robin straightened his jacket and his posture.

"Delighted." Elizabeth nodded and scurried to Cabin 1.

Robin heard her door close so he closed his own.

"May I confess something to you? There is something troubling me. I had to surprise Adam with my leaving this morning. He thought we had another day before I left. I feel badly that perhaps he did not get enough time to say goodbye to me." Robin moved his teacup to the left side of his plate. Then he moved his water glass.

"Why did you ensure the departure was so brief?" Elizabeth asked.

Robin crossed his legs beneath the table. They sat at a table for two while the other side of the train had tables for four. Most seats were occupied and the dining car was rather loud with conversations.

"Afraid to break his heart?" Elizabeth mused. "He has a wife to console him now."

Robin nodded. "He's been through a lot, in so few young years. I don't know how he… What you do not know, is that he and I were involved in a case in Amsterdam and it became very dangerous. He was assaulted and kidnapped for a time. And then they came after us at my brother's home. Adam and I had to shoot them."

Elizabeth sat back very seriously. "Adam shot a man?"

Robin nodded.

"You taught him about weapons?"

"I taught him to shoot and reload, yes. He became very dependent on me. I mean, at the same time he was coming of age. He was yelling back at me. He was sleeping with Zoey. He came into some money in the form of a bonus from me and a dowry provided by my brother."

"So financial independence afforded him the right to yell back at you. He knew he was born to be a gentleman and his status was his right. Why were you yelling at him?"

"He slept with Zoey," Robin admitted.

Elizabeth smiled. "Really? How did you know?"

Robin laughed. "I know. Trust me. Seen enough young men levitating from their first. And when confronted, he bragged about it to me."

"I'll bet that was a surprise. He was so infatuated with you."

"May I continue with this story? If it does not offend you."

"I hang on every word. Do go on."

Elements of their meal were set between them and Robin paused until they would have confidentiality.

"At first, he said he did it because I told him he should try a woman. But then he fell in love with her. Wanted her for himself. And she was infatuated with him from the day they met. I was afraid I pushed him into marriage."

"Sounds more like she pulled him into marriage." Elizabeth smiled. "Even if he did start this with Zoey for the wrong reasons, if they fell in love, you can still be credited with bringing a young couple together. And now they are a wealthy couple, set for life. You ensured that as well. I've known Adam for many years. For him to play the valet for years, never letting on that he was a Rothschild, there's an inner strength in him we knew nothing about. I imagine that came out when he had to shoot a man. He's done whatever he had to for survival before."

"Yes. Brilliant summary. You're right, of course."

"Why did you tell him he should try a woman?" Elizabeth leaned forward to whisper. Then she smiled at Robin's raised eyebrows.

"Mrs. Miller, I am not sure that you are aware that there are men who prefer the company of other men, and I would imagine perhaps women who prefer the company of only women," Robin said very quietly and slowly.

"Do you think for a moment that my household was not aware of Adam's attractions?" Elizabeth toyed with him. "It was only that he got on so well with the maids that we thought there was hope for him. That is to say, a hope that he could find happiness with a woman someday. You don't think I'm one of those women, do you?"

Robin nearly choked. He brought his napkin to his mouth. "I beg your pardon, no. Not at all."

"I have heard women talk that sometimes a young man is taken to those certain kind of establishments, for his first time. Were you suggesting that to Adam?"

"My what an imagination you have," Robin said.

"You would have paid for your valet to have his first?"

"Mrs. Elizabeth, please do not continue for I do not wish to blush in public while dining alone with you," Robin said quietly.

"Yes of course. It is quite all right for a lady to blush in public, especially with a wine glass in hand," Elizabeth said. "Change of subject then, sir. You're starting a horse business?"

As the ladies remained in the dining car to pass the hours until dinner, the men retreated to the smoking car.

"Mr. Van der Kellen is married to my best friend Marie. I've just come out of mourning and wanted so much to visit with Marie. They've just had a first child, whom I can't wait to meet."

"Oh, your best friend's husband. Is it proper to be traveling alone with him then?"

"I'm not alone. I have all of you here," Elizabeth proclaimed.

"Of course, darling. Perhaps you should stop dining alone with him then. You may both dine with us."

Robin held a tobacco cigarette to his mouth and puffed. He set his brandy snifter down on the bar top.

Beside him, some men gathered, ordered their whiskeys or gin and tonics.

"And you sir, your wife is that beautiful blonde?" One man said.

Robin smirked and set his cigarette down on the edge of an ash tray. "Forgive me for correcting you. I am traveling with the widow of a friend of mine, taking her back to visit with my wife for a time."

"Well. Wish my wife had friends like that."

By Susan Eddy

Robin let out a breath. "Regretting my decision to have her leave the mourning gowns behind. Would that have made you men stop snickering?"

"How long is your travel, sir? Constitution holding up?"

Robin walked away with his brandy snifter. He took a seat by the windows instead.

One of the men brought his ash tray to him and sat across from him. "It's just that she's so beautiful. Or haven't you noticed?"

"Am I to endure two more days of this? Or shall I get rude and tell you to go fuck off?" Robin said plainly.

That stopped the laughter.

The seated man across from Robin offered a handshake. "Beg your pardon, sir. May I introduce myself?"

Robin returned to the dining car for dinner that evening, speaking French with some fellow travelers. Elizabeth overheard as he passed and gave a nod to her, overheard them discussing steamer travel.

She dined with her lady friends who only talked about children or knitting, while her eyes watched Robin make new friends so easily. He spoke French so fluently.

Following dinner, Robin was invited to a card game in the smoking car. Elizabeth was forced to endure more feminine conversations.

Robin returned to their car and after a moment of thought, went forward to Elizabeth's cabin to knock on the door.

She rose from her bed, pulled on a robe and went to pull open the pocket door just a bit. "Robin?"

"Are you well? Checking on you before I turn in," Robin said.

"Yes. Thank you. I'm fine."

"Good night, then," Robin stepped back.

"Good night, Robin."

He returned to his cabin right beside hers and opened his pocket door. Inside, he found his lamp lit and a carafe of brandy on the bar. He removed his jacket to hang it beside his top hat on the wooden pegs beside the door. He began tugging at his necktie to loosen it. That's when he found the letter on a tray beside the brandy.

He poured himself a glass and sat down to open the folded paper. He turned it to see the initials in the wax stamp. EM.

That made him let out a long breath.

Dearest Robin,

It is with my most sincere apologies that I write to you words I could not speak. I never meant to offend you so. If only I had known about Adrianna, I would never have asked. And I do not know why I so foolishly thought there was any possibility you and Marie would have accepted.

How you must have suffered on that train ride home, so soon after surgery. I suffered also, knowing that it was because of me you had to endure such torment.

I was so full of elation when I first saw you. You were so exotic, confident, and European. I cannot be the first woman who's heart you have broken. I want you to know, you have nothing to worry about with me. I have learned my lessons in life. I will do nothing to disgrace you again.

I long so to spend time with Marie again. I never had so much fun as when I was with her. I was free of cares then. Perhaps with Marie I can recapture a bit of that. And I cannot wait to see your darling Frida.

I know you can never fully forgive me. I do hope we can become friends.

Sincerely,

Beth

Robin took a good drink of brandy and sat back on his sofa, looking at the bunk beds before him. He would be alone that night, as the train rocked along the track toward Bridgeport, the city Marie was born in.

In the morning he knocked on Elizabeth's door. He heard her footsteps inside and then she slid the pocket door open.

"Good morning, Beth," Robin said.

"Good morning to you, Robin. I don't...don't think you ever called me Beth before. I'm delighted," she said.

"I thought before I escorted you to breakfast that we would talk," Robin said.

"Yes, of course. Do please come in?" She stepped back from the door and sat down on the far side of the sofa. "I heard your boots on the floor over there. I knew you were stirring."

Robin entered just inside the door and left it open, though with Elizabeth's cabin being the first one, only the engineer or conductor would be walking past. He smoothed his hands down his jacket. "You heard me pacing then. Rehearsing my opening statement."

As Elizabeth looked up at him in the doorway, she couldn't keep her eyes on his. She had to take in his crisp white collar and the way he tied his green silk ascot into a perfect bow. She observed the shine of shell buttons on his vest and the fact that the buttons of his trousers were hidden beneath a flap of fabric. His thighs looked muscular in slim trousers. His fancy ankle boots had a perfect shine to them.

"Elizabeth."

Now she met his eyes. "Waiting for your statement."

That made Robin shake his head. "Feel sorry for the man you finally do set your sights on."

Elizabeth stood up. "Why is that?"

Robin backed into the hallway, laughing. "That look you just laid on me, well you'd best be mindful of who you turn that on."

"How so?" She joined him in the hall and closed her door behind her.

"If he doesn't have half my experience with women, he's going to burst into flames on the spot." Robin gestured down the hall to the rear of the car.

"No harm in looking, I always assumed," she said as she walked in front of him. "Given that he has no valet at present, amazing how well dressed a man can be. What happened to that statement you were to make?"

"Moot point, I believe."

"I should warn you, the ladies on the train think that we should dine with another couple from now on."

"Oh?"

"Keep us from sharing confidences." She waited at the crossing to the next car for Robin to take her hand.

Without hesitation, he did take her hand and stepped across before guiding her over the gap.

"Come on. What were you going to say? You won't get to in the dining car," Beth said.

"I'm sorry we left so abruptly from you that day. I didn't want Marie to see in my face, that I'm as human as the next man, and not entirely so noble as to never meet temptation," Robin said.

Beth looked at him. "Well don't worry. You will never have a chance with me again." She entered the dining car.

"Mr. Hudson, a word if you will."

"Of course, Mr. Hobson." Adam followed him down the hall and into the library. He was surprised to see Hobson close them in by shutting the pocket doors.

"Mr. Hudson, you have the door locked to the room beside yours. The maids wish to make the bed," Hobson said.

Adam shook his head. "I won't have anyone inside that room for a time."

"And what explanation am I to give the maids?"

"Well, none, of course. I don't have to explain anything I do in my own house," Adam said.

"Of course not, sir," Hobson said. "Frankly, it has your mother a little concerned as it is to her the maids are complaining."

"She said nothing to me," Adam said.

"She wouldn't." Hobson met his eyes and saw that Adam teared up again. "I do apologize. You are not ready to let him go just yet."

Adam turned away and wiped his eyes.

"A dear friend to you, and he had to leave rather suddenly to escort Mrs. Miller," Hobson said.

"He saved my life, Mr. Hobson. More than once. And I his. It is a bond you cannot understand. And there is nothing untoward about it," Adam said.

"Then the bond is still there, young Mr. Hudson. You can let the bed linens go," Hobson said.

Adam ran a hand up through his hair and then fished a brass key out of his pocket. "Here then. Be done with it."

"I am sorry, sir. But you are making the right turn," Hobson said.

"I just didn't want his room disturbed. That's all," Adam said.

"Of course, sir."

"Mr. Hobson, all my security in the world is gone and I'm on my own. And worse than that, I have two women to look after while I feel this," Adam admitted, his back to the man. "I'm on my own at this. Every dawn delivers another torment that I don't know what to do about."

Hobson took a deep breath. "May I tell you what I think?"

"If I can bear it. No one tells me the truth anymore. It's yes Mr. Hudson this and yes Mr. Hudson that. What is it? Really?"

"I find you to be a very strong young man to have survived all you have. I find you to be behaving honorably. Admirably. Allow yourself time to absorb what you have done. Allow yourself time to heal from old wounds. And enjoy all your fortune and your pretty wife."

Adam straightened his posture. "Anything else?"

"Many eyes are on you these days. I suspect you know that. You've had a fine example of how to be gentleman. You just have to do as he would."

Adam reached for his pocket watch and let out a long slow breath. "If you don't mind, we will have these talks from time to time."

Robin entered the café and immediately saw Elizabeth sitting at a table near the windows, her blonde hair illuminated in the sunlight and rose-colored dress extending beyond her table into the aisle. Robin nodded to the host and passed, pulling off his top hat. He pulled out the chair across from Elizabeth and sat down. "Good news. I have purchased a horse and carriage."

"Purchased? Oh I'm sorry to be such a bother. I wondered if we would be here for days waiting for someone to come for us," Elizabeth said. "I hope you don't mind. I bought a few gifts for Marie and Frida."

"Oh?" Robin looked beside her and beneath the table. There were wrapped packages. "How kind of you. I believe they will fit all right."

She laughed at first. Then she stifled it. "You're serious. Oh my. I should have asked first."

"No. No. This is very kind of you. I am far too practical," Robin admitted. He glanced up at the waiter as a first course was served to him. "Thank you. Would you be so kind as to bring me a brandy? A carafe please?"

"Yes, sir. My pleasure."

"You ate already? I'm glad. Most women have an aversion to dining alone," Robin said. "Are you up to a long ride? We would make it to Chester before nightfall."

"Absolutely ready for adventure. Already accomplished dining alone in a café. My first time, I would have you know." Elizabeth indicated her empty wine glass to the waiter. He refilled for her as he set Robin's brandy snifter down on the table with a carafe of plenty of brandy for him. "Chester? That's along the river, isn't it?"

"A horse can go no further than about 35 miles in a day. We'll rest it overnight, then cross the Connecticut River on the Hadlyme ferry, and continue on the next day." Robin began eating his meal of roast duck and potatoes. "You've taken a stagecoach across the river before?"

"Yes. With Edward. We had to get out of the carriage for the crossing."

"This will be the same for us," Robin said. When the waiter returned, Robin looked up at him. "Would you pack a meal for us to take with us? Whatever you think travels well. We shall be taking supper on the road to Chester."

"Yes. I can do that for you. For the two of you? Shall I include a flask of this brandy for you? Water? Fried chicken?"

"Sounds wonderful. Whatever you think is best."

Robin's new Brougham was shiny hunter green with black top, two doors, windows between the driver and the cabin, and an attractive Hackney horse to pull it. Elizabeth's trunk and Robin's cases were strapped onto the boot. Her packages were inside on the backwards facing seat.

"Do you mind if I ride with you up front? I'd like to see a bit of the countryside," Elizabeth said.

"Of course, but you'll tire up there. You let me know when you need to recline inside," Robin agreed.

"Are you going to keep this? It's attractive." Beth began searching for how to climb up over the front wheel up to the driver's seat.

"I could always use another, especially for wet weather. I don't have an enclosed carriage at home, actually." Robin bowed and set his hand on the axel of the front wheel. "I want you to put your left foot firmly here. You will set one hand on my shoulder and grab the handle with your other. Lift right foot up to the top of the wheel when you can. Don't worry, I have the brake on."

"Oh." Elizabeth considered this. Then she stepped forward and reached out to Robin.

He pulled her hand onto his shoulder. "Hold on tight. Up you go."

She managed to step up and pull herself up.

"Left foot up into the carriage. Hold on," Robin coached. "Keep moving forward."

"Whew. Won't be doing that again any time soon." She held onto the seat and moved across to sit on the other side, smoothing her skirt and coat beneath her.

Robin collected the reins and popped up onto the wheel.

Beth looked down at the seat, realizing there was just enough room for the two of them side by side.

"Changing your mind?" Robin questioned.

"Not at all. I just never sat up front before," she admitted, looking around.

"Keep your right hand on the railing beside you there." Robin rose and slid onto the seat beside her. "Forgive me."

"Not at all." Elizabeth looked ahead, over the horse at the road beyond. "You know the way?"

"I have done it before." Robin reached down with his left hand to release the brake. "Walk on now." He tapped the reins, holding them in his right glove.

"Do you think in time, in the country, that I could learn to do that?" Elizabeth asked.

"We will get out of the city and I can let you drive," Robin said.

"No. Really? I couldn't." She laughed.

"The horse does all the work. I'll teach you," Robin said. "But not in this traffic." He looked over his shoulder and pulled them out away from the storefronts. Many other carriages and wagons traveled with and against them.

Elizabeth held onto the rail on her right side. She glanced far down beside her at the cobblestones below.

Robin pulled her back to the center. "Don't do that."

"Do what?"

"Lean too far out. Someone might be riding by. You might fall out," Robin said. "Sorry about that."

She smoothed her coat down. "It's all right, Robin. You know it really amazes me how many talents you do possess."

"Driving a carriage?" Robin asked.

"Keeping a foolish woman from doing stupid things," Elizabeth corrected.

Robin burst out laughing.

"Eat this with my fingers?" Elizabeth looked down at fried chicken in the unfolded napkin on her lap. "You won't tell anyone, will you?"

"Only if you fail at it miserably," Robin said.

She laughed unexpectedly, sitting on a rock beside a stream where their horse was drinking.

"Here." Robin offered her the flask.

"Drink from that? What is it? Brandy?"

"Don't tell me you never had brandy before."

She took the flask, sniffed it and then took a drink. She cleared her throat after. "I've had better." She handed it back to him.

Robin sat down on a rock across from her and took a sip. "Jesus. So have I. It's like turpentine."

She laughed. She daintily picked up a chicken leg with two hands and tried taking a bite.

"What else is there?"

"Um. Biscuits. Peaches. Something in a tin. Let me look. Pastries," Elizabeth said.

A gentleman came out of the inn and held a hand to catch the harness of Robin's horse. "Welcome. Would you be needing a room for the night, sir?"

"Yes. Two rooms, if you have them," Robin replied.

"Absolutely. Welcome. I have several rooms. How many besides you and your wife, sir?"

Robin set the brake. "I am Robin Van der Kellen. With me is the widow of a good friend of mine, Mrs. Miller. I am bringing her to visit with my wife for a time."

"I beg your pardon, sir. Two rooms, of course. My boy will tend to your horse after we get your bags inside. We have no other guests tonight. How would you like to choose your own rooms?"

"No need. Give the best to Mrs. Miller. And I am not particular." Robin climbed down and opened the door for Elizabeth. "Why don't you go on inside and select your room?"

Elizabeth took his hand and climbed down. "Thank you, Mr. Van der Kellen." She looked up at the porch of the Inn. Lamplight came from inside where a woman was at the door.

"Right this way, honey. Let's get you a room and then offer you a glass of wine, a bath, anything that we can get you."

Beth picked up her skirts and carried one small bag with her toward the porch. "Just leave the packages in the carriage. Don't need them tonight."

Beth entered the inn, glancing at the simple fireplace and furnishings, the candlesticks on the mantel. She followed the woman through and up the stairs.

"I would say this is the nicest room. Do you like a canopy? This one has the nicest canopy."

"I like this one just fine. May I see which room you will put Mr. Van der Kellen in?" Beth asked.

"He's not your husband?"

"Oh no. He's my best friend's husband. I'm a widow. I've just gotten out of mourning," Elizabeth explained. "Show me the other rooms for him."

"I am so sorry, ma'am." The woman let her look into each of the other rooms.

Elizabeth returned to hers. "Put him in the one with the big bed on the end. He will like it best."

"Of course, ma'am."

"Could I trouble you for a hot bath? I've been on a train for two days," Elizabeth said.

"Come right this way. Right back here."

"Mr. Van der Kellen, may I intrigue you to a glass of whiskey with me?" the inn keeper asked.

"I would be delighted." Robin folded Connecticut paper money into the man's hand.

"This is too generous. The rate is only fifteen dollars," the man said.

"Keep it. Traveling season is nearly over. Until Christmas, you may not see another," Robin said.

"Are you a rich man then?"

"Well..." Robin shrugged.

The man smiled and pocketed the money. "Of course, you are, or you wouldn't be traveling with a carriage so fine." He picked up the whiskey and poured two glasses. He handed one to Robin.

The wife came down the stairs and insisted, "Albert, you can't let them stay here if they're not married. What will everyone in town think?"

"Martha, sit down. She's a widow."

"Then why did she want to know what bedroom to find him in? And chose the one with the biggest bed?"

"Martha, sit down."

Robin drank a gulp of whiskey. "My wife would thank you to hide me in another room then."

"Your wife?" Martha said.

"I told you. The widow is a friend of his wife's. He's just escorting her to their home," Albert said. "Calm down, Martha. Where is she?"

"She's taking a bath upstairs. Said she was going to bed after," Martha said. "And you will not be going to her room tonight, sir."

"No ma'am. Like I said, I have a wife and child at home. I am married," Robin insisted.

"Martha, you should see what he paid us before you make him sleep on the porch." Albert laughed.

Robin had another drink. "Pretty cold on the porch tonight, ma'am."

The couple looked at each other.

"No funny business tonight, mister," she insisted.

"You have my word," Robin said. "Mrs. Miller is likely very tired. She's not used to such a long carriage ride preceded by two days on a train. She's accustomed to a very...plush life in New York. Whatever she said, I'm certain she did not intend it that way."

By Susan Eddy

Martha finally relaxed. "Are you hungry? Would you like some pie?"

"I...I would love some. If it is not too much trouble," Robin said.

"Have a seat."

Robin and Albert sat in the parlor. Albert refilled his glass.

"What is your line of work, sir? Or are you a gentleman?" Albert asked.

"I am a lawyer and I own a horse farm in Canterbury," Robin said. "I am returning home from trying a case in New York."

"A murder case?"

"Inheritance." Robin shook his head.

Robin was shown to a room down the hall on the lower floor. His two cases were inside already. With a bit of a smirk and the remainder of that bottle of whiskey in his hand, he entered his room and closed the door. He set the bottle and glass down on the chest of drawers. Then he removed his jacket and hung it over the bed post. He began to untie his ascot. "Home to you tomorrow, Marie."

His room was adequate, with a feather bed, oil lamp lit, place to set his suitcase. He laid out a clean shirt and underclothing for tomorrow. Then he removed his boots, vest, and trousers. He set his stockings in the boots. Then he pulled out a sleep shirt for the night. He sat on the bed to finish his whiskey.

Chapter Two Amazing Creature

In the morning, Robin heard Martha and Albert getting up and sounds from the kitchen just down the hall. He slid out of bed and dressed. He repacked his suitcase. And then he carried his two bags out to the parlor to set them near the front door. Then he strolled into the kitchen.

"Mr. Van der Kellen, good morning, sir. Please have a seat. May I get you a cup of coffee?" Martha said happily.

"Good morning, Ma'am." Robin was taken aback but sat near the fireplace just the same. "Might you see that Mrs. Miller is awake?"

"I will, sir. Here. Coffee. Cream and sugar there." Martha set them on the table for him. "Breakfast will be ready shortly. I'll knock on Mrs. Miller's door."

"I apologize for any impression I may have given evening last," Robin said.

"I apologize, sir for assumptions. You are a gentleman. Please, enjoy your coffee." Martha went upstairs.

Robin was alone in the kitchen, and stirred cream into his cup.

Albert entered through the back door. "Ah, you are up, Mr. Van der Kellen. My son is hitching up your horse. He was just feeding it a bit of grain and hay for the road."

"Thank you. I'm very grateful," Robin said.

"Wouldn't you rather sit in the dining room?"

"The fire is nice and warm here. I'm quite at home in the kitchen," Robin said.

"Bundle up when you do leave. It's turned chilly this morning," Albert said.

"At least it is not snowing," Robin said.

"Indeed."

Elizabeth took a look out the parlor window. Then she joined Robin at the kitchen table. "Frost on the ground. Can we travel in that?"

"We need to get moving if we're to make it home before dark today. Have a hot meal." Robin rose from the table. "I have to check on my horse."

She watched him exit out the back door and the woman enter from the hall.

"Ah, Mrs. Miller. Good morning to you. Did you sleep well?" She brought a plate of breakfast and set it before Elizabeth.

"I don't think I have ever slept so well as last night. I was so exhausted," Beth said. "And your feather bed was the most wonderful thing after that train ride."

"I'm so glad you enjoyed it. I'm sending a warm blanket with you to keep you inside that carriage. You'll be needing it."

Down the road, toward the ferry, Elizabeth opened the window between herself and Robin.

"What is it?" Robin questioned.

She pushed the blanket out through the window. "Wrap up in this. I can see your breath out there."

"Are you sure? You need this," Robin said.

"I'm fine in here. You're in the wind. Take it."

"Thank you. Close up that window." Robin wrapped the blanket around his legs and up to his waist. He tugged his leather hat down and secured the wool scarf about his throat.

Robin drove the carriage onto the ferry, put on the brake, and then climbed down to secure his horse to one side rail. Some boys ran forward to block his wheels with cobblestones. Robin gave them a few coins.

The ferry driver's wife opened the door for Elizabeth to emerge. "Best if you wait out here, ma'am."

"Thank you." Beth slid hands deeply into her coat pockets, into the fur lining and looked up at the cliff on one side of the river.

"Where are you heading?" the woman asked her.

"To Canterbury, hopefully by tonight." Elizabeth watched Robin leaning against the horse.

"Hot cup of coffee then? And one for your mister?"

"Yes. I'll bring it to him." Elizabeth accepted two cups. She glanced up at the clouds overhead and then approached Robin. She offered one to him.

"Thank you." He wrapped his gloved hands about the tin cup and had a drink.

"Robin, should we stay somewhere along the way? There's weather coming in," Elizabeth said.

"Ahm."

"Don't feel that you must get safely back to Marie on my account. We will get there today or tomorrow," Elizabeth said.

"We will try for tonight," Robin said.

The ferry slowly drew them across the Connecticut river.

Rain came down hard and slowed travel. Robin finally called it quits for the day when an inn presented itself in a small town called Salem. There were several taverns, a blacksmith shop, a number of homes and churches.

Robin climbed down and tapped on the carriage window. "Wait here."

Elizabeth wiped at the fog inside the glass, to see Robin walk into the inn. Cold rain poured down. She waited.

In another moment, Robin returned with an umbrella and two men. The men went to the back of the carriage for the trunk and bags. Robin opened the door for Elizabeth. "Let's get you inside and get dry."

"Oh Robin, I'm so sorry. You've been out in this for hours. You did the right thing pulling in here." Elizabeth ducked beneath his umbrella and hurried onto the porch with him.

Then he turned back toward the carriage. He mounted the buckboard again and drove the carriage around the building.

Elizabeth shook the rain off her coat and went inside.

"Give me your wet clothing, sir. I will get it wrung out and hang it all by the fireplace in your room."

"Yes, miss. Thank you." Robin closed the door to his room to undress, towel off, and pull on dry underclothing, trousers and shirt. Then he passed the wet things through the door to the maid. He returned to dressing with a pair of stockings, his ankle boots, vest and jacket. His riding boots, he stood beside the fireplace to dry them. He toweled his hair as much as possible, but there was no use. He would go downstairs as he was. It was only five o-clock and already getting dark out. The dining room was lit by oil lamps and the fireplace.

Elizabeth was the only one in there. She watched Robin enter, pull out the chair in front of her, and sit down holding his right shoulder with his left hand. "Oh, you must be miserably cold. Here. Hot chowder. Tea."

"Wonderful. Thank you, Elizabeth."

"Mr. Van der Kellen." The inn keeper entered. "I'm told you are headed for Canterbury. You best find another route than Governor's Road. There's a bridge out, North of here."

"Oh? Thank you for that. Perhaps I should make for Norwich then and turn North there," Robin said.

"I would advise that. Where's that maid? She did not put bread on the table."

"She is tending to my wet clothing, I believe." Robin spoke up for the girl.

The man left them.

Robin picked up a spoon with his left hand and got into his crock of chowder. "I wonder if I should go to the tavern next door and seek more information about roads around here." Robin's hair was wet as if he'd just stepped out of a bath.

"Wouldn't that be dangerous for you alone? To visit a tavern here?"

"Me? You're not serious. You wouldn't last five minutes."

"You're teasing me," she realized.

Robin smiled. "You had better stay here. I can't have you telling Marie that you went to a tavern with me. You'd be the only female there who wasn't waiting tables or dancing on them."

She burst out laughing. "You've been to such places? With dancing girls, have you?"

"Me?" Robin only smiled.

"Hmm. Perhaps it is not the travel conditions that tempts you to the tavern then. I won't tell Marie," she said.

"No. I have never seen a drinking establishment in this country that holds any temptation for me other than brandy," Robin admitted. "Not compared to the ones in Europe."

"Really? Edward frequented some in France. What sets them apart?" Elizabeth asked.

"You do not know?" Robin looked at her. He glanced around to see that they were alone in the room. "It's not the gambling. It's not the music. It is the women."

"Are you saying European women are prettier?"

Robin laughed this time. He shook his head. "I'm saying there's nothing you can see from a dancing girl in Boston that you can't see on the street. So don't charge me for looking."

"I believe I'm proving how naïve I am, getting married so young as I did," Elizabeth said. "What have you paid to look at?"

Robin's mouth opened.

"Ah ah." She laughed. "Does your wife know?"

"She knows, all right."

Elizabeth put her hand over her mouth and nose and giggled.

Hearing whispering and a bit of a commotion in the next room, Elizabeth slipped from her bed to slip quickly to her door. She opened it a crack and then wide open to stand in the hall. She tied her robe closed about her.

Robin had a maid in his arms and was trying to extract her from his room.

The girl looked in horror at Elizabeth. "Ma'am, that was not what you think. I am so sorry. All a misunderstanding, Mr. Van der Kellen."

"Your tongue in my mouth was a complete misunderstanding." Robin put his hands on the hips of his trousers.

"So sorry, Ma'am. I didn't know he was…that you were…so sorry." The maid scurried past Elizabeth and down the back stairway.

Robin didn't even bother to do up his untucked shirt at that point. He just turned his eyes on the blonde.

She just smirked and shook her head. "Boy, are you in trouble."

Robin stepped forward. "I am not in trouble. I…was attacked."

"Did you enjoy it?"

"I didn't have time to enjoy it."

"Did she just enter your room?"

"To bring my wet clothes back to dry by my fireplace," Robin said.

"And her what ended up in your mouth?" Elizabeth teased. She reached forward to bring the two sides of his shirt back together. She meant to tease him further but caught a glimpse of the scar on his upper right chest. Then she pulled his collar back to observe it better.

Robin straightened up properly and stepped back from her, buttoning his shirt.

"Get some sleep, Robin, and have no worries. We'll have you back to Marie tomorrow."

"Good night, Elizabeth."

"Good night, Robin."

"I think Elizabeth may be most comfortable in Adam's old room on the end. That entire wing will be only women," Marie suggested.

"Any room will do for me. I am a surprise and I do not want a fuss over me," Elizabeth insisted, still looking about at the overhead baskets in the kitchen and the worktables.

"Come, let's have a look at it. June, grab her bag there. The men already put her trunk up in the end room." Marie led Elizabeth and June to the stairs and up. They passed Robin coming down.

"Beg your pardon, ladies." He backed against the wall on the landing as they passed him. "Is there anything else I can do?"

"Please check on the house, Robin. I'm not sure what Miles had them do with the construction while you were away. He was in charge outside," Marie said.

"I will do exactly that, my love." He gave Marie a kiss as they passed.

The women continued up and around into the servant's wing. "June is in here. Marta here, and Louise is in this one. So if you need anything they are right here."

Elizabeth entered the room on the end, knowing it was Adam's room. She looked around at the simple bed, dressing table, armoire, fireplace and the windows on either side of the house. She looked out at Robin crossing the circle drive below, toward the new house construction. "This will be just wonderful."

Robin wore no hat, and so his hair shined in the sun and he shaded his eyes against it with a hand as he spoke to the men out there.

"Pull her trunk over here and unpack her dresses, if you would," Marie said.

"I can handle that," June told her. "We'll stock this up with firewood for the night as well."

Marie took Elizabeth's hands. "What else do you need?"

"Oh. Nothing. This is fine, really. How about a tour of the house? I hope Frida won't be napping much longer. I can't wait to meet her," Elizabeth said.

"Come on. I'll show you everything," Marie said.

June moved over to glance out the window where Beth had been staring. Robin was down there talking to Miles and the Mohegan supervisor. Then she went about the unpacking of dresses.

Marie gave her friend the tour. "Miles is in this room. Jasper here. This is Frida's nursery but she's sleeping down in the kitchen to be watched by Marta and Louise. I turned this room into a dressing room like you have."

"Oh yes. That room is perfect as it is too small for anything else. Oh look at this nursery." Beth wandered into that room to look over the cradle and the baby clothes.

"How have you been lately? Are you ready to go back into society?" Marie asked.

"Not yet. Haven't even thought about it until I saw Adam's story in the papers. And then I thought I might see you and Robin at the trial. That's why I went," Elizabeth said.

"I'm so glad you helped him in the trial, Adam. He's such a sweetheart." Marie led her into Robin's room where Elizabeth was drawn to the crossed swords over the fireplace and the windmill clock.

"How did he end up with his pretty little wife?" Beth turned and looked at Robin's mahogany 4-poster bed.

"It was a surprise to us all. Robin said he caught them kissing. And it was a passionate kiss. They were embraced and everything. He warned Adam that he had to be a gentleman. The next thing we knew, Robin said he could tell they had slept together. Adam was being very evasive about where he had been. Robin tried to force Adam to marry her, but then the shooting happened. Zoey was afraid of Adam then," Marie explained.

"Robin told me about the case and the shooting. I'm shocked one so timid as Adam could do such a thing," Beth said. "Or that anyone could be afraid of Adam."

The two women sat down in the high-backed chairs by the fireplace.

"Robin had taught him how to shoot here last fall. In Amsterdam, Adam purchased a pistol of his own. We brought Zoey along with us when the king summoned Robin to the palace," Marie said.

"I can't wait to hear your side of the palace story. It must have been amazingly beautiful." Elisabeth glanced over at the VOC trunk at the foot of Robin's bed. There was a wool blanket folded up on top. A pair of his shoes was beside it, shoes she'd seen him wear in court.

"Oh yes it was."

"You must have some of the latest fashions from Europe. I can't wait to see them," Elizabeth said. "Men are wearing shoes like that? With a heel that high?"

Marie looked over her shoulder. "Oh I can't wait to show you the gowns from Amsterdam and London. I never thought I would get Robin to shop in London. Thought he was violently opposed to the English. But he bought two suits there, very English looking. Those shoes were from Paris, though we did not go there. He got those with a new suit in Amsterdam, made by the same tailor he always used. Remember the suit with tails that he wore in New York? That tailor made more for him. You know, he puts secret pockets inside for Robin? He has a dagger pocket."

"A what? I have to see that."

Robin walked with Miles and Jasper to see the area marked out for the barn. He pulled his scarf about his neck and his coat closed against the breeze. "This is just the location I had in mind. This is wonderful. Is this going to be big enough?"

"Well, my thinking was we could extend it further that way. If we close in this part before snowfall, we can work with this through the winter and add on in the spring," Miles said. "Hope that is agreeable with you. It seems getting enough men to help will be the problem."

"I will see what I can do about that. I can certainly go farm to farm and gather up all available hands for particular days. I will exert my influence, such that is," Robin told them. "Otherwise, I think your judgment is the wise one. May I just ask a favor of you men, as it comes to Mrs. Miller?"

"You have nothing to worry about with us," Miles said.

"I know I don't. I just want to say that she is a widow and she is Marie's friend. And...do not be alone with her. Always be certain there is a maid present. I will speak to them about this as well," Robin said.

"And yourself? You worried about being alone with the widow?" Miles asked.

"Of course not," Robin said. "When will the lumber all be here?"

Jasper and Miles looked at each other.

"Lumber is being delivered tomorrow and the next day. Thought Jasper and I would also take your wagon and pick up more tomorrow."

Robin pointed down the hill. "You see all the oak trees down there? I know some of my neighbors have the log strippers and sawmills to make the support beams out of those trees. Will that help?"

"Well, hell yes. If all we have to haul in is the planking, we're in business. It's the timber supports that we can only haul so many. They're too big and heavy." Miles said.

"And tall," Jasper added.

"Saddle up my horse, Jumper, and I'll take a quick ride to a couple neighbors before dark. Tell the women I'll be back for supper," Robin said. "You can take any of those trees that will suit you."

"It's a plan," Jasper agreed.

"If I can get every available man here this Saturday, and they can cut timbers out of those trees down there, can we raise a barn this weekend?" Robin asked.

"This weekend? Maybe next weekend too," Miles said.

"Press on. For all we know snow can come next weekend. All right? That's all I'm saying," Robin said.

"We need ten good men and timbers. We will get your barn basically up and framed," Miles said.

"Ten men."

From inside the kitchen, commotion from the native encampment could only mean one thing. Marie got up and went to the window.

Miles got up from the table and opened the door. "He's returned, all right. I'll help him with that fine horse."

"The Indians are cheering? For Robin?" Beth sat down at the table with little Frida in her arms.

"Have you known any group of people who didn't?" Marie questioned.

"I'll get the table set," Marta declared.

Louise began dishing out beef pot roast in celebration of their new quest, potatoes into one bowl, carrots into another. Gravy went into two decanters. "June, get the rolls out of the oven quick."

"I got em," June said.

"Let's bring Frida into the dining room, before the commotion in here," Marie suggested. She brought Elizabeth across the hall into the grand dining room. There was a highchair ready for Frida at one end. Marie and Elizabeth on either side of it.

But Elizabeth looked to the far end which would soon be filled with Robin and the men in excited conversation about the neighbors who would be coming on Saturday, including Constable Poole and his son, the Lee boys, Sharp and his boys, and most importantly Mr. Phillips and his log stripping and planking equipment.

"It will all begin at dawn. Even the Mohegans are coming. Oh and the women are coming with food for the workers, for the whole weekend. Some will be going home but those with longer travel will be boarding up at the Lee's and the Sharps'," Robin said. "We can pile a few up into the empty two rooms on our side."

"How many hands in all, do you expect?" Miles asked.

"I count about thirty," Robin said.

Miles cursed in Dutch. "You do hold influence."

Robin flipped open his napkin into his lap. "Get markings out there for the timbers, where you want them. With this big of a crew, we shall split up into teams and more than one timber shall go up at once. Then we join them. Your call of course."

"I can handle it. Totally ready for this." Miles reached for the basket of rolls, selected one and passed it to Robin. "Ladies, on Saturday, we are raising a barn."

The men cheered.

Marie looked to Beth and said, "Just what I always wanted."

"Don't you knock it, Marie," Miles said. "Once we win some championships and build a show ring here, we will bring the competitions here, to Canterbury. We'll put this place on the map."

"I appreciate your enthusiasm, Mr. Champagne," Robin said. "Let's start with a barn."

"And then a trip to Boston to select horses," Jasper added.

"And New York. And Kentucky," Robin added.

"Let's set up a jump course," Miles suggested. "We should like to see you demonstrate your lovely horse."

"I'll have to train him," Robin said. "Then I would love to. He's only jumped things in the wild."

Robin, Miles, and Jasper walked out the following morning, their breaths showing in tiny clouds.

"Perfect spot for your new home there, on the edge of the hill. You can build a new entry drive to it, off this one. Unobstructed view of your whole valley below from that house," Miles said.

"Yes. Remember the terrace and balcony off the back of Robert's house? I'm having the same here," Robin said.

"Given that and the layout of the hillside, the new barn will go over that way, right there. Winds mostly come from the west here, and you don't want the barns upwind of the house," Miles said.

"Oh? Good thinking. I never minded the smell of a barn, myself. But the ladies...." Robin said.

The men laughed.

"Looks to me as if your home will be almost dried in before winter," Jasper commented. "Stone masons are almost done. Windows can start to be set in place."

"Yes. I made one addition of a solarium on the west side. But that can be added on later," Robin said. "I have enjoyed the balcony off my bedroom so I'm adding that on also to the upper west end, a private master suite balcony."

"So what else does that little Adam have in his mansion? Unbelievable how rich he is now," Miles said. "Bout half as rich as you, I heard."

"He is set for life, and safe," Robin said. "His father's influence on that mansion is bothering Adam. He's replacing furniture. But as for what his house has that I want in mine...the solarium to extend the seasons a bit, a lovely bathing room that Marie will enjoy, a modern kitchen..."

"Is that staff taking to Adam? Will they listen to him?" Jasper asked.

"I believe so. Only one there from when Adam was a child, the butler. The man seemed to be kind to Adam," Robin said.

"Adam's wife is lady of the house. How does that sit with his mother?" Miles questioned.

"His mother wants grandchildren. I think she'll be welcoming to Zoey."

"Mr. Hudson. You do not remember me from your childhood, do you?"

Adam looked at the butler at length. "A little bit."

"I was here all along, you know?"

Adam met his eyes and stepped back. "What do you mean?"

"I was here from the time you were born until today. I am very happy that you returned and saved your mother, if I may say so," Hobson said. "You were called Teddy, then."

Adam smiled a bit. But he stepped back further.

Hobson held up a hand. "Sir, this is your home. I just hope to continue to work here, as long as your mother lives. I would hope you would not put an end to my service to her."

"I don't mean to," Adam said.

"Did you think as a 14-year-old boy you could evade everyone? I knew you were at the Millers. I saw you there," Hobson said. "Many times."

At that, Adam had to sit down. He ran a hand up through his hair and looked away. "How so, given that you never exposed me?"

"I never let on that I knew who you were. I suggested to Jonas that you should be sent to school. You would be a more beneficial employee. It would benefit everyone." Hobson sat down too.

"Why didn't you tell my father?" Adam said into his hands. "Oh my God," he sighed.

Hobson waited until Adam looked at him. "Beat you to within an inch of your life. Stopped him from continuing, I did. My pay was held for some time. I searched for you for weeks. It was only by chance that I ran into Jonas at the mercantile. Saw you in the back of his wagon. Thinner. Pale. Short hair."

"Why didn't you tell my father?" Adam repeated. "Or my mother?"

"I knew what they did to the other boy," Hobson said. "It was my opinion that the boy being older than you, may have taken advantage of you. You returning here with a wife seems to have proven me right."

"Lucas should not have been killed for me," Adam said.

"No, he should not have been. As long as you were at the Millers, I kept eyes on you," Hobson said. "It was only when you left suddenly, that I realized your mother would have no way of finding you ever again. She was never more delighted than the day your letter arrived. I look after this family, Mr. Hudson. I will until I die."

Adam nodded. "I wouldn't want to keep you from it. Am I to trust you now? How do I know you are not loyal to my father and not my mother?"

"If I was, you would have been dragged out of the Millers," Hobson said. "Seven years ago."

Adam wet his lips. He sat back further in his chair and looked at the butler.

"You were safe there and I knew where you were," Hobson said. "I hope you know in some very small way that I was looking after you. Your wife is lady of the house now. She does not speak English. How do I seek her orders?"

"I need your help hiring us a translator. I would prefer a woman of similar age to Zoey, someone who can teach me Dutch and Zoey English," Adam said. "I believe the way to smooth this over with my mother is to explain to her that Zoey is only 19 years old and does not know the customs here. Zoey would prefer my mother continue as lady of the house and instruct her on what is to be done."

"You got all that from her without a translator?" Hobson asked.

"Mr. Van der Kellen used to translate for us."

"That must have been awkward," Hobson said.

"You have no idea," Adam sighed.

"I will smooth this over with your mother. The house is yours. What would you have me do?"

"All that furniture in my father's room must go. I'm shopping for something else soon. The shit gives me nightmares," Adam blurted out.

Hobson actually laughed. "I shall have it removed when your new things arrive."

"What room in the house can I convert into an artist studio?" Adam asked. "The one beside the solarium would be ideal."

"Then take it. It is only a guest room."

"It has excellent light. Plus, I could always take an easel into the solarium and paint there," Adam said.

"Are you an artist, sir? I do recall your drawings as a child," Hobson said.

"Well, I will be. I also need a painting instructor. Translator first. Find me some women for us to interview and the sooner the better," Adam said.

"Is it very difficult, the communication with your wife?"

Adam winced. "Anything complex is impossible. Ik spree keen beetje Nederlands."

"In just a few months you are picking up the Dutch?"

"Trying to. What other concerns of the house are there? What are the staff saying about me? About Zoey?" Adam asked.

"Your wife is much adored. She is lovely and sweet. You, they are curious about. They do not know you as I do. They admire the way you handled yourself in court. Of particular, the way you kept your sisters from being called as witnesses. Even with how rude Gerard Rothschild was to you, you protected your sisters from his wrath. That goes a long long way here. You are a true gentleman."

"Gerard and Bernard are not to step foot on this property. In fact, no one is to step foot on this property that you do not know and approve of. If in doubt, I am to be asked."

"Yes, sir."

"My mother is to be protected," Adam said.

"Will your wife continue to sleep in your room? She can take the room on the other side of yours," Hobson said.

"She is sleeping with me. She barely speaks any English. She needs my comforting," Adam explained.

"And you have just married."

Adam smiled. "You can have the valet tend to my suits the night before. It's a simple adjustment. Then there is no need to disturb us in the morning."

"Of course, sir. I am very much impressed with you. Not that the opinion of a butler counts for much. But all on your own, you have become a fine young man. And you were brave in court."

"I do value your opinion, of course," Adam said. "I have the example of Mr. Van der Kellen to aspire to, remember?"

"And what an amazing creature he is," Hobson said.

Adam looked at him. "Yes."

Chapter Three   Barn Raising

Miles got up from the table and fastened a bright yellow scarf around Robin's upper left arm.

"What is this?" Robin held out his elbow and watched him tie it on.

"You understand rank, do you not?" Miles said.

Robin looked up at him. "Excuse me."

"Jasper, Mr. Sharp, and myself will have red ribbons. You alone will have the yellow. There's going to be some thirty work men out there, heavy lumber carried about, and all these men in dark clothing. Red ribbons lead teams of workers. We need to be easily identified," Miles explained.

"And me?" Robin asked.

"You own the place. We need to make damn sure nothing happens to you," Miles said, to a burst of laughter from around the breakfast table. "Of course, you have final say in anything. That ribbon might well as be made of gold."

"Shall I wear it about my head then?" Robin questioned. "Like a crown."

"No." Miles laid his hand on Robin's shoulder. "Now, ladies, we will set up a table just outside the kitchen door. When those wives arrive with the food, you are to inform them that no lady goes beyond that table. None of you. We're raising a barn out there and that's men's work. It is too dangerous to have any of you go beyond that table. Now on the table, we will need water, cups, food to be grabbed up and taken. Keep it supplied all day long. Marie is in charge of the women. Any questions from the ladies?"

"You want coffee out there, don't you?" June asked.

"You bet we do. If you could please," Miles said.

"You'll take a sit-down lunch?" Louise asked.

"We will not. We will work until it is too dark to work anymore. Men will be taking breaks in shifts. You could have a few chairs out here, but mostly they're going to eat on the run," Miles said.

"What about the Indians?" Elizabeth questioned.

"Ma'am, Mrs. Miller, from my understanding the Mohegans have a couple men who speak English. Those men will translate for the others who work best as their own team. We plan to use most of them to fell the trees down below, and drive horses to haul the timbers up to the build site. Robin's instruction is that they are to be fed and given water or coffee just like any other man out there," Miles said. "Don't you be frightened by those Indians. There are plenty of us gentlemen to look after you."

"Can we use your Friesians?" Jasper asked. "To pull timbers up the hill?"

"Yes. Both will do it. Klootzak will pull like you wouldn't believe but you really have to swat him hard to get him to move," Robin said. "Genie will do it. And together, they can haul the largest of trees up the hill."

"I've handled Friesians before," Miles said. "Won't be using Jumper. Don't you worry."

"No. That animal is not for pulling," Robin said.

"In fact, if you want to exercise him, you can supervise the mission from horseback today," Miles said.

"Some of it, perhaps," Robin said. "Klootzak may be more likely to pull if I'm beside him with a hand on his throat latch."

"I don't want you with a hand on him, sir. You can ride beside him, but that animal will break your arm when he bolts and you know it," Miles said.

Robin raised eyebrows. "You may be right." Then he indicated Marie at the other end of the table. "Did she tell you not to let me do anything?"

"I hear horses outside. Time to go to work," Miles said.

Robin pushed back his chair. "Chicken, Miles."

The gentlemen hurried to get out the back door. Robin would meet each man and boy with a handshake. Then he strolled to the group of Mohegans to shake their hands as well. He would then ride on the wagon with Mr. Phillips down to the oak grove to indicate the trees to come down.

Marie looked about at the women. "Marta, your number one job is Frida. Beth can help you with her. Beth, I'm so sorry about this. I don't know what today is going to be like. Chaos most likely."

"I find this exciting. I've never seen a barn built, or anything else for that matter," Elizabeth said. "Perhaps I can help with something. I would be delighted to feed little Frida."

"Stay in the house or behind those tables."

Daylight was just breaking and there were already twenty neighbors and a dozen Mohegans ready do to work. Miles sat on Jumper to lead

Klootzak and Genie down the hill. He found Robin down there, and dismounted to hand the horse over to Robin.

Mohegans were chopping the first tree down, and they all stood behind with Robin and the horses when it crashed down. Then quickly with axes, the Mohegans went in to remove the branches.

The two Friesians were connected to the tree by chains. They were to pull the trunk into the tree stripper/timber cutter. And then Robin rode in beside Klootzak to howl in Dutch at him, "Lopen op! Gaan! Gaan!"

Miles and Jasper each swatted one of the Friesians on the rump with their switches, and once Genie took off forward, Klootzak bolted. The giant log was pulled forward and up onto the tree stripper, almost dragging the wagon it was on.

"Stoppen! Stoppen!" Robin halted the Friesians.

And the men cheered. The first timber was about to be cut.

Miles and Jasper moved the horses out of the way.

Mr. Phillips went to work, taking charge of the timber operations.

Elizabeth came down from upstairs to report, "Robin is riding his horse up the hill. Men are digging where the barn will be."

Mrs. Sharp said. "They'll have the first timber up the hill in an hour. You'll see. Right now they'll be digging the timber holes. Let's bring more coffee out to the girls. You grab this, Mrs. Miller."

"Oh? This coffee pot too?"

"Use the towel. It's very hot."

Elizabeth grabbed a towel and picked up the coffee to follow Mrs. Sharp out the kitchen door.

Marie had June and three Sharp girls, one girl from the Lees all serving men from behind a row of tables. And these tables were made from planking on sawhorses with tablecloths over them. They had tin cups, tea, water, biscuits, sausages, cakes, and cookies all laid out for the men to come by and take what they needed.

The young girls all looked at the blonde Mrs. Miller. The teenage Jane Lee helped her with the coffee and poured it into waiting cups. "You're Mrs. Miller from New York, aren't you?"

"Oh? Yes. And you are?"

"I'm Jane Lee. I live over there in the white house. I knew Robin and Marie when he was sick and they needed help."

"Is that right? I heard about his illness. Tell me all you know, honey."

"Oh I know all sorts."

"Oh we have all day."

"Tell me about New York. I've never been to the city."

"Well, I shall have to speak to your mother about that. I'll be needing a companion on my trip home, when I go home that is," Elizabeth said.

"Really? I'd love to. But she'll never take me out of school," Jane lamented.

"We have schools in New York, fine ones for girls. Besides, I can tutor you on most anything," Elizabeth said. "Now, tell me about the first time you met Robin."

Robin Van der Kellen with the yellow silk fluttering off his left bicep, came riding his fine black horse up the hill from the oak forest below, into the circle to observe the teams of men digging post holes, men stacking lumber, and men unloading wagons. He glanced over at the house and smelled coffee and sausages. He rode toward the circle drive in front of the women's tables.

"What can we get you, Robin?" Elizabeth asked.

Robin gracefully dismounted in a long coat, riding trousers and tall black boots. His wide brimmed leather hat remained on his head. His horse remained diligently beside him. "Oh, cup of coffee, if you would. Oh and..." He reached into a bowl and grabbed up a sausage to eat it quickly. "Forgive me."

"You're working hard today, sir. You need sustenance." Elizabeth handed him a tin cup of coffee and a napkin.

Jane Lee handed him more sausages. "We have plenty, Mr. Van der Kellen."

"Thank you. Thank you, ladies." Robin gulped down his coffee and then remounted his horse with sausages wrapped in a napkin. He turned the horse to observe the work men. And he munched on the sausages.

"Robin." Elizabeth risked a moment beyond the table to hand a muffin up to Robin.

"Thank you. Best get back behind the line before Miles catches you." Robin rode his horse away.

The teenage girl swooned. "Nobody sits a horse like that. Isn't he wonderful?"

Elizabeth filled a cup of coffee for herself. "It is a very exciting day, is it not?"

Marie heard the cheering of men and hurried out from the kitchen to see that the first corner timber was set in place. Not a half hour later the second one was up and they began to join them to stabilize one end. "Well, it's a good thing we have a fine day for their work."

"It is a fine day," Mrs. Lee said. "Marie, you should sit down for a bit. You've been going since daybreak."

"If the men don't rest, neither do we," Marie said.

Mrs. Lee took Marie by the arm and whispered to her, "How do you know you're not expecting? You should rest, just in case."

"Maybe just for a few moments."

"You go on inside and chat with your friend Elizabeth. I have the table under control."

Hours and hours later, the men were roofing. Men were relaying roofing lumber up to the top and Robin was one of them on the ground. It was about then that Miles saw Robin double over and hold onto his right shoulder.

Miles hurried forward. "Take this for him. Robin, step aside. Robin…"

Van der Kellen stepped out of the line of men. "I'm all right. Just sore."

"I see that." Miles moved closer to him and took him by the arm. "Robin, you're too important for manual labor. You don't want to be in a sling tomorrow, do you? I have another job for you. I need you to walk back to a distance and tell me how straight the walls look to you." He pointed toward the house. "You have good eyes. We need you for this."

"Very well then." Robin looked up at the tall barn looming over them. Timbers were up, cross braces were up, trusses were in place, and roofing was going on. But the walls were not fully planked up yet. Darkness was coming down.

Robin walked toward the circle drive and the house. There was a bon fire in the middle of the circle, burning the scraps and barks from the oak timbers.

Marie stepped around the table and met Robin near the fire. "Nice barn, Robin."

"Yes. Amazing what they've done today." Robin turned around to look at the barn. "It is straight. It is perfectly straight. He just sent me over here to you."

"Because you hurt your shoulder?" Marie asked.

"A bit."

"Need some laudanum?" Marie slid beneath Robin's arm and wrapped hers about his slim waist.

"Need a bottle of brandy, but not yet."

"No. Not yet."

It was well after dark before Robin, Jasper, and Miles came into the house. All three of them sat down at the kitchen table, dirty, exhausted, and almost too tired to eat anything, though Louise and Marta set plates of food before each one of them.

"How's the encampment?" Marie asked them.

"They're fine. Grateful for all the food you set out for them. They thought they had to cook tonight, but now they do not," Miles answered. "Oh your last two guest rooms upstairs on this side are about to be filled with about ten fellows. They'll be in shortly."

"They'll be needing to eat then." June got up from the table and returned to the kitchen with the other two maids to dish out more food.

"Poole and his son are taking my room. I'm bunking up with Jasper," Miles said. "Jasper's sleeping on the couch cushions from your room."

"Oh?" Robin said. "That's kind of you both. Really."

"Well, amazing what got done today. More to be done tomorrow," Miles said.

Michael Poole and his son Travis entered then, taking seats at the table.

"Eight more?" June asked. "Shall we set them up in the dining room?"

"Yes. I'll help you," Marie said. "Just set the plates and silverware here. We'll have them fill up and carry it into the other room for themselves."

"Line them up," June said.

"You all right, Robin?" Miles questioned.

Robin let out a sigh. "I'm just sore and exhausted."

"That's a big barn. Very impressive," Poole said.

November 15, 1841*

Mr. Hudson,

Your presence is requested by invitation of Mr. Bernard Rothschild, to dine with him at Pied a Terre, five o-clock on Friday, November 19.*

Please do be prompt.

Sincerely,

Mr. Sinclare, Valet to Mr. Rothschild

Adam had taken the letter off a silver plate and read it. Hobson remained standing over him. Adam raised blue eyes up to look at the butler over the breakfast table. Adam held one finger to his lips and glanced at his mother and wife at the table. He replaced the letter on the plate and picked up his coffee cup. "Mother, is it too soon for you to get out of the house and do some shopping with Zoey on Friday?"

"Shopping? I can't be seen shopping now," Lena Rothschild said.

"I just thought for Zoey's sake it might be acceptable," Adam said.

"One of the maids can take her. What does she need to shop for?"

"Um, evening gowns. She only has the pink one," Adam said.

"Oh yes, a lady must have half a dozen or so. She cannot wear the same one to the same venue again. Yes, I will see that a maid can take her on Friday."

"Excuse me, darling. I have to talk to Mr. Hobson for a bit." Adam left the breakfast table and followed the butler into the kitchen. Cooks and maids scrambled to clear the breakfast plates and leave them some privacy in the room. "Did you read the letter?"

"Of course not, sir."

"Read it." Adam waited while Hobson opened and read the letter. "Would you recognize the writing of Mr. Sinclare?"

"Yes. This is his hand." Hobson refolded the letter. "Do not go. At the very least, do not go alone. What is to come of this for you?"

"Nothing for me, that much is certain."

"I shall draft your rejection then," Hobson said.

"But wait a minute. Why would Bernard want to see me?" Adam asked.

"Why did you want your wife out of the house that day?"

"Ha. I didn't. I wanted my mother out of the house that day," Adam admitted.

"Take your wife shopping. I shall draft your rejection letter."

"No. I will be there. But I will hire some security," Adam said. "Get me those men who took me to the factories. I'll pay them well to make certain nothing happens to me."

Zoey slid into bed with her husband and snuggled up against his back, wrapping her arm around his arm and chest. "What is this trouble? This bad letter?"

Adam let out a breath. "I did not want to worry you." He rolled onto his back to wrap his arm around her. "Bernard wants me to meet him at a restaurant."

"Mean Bernard?"

"Yes. My cousin."

"Do not go," Zoey said.

"I was going to hire men to go with me," Adam said. "I should just say no."

"Why go to him? Why?" Zoey asked.

"I'm curious. I wonder what he wants."

"So?" Zoey rose up on her elbow to look at him. "He will be mean to you again."

"I will have Mr. Hobson send my regrets in the morning."

"Good. Do not go."

Adam entered a furniture store with Zoey on his arm. They were both finely dressed, Adam in a Dutch suit and Zoey in a dress from London. With him being twenty-one and her only nineteen, they drew immediate attention from a salesman who strolled toward them.

"Good morning. How may I help you, sir?"

"Good morning. My wife and I are looking for a new bedroom set, Mister..." Adam extended a hand.

The salesman shook his hand. "Mr. Andrews. And what may I call you, sir?"

"Mr. Hudson."

"Hudson? Hudson?" Andrews mused. "Oh. The Rothschild inheritance?"

Adam frowned. "I see you read the papers."

"And I can see why you are looking for fine furniture then. We have many fine bedroom sets upstairs. Would you come this way? I'd be happy to show you what we have or acquire for you anything we do not have."

Adam met eyes with Zoey. "Lead on then, Mr. Andrews."

"Right this way. May I ask you, what are your tastes? We have many fine sets from France, the very latest styles. French, English, Italian...."

"Italian," Adam said. "Let us begin there. I am half Italian, after all."

"Right this way." He brought them through living room sets toward the stairs.

"Wait? What is this?" Adam stopped them at an ornate golden chair with blue silk cushion. It had carvings in the back with inlayed stones of lapis and amethyst. The arms were gilded with the paws of tigers.

"This was found in India. Said to be an emperor's throne," Andrews said.

"Mark it sold. I'm taking it," Adam said.

"It's very expensive. Are you sure you don't want to...."

"Mark it sold," Adam insisted.

Andrews gestured to other assistants in the room and indicated the chair. "There is a table that came with it."

"I want that as well."

"Oh delightful. Get the table with this as well. Set them aside for Mr. Hudson."

Up the stairs and into another layer of displays, the salesman led them toward the Italian section. "This is the Cortina sleigh bed, recently acquired from Cortina, Italy. Made of honey walnut and marble inlays, it is sure to be the statement piece for your home that you are seeking.

One thing to keep in mind, however, without a canopy the winters may be chilly for such a bed."

"There are two fireplaces in the room. I think we'll be very happy in this. I mean, with this," Adam said. "Do you like this one?"

"I love it," Zoey said. "We can have?"

"We can have anything you like," Adam said. "Do you have wardrobes and chairs to accompany this? How about those?"

"Those right there would be lovely in the same room with this magnificent bed."

An assistant came to whisper to Andrews while Adam and Zoey examined the bed more closely and the marble inlays in the head and foot.

"Might I suggest this rolled desk also in honey oak. It will complement the bed, even though it is Dutch."

"Dutch? Yes, I need that. Zoey is Dutch, you see?" Adam said.

"I shall need to start tagging all of these. I'm going to need some help," Mr. Andrews said. "Mr. Hudson, would you like to see more Indian antiques? I am told we have a chaise lounge and some candlesticks. Oh and some chests."

"I would. After we decide on these, of course."

As they walked back downstairs, something on the far side of the lower room caught Adam's eyes. "What is that?"

"It is not assembled yet, but it is an ancient Indian hand carved swing, sir. We are reupholstering the swing cushion in..."

"In silk from India, of course," Adam said. "Lavender silk, with gold thread. I want that in my solarium. Do you have anything to go with it? Anything with elephants on it?"

"Why, yes we do. Some vases and oh and this unique table, with feet that look like those of an elephant."

"Oh I love that!" Adam declared. "I want that too."

"You've been on the grand tour then?" Andrews asked.

"Not yet. But anything Indian reminds me of a very good friend of mine."

"You are that rich young man from the Rothschild fortune, aren't you?" Andrews asked.

"You see that man waiting patiently at the door? That's my butler, Mr. Hobson. He's going to pay you for all of this. I just want to let my wife stroll around and pick out anything else she likes."

"Wonderful. May I get you some tea, sir?"

"Tea would be lovely."

Robin went down the stairs as early as possible, Sunday morning, just as the sun was coming up.

Miles and Jasper were at the table. June was pouring them coffee.

"Told you to sleep in, didn't I?" Miles looked up at him.

Robin sat down with them. "Couldn't sleep once the sun began to light the room. Dreamed of horses all night long, wonderful horses."

"Sorry for Marie." June set a cup down in front of Robin and filled it with coffee.

The men laughed.

"Well, I do not have to dream of Marie. She's lying beside me," Robin remarked.

"How's your shoulder?" Jasper asked.

Robin looked at them and up at June. He just drank his coffee. "Would you have any cream?"

"Yes I would." June went to the pantry to retrieve a ceramic of cold cream.

Travis came down the stairs and sat down with the men. "So glad you're back from Europe, Robin. I didn't get to hear anything about it yesterday."

"We have all winter for that. I'll tell you everything," Robin said.

June poured cream into Robin's cup.

He stirred it with his left hand and picked up the cup with his left.

"How is your shoulder, Robin?" Miles asked again.

"You know, I feel so grateful and so guilty with all these men building my barn. Of course I want to help," Robin said.

From the doorway, Constable Poole said, "The town judge is back. The town Indian agent is back. The nearest thing to a horse doctor, the only lawyer for miles....and you don't feel you're doing enough? You can sit your crazy Dutch ass down and watch your damn barn being built."

That broke up the room with laughter.

Miles pulled out the chair beside Robin and poured his own coffee from the pot June left. "He needs that arm in a sling, if only to keep him from doing something stupid with it."

"The stories about Poole do not disappoint," Jasper said.

"I know, right?" Robin nodded.

"I hear horses. Someone's here already." Jasper rose and went to open the door. "It's women, for those of you who were waiting."

"That'll be today's cooking." June moved past him and out the door.

"Your wife is here," Jasper said to the constable.

Robin looked at Poole. "Straighten your American ass up."

"Why is it you never married yet, Miles?" Poole asked.

"Just haven't knocked any of them up yet," Miles said.

That make them all laugh.

"Maybe you're lacking fortitude," Robin teased him.

"Or opportunity," Jasper teased.

Then women began hauling in bowls and crocks of food to set on the work tables and hang over the fire. Within all of that commotion, Marie and the other women dressed quickly and started down the stairs.

The men who stayed over the night also dressed and followed them down.

"I'll get you coffee or tea for now. Food will be outside on the tables in just a few moments," June announced.

When Elizabeth carried a bowl of ham sandwiches out, she was startled to find a dozen or so Indians standing just outside the house. She collected herself enough to set the bowl down. Beside her, Alice set down baskets of hard-boiled eggs.

Alice gestured to the Mohegans to come on forward and take what they wanted. She laid a hand on Beth's back and said into her ear, "Don't worry, hon. They ain't seen too many blonde women is all."

"Oh? Really?" Elizabeth back stepped.

"Let's bring out more. There's tons of food today."

In the parlor, Marie took Robin to the side and held onto his right arm. "Please do be careful today. You don't have to lift heavy things. There are plenty of men for that. You need to ride around on that horse and look resplendent."

Robin smiled. "All this time and you only think me a pretty face." He kissed her mouth.

"It's not just your face that looks pretty on a horse, darling."

"Oh? You like my English riding trousers, do you? They are comfortable. Are you working too hard? You have much help yourself, you know? Was someone minding Frida yesterday?" Robin said.

"Everyone wants to mind Frida. Don't you worry. There's a rotation of young ladies who can't stop cuddling her," Marie said.

And then it was quiet in the kitchen.

Robin looked over. "They're all outside. I better get to work then."

By late afternoon, Robin's good luck with weather had reached its crescendo in the coming of dark clouds. Men quickly sheathed up the wayward side wall of the barn and began working their way around the outside. All men were called to work on the outside first.

The log stripping crew had changed tactics to making planks from the other oak trees they had felled the day prior. Mr. Phillips had a crew of Mohegans feeding logs in and transferring planks around the barn to where they were needed.

The ladies had to pack up the tables and move food inside the house to the ballroom.

And then there was thunder.

Robin rode Jumper into the old barn and handed him over to Travis.

"I'll unsaddle him and bed him down. I fed the others already. I'll feed him next," Travis announced.

"Thank you." Robin laid a hand on his shoulder. "Appreciate it."

More thunder shook the farm.

Robin tugged his hat on firmer and hurried toward the new barn. "Get those men off the roof! Now!"

Miles looked up. "Still got men up there? Get them down now!"

And just as the sky let loose in a heavy down pour of rain, several men were climbing down ladders from the roof where they had been shingling. Robin and Miles jumped in to hold ladders for them. But everyone made it down and safely inside the new barn before the lightning.

There was a roof and two sides closed in. The other two sides had vertical timbers and cross bracing but nothing else.

"Have to stop making planks in this. Saw doesn't work when wood is wet," Phillips said.

"I don't wish anyone to work outside in this, or be injured due to wet lumber," Robin said. "I'm afraid most of the work may be done for the day."

"We can begin stalls, with wood not suited to wall planking," Mr. Sharp said. "Got plenty of that stacked inside here."

"And stalls built will help stabilize the open structure, should winds pick up," Miles said. "Jasper and I will lay out boards to indicate where the stall walls will be. Some men can bring stacks of lumber down to this end to get started. Some men can take your lunch now. Just be a wet dash across the courtyard."

"Miles, some stalls need to be larger than others," Robin reminded.

Miles nodded. "I'm planning for some large horses like yours. Don't you worry. You can't lift this lumber. Now go lead a group across to have a meal, Robin."

"There is too much lightning. We must all wait here for a bit," Robin said.

Mr. Hudson,

Mr. Bernard Rothschild requests to join you at his sister's home for dinner Monday evening. Do come at seven. Your wife is invited of course. Please send your acceptance.

Sincerely,

Mr. Sinclare

"Excuse me. You speak English, do you not?" Elizabeth paused on one end of the line of tables in the ballroom.

The Mohegan Indian, wearing white man's trousers and a buckskin tunic, turned to look at the rich woman. "Yes, ma'am."

"Can you tell me, why do they look at me that way? What do they say about me? Something bad?" Elizabeth asked quietly.

"They say you are beautiful. You and Van der Kellen's wife. You never saw an Indian before?"

"No. I have not," Elizabeth said.

"You have now." The man just took his plate away and joined his group sitting on the floor in the corner of the room.

"Making friends?" June startled her.

"Um...Trying to keep this table full."

"It's full enough. You can sit down now back in the kitchen. You came here for holiday, didn't you? Not to work," June said.

"My whole life has been a holiday. It is very satisfying to get work done," Elizabeth said.

"You've worked very hard these days. Thank you, for the help," June said, escorting her back into the kitchen.

Elizabeth looked around and found Marie with Frida in the dining room. Robin was sitting at the end in absolutely wet and dripping clothing. Water was puddling on the wooden floor beneath Robin and the other men.

"Beth, sit down. You need to eat something," Marie told her.

Alice Poole pulled out a chair to invite her. "Plenty of food here. I'll get you a plate, Mrs. Miller."

Elizabeth entered and took the chair offered. "Thank you. Please call me Beth."

Lightning stuck again and for a moment the room lit up white.

"That was close," Robin remarked. "Hate to have my barn torn down when it's hardly up yet."

"It will be fine. There's no wind out there and it's too wet for anything to burn," Phillips said.

Chapter Four   The Protégé

"This one," Zoey whispered to her husband.

"Are you certain? I like her too. You like her?" Adam said.

"Yes. Now."

Adam turned and walked across the office to where the young woman was seated across from Adam's father's desk. "Miss Hendriks, we would like to offer you the position. Sophie Hendriks, is your name?"

"Yes, sir, Mr. Hudson. Sophie Hendriks. I can start right away. May I move in right away?" the young woman asked.

"Yes, if you would like. Your salary will be fifty dollars a month, ample enough for you to get a room nearby, if you like. But of course you can take a room in our servants wing," Adam said.

"I'm new to New York. It is a little frightening for a girl to look for a room on her own. If you don't mind, I will move in here. I will just pick up my things at the boarding house and bring them back here tonight," Sophie said. "Did you say fifty dollars a month?"

"For your confidentiality," Adam said. "Yes."

Zoey strolled closer and took a seat near the desk. She said in Dutch, "We would love to have you move in. And do not feel that you will have to work all day and all night, of course."

"I would be delighted to work for you, Mrs. Hudson," Sophie said.

"One question for you, do you embarrass easily?" Adam asked.

"No sir. Not that I know of," Sophie said.

"Well I sure do. So does my wife," Adam said with a great big smile. "You will keep these translations private?"

"Oh, absolutely private. I won't tell a soul the things you need to say to each other, least of all those reporters outside," Sophie said.

"Reporters?" Adam's smile evaporated. He strolled to look out the window. "Not again."

"Why do you have news papermen out there?" Sophie Hendriks asked.

Adam opened the top drawer on the desk and pulled out a newspaper. He laid it on the desk in front of her. The headlines read, "Adam Hudson Wins Rothschild Fortune in Heated Court Case."

The girl's eyes skimmed the article. "That was you?"

"You heard about that?"

"Yes. Your lawyer was that bank robber catcher, the one who got shot on that case?" she asked. "The handsome one."

"Yes. He's a good friend of mine," Adam said. "Say nothing to the reporters."

"Of course, sir. You are going to learn Dutch, and Mrs. Hudson is going to learn English. When do we start?"

Adam reached into his pocket and pulled out two ten-dollar coins. He set them on the edge of the desk in front of her. "This is in addition to your salary. Get yourself some new clothes, whatever you need. Get yourself moved in upstairs. Hobson will show you to your room. Join us for dinner and finally I can have a conversation with my wife. Hobson, I have hired Miss Sophie Hendriks. She will need a room in the other wing. Will you show her the way?"

"I will be delighted," Hobson said from the doorway.

"Thank you, sir. And thank you, Mrs. Hudson." Sophie picked up the coins.

"Was your marriage arranged?" Sophie Hendriks asked.

"No, it was not," Adam replied. He and Zoey were dining alone that evening at a special table set for them in the solarium. The table was set for three, with white linen cloth, gold rimmed china, and crystal glasses. A floral arrangement and lit candles were in the center.

"Then how did you...court, if you could not speak to each other?" Sophie asked.

Adam smiled shyly, lowering his chin. "I met my wife in Amsterdam, visiting Mr. Van der Kellen's family there. It was love at first sight, I believe."

Sophie smiled and translated that for Zoey, who leaned over and put a kiss on her husband's cheek.

"How long have you been married?"

"Two months."

"That's wonderful," Sophie said. "I always hoped love was real. Anyway, I am here to work, am I not? Allow me to translate and not really be here, except that I do want to eat this. It looks amazing."

Adam smiled. "Please enjoy your dinner. Um… is she comfortable here? Is there anything in the home that she would like to see different?"

The young lady translated into Dutch, and continued for them through their conversation until they almost forgot she was there. Sophie found young Adam to be shy and empathetic. She found Zoey to be enthusiastic and completely infatuated with him. As she looked at him, she began to see why. The way he fussed with his hair when he searched for answers, the way he blinked blue eyes with such long lashes as he thought, he was extremely handsome. But there was something almost delicate about him. She couldn't place it yet.

"Everything is wonderful, especially now that the new bed is here. I love it," Zoey said.

"You do love it? You don't think me a bit crazy with new money? Spending too much at once?" Adam asked.

"Seems to me that you deserve it. What is that thing they are assembling over there? In the corner?" Zoey pointed toward the carved wooden item on the other side of the solarium.

Adam laughed. "Oh the swing? Do you have a word for swing? It is an ancient Indian one. They are making a new cushion for the part you sit on. It's silly, I know. But when we sit on it together, you'll get it."

Zoey laughed too. "Swing? Schommel? Now that is silly. Why did you buy that?"

"I did not have a lot of fun growing up. I will have it now," Adam said. "I know we talked about this before Robin left. My mother is still acting as lady of the house. You are entitled to that role. Are you still okay with this?"

Zoey laid her hand on Adam's arm on the table. "You must respect your mother. This is her home as long as she lives. And I have absolutely no idea what to do, if it was up to me. I have to be able to communicate better with the people before I can even learn what is to be done. Adam, I was marrying a valet and assistant to a lawyer. All of this is overwhelming. This is a little frightening."

Adam took her hand into his. "She said that? Frightening?"

"Yes, sir. Beangstigend."

"Ask her what is frightening? And I will fix it."

"All of the people, the reporters outside, the maids when I am not used to anyone helping me with such things. Inside the house, these things are all very nice of course. I'm afraid your butler or valet will walk into our bedroom at any moment," Zoey said.

"Zoey, they've been instructed not to enter our bedroom when the door is closed. Now you have that. I told them we have just been married and we will have our privacy," Adam said. "You have no need to clean or iron again. Let them do their work."

"What will I fill my day with then? I have no work, no children, and all this time." Zoey looked down.

"You can learn what it is you enjoy doing. Maybe it will be arranging flowers or embroidering or something else. What did you love to do as a young girl?" Adam asked.

"I had a garden. I grew flowers," Zoey said.

Adam indicated all around them. "Do anything you want in here. My mother never comes in here. She just wants fresh herbs for her food and flowers on the tables. Zoey, you can have children if you want."

At that, Sophie blushed as she translated.

And Adam added, "Sophie, I apologize. There are far more personal things we need you to translate than that."

Sophie nodded. "I will do so, sir. And these are your secrets."

"You've never been married?" Adam asked.

"No, sir."

"Well, until a couple months ago, we never did either," Adam said.

Sophie translated what he said and they all three laughed nervously.

Zoey had questions, "What about Bernard? I have seen more letters."

"He keeps inviting me and us to dine with him. He wants something," Adam said.

"Don't go. I don't want you hurt," Zoey said.

"I am not impressed enough or curious enough to meet with him." Adam looked up as his empty plate was removed by a maid and a dessert plate of cake was placed before him. The plate itself was a colorful flowered china with a gold rim.

Zoey and Sophie's plates were replaced with dessert as well. Conversations paused until they were alone again.

Zoey wasted no time in asking, "Adam, are you missing Robin very much?"

Adam sipped from a crystal glass of wine first. He set that down. "I am. The way he left, I think he means to not see me again for a very long time. Years, maybe."

"I thought you planned to visit in the spring? Have you left anything unsaid?" Zoey asked.

Adam shook his head. "When I suggested a visit he said we should do the grand tour, see more of Europe and such things. I didn't leave anything there except for $700 in the Norwich bank. I need to retrieve that."

"I'm sure he just means that he will be busy with his horse business," Zoey said.

"How much work can that be? Even if they start now, it takes almost a year to have a foal born and then another two years to grow his first horse. He intends to enter competitions with those horses. It sounds like an awful lot of waiting to me," Adam said.

"You think he means to not see you again? I do not think so. I think he cared for you very much," Zoey said.

Adam looked down at his chocolate cake. "Not as much as I." He took a deep breath. He met eyes with Zoey. "But I have you. And I have all this. I'm happy. I am. I just feel like he hurt me, the way he left. I get it. He had to. He has a wife and baby to get home to. It wasn't his fault."

"Your room in his house, he put you in a servant's room. Are you sure he thought of you as a friend?" Zoey asked.

"Oh I was a servant then, before we went to Amsterdam. I was just a valet and butler. In fact, June ran the house so I had few butler responsibilities. Even my valet responsibilities were restricted by Marie. I thought working together in Amsterdam on Wout's case, we became friends. I thought he began to see me, well as he put it, growing up," Adam said. "He is almost fifteen years older than I. At first, he often saw me as just a boy he had to look after."

"Why did you argue so? You didn't want to get married?" Zoey asked.

"Oh. Before I met you, I could never see myself married. But you came along and changed all that. As for our arguments back then…" Adam looked down and smirked. "From that moment he caught us kissing, he insisted we get married. He was worried about his reputation, that my behavior would reflect on him."

Ezra August

Adam strolled into an art gallery, looking about at paintings. He glanced back at the door to see his two security companions waiting.

There was a young man sitting in the back of the room, sitting cross legged in an armchair with a book in his lap. He made eye contact with Adam briefly. And then as Adam continued to look at paintings, the man began intensely observing Adam.

Most of the paintings were of landscapes, flowers, or bowls of fruit. They were oil paintings with various kinds of elaborate frames. And then Adam found portraits. He moved toward them, examining them from up very close to appreciate the brush strokes, and then standing back to take in the perspective and the arrangement.

The man got up from his chair then and set his book down. He was not much older than Adam, wearing a black suit of poor cloth. But what

Adam noticed about him was the purple silk vest paired with a red ascot tied about his collar.

"Painter?"

"Ah...no. Not yet anyway," Adam said.

The man glanced at the door where through the window he could see Adam's two security men. "Are you looking for a portrait artist?"

"In a way. You see, I make very good drawings. They look very much like the man I am drawing. But I want to make this. This is very impressive." Adam indicated the portrait of a young woman beside a sunlit window. "The way the brushstrokes convey the look of fabric and folds is amazing. How do I talk to this artist? Is he...is he in New York?"

"He is. I doubt he would give away his secrets," the man said.

"I wouldn't say give away. I will pay for lessons. I need lessons. And I'm not interested in painting fruit bowls," Adam said. "Where do I find this gentleman, or someone like him?"

"Who are they?" The man nodded his bell of black hair toward the door. "Police?"

"No. No," Adam said. "They just work for me."

The man circled around Adam, looking him over. "What are you interested in painting then?"

Adam changed his posture and looked at the art gallery man and the clashing of his red and purple. "I have portraits I need to paint before I can't see them anymore."

"Before I can't see them anymore..." He repeated Adam's words. "You said you draw?"

Adam nodded. He pointed toward the portrait of the woman. "Do you think the artist will teach me how to paint?"

"On one condition."

Adam and the man were face to face then, but not making eye contact. Adam felt very examined, studied. But he noticed paint around the fingernails of this gallery man. The man was only a few years older than Adam was, slender and had a rather deep and raspy voice.

"May I see your drawings?"

"They're at home. Who is the artist?"

"I will tell you who painted that portrait if you buy me lunch," the man said.

"Is that the one condition?"

"No, it is not," he said. "Your minders are not joining us. I would talk to you alone. There's a café on the corner."

Adam walked out first and spoke to his hired men.

The man from the gallery came out and locked the door. Then he started down the walk toward the café. "Come along."

Adam caught up with him.

The two men followed at a distance.

"After you." He held the door for Adam.

Adam entered the café.

"Table sir?"

"Yes, please."

The man followed Adam to the table where the host stopped him with a hand on his purple vest. "What are you doing?"

"Having lunch with a client."

"You don't have any money," the host said.

"Wait. What?" Adam blurted out.

"He's a friend of mine. He's just being a dick right now," The gallery man said. "Pierre, go back into the kitchen and bring out the special, for two."

"Somebody had better pay for this. I can't cover for you again," Pierre said.

"I'm paying for this," Adam insisted. "You two are friends?"

"That's debatable," the gallery man said.

"Are you cheating on us?" Pierre leaned close to the gallery man's ear to say.

"I wish."

"Oh shut up, Ezra." Pierre exited for the kitchen.

Adam sat back and remarked, "I'm buying you both lunch."

Ezra leaned elbows on the table. "So what is your name?"

"Adam. And you are Ezra. The painting was signed Ezra," Adam said. "You're the artist."

Ezra nodded. "You're a regular genius, Adam. What's with the two apes?"

Adam laughed out loud. "They just work for me."

Ezra laughed. "So you're that rich? They don't let you out without those two apes? Adam, what's your last name?"

"You read the papers at all?"

"Sure, just in case the police are looking for me," Ezra said.

Adam smiled.

Pierre returned to fill their coffee cups and set a bowl of fresh bread on the table. "The special today is lamb with potatoes and the soup is vegetable."

"Thank you, darling. Adam is buying you lunch too." Ezra picked up a slice of bread and started to butter it with a spoon.

Pierre met eyes with Adam. "They won't let me sit out here. Thanks anyway."

"Eat it in the kitchen then," Adam suggested.

Pierre looked to his friend. "Is he for real?"

"I'm getting that a lot lately," Adam said. "My name is Adam Hudson, gentlemen."

Ezra dropped his spoon on the floor. "Prove it. Give me a haircut after lunch."

"What?" Pierre said.

"He's the valet that just inherited a fortune." Ezra leaned under the table to retrieve his spoon. And then he handed it to Pierre. "A clean one, if you don't mind. Don't just wipe this off and hand it back to me."

"I'm not cutting your hair. It's absolutely perfect." Adam shook his head.

"That was the test. My hair is perfect today." Ezra ate the first piece of bread and reached for another. He indicated the remaining bread to Adam.

Watching Ezra eating the bread made Adam lower his eyes. Ezra's hands were shaking. "Are we going to talk about painting lessons?"

Ezra selected another slice of bread and buttered it quickly. He ate that quickly too.

"I can pay, of course," Adam said. "I have to make these portraits."

"Wouldn't it be easier to just hire a portrait artist?" Ezra asked.

"Not when the man I need to paint is in my head," Adam said.

Ezra studied him across the table.

"You said there was one condition. I'm guessing it's the money, and that won't be a problem," Adam said.

"Actually, it wasn't money. I can see you have that." Ezra sat back to look at him. "Here is the deal. You must let me paint you."

Their meals were brought to them and Pierre set another spoon down for Ezra. Ezra's plate was cleaned before Adam was halfway into his. This painter was thin but handsome in an exotic way with black wavy hair and fair skin. He had high cheek bones and thick eyebrows.

"I never met another Ezra. What is your last name?"

"I need to see your drawings before I agree to teach you anything," Ezra said. "I'm Ezra August. Formerly Ezra Arikan, but that name kept getting me beat up. And your last name was...Rothschild. What an awful thing. It just oozes snobbiness."

"And that got me beat up as well. Ezra, come to my house tomorrow. Bring paints and brushes. Show me how to stretch a canvas." Adam pulled out his leather purse and selected twenty dollars which he set on the table between their plates. "This is just for supplies. If you agree to teach me, I will hand you one hundred in gold."

Ezra looked up from the New York paper money. "I will bring everything you need, Adam. I will close up the gallery and gather those paints and brushes and such. You live where?"

"Number five, William Street," Adam said.

"William Street? You are wealthy," Ezra said. "What time tomorrow?"

"Ten o-clock?"

"Thank you for not making it eight o-clock. I paint all night. Oh and I should warn you I will probably be late. I have to take a trolley to get there."

"Late is fine. Just be there."

Ezra August sat down on the sofa in Adam's art studio, bouncing up and down on the cushion for a moment. He scanned around at large windows, purple velvet drapes, cushioned chairs. "What is this? The lady's parlor?"

"I think it was. My mother hasn't used it in years." Adam coveted a leather-bound book in his hands. He looked down at it.

"Live with your mother?" Ezra asked.

"My uncle was trying to throw her out into the street. I had to prove who I was to inherit the estate and now I look after her," Adam said.

Ezra uncrossed his legs and sat forward, gesturing to bring him the book with those slender fingers of his.

Adam reluctantly handed it over to him. "Be careful with this."

"You don't need to tell me that." Ezra opened to find it was fine art paper bound into a book. There were drawings, hundreds of them. He found poems and notes. He reached into his pocket for a long skinny box, and removed from this some gold spectacles. He put those carefully onto his nose and wrapped behind his ears. He examined more pages in the book. His head tilted.

Adam was examining the jars, pigments and oils arranged on the table. He picked up sable brushes to feel them with his fingertips. "No purple vest today?"

"This is the man you need to paint?" Ezra asked. "Are you in love with him?"

Adam shot him a look.

"Stupid question. Never laugh at my purple vest." Ezra continued to turn pages.

"Did you have any formal art training?" Adam asked.

"In Paris. Made a far better living there than I do here, that's for sure. Tourists would buy them before they were even finished." Ezra stood up. He set Adam's book down on the sofa. He selected some paper and pinned it to a drawing board on the easel. Then he handed a stick of charcoal to Adam. "Prove to me you drew those. Draw me and it had better resemble me. You've got ten minutes. I'd get started if I were you."

Adam took the charcoal and stepped up to the easel.

Ezra stood in front of him and posed with his chin up and a smirk on his full lips.

Adam hardly looked at the paper. He was looking at his subject, drawing, shading, blending with his fingertips.

"Are you using the whole paper? You are not making a little stick figure in the middle, are you?" Ezra said.

"Shut up and hold still. Lift your chin just a bit. There."

"Five more minutes," Ezra said.

"Six." Adam continued his portrait. His left hand was quite blackened. His right held the charcoal stick.

"You use both hands," Ezra observed. "You were taught that?"

"No."

"You had no lessons before today?"

"No. No training. Used to get smacked with a ruler for drawings in school," Adam said.

"So did I. Time's up." Ezra burst over to see the drawing. It was a bust of him, head and shoulders. And the face looked exactly like his, lit from the windows on the left. It had his sideburns, his long black hair with shine implied by omission of charcoal. "Holy Jesus. You're a natural. I never expected all this. Holy fucking Jesus God."

"I thought you were Turkish, Arikan. Aren't you a Muslim?" Adam looked down at his ruined hands.

Ezra handed him a towel. "Wet that in the bowl. Clean up your hands before it gets all over you. Stop wearing white shirts in here. Just stop it. Holy Jesus."

"You do speak frankly." Adam started to clean up his hands. It was the right cuff of his white shirt that was blackened.

"Art is my religion and my blood." Ezra was watching him. "You have perspective. You have observance of light and shade. You have composition. You used the entire paper. You did not outline. You even have each corner different. And it looks like me. I have mirrors you know. Enjoy them quite a lot. Holy fucking shit."

"There's a whiskey over there if you need one." Adam pointed.

"I might."

They both laughed.

"I have been drawing my wife but I can't show them to you," Adam said.

"I met your wife. They don't look like her?" Ezra asked.

"Oh they look like her, every inch of her if you get my point."

Ezra burst out laughing. "All right, normally I would begin with color mixing and basic brush techniques. For you, for now, I'm going to mix your paints. And then we're going to get Pierre to mix your paints because he's a wizard with pigments. Going to die before he's thirty because of it, but a wizard. Let's get a canvas stretched and primed for you. You get a painter's smock on. Roll up those sleeves. And your first painting will have to be what you see here in this room. That's just the way it is."

Adam picked up his book and selected a particular drawing of Robin Van der Kellen. "My first painting will be this."

"It's going to be hard to add color to a black and white drawing. I don't want to discourage you. Better to practice with what you can see."

"You think I don't see every color in his face? The green in his brown eyes. The blush on his cheeks. The shadow of his beard starting to grow in very late in the day."

"I'm just saying do not be discouraged if at first you can't make it look as you see it in your mind. The technicalities of oil paint must be learned. Layers. Transparency. Opacity. Blending. These things you must learn."

"I'm willing. I'm not afraid to muck it up at first. I'll get it."

"Yes. I believe you will."

"This has to dry?"

"Yes. This prepares and shrinks the canvas tight making a perfect surface to paint on. We made two. You'll start one tomorrow," Ezra said. "There are some more paintings I want you to see. More artists to meet. You're coming out with me tonight. Don't wear all that gold. Leave that watch behind. You're not going into the best of neighborhoods tonight."

"I'm not?" Adam questioned.

"They're my friends. You'll be all right. No need for those armed guards minding you."

"Do they know anything about me?" Adam began to clean up his hands with a bit of linseed oil and a rag. "I don't want them to know I'm rich."

"You hungry?" Ezra moved about, picking things up and closing lids of pigment jars on the table.

"Yes. Been a while since Hobson brought the sandwiches," Adam said.

"Bring a few dollars. Five at the most. We'll get something at the tavern where we hang out," Ezra said. "Do you drink? You said whiskey."

"Oh, I keep it here for sentimental reasons. I can't really drink that myself," Adam said.

"So he did?" Ezra pointed at the book. Ezra looked at him closely and then examined his hands. "This stuff starts fires. No smoking in here. Be very careful with lamps and candles. Tell your people."

"I will."

"Tell your wife you are going out to meet some other artists with me. You'll be back late," Ezra said. "Can you do that?"

"Well, yes."

Ezra pulled the smock off Adam. "Go on and talk to your wife. Leave that watch and jeweled necklace here. Got anything else on you that makes you look filthy rich? Those shoes. Have any older, less shiny? Lose the vest. Lose the silk ascot."

"Yes. You know I grew up here but I lived in the streets for a time when I was fourteen. I do know how to get along in the less polite neighborhoods," Adam said. "I just don't look it."

"No. You don't. You best look like it tonight. Does your hair have to be so perfect? Wear a hat."

Ezra put his beret on Adam's head. "I told you to wear a hat."

"I do not have perfect hair." Adam adjusted the beret to the right angle, walking down the street with Ezra. "Does the rest of me look all right?"

"Well, I don't see a glint of riches on you anywhere." Ezra looked him over. "Don't look so terrified. We're only going to a tavern. It's not one like you've ever been to, I'd imagine."

"Why? I've seen dancing girls."

Ezra shook his head. "Furthest thing from it. Why? Have you been to one of those?"

Adam laughed. "I can tell you stories of places overseas, the likes of which you won't find in this country."

"I'm born in Ankara," Ezra said. "Traveled through Constantinople to Rome to Nice... In very plain English, you can't shock me, New York."

"Rome? My mother is from Italy," Adam said. "How old were you then?"

"You didn't let me finish. I studied painting in Paris for three years. I was sixteen," Ezra said. "There was war at home, always war with Greece. I left everyone behind or I would have serve in the army. I made a living in Paris as a painter. Then I came here where nobody wants me at all."

"You're a really good painter. Must be the neighborhood."

They rounded a corner and passed some street vendors. Adam realized they were heading for the trolley stop. "Where are you taking me?"

"Don't worry. I'll take you back home later. Open your eyes, Adam." Ezra stopped him on the street. "You've never seen this side. But you know it exists. You know you're one of us."

"I'm not going anywhere."

"Yes you are."

"I'm not going anywhere."

"Aw come on. You don't have to do anything with anybody. It's just a tavern. And there are artists for you to meet," Ezra said. "Give me two bits."

Adam shook his head and paid for the trolley that they both hopped onto. They sat side by side. Ezra's thigh was against his. Adam watched what streets they were taking.

Ezra reached over to feel the lapel of Adam's jacket. "I'm not kidnapping you. You know?"

"I know."

"You look terrified. What is that?" Ezra turned to look at him. He reached into Adam's jacket and his hand was blocked. "It is what I thought." He leaned his mouth to Adam's ear. "You're carrying a gun."

"I know that."

"Trust me that well?"

Adam pushed his hand away. "I'm sorry. You don't know what I've been through."

"I see you came through it all right."

Adam followed Ezra down from the trolley and walked with him on the cobblestones, past some prostitutes, round a corner. The women called Ezra by his name. Called him sweetheart. Ezra started into an alley but Adam stopped. Ezra looked back at him. He gestured for Adam to come to him.

Adam walked into the alley, checking the corners and holding onto that gun. He stepped around puddles.

Ezra stooped and knocked on a coal door about halfway down the alley.

The door opened upward from inside. A man looked up at him. "You can enter. Not him."

"He's with me," Ezra insisted.

"I don't know him." The man looked up at Adam.

"He's with me." Ezra stepped into the opening and reached back to grab Adam by the arm. "C'mon."

The man inside backed down the stairs, allowing Ezra and Adam to pass, and then reached up to close the door again.

Adam looked about at dimly lit tables, chairs, patrons, beer glasses, wine glasses. The servers were men. The patrons were all men.

Ezra put an arm around Adam's shoulders and drew him toward a table in the corner. "Albert and Pierre, here he is. Have a seat, Adam."

Pierre pushed a chair back for Adam. "Hello again, Adam."

Ezra took another chair on the other side of Adam. "What's the special here tonight?"

"You're hilarious. Oyster stew. Same as every other night," Albert said. "So this is the protégé?"

Adam sat down at the bare wooden table. A bowl of stew was set in front of him, just as it was for Ezra. Spoons were just tossed into the center of the table.

Pierre began opening a bottle of wine.

Adam saw two men kissing at the next table. He leaned closer to Ezra. "I can't be seen in here. What if this place is raided?"

"You're fine. Nobody knows who you are. They're not letting anybody in they don't know," Ezra whispered back. "You're fine."

"Why did you bring me here? You know I have a wife," Adam whispered.

"I know you're in love with that Dutchman too," Ezra said. "Albert paints the other portraits you saw in the gallery. Pierre is the landscape painter. You can't have a better man mixing paints for you. He has a great eye for pigments."

"What Dutchman?" Pierre set a simple water glass with about two inches of wine in it, for Adam. "So you want to learn how to paint? And you draw very well, I hear." Pierre grabbed Adam's right hand to look at the charcoal beneath his fingernails.

Adam pulled his hand back.

"Scrub brush. Scrub brush and soap will get that out," Pierre told him.

"He has a book of drawings that are amazing," Ezra told them. "I mean like this guy comes to life, when he draws him. And different emotions on this guy, every kind you can imagine. But I think his favorite to draw is sadness. He drew that a lot."

"Who is this man?" Albert asked.

They all looked to Adam. And Adam just wet his lower lip. His eyes darted a bit. When Adam almost teared up, all three of them returned to eating their stew of potatoes and oysters. Only when they thought he would never answer, Adam told them, "I see him so vividly. I can hear his voice in the air. I can feel his sideburns against my finger. I can't touch him except to put his jacket on or sometimes cut his hair. I would give him a shave sometimes. I held everything back for so long...the only way I can express everything I feel for him is to paint him. The only way to touch his mouth, his neck, his hands... The only way to hold onto him while I still can."

Pierre wiped his eyes on a napkin and Albert elbowed him. "More sentimental than my mother."

Ezra laughed out loud then. Pierre laughed a bit. Finally Adam did too.

"What's his name?" Albert pushed a spoon across to Adam.

"I won't tell anyone his name. He's too famous." Adam picked up his spoon and tried the stew. "Would you have any black pepper?"

Chapter Five   August Gallery

Ezra August arrived at Adam's house and was stopped at the door by Mr. Hobson. "I know very well who you are and what you are here for, Mr. August. But I cannot let you in. Not with consumption."

Ezra's eyes opened wider. He felt a hand to his mouth to find blood on his lip. "No. You don't understand. I was beat up on the way here. Robbed. I'm not sick at all."

"Wait right there, if you would please." Hobson turned to find Adam standing in the hallway.

"You're stopping my friend from entering?" Adam questioned.

"Stay right there, sir. He has bleeding from the mouth. I made the assumption that he was terribly ill of a contagious disease of the...."

"Of the poor?" Adam asked. "Send for the physician. Immediately." Adam moved round him and held out a hand to Ezra. "Come in and sit down. Are you all right?"

"Ah, it's nothing. He's afraid I'll kill the whole household because I'm poor," Ezra remarked. "It's nothing. Some fool tried to rob me only to find I have nothing but paint brushes and pigments in my pockets."

"Fetching the physician, sir," Hobson called from the hallway.

Ezra sat on the sofa in the grand parlor. Green knit vest today with the red ascot tied about the neck of a white shirt. His eyes darted about at embroidered pillows and oriental rug.

"You got hit in the mouth? Where else?" Adam sat across from Ezra. "What did he take from you? My hundred dollars? I shall replace it."

"Oh no. We paid the rent with that. It's gone already. Thank you."

A maid brought in a tray of tea and cookies. She placed these on the table between Adam and Ezra, not making eye contact with either of them.

"Thank you, Ellie," Adam said to her.

"Yes, sir, Mr. Hudson."

"How far behind in the rent were you?" Adam asked.

Ezra looked at him. "All the way I suppose."

Ezra was examined by the physician in a guest room beside the art studio. Then the physician emerged to find Adam and Hobson waiting.

The doctor walked with them away from the guest room, toward the conservatory. "He is not sick, not with anything contagious anyway. And he was not beaten up as he claimed."

"Is he all right? I saw his mouth was bleeding," Adam said. "Can you help him?"

"His mouth bleeds because he is malnourished. If he doesn't eat properly he will begin to lose teeth. I gave him a bit of laudanum to apply a bit on his fingertip where it hurts," the doctor said. "His abdomen also gives him some pain from not eating. I saw this many times when I visited the poor houses in medical school. He is an otherwise young healthy man but with nothing to eat, it would seem."

"If you give him too much laudanum, he'll just sell it." Adam started toward the guest room. "If that's all it is, we can fix it. Mr. Hobson, early lunch today if you would please." He knocked on Ezra's door and met him face to face when he opened it. "Ezra, I apologize for the reaction of a privileged household. Can I make it up to you with some lunch before we work today?"

"You're too kind, Adam." Ezra finished tucking his shirt in. "Let's get started."

"Said he gave you laudanum. Let me see it." Adam blocked him. "It's my house. I would see it."

Ezra produced a tiny glass bottle from his inside pocket. It only contained a couple teaspoons of yellowish liquid.

"Put a touch of that where it hurts you, especially for sleeping. You don't look as if you slept much last night." Adam gestured for him to put the bottle away. "Don't sell it. I have plenty of money to give you."

Ezra shook his head. "I can't pay this physician."

"You have a rich friend," Adam said. "Don't give it a thought."

Ezra's painting of Adam Hudson

They set up the paints for the day and Adam sketched out his Robin Van der Kellen on the large canvas. Then they broke for a lunch set up in the conservatory. They painted all afternoon, with hours passing like moments. They shared ideas with each other, about what colors looked best beside each other and how to make a figure pop forward from the background of the painting, how cool colors recede and warm colors come forward. Ezra demonstrated many techniques by starting his painting of Adam on another canvas.

By Susan Eddy

And in the midst of this artistic exchange, passing back and forth from the two paintings, Ezra delved his hand into Adam's curls. He examined his blue eyes, and then kissed him on the mouth.

Adam froze.

Ezra stepped back, still holding Adam by the neck gently. But he suddenly smiled. "You're a little too straight for me, but it can be managed."

Adam tried to smile. "I have a wife. Why did you do that?"

"A lot of queer men have wives." Ezra shrugged. "I have two myself."

"Yeah, Pierre and Albert," Adam said.

Ezra smirked and nodded. "Yes. But they're more married to each other than to me. Being part of a triangle has that disadvantage, you know?"

"Are they more together than with you?" Adam asked.

Ezra poured out some titanium white powder and began mixing it with potions and linseed oil. "Well, yes. But I'm like this binder here, that allows oil to mix with water, as it were. Without the binder, those two would fight and be jealous all the time."

"Are you in love?"

Ezra pointed at the canvas. "Not like you are. No. I only find you attractive, sweet, and naive. No that's not entirely true."

Adam folded his arms. When he looked at Ezra he found him to be only inquisitive, optimistic even. "What do you mean?"

Ezra's eye contact was comfortable. "Adam, that agony you have over the Dutchman might just be the most beautiful thing I've ever seen. I'm going to paint it."

"Aren't you ever afraid to be...what you are in public? Isn't it dangerous to be...."

"Queer? I'm not in public. I sure don't think you're going to call the police on me," Ezra said. "Riding the trolley, you think anyone can tell? You want to know? Sure, I live with two men. I'm...in a relationship with two men."

"Do they exclude you?"

"Sometimes," Ezra said.

"What if I took you to get new clothes? Would they be jealous?"

"Yes, but who gives a fuck?"

Adam burst out laughing.

Ezra smiled. "You really hate my vests. Is that it?"

"It's the combination of vest and clashing ascot that I hate."

"Oh well you're so well coordinated," Ezra said. "What's in your closet, New York?"

"Adam, this is magnificent." Ezra held up a jacket from Adam's armoire, a black jacket with silk lining and tails.

"It was his," Adam said.

"His?" Ezra lowered his chin. "As in the Dutchman? His? How did you come by an article of his attire?"

"He dressed me up in two of his older suits so that we could go persuade the Dutch king to help on his law case. I couldn't very well go in there looking like a servant," Adam explained. "You have to see this."

"Can I try this on?" Ezra asked. "I'll be mindful."

"Sure."

Ezra pulled on the jacket and then looked at himself in the floor length mirror. "So he's not a big tall man? I look wonderful in this. Who wouldn't? But not as wonderful as he did."

"Not at all." Adam handed a small, folded handkerchief to Ezra.

The artist wrinkled up his mouth and unfolded the linen to see the embroidered RVK in the corner. "He gave this to you?"

"Well, he made me cry so it was the least he could do," Adam said. "Caught me with Zoey and said I had to marry her."

"Did you want to?" Ezra returned the precious handkerchief to Adam who returned it to the secret place in his drawer.

"Marry her, yes."

"He was hopelessly straight?" Ezra slid his hands down into Van der Kellen's pockets. "You know I never believe anybody when they tell me they are straight. Did you ever kiss him?"

"Not ever. No. Wouldn't be able to stop."

"Well, I know how I rate then." Ezra removed the jacket and returned it to the armoire. "Does he have a wife?"

"Yes. Marie is absolutely wonderful."

"Of course. What else would he have?" Ezra sat down on the edge of Adam's bed. "Did he send you away?"

"No. We parted as friends at the end of my trial. He had to return home to Marie and his horse farm. I had to stay here to look after my mother and Zoey."

"Parted as friends? Did he even know you were in love with him? Men aren't that bright, you know." Ezra looked about at the Italian sleigh bed and other furniture.

"I told him, yes. Couple times I think. You wouldn't think a man like that could be more uncomfortable with any situation and there he was, unraveled," Adam said.

"By you? Afraid of you planting one on him the way I did you?" Ezra said, not exactly teasing. "No I suspect he was quite safe that wouldn't happen."

"Take a hot bath, next door, and I'll give you clean clothing to put on. We're going clothes shopping," Adam told him.

"I don't smell. Do I smell?" Ezra smelled his own arm. "I smell like a hookah bar. Cause I wore this shirt into a hookah bar."

"Bath. I'm not having my tailor measure you and you...."

"I'm not crawling with creepy things. But all right. I shall force myself into the luxuries of your guest accommodations. I want my hair to smell just like yours."

"So afraid of where you were going with all that."

Ezra August returned to Adam's house with his two friends, the painters. Adam had been to their attic studio and seen their work. He'd dined and gone drinking with them. But now, he drew Ezra aside to whisper, "I'm afraid to let them see my paintings. They're not done yet."

"They're incredible, Adam. They're fantastic. I want them to see these. Don't you worry." Ezra took Adam under his arm. "Gentlemen, my new protégé is getting cold feet. We're only encouraging in this company. Right?"

"Absolutely. If Ezra says your work is fantastic, we need to see it," Albert said.

"Yeah, he doesn't praise very liberally," Pierre said. "Shitty, actually."

"In fact, the last time he did praise a painting, it was his own."

"Very well. Remember, I am new at this." Adam brought them down the hall toward the art studio.

They walked past Hobson who asked, "Would your friends like refreshments, sir?"

"Yes. Good idea," Adam agreed.

They were all young men near Adam's age. The friends wore suits and over coats of poor cloth. Most had spots of paint on sleeves or boots. None of them looked as if they had any money, except for Ezra because of the new clothing Adam had bought him.

Adam opened the studio door and entered first. "Please, remember. I've only just started two paintings."

"Don't worry." One patted Adam on the chest as he entered.

Soon they had poured into the studio and circled the easel to see the painting Adam had turned away from the door. Ezra picked up the other from the table and stood it up against the wall. "And you guys have got to see this book of his drawings. Be very careful with it. I'm calling it the Dutchman codex."

"Does he really look like this?" Albert asked.

"If a couple hundred drawings of him are truthful, I'd say yeah he does," Ezra said. "It's an interesting face."

"I know. Handsome but there's something else. I mean, it's not a perfect face," Pierre said. "But I see why he studies it."

"No. Adam's face is perfect," Ezra said. "This man has a pointy nose, deep set eyes, maybe full lips, not as full as mine of course. There's something about him. And Adam captured it on both of these portraits. There's an air and manner of..."

"He's got the light. Great sense of light and direction. What are the plans to finish this one?"

Adam realized they were expecting a response from him. "Uhm, he has a pistol on his hip. That's why the jacket is open. I'll just hint at it being there. He's sad because he has just moved to Connecticut and he doesn't know anyone."

"Sad. Yes. I'm getting that," Pierre said. "But something else."

"Why do you like to draw him sad?" Albert had his book open and was taking in the many drawings. "He's fascinating. Only barely a smirk. Never smiling in these."

Pierre walked over to look over his shoulder at the drawings. "Wow. Look at that one. Jesus. You weren't kidding about this guy, Ezra."

"What does that mean?" Adam asked shyly.

"You, Adam Hudson. You're a natural."

"You know portraits don't sell. Unless you are going to sell them to him, your subject."

"I don't care about selling them. I don't even want to. I just want to make him look the way I see him in my head," Adam said. "Before I forget. I may never see him again."

"I'm mixing pigments for him. I get his palette all set up and then he paints, but he'll learn it all. Right now, I'm trying to keep him from laying thin paint on top of thick. Trying to keep him from painting thick at all really," Ezra said.

"Yes. Will crack when it dries. You don't want that," Pierre said. "We'd better help you. You're going to varnish this when it's done, right?"

Albert remarked, "This guy is... I see confidence like you wouldn't believe. I see intelligence in his eyes. What was he doing when you were drawing these?"

"He didn't know. We were sailing for Amsterdam and I would draw in my cabin. A British privateer fired on us. He took a rowboat over to a nearby French Naval vessel. He convinced the French captain to move his ship in between and let us escape in the fog. He saved our ship. He is a lawyer in two countries. He also served as a Captain in the Dutch cavalry. He's a marksman. I believe he did some very crucial assassinations in the Anglo Dutch war." When Adam found them all hanging on every word and studying the face of Robin Van der Kellen on the two canvases, he continued. "He's got a horse he likes to jump fences with. And you should see the ladies everywhere he goes. He's hard to look away from."

Hobson opened the door and two maids carried in trays of glasses and snacks, cakes, pastries. There was a pitcher of beer. They set them on the empty table beside all the paints. "Enjoy, gentlemen."

"Is Zoey at home?" Adam asked.

"Out shopping with your mother's maids, and Miss Hendricks."

"Wonderful."

The artists were left alone again.

Adam indicated the refreshments. "Well, help yourselves gentlemen."

"You super rich, Adam? A gentleman?" Pierre said. "I'm tending bar later tonight."

"I work in a market but I'm off today," Albert said.

"Ezra sells enough at the gallery to get by. He doesn't have to work two jobs."

"We read about you in the papers, Adam."

That turned Adam's head. "Don't believe everything you read. I read that I'm not me."

That made the men laugh.

"It's all right. You can be rich. We'll drink your beer and whiskey."

"Does this guy know you are painting and drawing him?" Albert asked.

Adam accepted a beer. "It's a little early for this. But I'd be a poor host if I didn't join you. He found the book once."

"Wait a minute. What?" Ezra said. "This man found that book of drawings?"

"What did he do?" The artists gathered around Adam, still looking at his paintings of Robin.

"I...was mortified. I think I burst into tears. Naturally. I think he said something like they were very good. And then we didn't speak about it for a time. We road into town, attended to his business. Then on the way home he stopped into a store. Kunst Winkel, I think it was called. Artist shop. He came out with a large drawing book of fine paper, graphite and charcoal. He gave it to me and said it was more worthy of my talent," Adam said. "Said I should draw Zoey and impress her."

"And you did." Ezra burst out laughing. "Won't show me that one. He drew her naked."

They all laughed. "Which one was naked? Both of them?"

"Those will sell in your gallery, Ezra."

"Are those in here?"

"What happened when you drew her? Adam?"

Adam almost spilled his beer laughing. "I'm not telling you. She's my wife."

"So your wife knows about your obsession with this man? Who is he?"

"Well, I wouldn't call it that. But ah...she's here with me and he's over a hundred miles away," Adam said. "He is my friend. I saved his life. He saved mine."

"He was a marksman, a cavalry officer. How did you save his life?"

"I shot two men." Adam looked at the paintings. "To save him and me."

The artists look at each other. "Well then. Adam, some would say your two souls are bound."

"That's why you paint him."

"You're trying to conjure him."

Adam nodded. "Yes. Right. I'm a witch. Paint him well enough and he will appear."

"Well, he already has." Ezra indicated the two paintings.

"If only."

"What's his name?"

"You will know him only as the Dutchman."

The next time the artists gathered in Adam's studio, Adam had three men setting up his pallets, brushes, and pigments. They brought more easels and canvasses. And Adam provided the food.

Adam painted his portraits of Van der Kellen, and the other artists drew or painted Adam. And one day, they drew and painted Zoey. And through the course of the winter, they filled Ezra's gallery with new work, work that began to draw attention, especially the many paintings of the Dutchman.

As they painted, they began to bring musician friends too who would serenade the artists. They brought some of their women friends to be models. They ate food. They drank Adam's wine and whiskey. His rule was, they would not sleep over. Everyone left at some point after midnight. It was always then that Adam would go upstairs to bed with his wife. But of course, eventually that rule would be broken and the artists began to sleep in the studio after too much whiskey or because it was snowing too badly for the trolley to run.

A blonde woman, bundled up for the cold weather, entered Ezra's gallery one day and wandered inside. A man waited for her just inside the door. She stared for some time at one of the paintings. Then another painting caught her attention. And another. She gasped.

Ezra August dropped the book he was studying and hopped off the top of his desk. "Hello, Ma'am. Can I help you?"

"I know him. I know that man. And that man!" She pointed. "Who is the artist?"

"The artist does not wish to be known."

"Doesn't wish to be known but does not mind being painted himself." She pointed at a portrait of Adam. "Did he paint this? Who else could know what this man looks like? I would buy this one."

"These are on display only. He is preparing for a show in Paris." Ezra hid a smirk behind his hand. His dark eyes took in this wealthy blonde woman as he moved about her, taking in fur muff, fur hat, jeweled necklace. Then he looked at the man at the door. He was plainly dressed.

"I want to buy this one. I'll give you two hundred dollars for it," she said.

"It is not for sale."

"I'll give you one thousand dollars for it," she said.

"Madam, you seriously compromise me," Ezra said in his rather deep and raspy voice.

Elizabeth Miller moved closer to him and forcefully whispered, "If I compromised you, you would be reeling from it."

Ezra stepped back, eyebrows raised. "As much as I would enjoy that, I think the artist would pay me that much not to sell it, in fact, he just about has."

"Nice vest. New suit," she said, "You know Adam Hudson."

"I..." Ezra stammered.

At Elizabeth's raised voice, the man at the door stepped to her side. He gasped also when he saw these paintings.

"That is Adam Hudson because I know him. Or I knew him, anyway. He painted this portrait of Robin Van der Kellen, didn't he? Oh my God, and all of those over there." She hurried around a corner to find several more paintings of the Dutchman. "I have buyers for these."

"What did you call him? The Dutchman?"

"That is Robin Van der Kellen, the lawyer," Elizabeth insisted.

"It definitely is," Jonas agreed.

"The one that got Adam his inheritance? That Robin Van der Kellen? He has no intention of selling his paintings. He wants them on display for public critique, as artists often do. So far there has not been much comment," Ezra said.

"I can fix that. Tell me, this one has a price tag hanging. How much?" She pointed at the portrait of Adam.

"Twenty dollars, ma'am. Did I say twenty? Fifty dollars."

She laughed. "Don't worry. I would have paid a hundred for it. Does his wife Zoey know he's acquainted with artists these days? I don't want to get him in trouble when he dines at my house the next time and this is on display. You tell him I want that Van der Kellen painting. And here. Wrap that one up for me." She indicated to Jonas. "Jonas, pay the man and carry this for me."

"Ah what was the agreed upon price, good sir?" Jonas questioned.

Ezra looked at Elizabeth and shrugged. "I have no idea, lady."

She laughed. "What is your name, sir?"

Ezra straightened up. "Ezra August, madam."

"August Gallery. I thought it had something to do with summer."
Elizabeth glanced again at the painting of Adam Hudson and the
signature in the lower right corner. It was just the elegant lettering of
the word Ezra. She went to Jonas and whispered to him.

Jonas began counting out paper money and passed it to Elizabeth.

She then folded it and placed it into Ezra's hand, closing his slender
fingers about it and holding his hand closed. "Do not say a word about
this to Mr. Hudson. Trust me," she said to him.

"Implicitly, madam." He would not see how much she paid until she was
gone.

The following day, reporters from a couple local papers came to the
August Gallery to view the paintings of the Dutchman, the famous bank
robber catcher. They told stories of the Dutchman to Ezra.

The day after that, two wealthy women came in together and marveled
over the Dutchman series. They argued over which one they each
wanted. "Our husbands were consultants of his. You have to sell these
to us. We dined with Van der Kellen at the Miller's home. Isn't he
magnificent?"

And Ezra lay in bed that night, dreaming of the Dutchman, Robin Van
der Kellen.

After that came a caller to Adam's house. He was a well-dressed man, if
not overdressed. He presented a calling card.

Hobson read it. "Wall Street Gallery? The one just down the road there?
Near the corner bank?"

"That's the one. We want to display the Dutchman series. Will you ask
Mr. Hudson if he would speak with me?"

"Wait here. I will ask if he is receiving visitors today." Hobson went to
the stairway but turned to look at the gallery man.

The man sat down there in the hallway, holding his hat in his hand. He waited a few moments before a maid came to offer him some tea in the parlor. He strolled to the parlor and handed his coat and hat to the maid. He waited, sipping tea.

Finally, the notoriously reclusive artist himself, who doesn't sell his paintings, entered the room. Hobson the butler was with him. The artist stood there, a willowy adolescent with brown curly hair. His trousers had some paint spots on them. His black shirt had sleeves rolled up. His hands, though rubbed on a towel before entering the room, had paint about the fingernails.

The man stood up. "Mr. Hudson, I presume. I am Steven Jones, curator of the Wall Street Gallery. You have some spectacular paintings showing in a little known gallery on a poor side of Manhattan Island. Your frames are not quite suitable for such fine portraits."

"They're not," Adam said.

"You see the frame on that mirror over there? That's what I would put on your Dutchman paintings. Gold. He needs gold."

"He does. I just didn't know where to get frames made like that," Adam said.

"Are you familiar with my gallery?"

"Yes. I've been there many times. No one even spoke to me."

"My apologies. We didn't know who you were, sir. How would you like your own show in that gallery? Your paintings framed in magnificent gold?" Steven Jones said. "Frames worthy of that gentleman?"

"We have one problem. Galleries make their money by selling paintings. Mine are not for sale," Adam said.

"I will charge admission just to look at them, one night only, in a grand party. What do you say?"

"Wh...how did you find my paintings? How do you know about them at all?" Adam asked.

"Mr. Hudson, I stay on top of what is in local galleries and in the newspapers. Paintings made by the recent Rothschild heir will garner great interest among the banking community, as you can well imagine," Mr. Jones said. "Particularly paintings of Van der Kellen, the bank robber catcher. Perhaps we can even enchant him to attend. They'll pay double if he shows up."

"On one condition."

"You already said that none of them are for sale."

"Correct. The show must be staged by my art dealer. Ezra hangs the paintings, or no deal."

Dear Robin,

I have done something terrible for which I first must apologize and then explain. You recall my book of drawings? Well somehow in the course of painting lessons I seem to have contrived a series of paintings using those drawings. And now, people have seen them. Before I knew what was happening it snowballed. I have not even asked your permission.

It seems that a gallery on Wall Street wants to display my paintings of you. It has everything to do with those banking friends of Mr. Miller. I can refuse, of course. Between my headlines in the newspapers and your fame as the Wall Street bank robber catcher, these paintings have become very locally famous. They even want me to invite you to the party. I am terrified of what you must think of me. I'm not even trying to sell these or to make money. I simply wanted to learn to paint.

I'm certain the popularity of these paintings has more to do with your fame than my skill as a painter. But let me share with you that they do look exactly like you, and as I saw you at that moment in time. You saw the drawings, however briefly.

I'm folding up and posting this letter now before I tear it up and hide the paintings away in my attic. Please advise me at your earliest convenience.

Adam

Self portrait by Adam

Dearest Marie and Robin,

I have arrived safely back in New York and am enjoying the comforts of the city in winter. I do hope that your barn is filled with wonderful horses and your home filled with more wonderful children.

A mutual friend of ours has made an amazing transformation from valet to legal assistant and now to artist. He is apparently having great success with fellow artists as well because I just purchased a portrait of Adam Hudson created by a beautiful creature otherwise known as an artist. A friend of Adam's no doubt by the unusual name of Ezra.

And guess what Adam has been painting? Breathtakingly beautiful portraits of the Dutchman, an unnamed individual whom we all recognize. In fact I brought some of Edward's banking friends' wives to this little gallery and they caused quite a clamor as none of them were for sale. Adam apparently has the nerve to tantalize us with these lovely images but yet keep them all in his possession.

There is to be a gallery presentation and celebratory party for these at the Wall Street Gallery March 12. 7:00 PM. I will be there of course. Would shock the pants off the banking world if you were both there not to mention what it will do to a Mr. Hudson. If you let me know you will attend I will not spoil the surprise. I caution you however Robin might make the little artist pass out unless he told you about them already.

Hoping to have you as my guests in March. Your room is always ready.

Love, Elizabeth

Seeing Adam Hudson again, after six months apart, and seeing the results of the transformation from shy valet to famous artist, made Robin pause in the gallery entrance just to enjoy the moment. Across the room, there was Adam in long burgundy velvet jacket, pink silk ascot about his neck, ruffled white shirt, black trousers and shiny black top hat. His hat bore a peacock feather on one side, held on with a gold VOC pin. Even across the room, Robin could make that out. He leaned to Marie to whisper, "Now where did he get the Dutch pin?"

Marie wrapped her arm about Robin's. "Are you missing one? He always was a little peacock."

"Yes. I believe it's time I do as I always did," Robin said.

"Don't you dare," Marie urged.

The crowd began to part down the middle as more and more attendees recognized the guest at the door. The typical party chatter dimmed to a gasp. Even the violinists ceased their music. The pianist halted and stood at his chair to see who had entered.

It was the Dutchman himself.

Adam Hudson inhaled deeply. He straightened his shoulders.

Robin and he made eye contact and held it across the room.

Ezra August seized the opportunity to stroll into the gap between Robin and Adam. He spread his arms out wide. "Ladies and gentlemen, it is my honor to welcome you to the gallery opening of the Dutchman series by Adam Hudson."

The party guests applauded.

Robin walked toward Ezra, Marie on his arm, and he looked about at canvas after canvas, all portraits of him.

Adam stood near the hearth with Zoey and his artist friends around him. His mother, sisters, and cousin Erica were there. "I shall faint," he was heard to utter.

Ezra turned back to Adam to pull him under his arm. "Don't you dare. You stand there and look like a famous painter, because today you are one."

Van der Kellen strolled ever closer, still taking in the portraits. He stopped before a full length one, not even knowing it was Adam's first.

There was a blush to Robin's cheeks, the kind of blush his fair skin took on after a few drinks. Was he embarrassed or had he taken a few drinks at dinner before arriving?

A similar blush also rosied Adam's cheeks, and his definitely was from the champagne he'd been consuming for the past hour. He waited where his boots were glued to the hearth. He shook. "Ezra, he's gonna kill me."

Ezra hugged him about his neck briefly. "He's so fuckin beautiful I'd let him." He then bombed straight through the gathering toward Robin. And Ezra wore a very dark plum suit with white shirt, black vest, and light purple ascot. His top hat was deep red with a purple band.

The crowd was watching the Dutchman making his way closer to the artist. Reporters moved into position hoping to capture the first remarks between the artist and the subject. One of them blurted out, "This is the famous bank robber catcher, isn't it? Robin Van der Kellen? This is whom you have been painting? Did you know it, sir? Did you know the artist was painting you, sir?"

Ezra stopped Robin, blocking his path, studying his face from front and side. He studied Robin's eyes and saw something in them that made everything all right. Acceptance. With grand sentiment, Ezra spread his arms wide again and announced to the room, "Ladies and gentlemen, allow me to present to you, the Dutchman himself. May I escort you to meet the artist, sir?"

"As if I haven't before," Robin said to Ezra.

"Do you like the show, sir? The arrangement? The drama? It's leading you right up to the best pieces." Ezra held Robin by the shoulders to stop him. "Allow me to show you."

"Excuse me, if you would, my friend." Robin patted Ezra on the arm in passing. "Adam first."

Ezra released him and turned to watch him walk up to Adam. Then he scurried through the crowd again to get close enough to hear the encounter, to slip in beside Adam. He couldn't take his eyes off Robin. It was as if Adam's paintings had come to life.

Robin now stood before the hearth, and squared off with Adam Hudson. Neither said anything at first. But Adam began to smirk.

"I believe you made me younger, Mr. Hudson," Robin said. "Might have asked first."

"If I could make you younger?" Adam quipped.

Robin burst out laughing and opened his arms to him.

Adam wrapped about Robin's shoulders and hugged him hard. "I'm so terrified at this moment."

"I know. I meant to tell you they don't look a thing like me, but I just couldn't," Robin said.

Marie hugged them both. "Adam, I love them!" Then she hugged Zoey.

"I knew you could draw, but Jesus," Robin said. "You painted these from memory?"

Adam stepped back, took Robin by the lapels and kissed him on both cheeks. "My long-lost Dutch friend."

Robin stood back smiling.

A reporter pushed in. "You appear to be the subject of these paintings. Did you know the artist was painting you, sir?"

"I had no idea. I'm delighted. I'm humbled in the presence of an artist," Robin said.

The reporter scribbled that into his tablet. "What is your name, sir? You're the Dutchman?"

"Robin Van der Kellen, the bank robber catcher!" The crowd cheered together. "The famous lawyer. The Dutchman, Robin Van der Kellen!"

"Don't you see, he was Adam Hudson's lawyer," someone said.

"Adam Hudson's friend." Robin slid his arm about Adam's shoulders. "Breathe, will you?"

"I'll breathe tomorrow. Why didn't you send word you were coming?" Adam asked. "I was heartbroken that you weren't."

"Elizabeth wanted to surprise you. Marie wanted you to know the paintings were okay but surprise you with the visit. I would have you told everything," Robin replied. "So...surprise."

"Fuck me," Adam deflated in a breath.

"Don't you wish." Robin now looked around at the paintings. "I got lucky that the foal came a little early. It was healthy. So Marie and I hopped on a train."

"Adam, introduce me. I can't wait any longer." Ezra leaned in, eyebrows up.

Robin glanced around at the artists.

"My friends have been teaching me to paint, mixing my paints, stretching canvas for me," Adam said. "Ezra August, please welcome Robin Van der Kellen, the real-life Dutchman."

Ezra grabbed Robin's hand and wouldn't let go. "Holy shit."

"And Robin, Ezra is an amazing painter who studied art in Paris," Adam said.

Robin endured the extended handshake. "I'm going to need that back at some point, unless you're going to hold my drink for me."

"Drinks? Yes. Bring some champagne over here for our guests." Ezra released Robin and gestured to the girls with the trays of beverages.

Robin shook hands with Pierre and Albert. "Our pleasure to meet you, sir."

"Adam, they are spectacular," Elizabeth said.

"Thank you, Elizabeth." Adam hugged her as well.

Marie whispered to Elizabeth, "Is this the beautiful creature you wrote me about? The one from Adam's gallery?"

Beth gave her a little push and laughed. "Isn't he though? Love his little ass in that purple suit. He studied in Paris? Did you hear that?"

"Mr. August, would you show us the paintings?" Elizabeth asked.

"Yes. Mrs. Miller, isn't it?" Ezra's eyebrows rose.

Behind him, Pierre slapped Ezra on the backside, making him jolt.

"And this is Mrs. Van der Kellen." Elizabeth pushed Marie forward. "Are you in charge of this display, Mr. August?"

"Yes, Ma'am. I hope you enjoy it. Let's get you some champagne and I will walk you through the show, personally," Ezra said.

Ezra drew Elizabeth and Marie about to view all of the paintings, one woman on each arm. He explained the composition or special features of each work of art they paused before. The ladies held glasses of champagne and chatted with the banker's wives about which painting they loved best. Elizabeth glanced up at Ezra, her mouth at his shoulder. He smelled deliciously of aftershave and a bit of tobacco smoke. He was so neatly shaven and yet his sideburns went down to his tall collar and there was a curious bit of facial hair beneath his chin, just enough to tickle one's tongue on, she thought. Elizabeth wet her lips as she looked up at him.

Violinists were playing in the corner. The bankers, including Gregory, Markus, Victor, and Enri, all wanted to shake hands with Mr. Hudson. Noticeably absent from the Wall Street banking tycoons was Gerard Rothschild, Adam's infamous uncle.

"Mr. Van der Kellen, I need your help." A young man grabbed Robin by the arm.

"Aren't you..." Robin stared at him.

"Bernard Rothschild. Yes. I'm Adam's cousin," Bernard said. "I was hoping you would attend tonight. I must talk with you."

"You can visit me tomorrow, and tell me what it is you need then," Robin said. "I am staying at the Millers. You know where they live."

"Yes, sir. I would be delighted."

"One thing." Robin leaned in closer to him. "What is it about?"

"I need to hire you. It is urgent," Gerard said.

"You need a lawyer? Don't you have four already?"

"My father does. I need a lawyer who can beat them. I'm denied my inheritance just like Adam was," Bernard said. "I've been trying to contact Adam for months. He refuses to talk to me."

"I can't understand why. I will take your visit tomorrow." Robin moved away from him in the crowd. "Tonight is for Adam. If you will excuse me."

Finally, through the gathering among the paintings, Elizabeth and Adam came face to face. She grabbed his hand. "I'm so angry. I never knew you were an artist. I would have commissioned a painting of Edward. Well, and I would have bought one or twelve of these a year ago."

Adam laughed. "I had never painted until I met Ezra. But I can still paint your Edward if you wish."

"Can you? So this Ezra character taught you to paint?"

"Yes. I remember Edward's face very well," Adam said. "My problem is, I may have to be in love with what I paint, to make it magic. It may look like him. But it may not be magic."

Elizabeth looked at Adam for a moment, and then at one of the Robin portraits. "Resembling Edward would satisfy me. As for magic, I think that...came from your subject."

Adam saw Robin talking with reporters again. He nodded. "There is a celebration at my house following this. You will join us, I hope, and bring your house guests along?"

She smiled. "I would be delighted. Will your artist friends be joining? Tell me about the one who painted the portrait of you that is hanging in my parlor now."

"That would be Ezra. He's a far greater artist than I. I believe you already met." Adam drew Ezra over to them.

Elizabeth fondled her champagne glass as she looked up at the black haired, purple suited young man. His suit was such a dark purple that it was almost black except for a shimmer in the light. "Can you paint from memory? I would give anything for a painting of Robin."

"For your boudoir, madam? Or for the parlor?" Ezra smiled and kissed the back of her hand a bit drunkenly. "I need to know how much skin tone to mix up."

"You're a very evil young man. Come have a drink with me. I would like to hear what else you paint." Elizabeth pulled Ezra away with her and he looked back over his shoulder at Adam in terror.

At Adam's house there was a great celebratory ball, with musicians playing and a lavish buffet to be enjoyed.

Elizabeth snuggled up with Marie and Zoey. "What do you two know about Mr. August?"

"Ezra?" Zoey asked.

"Is he married? Has he a nice carriage?" Elizabeth asked.

Marie and Zoey looked at each other.

"Go ahead," Marie encouraged.

Zoey held Elizabeth close. "He's a wonderful painter, very sweet, very funny, but quite poor. Adam bought him suits and food. He was going hungry when they met."

"Really?" Elizabeth asked. "Is he all right? He looks fit enough."

"He's much better now," Zoey said.

"A bit drunk, I'd say," Marie said. "But he was in charge of that entire gallery show. Quite a lot of pressure on him, I would imagine. A lot of money involved. They were charging $20 just to enter, not to us of course. And there had to have been a hundred people moving through. Now that the show was a grand success, he can celebrate."

"And it was so magnificent. I think I shall tell him," Elizabeth said.

"You will?" Marie asked as Beth slipped out of her grasp and crossed the room toward the laughing artists. Ezra seemed to be the center of their attention, gesturing with his hands as he said something to make them laugh.

They parted to allow her into their circle, all young men about Ezra's age. He was dressed far better than they were.

Elizabeth singled him out. "Do you dance, Mr. August?"

Ezra met eyes with Pierre and Albert over her head. "Don't you dare say anything. Quite poorly. Do you wish to take your chances?" He gave her a devilish smirk.

The artists laughed.

"Do your worst, Mr. August." Elizabeth extended her hand.

Ezra waggled his eyebrows and led her away toward the ballroom. "Now, I warned you, Madam. Miller, isn't it?"

"Yes. You remembered. Let us see." Elizabeth held out her hands and he took them. She moved one of his to her waist and held the other in her hand. When they began to move, he bumped chest to chest right into her and turned away laughing. Elizabeth doubled over laughing. Couples around them made room and laughed, including Robin and Marie.

"Follow me, will you?" Robin told him.

Ezra took Elizabeth again and they danced. "I'm leading," Elizabeth told him. "This way, Mr. August."

Across the dance floor, as they swirled around, Ezra met eyes with Robin and laughed. He soon got the hang of it. "All right. All right, I'm getting it. Now twirl." He let Elizabeth do a twirl and then took her into his arms.

"Wonderful." Her hands were on his shoulders. "You know, you made a very wonderful gallery opening. I was very impressed."

"I did? I mean, you were?" He held her tiny waist.

"Well, yes! Adam said that you arranged the paintings and were in charge of the whole event." She looked up at him.

"Well thank you. It's what I do. I did not think it so much," Ezra said.

"My banking friends, who know Robin, cannot stop talking about it. The champagne and hors d'oeuvres were perfect. Your choice of what paintings to hang on each wall was genius."

"Madam, you flatter me too much. Please continue."

At the end of the song, Ezra bowed low before her. He thanked her and they separated. Their eyes met from time to time, across the room throughout the rest of the evening.

When Ezra saw Elizabeth and Marie being handed their shawls and furs, he hurried across the parlor. He met Robin there to offer an eager handshake. "Mr. Van der Kellen, I just want to say again what a pleasure it was meeting you at last, sir. I felt I knew you from all of Adam's stories."

Robin shook his hand warmly and patted him on the arm. "I shall look forward to seeing your paintings, Mr. August. The one you made of Adam captured his personality as well as his likeness. I'm sure you are very accomplished if you can teach Adam to paint in only a few months."

"Mr. August, I absolutely love that painting of Adam," Marie spoke up.

Ezra kissed the back of Marie's hand. "Thank you. Pleasure meeting you, Mrs. Van der Kellen."

Elizabeth pulled her hand from its glove and fur muff to slip it right in beside Marie's so that Ezra could not miss taking hers next. When he did, their eyes met and Elizabeth could not restrain a girlish smile.

Ezra grinned and kissed Beth's hand as well. "Thank you for the dance lesson, Mrs. Miller."

"Is your foot all right? I didn't mean to stop on it so," Elizabeth gushed.

The painter gave a quick glance down at his new fancy leather ankle boots. "It's all right. I have another."

She burst out laughing.

"Good night, Mr. August." Robin turned his women toward the door and they made their exit.

Adam crawled into bed with his wife at nearly four AM. Zoey awoke and kissed him.

"The last just left. I let Ezra, Philippe, and Albert stay over in rooms. They live too far away and were too drunk."

"And Robin and Marie?"

"They left a couple hours ago with Elizabeth." Adam sunk his head into a pillow.

Just a few hours later, when Zoey got up, she closed the drapes to allow her husband to get a few more hours of sleep.

"I wish he would sell them. I would take any one of them. Of course I have my favorite," Elizabeth said. "Which one do you like best, Marie?"

"The one of just his face and chest in the white shirt that he painted with blue shadows. I love the light on his face in that one," Marie said. "And you?"

"Oh I love that one too. But I'd have to have the full length one of Robin in the black suit and that pistol just showing inside his jacket. I mean, that is classic Robin," Elizabeth said enthusiastically.

"Which one do you like best, Robin?" Marie asked.

Van der Kellen rattled his teacup into the saucer with his left hand.

Jonas entered the room. "Excuse me. There is a visitor for Mr. Van der Kellen."

Robin smiled at the women. "Thankfully."

"You're not off the hook," Marie told him.

"Who is it, Jonas?" Robin slid his chair out and stood up.

"It is Bernard Rothschild, sir."

"Holy...." Elizabeth said.

"May I borrow your office? Edward's old office?" Robin asked.

"Of course," Elizabeth said.

"Show him to the office. I will speak to him privately. If you will excuse me, ladies." Robin left the dining room. "And Jonas, would you send us some coffee, please?"

"Yes, sir."

Robin entered Edward Miller's office or library in the home. He went immediately behind the desk to search for paper and ink. He found these in the top drawer and began setting them out on the top.

Footsteps were approaching.

Robin looked up to see Bernard Rothschild, a young man just a little younger than Adam, but stockier and no resemblance to his cousin at all.

Bernard entered the room and Jonas closed the door, leaving them alone.

"Bernard, before you begin you should know..."

"You will not take my case?" he asked.

"That Jonas is bringing us some coffee. You may want to wait a bit for beginning your story," Robin said.

"Oh. Thank you," Bernard sighed.

"Have a seat, please." Robin indicated the chair in front of the desk. And then he sat behind the desk.

Bernard sat in front of the desk. He wore an expensive tailored grey suit and set his top hat beside him on the next chair.

Robin sat back with his arms resting on the chair arms. He observed the young man quietly. "May I ask your age?"

"Eighteen, sir," Bernard said.

"So Adam is almost three years older than you," Robin said. "You never got along, is my understanding."

"That is correct," Bernard said.

"Your sister is older than Adam?"

"Correct." Bernard nodded.

"And you have only the one sibling?"

"Yes."

There was a knock on the door. Then Jonas brought in a tray.

"You can set that on the desk. Thank you, Jonas." Robin moved the paper and ink supplies to the side.

"Anything else just ring the bell there." Jonas indicated a decorative little chain in the wall with a ring on the end.

"Oh. Thank you." Robin watched Jonas' exit and shut the door again. Then Robin poured the two cups with coffee. "Cream?"

"Yes, please. Though I'm not much of a coffee person," Bernard said.

"Well, I got about three hours of sleep last night." Robin slid Bernard's cup across the desk and picked up his own. He tasted it.

"Quite a party then," Bernard said.

"Yes. Well, it was my one-year-old that would not allow me any sleep last night." Robin drank some coffee and set the cup down on the saucer. "What can I do for you, Mr. Rothschild?"

"Following Adam's trial, my father was quite angry with me. As you can well imagine," Bernard said.

"Why would he be angry with you? He lied more than you did," Robin said. "Under oath. You do realize that makes it difficult for me to trust you."

"I do, sir. But you must understand the influence of my father that I was under, the pressure, the threat of losing everything. I had to do as he said," Bernard said.

"Were you 18 at the time of Adam's trial?"

"No, sir. Just turned 18 this winter. December," Bernard said.

"So as a minor child you lied under oath as instructed by your father?"

"He's the one who wrote the affidavit my mother and sister had to sign," Bernard said. "He told me I had to deny who Adam was. But the point is, I was to inherit $25,000 on my birthday in December. I once saw it in writing. My father said I will never see that money now, because I embarrassed him in court."

"You saw this in writing? Can you get that document?" Robin asked.

"It's in his safe. If he has not changed the combination, I might be able to get in there, look for it," Bernard said.

"The fact is that until your father passes you will not inherit unless you can produce this document, this trust set up to provide you with $25,000 upon reaching the age of 18," Robin explained. "And you must be told that if you do sue your father for it, assuming you can prove he signed this trust to you, that you may not be on speaking terms with him the rest of his life."

"I'm not speaking with him now. Never have really," Bernard said. "What if he has torn up the document?"

"Then you do not have a case." Robin drank more of his coffee. "And should you murder your father I'm going to provide the police with your motive."

"Jesus. I'm no murderer," Bernard said. "I thought what you tell a lawyer is private and you can't tell anybody."

"I haven't taken your case yet. You have not paid me anything," Robin said. "I cannot legally advise you to break into your father's safe."

"But if he gave me the combination and has not yet changed it, then I am not breaking in," Bernard said.

"It's weak. Very weak. Add to that the lying under oath previously. Would someone else have a copy of the document? A law firm who drew up the trust? A trustee? A secretary?"

"Yes. Mr. Andrews. The lawyer who wrote up the trust," Bernard realized. "I can go ask him."

"No, you can't," Robin said. "Should you go anywhere near that man, you will tip off your father and he will destroy his copy and tell Andrews to do the same to his. Then the trust disappears. What money do you have?"

"I...I can give you one hundred dollars now to start with," Bernard said. "I can get another five hundred...."

"Put the one hundred on the desk. I will visit this Mr. Andrews. If he does not have a copy of this trust or if your father has dissolved it already, you have no case and I will return you the hundred dollars," Robin said. "Should I discover this document, you're going to need the other for court costs and my retainer."

Bernard was already opening his leather pocketbook and counting out paper money which he laid on the desk. "You can keep the hundred for your troubles if there is no proof."

"My troubles are worth a great deal more than that," Robin said.

Bernard looked at him in shock.

"If I take this case, it is because the trust exists and you have a legal right to the money. If I take this case, it's because it's the right thing to do," Robin said. "Despite how cruel you were to Adam your whole life."

"Adam was weird. He was not like other boys. And did you see those characters he associates with?"

Robin sat back with folded hands. "You're not helping your case. I'm inclined to tell you to leave."

"No. Mr. Van der Kellen, please. I am begging you. He can cut me off with nothing at this point. What if you get this document but my father tears up his copy?"

"Have you considered earning a living?" Robin said. "I am going to see Mr. Andrews and walk the document immediately to the courthouse to file your case. From that second on, it is evidence. You will go down this street to Adam's house and you make it up to him, for years of abuse. You'd better be sincere. Let me tell you something about your cousin, Adam. He is the kindest, smartest, bravest young man I may have ever met. My family is far away overseas. Your cousin is just down the street. Do something about it."

"I will. I swear I will go right down there to see Adam and...and congratulate him on the art show," Bernard said.

"Good. You do that. Do you know the address where I might find Mr. Andrews?"

"Yes. I will write it down for you." Bernard picked up the quill and slid the ink well closer. "So you'll take my case with this hundred dollars? Is that your fee?"

Robin laughed. "My fee is ten percent."

Bernard looked at him. "Two thousand, five hundred dollars?"

"Minus one hundred." Robin picked up the cash off the desk and pocketed it.

"But I thought you were rich."

"And I'm worth every penny," Robin said.

Zoey returned to her bedroom, opened the door quietly, and stood beside her bed to look on Adam still sleeping. He was laying on his back with both arms up above his head on the pillows. A few rays of sunshine made their way through the drapes and across the bed.

Zoey moved closer and rested her hand on Adam's chest. "Are you okay?"

His eyes blinked. He jerked a bit and looked up at her. "Zoey? Did I over sleep?"

"Big party last night. You needed to sleep." Zoey sat down on the edge of the bed with him. "Are you okay?"

"Yes. I did not drink that much last night. Everyone else did." Adam rose up on his elbow and smoothed a hand down Zoey's arm. "Come here. Why don't you come back in here?"

She giggled.

There was a knock on the door.

"What time is it? I thought I told everyone not to knock," Adam said.

Zoey looked at the clock on the mantel. "It is almost one o-clock."

"Really? That's why I'm so hungry."

Another knock.

"I will go see," Zoey said.

Adam flopped back down on the bed.

Zoey opened the door just a bit.

"Mr. Hudson has a visitor," Hobson said. "I think he should know, it is his cousin Bernard."

"What?" Adam threw back the covers and grabbed his robe off the foot of the bed. He wrapped the robe around himself and went to the door. "What does he want?"

"Says he came to apologize and congratulate you on the art show," Hobson said. "What shall I do, sir?"

"Um...I'm starving. Tell them to set up lunch and have Bernard wait for me there. Are Ezra and the others still here?" Adam said.

"They have not left their rooms yet, sir."

"Set up lunch for all of us then. Tell Bernard I will be down in a few minutes," Adam said.

"Very well, sir."

Bernard rose from the table when Adam and Zoey entered. Adam paused. He met eyes with his cousin, and then strolled toward him.

"Teddy?"

"Bernie..."

That made Bernard smile a bit.

"Um, have a seat. They're bringing in lunch. I confess I'm starving," Adam said. "I have a couple friends who stayed over. They'll be down shortly. But if you'd like to talk, we can talk after."

"All I want to say is, congratulations on your art show. It sure had a big turnout. Lot's of people and all," Bernard said.

"Thank you," Adam said. "Zoey." He gestured her to come to the chair he pulled out for her.

"So, married man already?" Bernard said. "I never thought you would. Didn't think you...."

Adam pushed Zoey's chair in and sat at the head of the table. Zoey and Bernard were on either side of him. "Zoey, you remember my cousin, Bernard."

"Hello Bernard," she said.

"So you brought her back from Amsterdam, I heard," Bernard said. "You know I did a year of school in Paris and one in Austria. I did not get to the Netherlands at all."

"I really want to see Italy, where my mom has family," Adam said.

"You will love it, I am certain," Bernard said.

Ezra entered with his hand on his temple. He made his way in his purple suit to a seat at the table and moaned. He lifted a glass of water with both hands and drank with eyes closed. Then he held the cool glass to his temple.

"Ezra?" Adam said.

"Yes darling?" Ezra rolled the cool glass across his forehead.

"I'd like you to meet my cousin Bernard," Adam said.

Ezra set down the glass right onto the middle of his empty plate with a clang. Then he winced. "Cousin Bernard. Pleasure to meet you, any other day but this."

Bernard laughed. "Quite a party, huh?"

"Mr. Hobson, can you bring some hangover remedy?" Adam suggested.

"I'm hoping that means an ice box to put my head into," Ezra said.

Pierre and Albert arrived and took seats near Ezra. "Don't mind our friend here. He drank an entire bottle of champagne. And some scotch. And some beer."

"That champagne really goes right to your head." Ezra sighed. "I don't remember the beer."

"Remember the woman?" Pierre asked him.

"I remember a woman. I danced with a woman. Did I sleep with her?" Ezra squinted at him. "I'd remember that, right?"

Lena entered with Hobson and took the packet of hangover remedy from him. "Let me handle this. Come, Ezra boy. You take this and I will get you some sambuca."

Ezra looked up at her.

"Come. Come."

"Mother, don't you think he had enough to drink?" Adam said.

Lena gave her son a look. "Your father drank too much all the time. I know exactly what to do."

Adam walked Pierre and Albert out while Ezra was escorted back upstairs to sleep it off. Adam returned to the dining room with Zoey and Bernard.

Adam smoothed his hands down his jacket the way Robin would. "Bernard, if you would like to talk, no one will disturb us in the solarium."

Bernard nodded. "Excuse me, Miss Zoey." He followed Adam down the hallway.

The solarium on the top floor of the mansion opened up just past the room Adam used as an art studio. In the early March as it was, while cold and wet outside, inside the solarium of glass panels, it was warm and green with plants.

One side of it had Adam's antique Indian swing that caught Bernard's attention. He went straight to it. "What the hell is this?"

"My wife enjoys it. It's a swing from India. Reminds me of a friend," Adam said. "Try it out."

"Oh no. It does not look safe," Bernard said.

"Of course it's safe. Her and I swing on it all the time," Adam said. "Anyway, why did you want to see me?"

"I sent you several invitations. You refused them," Bernard said. "You are suspicious."

"Can you blame me? You looked me in the eye, in court, and swore that I wasn't me," Adam said.

"Well, speaking of which, that hasn't made my father very happy," Bernard admitted. "Is your marriage for real? Why do you have a wife?"

Adam's brow furrowed. "My marriage is legitimate. I wouldn't leave Europe without her. How dare you ask me that."

Bernard nodded. "Very well."

"So what do you want here?" Adam shot back.

"I need your lawyer. I just sent him to get a document from Mr. Andrews. My father is denying me my inheritance just as yours did."

Adam laughed out right. "You expect me to sympathize? Where did you send Mr. Van der Kellen?"

"Why?"

"C'mon. We are going to look after him. People keep trying to shoot him when there's money involved. Let me grab my pistol first."

Chapter Seven Cousin Bernard

Adam Hudson entered Gerard Rothschild's home for the first time in a decade. He paused in the entry hall, looking into a glass case of African artifacts. There was a mask and some wooden tools. Several daggers were pinned up inside, on display.

"Wait here. I'll be right back." Bernard moved past him and went up the grand staircase.

Adam slid his hands down into jacket pockets and quietly slipped into the library, out of sight. He began to hear voices upstairs, so he moved closer to the door, with his back to the wall.

The voices upstairs were male and it was getting louder. Bernard and some other man. There was a strange crash.

Adam drew his pistol and darted toward the stairs when he heard a gunshot up above. That made him stop on the carpet below the stairs, freeze and listen.

Robin was walking up the steps to that very home when the front door opened. Adam came scrambling out, holding his right arm to his chest. Blood was dripping from his arm onto the front porch and Adam fell to his knees.

Robin caught him by the shoulders. "Who did this to you?"

"He took my gun. He has my gun." Adam's head pressed to Robin's shoulder.

"Who? Bernard?"

"No. He was upstairs, arguing with his father. I heard a gunshot." Adam gasped.

"Who stabbed you?" Robin asked.

"Stabbed me?" Adam sat back to look at a large ivory handled dagger stuck in his right forearm. "Oh my God."

Robin called out to a passing carriage. "You sir! Stop!" Robin pulled that dagger out of Adam's arm and quickly tied Adam's ascot tightly around it.

The driver of the carriage climbed down and walked up the stairs.

Another gun shot rang out inside the house.

"Oh no way! I'm not..." The man ducked on the stairs.

"Get my friend in your carriage and take him to the nearest hospital. Send the police here. Go!" Robin grabbed Adam up by the other arm and hurried him down to the carriage.

The man opened the carriage door.

Robin lifted Adam up inside, onto the floor. Then he dropped the bloody dagger on the floor beside him. "See that the police get that. And here. This is my identity." Robin dropped a handful of calling cards into the carriage before closing the door. "Go man. What are you waiting for?"

The man climbed up and got the horses moving.

Robin dashed around toward the back of the house, drawing his revolver.

Adam awoke in a hospital bed, lying on his left side, with his arm suspended above in a sling from the canopy.

Zoey immediately went to him to kiss and reassure him. Behind her, Marie took Zoey into her arms, saying, "He's okay. Adam, you're all right. Are you in much pain?"

Adam looked about. "Some pain. Not too bad. Where is Robin?"

"He's at the police station, Adam. What can we get you? Can you eat something?" Marie said.

"Ik ben in orde," Adam said to his wife. The fingers of his right hand moved a bit. "Can I put my arm down?"

"No. I believe they want you to keep it elevated or it will throb again. You are still working on stopping your bleeding," Marie told him.

"I want to go home," Adam said.

"You will. Just not today," Marie told him.

"Send for the doctor. I want to go home," Adam said.

"I know what you want to do. You want to get to work with Robin and you will not," Marie told him. "Not yet. Robin is fine." She left the room for a bit.

Zoey leaned in and kissed her husband again. "Adam, rest. Please. Do you want water?"

"I can't."

The doctor entered with a nurse and Marie. "Mr. Hudson? How are you feeling, sir?"

"I don't know. How long was I out?" Adam asked.

"We are going to sit you up so that you can take some food. You have been out for nearly a day, sir." The doctor and the nurse cranked the head of the bed up. The young doctor helped Adam onto his back, keeping his injured arm in the sling and elevated somewhat above his heart.

Adam found himself unable to lift his head off the pillows. "Don't feel very good."

The doctor felt his forehead and then took his pulse. "Bring him a bit of broth and tea with the laudanum in it. And bring me the wrappings to change his dressing."

"Yes, doctor." The nurse exited.

"Would the ladies please leave us for a few moments. I need to tend my patient. If you would, please?" The doctor looked at them both.

"We will, Doctor," Marie said. "If you will reassure him that his arm will heal properly. He's worried about his painting. He's an artist."

"An artist? Of course, Mrs. Van der Kellen. But right now, he needs a lot of care."

Adam had to endure some additional stitches to the underside of his arm. He could take nothing but broth and tea for that first day. He brightened a bit when Robin visited that evening to take the girls home. But the following day, he had a fever. The doctors continually opened his bandages to evaluate his wounds.

Marie stopped the doctor out in the hallway. "Will he beat this fever?"

"Mrs. Van der Kellen."

Marie stared him down. "He can learn to paint with his other hand if he has to. You must make a decision and tell me the damn truth."

"Ma'am. You are much stronger than he is." The physician thought a moment and then redirected. "His infection is minor and we believe it is not progressing. He could fight this infection best if he would eat properly. He's young and otherwise healthy. He's very young in fact. He lost a lot of blood."

"You're saying he can keep this arm if he eats properly?"

"Most likely, yes."

"Then that's what we will do. But I'm bringing in food for him," Marie said. "He won't eat this."

"Anything you can do to make him eat, madam." Then the doctor added, "When your husband was here last night, he seemed to strengthen. He would not want to appear weak with your husband around."

Marie nodded. "I can use that."

Robin sat back and crossed his legs as he watched the police captain pace behind his desk.

"Mr. Van der Kellen, when they dig that bullet out of Mr. Rothschild, it had better not be a .36 caliber Colt. That's all I can say about you," the captain said.

"Even if it is, my weapon has not been fired. It was ice cold when they took it from me. The lieutenant even said so," Robin said.

"He did. It doesn't mean you didn't fire another one and then toss it. They are combing the house right now," the captain said.

"Taken from Adam Hudson was a Belgian made silver pistol with a walnut handle. Look for that, if you will," Robin said.

"Tell me again what Adam Hudson said when you found him."

"I've told you eighteen times. He said, 'He took my gun.' He heard Bernard and Gerard Rothschild arguing upstairs and a gun shot rang out up there. Some other man stabbed Adam and took the Belgian silver pistol from him," Robin said calmly.

Someone knocked on the door and leaned his head inside to say quietly to the captain, "Bringing the suspect in now. But get this, he claims that he wants his lawyer. Says that we already have his lawyer here."

"That would be me," Robin said. "You will not question Mr. Rothschild without me present."

"I don't know yet that you didn't shoot the other Rothschild, Mr. Van der Kellen." The captain let out a frustrated breath.

"When I got there, Bernard and Gerard Rothschild had argued upstairs. A third man stabbed Adam Hudson and took Adam's gun. A weapon was fired upstairs. I sent Adam off in a carriage and told that good man to get him to a hospital and send the police. Does that sound to you like I would then walk calmly into that house and shoot Gerard Rothchild? I tossed half a dozen of my calling cards into the carriage for Christ's sake," Robin said.

"Get over to the hospital to question Mr. Hudson if he's able. And find the good Samaritan so that I may question him. I want that dagger and those calling cards."

"Yes, Captain. What about the suspect?"

"Lock him up and don't question him until his lawyer is present."

"Yes, Captain." The lieutenant left and closed the door.

"Tell me again where you found the body?" The captain sat down at his desk and looked at the elegant Mr. Van der Kellen before him, blood staining his French cuffs and English suit.

"Gerard Rothschild was lying dead in the hallway upstairs, outside his bedroom. The son, Bernard was in his father's bedroom, attempting to open his safe. I warned him to freeze and to sit down exactly where he was. He did so. And I held him there until the police arrived," Robin said.

"Did he have a gun in his hand?"

"No."

"Glass case was broken into by the front door. Did he get a gun from there?" the captain asked.

"I suspect that's where the dagger came from that Adam was stabbed with, as he wrestled with another man there at the door. Lost his gun to him when he was stabbed through the gun wielding arm," Robin said.

"Tell me again what the younger Rothchild said to you when you entered the bedroom?"

"He said, 'Did you shoot my father?' Then he looked shocked at who I was and said, 'Oh my God, it's you'."

"You're saying someone else shot his father dead in the hallway and Bernard was still working the safe open?"

"That is correct. It is my opinion that a third man shot Gerard while father and son were arguing, and the son went to the safe. The shooter then went downstairs to take care of Adam. Adam Hudson, if you'll remember, is formerly Adam Theodore Rothschild the third. He and Bernard are cousins."

"You don't expect me to believe that your client didn't just shoot his own father while this third man went to stab Mr. Hudson?" The captain squinted at the lawyer in front of him. "Now I remember who you are. You're that brilliant bank robber catching lawyer. You got Adam Hudson his inheritance."

"That's correct. And Bernard Rothschild had just hired me to sue his father for a $25,000 inheritance he was being denied. There was a copy of that trust in that safe Bernard was opening. I also obtained a second copy of that paperwork from a Mr. Andrews, attorney at law," Robin said.

"That's one hell of a motive."

"Yes it is. Which is why I held him at gun point. Which is why you will let me defend my client, who is presumed innocent under the law, until we determine who killed Gerard Rothschild," Robin said.

"Looks more to me like the son and the knife wielding man were in it together to clean out that safe," the captain said. "One of them shot the rich man. That is, if you didn't."

Mr. Hobson arrived with a basket of food. "Good day, Mr. Hudson. Your mother has sent all of your favorites. I am happy to set them up for you."

"Wonderful idea." Marie smiled. "Zoey, let's get him a tray and sit him up so he can eat these."

Zoey raised the head of the bed, using the crank system she'd seen the nurses use.

"I...I don't want anything. I'm sorry," Adam said.

"Apparently even as a child he loved Dutch pea soup. We have that. We have focaccia. We have peach tarts just out of the oven," Hobson said. "Or, what about this? Your mother's famous three cheese risotto."

"Risotto?" Adam asked.

"Let's try that," Marie suggested. "When Robin comes this evening, you don't want him to see you looking weak, do you? Eat your mother's food. If you don't, she will come here to see that you eat it."

Adam looked at Marie, Zoey, and Hobson standing at the foot of the bed. "You must tell me. Tell me the truth. I will never paint again. I can't without this arm."

Zoey was frustrated. "What does he say? What is it?"

Marie put a hand on Zoey to move around her, up to the head of the bed. "Adam, listen to me. You know you have a fever. It's mild, they say. You can fight this if you eat just as much as you possibly can. You understand me?"

Adam sobbed.

And while Zoey dropped her head onto his knee and cried too, Marie laid her hand firmly on Adam's forehead. In fact, she depressed his head into his pillow a bit and leaned over him.

"Robin can always eat. You know that. So you are going to sit up, and eat all this wonderful food. Just like he would. Are you listening to me?" Marie said forcefully. "Do what he would do. You know you want to."

Adam wiped his own tears away with his left hand. He nodded a bit, when Marie released him.

Marie cranked him up more. "The only reason you're dizzy is because you need food. You draw and paint with both hands." She put a spoon into his left hand and slid the risotto closer to him on the tray. "You won't have any trouble at all with this."

Robin strolled in front of the judge and police captain. Then he looked back at the stand where Bernard was seated and handcuffed. "What caliber is that pistol you own?"

"I object!" Bernard cried out.

"You can't object. He's your own lawyer," the judge said.

"What caliber is the pistol you own?" Robin repeated.

"I don't know."

"You don't know? You have a Colt Walker, .44 caliber," Robin said. "Where is it?"

"In my packed suitcase back in the house," Bernard said.

"Send somebody to go get it. Wrap it in cloth and bring it to the munitions expert. I want to know if it was fired yesterday," the Captain said.

"Nobody can verify that. It has been too long to tell when it was last fired," Robin said.

"I can ask him, can't I?" the captain said.

Robin pulled out of an evidence box a large knife. He held it up and displayed it to the judge and captain. "Is this yours?"

"No! Of course not!" Bernard said.

"Why of course not? You've seen this before?" Robin questioned.

Bernard looked down and said nothing.

"Allow me to show this to you better. Who does this knife belong to?" Robin moved closer and held the large knife out in one open extended hand. "Don't worry. I've washed all of your cousin's blood off."

"I object!" The district attorney shouted out.

The judge looked to him. "On what grounds?"

"Here say."

"Bullshit," Robin said. "I personally pulled this out of Adam Hudson's arm just yesterday."

"Mr. Van der Kellen, you will mind your language in my courthouse," the judge said.

"Mr. Rothschild, you and I both know your father was shot and we are awaiting an examination of the bullet from the coroner. Your cousin, my assistant, who lies in the hospital right now, was stabbed with this very knife," Robin said. "Where did you see this knife before?"

"In my father's cabinet."

"Really? How do you know that?"

"From a safari in Africa. That's where he got it. I was with him. The handle is ivory," Bernard said.

"Ivory. A rare commodity here in America." Robin looked at the knife handle. "This is ivory, your honor."

"How do you know that?" the judge asked.

"I have in my collection an ivory handled sword from India, where I served as a distinguished captain in the Dutch cavalry. India and Africa both have elephants, your honor," Robin said. "The tusks of an elephant are made of ivory."

"I am aware of that," the judge said. "What is your point, Mr. Van der Kellen?"

Robin held up the knife. And he looked at it. "While you argued with your father upstairs, Adam Hudson waited near the front door. Why did you bring Adam there?"

"To collect a few of my things. I was going to move in with Adam for a time," Bernard said.

"When you asked me if I shot your father, who were you expecting to answer? You were surprised I was there," Robin said.

Another officer entered and whispered to the captain. "We have the bullet, sir."

"Bring it here and bring the munitions expert."

"Let us hold on this questioning until we see the size of this bullet," the judge said.

"Of course." Robin returned the knife to box and stepped back to patiently think to himself.

Bernard stared at Robin the whole time they waited.

Finally some officers entered with another man in a suit. This man was elderly with spectacles and carrying a wooden box of instruments.

The bullet was laid out on a table, on a white cloth, for all to see.

"All right Mr. Helms. What do you make of it?" the Captain asked.

The munitions expert bent over the table with his spectacles on and a caliper in his hands. He measured the bullet on a white cloth. "It measures .50 caliber. Half an inch. Best I can tell. Deranged a bit when it hit bone, I'd say. It's like something from an old flintlock or dueling pistol."

The police captain looked directly at Robin Van der Kellen. "We shall retain Mr. Bernard Rothschild in custody on suspicion of murder. Mr. Van der Kellen is free to go with the understanding that he remains in the vicinity. Return the Patterson Colt to Mr. Van der Kellen. We need a description of the man who stabbed Mr. Hudson. Hopefully he will be conscious enough to give my men a statement."

"Agreed," the judge said.

"May I speak with my client alone?" Robin asked.

"You may follow us down to a holding cell and speak to him in there," the captain said.

There was a knock on Adam's hospital room door. The police officer opened it a bit and asked, "Mrs. Van der Kellen. Men you asked for are here."

Marie appeared at the door. She looked, saw three young men in the hallway, and stepped outside. She closed the door behind her.

"Mrs. Van der Kellen." Ezra held his hat in hand. "We received your letter and came at once."

"You are Ezra, the painter. Of course. Officer, you may let these gentlemen enter. Thank you," Marie said. "Just before you do, Adam needs your encouragement. He needs to eat and get his strength up."

"What...what happened?" Ezra asked.

"Inside. We'll tell you," Marie said.

Witness for the district attorney took the oath and the stand. The DA began questioning with, "What can you tell us about how Gerard Rothschild II was murdered, doctor?"

"Objection. He was shot, not murdered. Not yet anyway," Robin said.

"Strike that. How was he shot, doctor?" the DA snapped.

"He was killed when a bullet passed though his chest, penetrating both lungs, part of the liver, and severing major blood vessels in the chest," the doctor said.

"And where did you find the bullet?"

"Lodged in a rib in the upper left side of his body."

"Thank you, doctor. Nothing further."

Robin stepped forward. "Do you know anything about assassinations, doctor? Trajectory of bullets or range of such?"

"I do not. I'm a coroner," the doctor replied.

"But your background was a medical doctor in the war of 1812. Did you not see bullet wounds back then?" Robin questioned.

"Of course I did, back then."

"Given then the context of your actual vast experience in bullet wounds, would you say that Mr. Rothschild was shot from very close or from some distance?" Robin questioned.

"Not from up close," he said.

"Why do you say that?"

"From up close typically the bullet passes through the body causing quite an exit wound," The coroner said.

"Would you say he was shot from 10 feet away, from the next room, or from elsewhere on the stairway?" Robin asked.

"Objection. Asking the witness to speculate," the DA said.

"I'd like to hear his answer, given his military experience," the judge said.

"Curiously, I would say he was shot from some distance and from below," the coroner said.

"Below, really?" Robin said. "Why?"

"The entry wound was very low on the right abdomen. The exit would was very high on the upper left back."

"Thank you, Doctor. Bernard Rothchild could not have killed his father then. He was standing at the same level just fifteen feet away at his father's safe," Robin said. "Gerard Rothchild was shot by a .50 caliber weapon from below, possibly from the doorway of the home where Adam Hudson was stabbed."

"Well, that may be. But your client Bernard asked you calmly, 'Did you kill my father?'," The DA said. "He expected someone else, not you to enter that room right after the shooting, someone he conspired with."

Robin entered Adam's room that evening, past the two police guards at the door. He set his briefcase down to kiss his wife and pat Zoey on the shoulder. And then his eyes took in the three artists. The leader of the gallery opening, Ezra, stood up by the head of the bed. The other two were sitting on the foot of the bed.

Adam watched him look on those friends from the perch of a hospital bed, but as if from a thousand feet above, seeing himself examined as well.

"Mr. Van der Kellen, it is our honor to see you again." Ezra stepped around to extend out the bold offer of a handshake.

Robin looked him over. "You would be the leader of this company?"

Ezra glanced around Robin's shoulder at Pierre and Albert. "Naturally."

Robin squared off with Ezra, finding him to be just a bit taller, just a bit older than Adam, and had very similar hair color and curls. But he was sporting a purple vest with red ascot. "You should learn how to tie one of those before displaying it so."

Ezra suddenly smiled. "Ezra August. We met at the gallery. It's supposed to be intentional."

"Robin Van der Kellen." Robin shook his hand. "It's supposed to be outside of your collar."

The guys laughed.

Ezra nodded. He turned to Adam to say, "You're right. Nothing gets past this guy. These are my fellow artists, Pierre and Albert. They're sort of a combined unit. Pierre and Albert as if it's one name."

Robin just turned toward Adam. "Well, you are looking better today."

"I am?"

Ezra spun about with both hands to his mouth and doubled over for a moment behind Robin. Pierre and Albert laughed. Marie burst out laughing.

"Little more color in your face." Robin moved closer and patted Adam on the knee through the blanket.

"What happened in court today?" Adam asked.

"The bullet that killed your uncle was a .50 caliber, from a flintlock or dueling pistol. The weapon has not been found yet. Bernard knows who stabbed you and who killed his father but he won't tell me. Bernard also recognized the knife being from his father's collection." Robin moved up closer beside the head of the bed. He folded his arms and studied the three painters further. "I proved that Bernard did not pull the trigger. The coroner testified that the bullet came from very likely downstairs."

Ezra moved down more toward the head of the bed to stand beside Marie.

"Bernard didn't pull the trigger but did he have his father killed?" Adam asked.

"I've always thought that he was involved. It didn't look as if they struggled over that pistol. It looked like an assassination from below. Bernard wanted money, but I do not think he's stupid enough to think he could get away with flat out shooting his father. There must have been a sudden fight argument with his father and another man fired the shot," Robin said. "I hate to ask you, but I'm required to, do you have any description of the man who stabbed you yet?"

"It was so dark. He came out of nowhere." Adam frowned.

"I know. I was hoping after some time you might remember something, the way you did with James Collins." Robin met eyes with Albert, Pierre and then even Ezra. "How soon will you be released home?" They were all three at least owning up to this eye contact.

"Oh, very soon. His fever is better. They are planning to put a splint on his arm when it comes out of that contraption," Marie said.

"Adam, I'm not bringing you back to your home when you do leave the hospital. I'm hiding you away someplace. Zoey too, of course," Robin said. "Until we catch the man, we need to keep you out of sight."

"I'm still in danger?"

"He doesn't know you can't recognize him," Robin said. "All I said in court was that you were still sedated."

"What if he signs papers stating that he could not see him?" Ezra asked.

"Ineffective," Robin said.

Ezra's chin dropped and his eyebrows rose. He placed both hands on his hips then. And immediately his chin rose level again. He met eyes with Robin.

"You do not think that will convince the man to leave me alone?" Adam asked.

"Not in the least. And I think it is a very good possibility that is the same man who killed Gerard. If you swear you did not see the man, Bernard is going to jail," Robin said. "Though I want to catch that man, I'm not sending you back to your home to endanger your family and you. I'm not using you as bait."

"Why not?" Adam asked. "He'll come for me again and we wait, ready with many hidden policemen?"

Robin held up one finger. "Do you trust these three men?"

Ezra snapped to attention. He looked across the bed at his painter companions.

"With my life, I do," Adam said.

"Are any of you familiar with the *Three Musketeers*?" Robin asked.

"Alexandre Dumas. I am," Adam said.

"Of course." Ezra he glanced at Marie to mouth the word, "What?"

Van der Kellen put his hand on Ezra's shoulder and shook him just a bit. "I need three recruits for a very dangerous mission and one hero among them. Are you up for it, D'Artagnan?"

Ezra August

Chapter Eight   The Three Musketeers

Adam Hudson was released from the hospital and assisted down the front steps by the famous Robin Van der Kellen, between a line of policemen toward an awaiting carriage. Reporters were being held back as they shouted questions.

"Tell them nothing." Robin held onto Adam's arm with the sling on it. "Nice and slow now. Just a few more steps. I know it's painful."

Adam Hudson looked down at the steps as he made his way, a hat low on his head. At the bottom step he even cried out a bit.

"Sorry. Pulled your arm too hard. Easy. Just get into the carriage and lay down on the seat." Robin opened the carriage door and guided Adam's foot to the carriage step. "Easy. Lay down now."

But it was Ezra August who lay down across the carriage seat.

Robin bounded inside with him and called, "Move out!" He sat down and drew his revolver. "You hear gun shots just roll onto the floor and stay down."

"Yes, sir. Gun shots?"

"It will go quickly at the hotel. Just do exactly what I tell you with no hesitation. We may have to improvise. You're doing fine."

"Gun shots? You just said this may be dangerous. You didn't say we'd be shot at."

"What did you think I meant?"

The carriage pulled up to the tenement housing located behind the gallery owned by Ezra August.

Pierre and Albert ran out to meet it.

"Zoey," Albert called. "Get inside quickly. We'll grab your bags." He held out his hand to her.

Zoey took his hand and then was quickly ushered inside the door to the building. She stood watching out the open door.

"Mother. What a delight to see you." Pierre held out his hand to the open carriage door while Albert took their bags and parcels.

Beneath a feathered hat, a white wig and a long brown dress, someone emerged from the carriage and took Pierre's hand. There was a black shawl around the person as well.

Pierre helped the person into the building. The door was closed. The carriage drew quickly away.

And in the hallway, the artists burst out laughing as they peeled away hat and wig to reveal Adam Hudson.

"Quit laughing. I've been stabbed, you idiots."

Pierre unwrapped the shawl to find Adam's sling and splinted right arm. "You've got a lot of stairs to climb. Can you make it? Mother?"

The artists laughed again.

Adam pulled up his skirt to reveal black trousers and boots. "How in this dress?"

Pierre took his left arm about his shoulders. "Well lift your skirts young man. Up we go. Up top, Zoey. Bring their things. Why so much baggage?"

"It's food. Hobson sent us all food for several days," Adam said.

They all started to climb stairs.

Zoey climbed up and around, up and around. She paused on each landing to look down at her Adam being helped up, Adam in that long brown dress.

On an upper landing, Adam had to sit down to rest a while.

Pierre sat with him. He looked up at Albert. "Well bring their stuff up top. We have a place all set up for you. You'll see. Honeymoon suite. How are you, Adam?"

"I'm...hurting quite a lot right now. I need to lay down when we get up there," Adam said. "Thank you for this. You know, I'm putting you in danger."

"No one will look for you here, mother."

Adam almost laughed.

"Nice dress," Pierre teased him.

"My sister got it," Adam said. "I just hope Ezra is okay."

The top floor attic of the building, four stories up, the artists lived in the long open attic space. Zoey wandered inside past paintings of nudes and cityscapes and portraits. She wandered past old couches set up for modeling with evidence in the corners of the attic where beds were set up. Either end had fireplaces. There were crates used as tables, displaying all manner of brushes and pigments. In some areas, the floor was splattered with colors. And there were windows all along either side, for most excellent artistic light but for frigid cold temperatures in the winter.

Pierre helped Adam inside and set him down onto one of the couches. He slid a foot stool in and lifted Adam's feet onto it. "Let's get you out of that dress."

"Bet you never said that before," Adam quipped, struggling to catch his breath.

Zoey saw their things carried past and behind a barricade of very tall 8 foot canvases. She stood with her hands clenched together in front of her.

"Zoey, it isn't much, but make yourself at home," Albert said. "No one will find you two here."

She moved forward and sat down with Adam. "Out of this gown now?"

"Please. I feel ridiculous." Adam sat up.

Zoey reached in and unbuttoned the dress down from Adam's neck. He wore a white shirt beneath it, no vest or ascot.

Albert and Pierre went back down for more crates.

Zoey untied Adam's sling to help get the open sleeve off his injured arm. "Do you hurt much?"

"Yes. Quite a lot. I need more laudanum," Adam said.

"I get." Zoey told him, unbuttoning the dress all the way to Adam's waist. Then she left the seating area for her bag that rested on what would be their bed. It was a mattress on the floor, with linens, quilts, and pillows.

"You know, Adam. You don't fill out that gown proper," Albert teased.

Adam looked at him and pulled an elegant British Cavalry pistol out of his pocket. "No but I am packing."

"I see that." Pierre reached forward and pulled the gown off Adam's feet. "Keep that laudanum away. There's a history. Stay away from the windows. Don't leave this floor. And anything we have is now yours, Adam. Not that it's much."

Zoey returned to Adam with a shot glass of liquid to offer. She sat beside him to see him drink his laudanum. "Where do you do cooking?"

"Either fireplace. Usually this one. We have some pots and dishes and stuff. I'll get what you need," Albert said.

"I can cook. I have many foods to share, for all," Zoey said.

Albert and Pierre brought up more baskets and bags.

"I'm told we have a bit of a feast for you, to thank you for taking us in for a few days," Adam said. "And be aware, Robin has some plain clothed officers stationed outside, watching the house."

"And very handsome ones, I noticed," Pierre said, to much laughter.

"We've never had a lady in here. Please forgive the general atmosphere." Albert indicated the nude paintings behind her.

"Zoey, they can turn those paintings around, if you like," Adam said. "Do they offend you?"

Zoey looked at the nudes for a moment. "She's pretty. Not her face."

That made the guys laugh.

"Was she here in this room? Not with her dress?" Zoey asked.

"Well, you could say that, yes," Albert said.

"Prostitute," Pierre added.

Zoey's eyes went wide.

"Oh, I think she knows that word," Adam said.

"Prostitute here?" Zoey asked.

"Just for us to paint her," Pierre said. "To paint her. Charged us by the hour and we never laid a finger on her."

"Zoey, you are safe here," Adam explained. "They only wanted to paint her. No sex. Only with each other."

While Zoey figured that out, the artists burst out laughing.

"Welcome, Mrs. Hudson, to the artist's lair," Pierre said. "We are delighted to have a real lady among us. Although you might become our new muse."

"If Adam does not," Pierre said. "Oh my God. You're so pale. You really did get your bell rung. I'm so worried about Ezra. I hope he makes it back here before dark."

Zoey sat down with her husband. "You need to eat. I make supper."

"I will show you how we heat things up over the fire. Pierre, get the fire going again," Albert said. "Let's get out the dishes."

"We brought. We have many things," Zoey said. "We have something for you. Adam, are you okay?"

"I'm okay right here. I'm so sorry about this, Zoey. I love you," Adam said.

Zoey leaned in and kissed his mouth. "Ik hou van jou." She rose and followed Pierre and Albert toward the baskets by the fireplace.

Pierre stacked firewood into the fireplace and worked to get it lit from the coals again.

Zoey unpacked dishware, cups and saucers, and some wine glasses.

Albert knelt beside Zoey and held the wineglass up. He ran his wet finger round the rim, making it sing. "Are you insane, Adam? This is crystal. You brought crystal here, to Chateau Taudis? To the slum?"

Adam laughed.

"You may not get it back," Albert said.

"I don't care. What's mine is yours." Adam shrugged.

"You warm enough?" Pierre asked. "Let's pull his sofa closer to the fire. Let's make a little seating area there. What can we make a table out of? Bring that drawing board over here and lay it out on these crates."

Zoey glanced at them setting up this bizarre little table in the midst of two couches and some foot stools. She returned to unpacking the food for dinner.

"This is clean. I washed it myself." Albert offered a pot to her. He held it out for Zoey to pour stew into. Then he hung it over the fire. "Is that beef stew? We haven't had beef in here in...."

"We never had," Pierre said. "I have an idea." He brought over a cloth they used for still life paintings and laid it out like a tablecloth. Then he brought over some oil lamps and candles. He began to light them about the area, on crates.

Albert began setting their little table with china and silverware. "Adam, we can feed you like a baby bird." He demonstrated with a silver spoon.

Adam waved him off. "You will not."

The guys laughed again.

And then Zoey set out two bottles of wine.

Pierre picked one up to examine. "This is from France. Did you know that?" He teared up a bit. He sniffled. "Ezra will love this."

Albert put an arm around Pierre. "I'll open it for you. You'll hurt yourself."

"Are you? Are they a...couple?" Zoey looked at Adam.

"The three of us are," Albert replied. "Sort of. Ezra cheats a lot. But he owns the gallery and has more of an income."

Zoey just returned to unpacking a basket of rolls, plate of sliced cheese, selection of sausages.

"When will we know he's okay?"

The young painter ducked his hat out of the carriage doorway and stepped down when all he heard, in his mind, were explosions. Ezra suddenly found himself face down on the cobblestones with Van der Kellen on top of him.

Right in his ear he heard, "Get up and run now! Stay with me!"

Ezra got up and held onto Robin's left arm. They were blocked by a man who got shot in the chest. Robin pulled Ezra to dodge and they ran toward the hotel doors, held open by police. They dashed straight inside, straight through the lobby, down a hall and out a back door.

Ezra found himself opening it up, running full out right beside Van der Kellen. Robin's coat fluttered open like a cape. Ezra could barely keep up with him, having an arm splinted to his chest. Robin grabbed him by that sling and pulled him through an alley slippery with snow, and suddenly there were men with guns in front of them. They skidded to a stop, reversed back around a corner.

"Are they shooting at us? C'mon!" Ezra jumped up to the bottom rung of a fire escape ladder. He put his right arm straight through the sling and climbed. "C'mon, Robin!"

Robin fired a few shots and yelled to him, "Go, go, go!" Then Robin had to holster the weapon and jump onto the ladder beneath Ezra. He climbed right up after him. "Inside anywhere!"

Bullets ricocheted off the metal ladder and the brick wall around them.

"Holy Jesus!" Ezra broke a window, and then rolled in. "C'mon. This way."

Robin dove inside, taking Ezra down again and they rolled into a narrow hallway. Robin just pulled a piece of glass out of Ezra's hair and looked at it. "No blood."

A woman blocked their passage, yelling at them.

Ezra pulled Robin up. "Sorry lady, bit of a hurry here." They squeezed past her. "Stairs! Stairs!"

"Up! Go up!" Robin hurried after him. They scrambled up several flights of stairs and came to the top with a door that was locked.

Beneath them they heard the commotion of those men starting up from the bottom.

"Now what, Captain?" Ezra caught his breath.

"Get out of my way." Robin ran his left shoulder hard into the door, crashing it open and he fell onto the floor inside an attic. Some people inside screamed. A woman came at Robin with a broom.

Ezra immediately took a blow in the right arm from that broom, blocking Robin's head. "Ow!" Ezra yelled back at the woman, "Alhijrat qadima! Kayf nakhruj min huna?"

She pointed and ran.

Several people quickly fled the room.

"Come on!" Ezra grabbed Robin by the arm and hurried toward a window on the far side. Through the opening he could see a wooden ladder laid out across the alley to the next building. A boy had just scrambled across and looked back at them from the window. Then he disappeared.

Robin looked over his shoulder at it. "You've got to be kidding me!"

"That kid just made it across. Come on." Ezra started onto the ladder and crawled ten feet across to the next building. Then he turned and put all his weight down on the ladder to hold it.

Robin made eye contact with Ezra and crawled out onto it. Seeing how far below the ground was, he froze.

"Come on!" Ezra shouted. "You can do it, Robin. Just look at me."

"I was listening, dammit!" Robin hurried to join him and Ezra pulled him in by whatever body part he could grab. "Knock the ladder down. Knock it down."

They both shoved it until it fell. For a moment they both sunk below the window and gasped to catch their breath.

"What did you yell at her?" Robin withdrew his arm from around Ezra's neck.

"Immigration is coming." Ezra detangled their legs.

Nose to nose with him, Robin pulled him to his feet. "Stairs down this time."

Robin led them, running down several flights and out the back door to again run full out through an alley. "Left, left, left!" Robin yelled.

They made several more turns and then slipped into the back door of another hotel. Two policemen hurried them inside to the stairway. Up three flights of stairs they ran together. And at the top, Ezra tripped and fell on the floor, gasping for breath, sliding against a closed door. The door suddenly opened behind him and he rolled, blocking his head with both arms.

The policeman said to them in a hushed voice, "Adam Hudson got away out the back of the hospital."

Ezra looked up at a police officer and Robin Van der Kellen.

"Get word to my wife that we made it." Robin held out both hands to Ezra. "Are you injured?"

Ezra grabbed his hands. "Amazing!"

Robin pulled him to his feet. "Let's get inside and stay quiet."

Ezra and Robin entered this hotel room with one bed in the middle. The policeman remained outside in the hall. Robin locked the door.

For several moments the two of them just struggled to catch their breath. While Ezra poured down to the floor beside the bed, Robin collapsed into an armchair. Ezra held a hand to his own heaving chest and laid his chin on the bedspread. "Did you shoot that man for me?"

"Yes, but he's not our man. We can only hope the one that stabbed Adam was there someplace and the police got him. Stay down. You may not be able to hear well until tomorrow. You will have bruises...from this. Sorry."

"You protected me...with your own body." Ezra laid his arm out across the bed, still kneeling beside it. "Did I do all right?"

"They totally fell for it. Yes. Adam got away." Robin walked to the side of a window and peeked out through the sheer curtain. He could see the police and the carriage at the hotel portico down the street. He could hear the sirens. And he held his right arm tightly to his side.

"Are you hurt, Robin?" Ezra said.

"It's nothing."

"How long do we wait?" Ezra asked.

"Long as it takes. Til it is dark."

Ezra crawled diagonally across the bed. Then he smiled and patted the other side. "Well, Aramis, however will we pass the time?"

"Didn't you feel me up enough already?"

Ezra rolled to his back, laughing uncontrollably. "Oh my God, that was more thrilling than sex, and you and I did it together."

"Spoken by a man who's clearly never had sex. Keep your voice down. Keep away from the window." Robin made his way back to the armchair and sat down to begin reloading his revolver.

Ezra rolled to his side to watch him slipping bullets into the carrousel of his Colt.

Robin spun the carrousel into position and then rose from the chair just enough to slip the gun into the holster on his right hip. He collapsed back and shut his eyes for a moment. He held his right arm in his left.

Ezra shrugged. "Are you injured, for real?"

"My shoulder is just in pain right now," Robin said quietly. "Are you all right, D'Artagnan?"

"No way that just happened." Ezra dropped his forehead down on the quilt. He let out a hard breath.

"Was that Arabic? Immigration is coming?" Then Robin laughed heartily.

Ezra laughed into the quilt.

"You got bystanders out of the way while saving us. Well done. You just became an officer."

Quick but quiet footsteps on the stairs made Adam duck down on the sofa, and Zoey move behind the paintings. The boys went to the door.

A raspy voice said, "It's me."

Pierre pulled open the door and Ezra rushed inside to be taken into Albert's arms. "Are you okay?"

Grabbing Ezra by the arm made him cry out in pain.

Adam sat up to look.

Pierre locked the door again.

"I'm all right. He was amazing, you guys. You have no idea what just happened to me," Ezra gushed.

Albert kissed Ezra on the mouth and then Pierre did and the three of them embraced. "We were so worried about you. Worried sick."

"What's wrong with your arm? Let me see it?" Pierre asked.

"Later for that. How did it go with Adam?" Ezra peeked out of their arms to take him in just as Zoey emerged. "Adam?" Ezra walked toward him and reached out both hands to grab onto the back of the sofa. He ducked down and wrapped his arms gently around Adam's neck from behind. "We were shot at and Robin threw me beneath him to the ground. I was sheltered beneath his body. And then you guys won't believe what happened."

Adam felt the excitement gushing from him, and smiled.

Ezra sat on the back of Adam's sofa. "He pulled me up and we started running toward the hotel with all these police around us and this man blocks our path. I only learned later that he had a gun pointed right at me. I just see the guy splattered with blood and he falls backwards. I had to identify the guy in the morgue later. Robin just pulled me up and we ran. And I mean, I never ran so hard in all my life. The next thing I know I am running out the hotel and down the alley side by side like a Musketeer with Robin Van der Kellen."

Pierre stood close beside Ezra, smoothing a hand through Ezra's hair. "Is this glass in your hair? Ezra?"

"Little bit, yeah." Ezra leaned back against him. "Together we ran through alleys, climbed fire escape ladders, climbed stairs. We crossed to the next building on a ladder four floors up. Then we ran downstairs again and into alleys. He led me into another hotel, up the back stairs, and into a room. He kept me safe in there while he reloaded this Colt and he monitored the situation down the road through the window curtains." Finally, he lowered his chin to his chest and sighed. "We talked for hours until the sun went down. I'm so in love that my heart is actually stunned. I'm so in awe of him. Aramis indeed. And he's so funny. You know I tried to get him into bed with me."

At that Pierre and Albert burst out laughing.

"You did not," Adam said.

"You ask him."

Ezra helped Adam get up and walked him round the canvasses to the little sanctuary they'd made for the married couple. Surrounding their mattress on the floor were crates for tables. Their belongings were on the side. It wasn't too far from the fireplace, and yet secluded by those tall works of art. One oil lamp was lit in the little sanctuary.

Ezra eased Adam down to the mattress. "Can I get you anything? Are you all right here?"

"Thank you so much. I'm fine here. Take a bit more laudanum and I will try to sleep some," Adam said. "Zoey will help me. Did he hurt you, when he threw you down?"

Ezra smiled warmly. "Only bruises I will covet as long as they last."

She was standing behind Ezra.

Ezra stood up and set his hands on his hips. "Zoey Princess, is there anything I can get you? Anything at all?"

"Thank you, Ezra. Thank you." Zoey patted him on the arm. Then she gave him a shy little kiss on the cheek that he had to stoop down for.

"I'm just over there. Get me if you need anything." Ezra exited their little corner. "Good night precious ones."

Zoey knelt down beside Adam. There was no door to close as there was no bedroom, really. She whispered to her husband, "Are they sleeping all together over there?"

He nodded. "I believe so. I think we have Ezra's bed." He set his pistol up on the crate where the oil lamp was.

"Did you ever sleep with them?" she whispered.

"No. No darling. I'm your husband." Adam slid toward the pillows and reclined down on the mattress. "It's cold in here."

"You want trousers off?" Zoey asked.

"No. Let's get under these quilts."

Robin sat down at the Miller's dining table at a place set just for him as it was nearly eight PM. Marie and Elizabeth sat down with him and they all had glasses of wine.

"Well, we made it. I have to admit, I'm not sure I could have done that without Ezra August. He looked just enough like Adam that we had shots fired at us. Had to identify a body at the morgue. That's why I'm late. Had to bring Ezra identify him also and then drop Ezra off at his home, immigrant neighborhood across the island from here." Robin held his right hand in his lap and picked up the spoon with his left hand. "I almost had second thoughts when I saw the place, with leaving Adam and Zoey in his care there."

"A body? What body?" Marie questioned.

"The man I shot, you could say," Robin said. "Gun was pointed at Ezra."

"What, um, what exactly did Mr. August do? How did he conduct himself on your harrowing escape?" Elizabeth asked. "Is he all right?"

"He was brilliant, actually. He fashioned two escapes for us, all on his own. We went up a fire escape ladder, firstly. And then when trapped on a fourth floor with the gunmen running up the stairs, Ezra led us across the alley to the next building on another ladder and some planking which we knocked down so they could not follow us or even see where we went," Robin said.

"You climbed ladders and crossed alleys on planking?" Marie reached for his right arm.

He resisted. "Yeah my shoulder is really hurting right now. But my point is, we're all right. We made it. And Ezra really surprised me. He really came through. And you know what else he did? He saved bystanders in the process."

"And he had to look upon a body in the morgue?" Elizabeth recoiled. "How dreadful. Did he faint? Was it so awful?"

"There's strength in him I couldn't have imagined, a quick intelligence. It's ironic that he said he ran away from home to escape conscription into the army, and yet, he would have made a fine soldier even an officer. Undisciplined though." Robin ate his chowder for a moment. "I had a long talk with him while we were in hiding. He learned to paint in Paris. He's had every odd job you can think of from fish monger to running a print making machine for a newspaper. No military experience. No weapons training and yet, I would have to say I actually hold some admiration for him."

"Well, you were looking for a hero." Marie smiled.

"I found a Musketeer."

In the early moments of sunrise, Adam rolled over and hurt his arm. He cried out in such pain that his companions came running.

Zoey was beneath the blankets with him and sat up, holding her covers up.

"Adam, are you all right?" Ezra stood there in undershorts hanging off his hips and his flat abdomen showing beneath a white under shirt.

Adam sunk his head down into his pillow, moaning. He had to catch his breath to say, "I just twisted my arm. Oh my God that hurt."

"Show me. Are you bleeding again?" Ezra entered their little area, rounding the mattress to Adam's side as if he gave no thought at all to how revealing his underclothing was. "Thought that splint kept you from doing that."

"So did I. Now I see why they insisted I wear this." Adam rolled back toward Zoey to sit up and examine his bandages and splint.

Zoey looked away from Ezra's beautiful body and the shadow of dark hair through his white undershorts.

"Came loose, it looks like," Ezra said. "I'm so sorry, Zoey. Didn't mean to intrude. If I had a proper bedroom to offer you, I'd be knocking on a door."

"They thought I was dying or something," Adam told her. "I'm okay. Just...bleeding again."

"I'll get the fire going." Albert backed out of their corner.

"What can I do?" Zoey asked.

"Help me get up," Adam told her.

Zoey looked up at the two men standing over their bed.

"Oh, sorry. We'll start some coffee. How about that?" Ezra pulled Pierre away. "Let her get dressed, you idiot."

"I'm an idiot? You're practically naked," Pierre said.

"There's a woman here now. We can't just barge in," Ezra said. "Sorry Adam. Just not accustomed to wearing proper attire. Next time I'll wear a top hat, I promise."

"Hey, Ezra, help me up. Then get some pants on, will you?"

Zoey had gotten dressed in one of her travel gowns and emerged from behind the partition. Her hair was still down, shiny black hair down to her waist. It swept around her as she turned.

All four of the men looked at her.

Adam was sitting on the couch while Ezra was opening his splint. As Adam was still in his sleep shirt and trousers, Albert wrapped a blanket around his shoulders.

"What? Should I make the coffee?" Zoey questioned.

"No. Pierre went for a coffee grinder and a pot. He'll be back with it," Ezra said. "She's beautiful, Adam. You're really beautiful with your hair down, Zoey Princess."

"Oh?" She smiled. "I didn't have time yet to…"

The attic door opened and Pierre entered, carrying the coffee grinder and a coffee pot of water. "How is he?"

"Bleeding a little. We're changing bandages," Ezra reported.

Pierre set up beside the fire, on their little table, to open the coffee Adam had brought. As it was whole beans, he had to grind it first.

"I'm so sorry." Zoey knelt beside Pierre to help him. "You did not have one of these?"

"We borrow stuff from downstairs all the time. We haven't had the luxury of real coffee up here before. And look at all the other food that you brought, the eggs and bacon, the biscuits…" Pierre said.

"This is your kitchen?" Zoey indicated the fireplace. Then she and Pierre both laughed.

"It is now," Pierre said.

Adam could barely watch as Ezra unwrapped the bandages. And they stuck a bit to his stitches, making him wince as the cloth peeled back. The more he peeled, the more Adam rose from the sofa.

"Easy. Easy. Boil some water, Pierre," Ezra said.

"Boil water? What for?" Adam stressed.

"Easy. Calm down. We're going to use warm water to wet this so we can get the bandage off. Then we'll clean the wound and redress it." Ezra supported Adam's arm and reached for the scissors.

"What are you doing with those?" Adam gasped.

"Cutting the rest of the bandage away. The weight of it pulling is hurting you," Ezra said.

By Susan Eddy

Zoey looked on, concerned.

"I'm not going to hurt you," Ezra insisted. "That knife was huge. Look at this. Three inches down the middle of your arm and went right through the other side."

"Tell me something I don't know," Adam said.

"It doesn't look too bad though." Ezra winced. "Zoey should do the clean bandages. She saw how they did it at the hospital. Zoey, come on in here."

Zoey sat right beside Adam. "Water is on."

"Hold his arm level here. Just like this." Ezra moved Adam's wrist into her hand on her knee. Then he worked with the scissors to cut away any bandage that wasn't stuck to him. "Were you cold last night? Slept in your trousers."

"We were okay," Adam said.

"We'll get some more firewood. Could you by any chance…" Ezra snipped at the last of the bandage and set the pile aside on the table. "I hate to ask you."

"Oh? What? Anything," Adam said.

"We burned the last of the crates we don't need last night," Ezra admitted.

"You need to purchase firewood? Zoey, give them a few dollars," Adam said.

"Yes. I have his purse," Zoey said. "What do you need?"

"Give them five dollars in small coins," Adam said. "Remember how we count money over here?"

"The small coins confuse," Zoey admitted.

"Just bring a handful and let Ezra take what they need," Adam said.

"Coffee is started," Pierre announced. "I'm starting on the bacon then. Right?"

"Yes, absolutely," Albert agreed. "You want some whiskey?"

"Bring it here," Ezra said. "You want to take some laudanum before we do this? Or a couple hits of whiskey?"

Albert brought the bottle and set it down on the table beside them.

Everyone was looking at Adam. "They would make me take laudanum in the hospital for this. Then they poured alcohol on the wound, dried it, and put on clean wrappings."

"Zoey, bring his medicine, please," Ezra said.

She nodded and set her hand on Adam's shoulder as she rose.

Once she was behind the divider, Ezra put the whiskey bottle to Adam's mouth and helped him drink liberally from it. Then he set the bottle down while Adam wiped his mouth with his left hand. Ezra was supporting the injured arm by holding Adam's wrist elevated.

Zoey returned with a shot glass of laudanum for Adam.

He drank that too. "God that's awful. Give me that whiskey." He then had another good drink from the bottle.

Ezra kept a straight face but Pierre and Albert had to turn away to keep from laughing. "Coffee. Focus on coffee. You cook that bacon."

Adam had a bit of coffee, some bacon, a biscuit, before the water was hot enough for cleaning his wound. By then he was drowsy anyway, needing to curl down on his side on the sofa. Ezra and Zoey could work on cleaning his wounds, removing the stuck cotton bandages, dabbing with whiskey, and then rewrapping his arm. They put the blanket over him and let him sleep while they entertained Zoey with breakfast and their fussing over Adam.

Albert and Ezra came in with bundles of firewood. Setting all of this down by the fireplace awoke Adam again. They got the fire going again and served Adam a cup of coffee. Adam sat up in his sleep shirt and blanket.

"There is something I would like to do for you guys. Zoey and I discussed it, last night," Adam said.

"You don't have to do anything," Albert told him.

"I want to buy you a place to live, a place with real bedrooms and beds and a kitchen," Adam said. "I own it. You live in it and make paintings. You won't have to pay rent any longer. I could hire you a cook and a maid."

"Adam, I...I don't know how we can accept. I don't know how we can refuse this either," Ezra stammered.

"I'm putting you in terrible danger right now. You risked your life for me, Ezra. And you so kindly are hiding Zoey and myself away in your home," Adam said. "Let me do this."

"You paid us so much for your lessons," Pierre said. "How do we?"

"And I see my money was spent on canvas and pigments. Certainly not on luxuries," Adam replied. "Such as warm blankets or a proper dining table, or wood for your fireplace."

Zoey sat down with Adam on the sofa, fluffing up his hair. "You just let him do this. You do. You are good guys."

"After Robin catches this murderer, we will look for a place together. Not something extravagant, but rooms for each of you and a place for your studio. You could have a gallery in a neighborhood where people actually pay artists and purchase portraits and such," Adam told them. "Do you own that gallery, Ezra?"

"I do. Barely. Adam, we've barely had enough money to scrape together for food some days." Ezra bowed his head. "Rent is always late. Pierre got beat up and robbed last month."

"And I have been homeless. I slept in an alley. I used empty wine crates to keep out of the rain," Adam said. "It would please me very much to spend my father's money on my friends."

Ezra looked at his artist friends. "Adam, I don't know how we came to be this. I came to America for the dream, you know? To be an artist and run my own show. How is it the three of us can't even afford food? We're not that stupid."

"Of course you're not. But this world is so hard. It is so hard to survive. Let me help you," Adam said. "You saved me."

Chapter Nine   Artist's Lair

There was a knock on the door. Adam met eyes with Zoey and they both retreated to their makeshift bedroom.

Ezra went to the door and opened it just a bit. "Oh hey Marco. No, sorry. We have a model and she does not want to be seen. Working on her all week. She's quite shy. Yeah, we'll see you in the tavern later. See you there."

"Model? I can't see the model?"

"No, man." Ezra closed and locked the door.

Zoey took Adam by the arm and walked him back to the couch he'd been sitting on.

Adam took his seat again. "You know, you should go to the tavern tonight and look as normal as possible."

"I can try," Ezra said.

"Without any mention of me. Your model is having a secret portrait made for her husband." Adam glanced over at the two paintings Albert and Pierre had started of Zoey.

"True enough," Ezra agreed.

"What's she paying me?" Pierre asked.

Adam laughed. "Zoey, what are you paying? I happen to know your husband will love those."

"Wait." Zoey returned to their space to her luggage.

Pierre sat down across from Adam while Albert poured more coffee for the guys.

Zoey came back to them and offered a gold coin to each artist.

Albert looked at his coin. "Does she know what this is?"

"I don't know. What did she give you?" Adam replied.

"Ten dollars," Albert said. "You?"

"Ten." Pierre nodded.

"Well, she's a rich woman. You'd better get those portraits finished," Adam teased.

"No. This is too much." Pierre tried to hand it back to Zoey.

She waved him off. "Keep. Yes, Adam?"

"Keep them. Have some drinks on me tonight. Buy a few things you may need," Adam said. "I don't want to give you more right now as it may draw attention to the attic. Just keep a lid on it."

"I'll stay here tonight. You two go to the tavern. Someone should stay to look after the situation," Albert said. "Don't show both of those coins. Just one of you cash it in for drinks."

"Situation? Is that what I am now?" Adam smiled.

"Hey, can I give you shave?" Pierre asked.

"I like his whiskers," Ezra protested.

"That? Those are not whiskers," Pierre said. "It's fuzz I can remove."

They all laughed.

"Zoey, want him to have a shave?" Pierre questioned.

"This?" Zoey reached out to touch Adam's light mustache. "It is cute. He looks older."

"Five minutes older," Ezra said.

Hobson, winded after climbing the three flights of stairs, entered the humble attic and for moment could only work to catch his breath. Ezra had let him in.

Adam rose from his sofa.

The artists stayed their brushes.

Zoey was sitting beside the east windows, in the morning sun, in her simple gown with a shawl about her, as their model.

"Hobson, no one saw you, I trust?" Adam said to him. "Get him some coffee."

"No, thank you. I came with more supplies for you. If you would send these fellows down to the wagon out back. There are boxes of more food." Hobson looked about. "So this is an artist's lair."

Zoey hopped up and went to stand with Adam.

"Any word from Robin?" Adam asked.

"He is still working on the case. Still hoping that you would remember any detail about your attacker," Hobson said. "Go get the boxes before they go missing in this neighborhood."

"The police are still out there?" Adam said.

"They are," Hobson said.

The three artists left then, down the stairs together.

"Do you remember anything besides dark eyebrows?" Hobson asked. "Dark hair color then, right? Well-dressed or poor?"

"No. White hair, almost. That's what struck me about the dark eyebrows," Adam blurted out.

"White hair and dark eyebrows? Sounds like Sinclare to me," Hobson said. "Thought he was good friends with Mr. Rothschild."

"Sinclare? Uncle Gerard's butler?" Adam asked. "What does he look like?"

"Tall slender fellow. About forty years in age. Gray hair and yet the most black of eyebrows," Hobson said.

"Deep set eyes. Bit of a mustache. Dark sideburns," Adam picked up. "Does he wear a funny after shave? Almost like a woman's lilac water?"

"Yes. A flowery smell, for certain," Hobson said.

"Oh my God. Why would...what would Sinclare stand to gain if Gerard was dead?" Adam questioned.

"Nothing except that with Bernard jailed for the murder, there is no one to claim the fortune, except for you. There could be some trust set aside for Sinclare in that case," Hobson said. "Surely Robin will figure that one out."

"You must hurry straight to Robin and tell him this," Adam said. "And do be careful."

"How is your arm, Mr. Hudson? Your mother worries so," Hobson said.

"Thank you for the food. My arm is better every day. Assure mother that I am well."

"And that no one can find you here. I almost didn't and I had a map from Van der Kellen himself to follow." Hobson paused and indicated toward the paintings of the nude woman. "Is ah...is she around?"

Robin was approached by a man, and Robin unbuttoned his jacket, revealing the pistol on his hip.

The man paused. "You have to be him. The lawyer."

"And you work for me, genius," Robin said.

"Detective March, sir. I beg your pardon."

Robin shook hands with him. "Robin Van der Kellen."

"Pleasure."

"Been quiet here?" Robin asked as they stood beneath the awning of a laundry.

"All morning. His butler brought supplies to them earlier. I would suggest he not return. He's been here twice now. He must send someone else the next time," the detective said.

"I'll tell him," Robin said. "Do you mind if I go up?"

"Be my guest, sir."

"Carry on then." Robin crossed the street, in the rain, and climbed the steps to the side door. The wooden door was not locked. He entered and pulled off his leather hat.

Two women were coming down the hallway.

Robin started up the stairs but gave the women a bit of a bow. "Good evening, ladies."

"Good evening to you, sir," one said. "Who are you looking for? Me, I hope."

"Thank you. There would be some painters making something for me," Robin said.

"The very top. And tell that idiot Pierre to keep it down the next time he comes in drunk in the middle of the night, would you?"

"Pierre? Again? Yes, I'll tell him." Robin began climbing stairs.

The women watched him from below.

A couple passed him on their way down, two children hurrying after them.

"Good evening," Robin said in passing them all.

The couple ignored him, herding the children and speaking Hungarian.

Robin kept climbing up and round. He knew it was the attic, so he kept climbing. Finally at the top, he knocked on the door. He heard footsteps inside on the wooden floor.

"Who is it?"

"I'm here to see Pierre," Robin said.

"He's not here."

"You are Pierre," Robin said.

"No, I'm not."

"Oh, knock it off and open the door!" Robin snapped.

There was laughter inside and the door opened.

Robin was standing with hands on his hips.

The laughter immediately stopped.

"Oh my God. It's you." Albert stepped back such that Robin might enter.

Robin met eyes with Adam, who was seated on a couch with a blanket over him and a big grin. Zoey got up from beside Adam.

"You don't know his voice by now?" Adam asked.

"Which one of you is Pierre?" Robin looked at the men.

"Me, sir. Me," Pierre said, still holding a long paintbrush with blue paint on it.

Robin shut the door and locked it. "You need to keep it down when you come in late at night. You draw too much attention."

"How does he..." Pierre looked to Albert and Ezra.

Adam smiled. "He knows everything."

"Can I get you some tea, Mr. Van der Kellen?" Ezra offered.

"Yes. Thank you." Robin walked to Adam and laid a hand on his blanket. "How are you?"

"I'm okay. Surprised you risked coming here," Adam said. "But glad to see you."

"With the rain out there, nobody saw me. I walked from the trolley stop." Robin went directly toward the nude paintings and started turning them toward the wall. "What is wrong with you men? There is a lady present. Seriously."

"Sorry, sir. You are quite right," Albert said.

"There is a gentleman present," Adam commented.

"I thought you were raised a gentleman?" Pierre asked.

"He was, but he turned feral," Ezra replied.

That made Robin just squint at Ezra. Only then did Robin turn to take in the attic in its entirety, the mattresses on the floor, the cooking pots near the fireplace, the big windows and paint supplies on the tables. One of the canvasses Robin had moved was still wet and Robin looked at wet paint on his hand.

"Oh, I'll get you something for that. Don't move." Pierre hurried to wet a rag with some oil and bring the rag to Robin. He wiped the paint off Robin's palm and finger. "Can take months to fully dry. Sorry about that. You have beautiful hands. He has beautiful hands. Have you seen these?

Of course, you have." Then he checked that the canvas was distanced from the wall enough, as it faced the wall now.

"Are...are you comfortable here? You were brought food. This I know." Robin looked to Zoey and Adam. And again he made sweep of the attic, seeing mattresses on the floor. His brow furrowed.

Ezra brought Robin the cup of tea. "Join us for supper, Robin?"

Robin held the saucer and teacup. "Thank you. Zoey, these are not decent conditions for you. I had no idea when I put you in their care that..."

"We're okay, Robin," Adam spoke up. "And we are well hidden here."

Ezra moved behind Robin and took a lock of his hair to sniff. Then he slid one hand down his back all the way until he picked up one of the tails of his jacket to turn it over and reveal the black silk. Robin turned and freed his jacket from Ezra.

Pierre and Albert burst out laughing and then stifled it.

"I'll give you that one, Ezra." Robin spun to look at him. "Are you done petting me?"

"Not for my part," Ezra said. "How's your shoulder?"

"How's your arm?" Robin moved away from him and took a seat across from Adam. "I had an agenda in coming to you. Are you certain you could pick out your attacker from a lineup of similar men?"

"Similar?" Adam asked.

"Say they all have white hair and dark eyebrows," Robin suggested. "I cannot guarantee the man has the same aftershave that he did the day he stabbed you. But I'll have our suspect in the line."

"I'll know him when I see him," Adam said. "Hobson talked to you?"

Robin nodded. "You never met this Sinclare personally?"

"No."

"I'm not certain he didn't come to your trial. He may have been there with your uncle. You wouldn't recognize him from the courtroom?" Robin questioned.

"I don't believe so. I'll only be going with what I saw when the man came at me with that knife," Adam said.

Robin set down his teacup on the makeshift table between himself and Adam. He reached into his inside jacket pocket and pulled out something wrapped in white cloth. They all watched Robin's hands as he unwrapped a dagger. It was ivory handled and the blade was about two inches wide and ten inches long. He laid it on the table, displayed there on the white cloth.

"Jesus." Ezra leaned over Robin to examine it.

The guys gathered around.

"That's what you pulled out of his arm?" Albert said.

Ezra moved behind Adam's couch and laid a hand on Adam's shoulder. "You poor doll. That is horrific knowing it came out of you."

"And you are the bravest man, to separate Adam from that," Albert added.

Robin glanced up at Albert. The eye contact made Albert shudder.

Robin said with icy coldness, "You were waiting inside the Rothschild mansion, near the front entrance. You heard the breaking of glass."

"I pulled my gun on him. White short hair. Bushy black eyebrows. Deep set eyes. Large nose. Dark sideburns." Adam picked up the story. "As tall as me. Heavier though. Hair wasn't purely white. Some darkness in it. Why isn't that in evidence at the police station?"

"I hold influence." Robin picked up his teacup.

"Don't have to tell me," Ezra commented.

"Bernard identified it. I saw the cabinet where it was housed. It was displayed with a number of African artifacts in a glass case in Gerard Rothschild's parlor. There's no other knife like this in New York," Robin went on.

"My mother sent her Tuscan chicken," Adam told him. "We are heating it now."

"Tuscan chicken? Is that garlic and onions I smell?" Robin asked.

Adam smiled. "And my mother's pasta."

"I knew you were half Italian. Tuscany? I traveled through Tuscany you know?" Robin said.

"Tell us what you remember about his homeland, Mr. Van der Kellen. Get you a glass of wine?" Pierre offered.

"Don't worry, we'll get you back to the trolley stop before they quit for the night." Ezra went to the fireplace to help with the supper.

Robin looked about. "You...you do not even have a proper dining table."

"Get off your high horse, sir. You've done with less," Adam remarked.

They burst out laughing. Ezra doubled over, laughing.

Robin finally laughed. He looked up as a plate of chicken, roasted tomatoes and pasta was offered to him over the incorrect shoulder. And then he was offered a fork. Robin accepted them. "This is very inappropriate. Running with wolves, are we?"

A glass of wine was set before him by Ezra. "Run on sir. I think you can handle it."

A plate was set for Adam and Zoey.

And they sat back and dined on good food.

Robin Van der Kellen pulled a Colt revolver from his pocket, laid it on the crate beside him, and laid his body down on the sofa. Ezra unfolded a wool blanket over him. And for a while, without the Dutchman knowing, Ezra, Albert, and Pierre were all watching him sleeping.

In the dawn light, Robin jerked awake and sat up to find the three artists all asleep on the floor around him, with sheets of paper all around.

Robin sat up, mindful of where he put his feet. There were drawings of his face as he slept, his hands, his hair, his expression. Drawings of his body reclining across their sofa.

The floor creaked behind him.

Adam was standing behind the sofa and put his left hand on Robin's shoulder. "You had a lot of wine last night. We couldn't let you take the trolley alone."

Ezra sat up on the floor. He began gathering the papers out of the way.

"Marie will be worried." Robin rubbed at his eyes.

"She'll know you were looking after me," Adam said.

Pierre scrambled toward the fireplace. "I'll get you a cup of coffee, sir."

"Ezra, I will have a word with you before I go." Robin nodded toward the far corner windows.

Ezra hurried to join him, giving Adam a look as he passed.

Robin waited and folded his arms with his back to the others.

Ezra stood before him, taller than Robin by about two inches. He said nothing.

Robin pulled something out of his pocket and held it out in his hand. It was a gold Ottoman cross on a chain. "You were as brave as any young soldier I have worked with. I would pin a medal on you, but I hope this will do. You spoke Arabic. You traveled from Rome to Nice to Paris. You ran away from home to avoid war with the Greeks. You're Turkish, aren't you? I made the assumption."

"My mother gave me one just like that, years ago. I don't have it anymore," Ezra said. "We speak a little Arabic and Greek, being from right in between them. You are exactly right. An Ottoman Muslim cross."

Robin stepped around him and fastened the cross necklace beneath his hair. "In honor of your braveness in battle, I present you with this medal and field promotion. May this keep you safe. May it remind you to keep your promises, to aim small, and to run fast. And while you're at it, let it be a reminder not to ever come on to me again."

The guys burst out laughing.

Ezra held onto his cross necklace. "Shouldn't have touched my hair then." Robin shot him a look, to which Ezra responded, "Sir."

Adam walked Robin to the door, smiling.

"I'll come for you tomorrow. Still have that gown?" Robin said confidentially to him.

"Yes."

"Put it on over your suit. Meet me at the back door," Robin said. "Ten o-clock. Ezra, you come with him to look after him, all right?"

"Yes, sir." Ezra still had his fingertips on that cross at his throat. "Do...I get a dress too?"

"I can't get it on over my jacket, but that's all right. I'll figure something out," Adam said. "I'll bring the jacket in a sewing bag."

"Are you all right, here?" Robin whispered.

"They'd do anything for me." Adam nodded. "We're all right here."

"Hang on for a few more days. It won't be much longer," Robin said.

"You should hire some protection for yourself. Don't be arrogant," Adam told him. "Please."

"I already have. Back door at ten. Okay?"

Adam reached his left arm up around Robin's shoulders and pulled him into a hug. "Be careful."

"You just get some rest." Robin hugged him and backed off. He took Adam's right hand into his to examine the fingers of his injured hand. Then he slid his hand up beneath Adam's bangs to feel his forehead. "You're healing. Keep the splint on. Get some rest."

Robin left, closing the door after him.

Adam locked it and listened to his boot steps sounding down the winding stairway. He listened there until he heard a door close below. Then he turned to find all of his artist friends gathered around him.

"All of you men are to stand still and face forward. Your blindfolds are to be left in place."

Robin took Adam by the arm and walked him down the lineup, behind the five men.

Ezra August leaned on the wall, his arms folded.

Adam already had one in mind, but he fully considered each. The deciding factor presented itself when Adam leaned closer to the back of one man's neck to give him a sniff. He quickly withdrew and tugged on Robin's coat. He nodded toward the exit. Ezra moved to intercept them.

Robin drew him silently out of the room and into a nearby interrogation room. The judge and prosecuting attorney were already waiting inside.

"Any conclusions, Mr. Hudson?" the judge asked.

"Number four. He's the man who stabbed me," Adam said solemnly.

"Number four?" Ezra jolted toward the line up room.

"Mr. August, calm down." Robin blocked him and grabbed him by the arms.

"Let me at him!" Ezra struggled.

"Calm down." Robin shook him, turned him, and pushed him to stand beside Adam. "And keep your mouth shut."

"Number four? Second from the end?" The judge stepped a bit further back from Ezra. "What if I told you he was our janitor?"

"You would be wrong. He's the man who stabbed me. I know that cologne anywhere. He smells like lilac water," Adam said.

"Jasmine, actually," Ezra said.

They all looked at him.

"What? You can't smell that?" Ezra snapped.

"Mouth shut, please," Robin urged.

"Any questions?" The judge looked to Bernard's prosecutor.

"It was dark. You saw dark eyebrows. You said he had white hair. Every man in there had such," the prosecutor said. "How do you know what he smelled like?"

"In the dark, when you cannot see, all your other senses become heightened. The breaking of glass. The grip he had on my throat. The smell of his cologne. Then he ripped the gun from my hand," Adam recanted. "I put my hands up in defense and took a knife right through my arm."

"Defensive wounds, his physician signed an affidavit," Robin added.

"Mr. Hudson, the man you identified was Mr. Sinclair, butler to Gerard Rothschild," the judge said. "Are you absolutely certain?"

"I am positive, your honor."

"He had access to the house. He had motive to eliminate Bernard Rothschild and Mr. Hudson," Robin said seriously. "He has the Rothchild safe combination and sign off rights to Gerard's accounts. He's probably cleaned them out already."

"I will remand him into custody," the judge said.

"I want his residence searched. I want that flintlock found, and Adam's Belgian pistol," Robin said. "And more security for Mr. Hudson and his family."

"You've got it."

"Ezra, you make sure there are police to accompany you home with him."

The artists sat cross legged on the floor, with Adam and Zoey joining them. The light of oil lamps and candles flickered and the meager warmth of the fireplace reached out to the little circle. A bottle of brandy passed from Ezra's hand into Adam's. Adam poured five crystal wine goblets with brandy. Each of them took a goblet and a drink.

Zoey coughed from hers.

"Sorry." Adam put a hand on her knee.

"Have you ever seen Robin?" Albert questioned. "Declothed? Sans vetements? Or for you, senza vestiti? Have you?"

"Why would you ask me that?" Adam

"What does he look like? Is he wonderful?" Ezra asked.

"What have you seen?" Pierre asked.

"I was his valet for a year. What do you think?" Adam said.

"I think he was modest," Albert said. "I don't think that man would ever, ever reveal himself to you, knowing how you are. Were. I mean. What are you doing?"

Ezra had drizzled some brandy on the back of his hand and was slowly licking it off while eyeing Adam.

Albert burst out laughing.

"That's not funny," Pierre said.

"Nice," Albert told Ezra.

Ezra smirked.

"Well, now that we know what somebody wants to do to Robin...and brandy is ruined for me." Adam sipped his brandy however, thinking how Robin would find this an inappropriate goblet and conversation. "I only once saw him completely nude but he was drugged on absinthe and would have torn his clothes off in front of anyone. He said he was hot. And it all came off. Every stitch. And practically a dance. I never saw a more graceful removal of trousers, followed by a more productive night of vomiting."

Ezra burst out laughing.

"What did you do? Did you have absinthe too?" Pierre asked, through the laughter.

"No. No. No. He was poisoned with absinthe by the British commander. Robin didn't know it was absinthe in his glass when he drank it. He knocked mine out of my hand, in fact," Adam explained. "He kissed me on the forehead once. It was the kindest, most heartfelt affection he ever afforded me."

"Did you ever kiss him?" Ezra asked.

"Couldn't dare to," Adam admitted.

"No?" Zoey asked.

"Oh my God she understands," Adam realized. "I'm sorry, my love. We were talking about Robin."

"I know. You saw him without his clothes? Is he lovely?" Zoey questioned, smiling.

The guys burst out laughing.

Adam laughed too. "Every inch of him, beautiful. Yes. Marie is a lucky woman."

"What did he look like?" Ezra persisted. "Any remarkable features? Snail trail? Circumcision, I hope?"

"I didn't look that closely," Adam said.

"Yeah you did. Draw me a picture later," Ezra said. "You know, I've been taken by a lot of men, but that one...he could do anything he wanted to me. He could throw me down hard, like he did in the street. He can get on top and I don't care what..."

"Enough, don't you think?" Albert reached for more brandy.

Ezra reached for cake from the plate between them. "Am I not allowed fantasy? While you two have each other right in front of me."

"Have you not had enough reality of your own?" Pierre said. "The waiter at Jackson's. The wine dealer on twelfth? That guy you sold the landscape for his office?"

"Pierre," Albert scolded.

Adam looked from one to the other.

Ezra brought the piece of cake to his mouth for a bite. "I never touched that landscape guy. He was straight, I told you."

"A triangle is difficult, I would think," Adam said. "Isn't one of you always left out?"

"Just me," Ezra said.

"It was the two of us who invited Ezra in, in the first place," Pierre said.

"Really? It wasn't the two of you chasing me down the street?" Ezra asked. "Memories are subjective, don't you agree?"

"We are intruding. We should go to bed," Zoey said.

"What a keen sense of emotion, Zoey princess has, when others around her have not," Ezra said. "Please stay, Zoey, that we might finish this discussion in a polite manner."

"We are imposing. The danger is putting stress on you," Adam said.

Ezra put a hand on Adam's shoulder. "Don't you dare get up in your condition, just because Pierre is being rude."

"He was jealous of the way you talk about Robin," Adam suggested. "Clearly they both care for you."

"I'm being rude? Who shoved who out of the bed this morning?" Pierre got up and walked away toward the mattress he shared with Albert. He dropped down and crawled into the covers. "And don't you even think about sleeping over here tonight."

"I am sorry." Zoey got up and patted her Adam on the shoulder. "I have to lie down."

And so Albert got up, and leaned to whisper to Ezra, "Let him fall asleep and come to my side." He went to the mattress on the floor with Pierre.

Ezra repoured and drank the expensive brandy that Adam had afforded them. When not sipping, his mouth was pursed tightly. His eyes were narrowed. His back was turned toward the side of the room where Albert lay with Pierre.

"You gave up your bed for us," Adam whispered. "Sleep with us tonight. When Zoey is asleep you lay beside me. She won't know."

"No. I'm afraid it is the cold couch for me, or the alley really. Could it be more clear than that? At least I have the memory of Robin lying there to keep me warm," Ezra said quietly. "Some people can only dream about what others have. Robin is straight as an arrow just for Marie and they have a child. I will never have any of that. Do you have any idea how much I love children? I had nine younger brothers and sisters."

"You have a very romantic view of love. Robin has his temptations. He hasn't taken any yet. Maybe he never will," Adam said. "But it is hard for him when women offer themselves to him so often. He loves Marie alone."

"That is what I mean. It is that which is unobtainable to me." Ezra looked down at his own hand as fingers came together as if grasping something. "Some people are meant to be alone. Obviously if I secretly marry a man, I'll never have children. Who am I kidding? I can't even afford a dog much less children."

"You just have not found the right one yet," Adam told him. "Man or woman. You don't know. Keep your heart open. I promise you."

Ezra and Adam drank quite a lot, whispering together into the night. And when time came to help Adam down onto his mattress, Adam would not let go of Ezra. In the dark and cold of night on the floor, Adam scooted down under the covers and wrapped his arms about Zoey. Behind Adam, Ezra lay on his back, staring up at the rafters. He pulled their covers up to his chin. He shared a mattress, blankets and pillows with them, but he couldn't have felt more isolated.

"Ez..." Adam heard him weeping quietly. "Did you get hurt in the escape?"

"Feeling a few sore spots, yes." Ezra smoothed his hands down his chest. "Robin's knee in my ribs. At least it wasn't my crotch."

"You risked your life for me," Adam said.

"Wouldn't you do anything Robin thought you could do?" Ezra rolled over with his back to Adam.

"I just...want to say how much I...really care about you," Adam whispered.

"I'll bet you'll be going home soon."

Adam put a hand on Ezra's back. "Then I'm buying you a building."

"Will you do me a favor?"

"Anything."

"Buy me a bed."

"Where did you get that bruise on your arm?" Adam asked him.

"Old lady hit me with a broom," Ezra said.

That made Adam burst out laughing. Then they were both crying laughing.

"You boys. Go to sleep." Zoey sat up.

They laughed even harder.

"Hey Zoey, by the way, can Ezra sleep with us?"

"You are both drunk boys," Zoey said.

"Did you ever sleep with a woman before?" Adam whispered.

"I had a girlfriend in Paris once. But I never slept with her. Well now here is something Zoey can brag to her friends about," Ezra said.

"What is that?"

"Zoey slept with two men," Ezra said.

Even Zoey laughed. "You not telling anyone."

"You want the middle, Zoey princess?"

Chapter Ten   Court a Woman

"My first witness will be Friedrich Schneider." Robin Van der Kellen stood up at his desk in the court room. He gave a glance to Marie, Zoey, and Elizabeth all sitting behind him with Adam and Ezra.

Adam whispered to Ezra, "Are you nervous?"

Ezra shrugged. "Nope."

An older man in plain suit rose and walked forward to the witness box. He entered, turned and raised his hand to swear to tell the truth. Then he took his seat.

Robin strolled closer to him. "Mr. Schneider, what is your profession at the estate of Gerard Rothschild?"

"Head cook, sir. I'm the head cook and I have served that household for two years."

"Thank you, sir," Robin said. "What did you witness on the morning following the shooting of Gerard Rothschild?"

"I entered the kitchen very early to begin to prepare the breakfast, knowing that mistress of the household, Mrs. Rothschild would need to keep her strength up. Others in the house would also need to eat," Schneider said.

"What made you go to the laundry shoot?"

"I heard one of the maids shrieking. Given what happened in the house the day before, I grabbed up a kitchen knife and ran toward the shriek of the woman." Schneider paused to take a breath.

"Take your time, Mr. Schneider."

"There were bloody things in the laundry. Of course cloths had been used to clean the floor. But that was not why she shrieked and fainted. As she lifted items from the basket, a gun had fallen out onto the floor," Schneider said.

Robin strode to the evidence box and picked up a walnut handled silver pistol. He carried this and showed it first to the judge and jury. Then he showed it to the witness. "Is this the gun?"

"Yes. This is the gun." Schneider nodded.

"Did you recognize the weapon at all?"

"No, sir. Never saw that before in the house, and I have handled Mr. Rothschilds guns as he has quite a collection of German and American weapons."

"How can you be certain the maid found this gun there among the bloody cloths and did not place it there?" Robin asked.

"Because she fainted upon sight of it, as if this was the gun that killed Mr. Rothschild. I thought it was too, when I saw it."

"And that is exactly why I did not call or even name this young lady. She is under medical care now. Let the record reflect that this gun belongs to Adam Hudson. It was ripped from his hand when he was stabbed that day. And this gun is not the same caliber of the weapon used to kill Gerard Rothschild. But someone who knows where the laundry shoot lands thought it would be burned or discarded with the bloody laundry. I have nothing further for Mr. Schneider." Robin returned the gun to the box on the judge's desk and then took his seat at the desk.

The district attorney rose and strolled up to the witness box. "Mr. Schneider, where were you when the shootings occurred? Did you not hear them from the kitchen below?"

"I was at the mercantile and then the butcher. You can ask them," Schneider said.

"I will. Nothing further for this witness."

"I call my next witness, Ezra August, to the stand." Robin Van der Kellen strolled right out into the courtroom.

"Very well. Mr. Ezra August please."

The bailiff opened the gate and Ezra walked onto the floor in a suit that Adam bought him. His long black hair was pulled neatly into a ribbon at the back of his neck. He crossed the floor to the witness box, stepped up into it and turned to face the courtroom with hands in his pockets.

"Raise your right hand and swear to tell the truth."

Ezra raised his right hand. "I do."

"Be seated."

He sat down in an armchair inside the box. To his right and up another level was the judge. He glanced up at him.

Robin walked toward him. "State your full legal name, please."

"Ezra Agustos Arikan," Ezra said.

"Hm. I learn so much when I do this." Robin muttered. "Mr. Arikan goes by the name Mr. August, therefore that is what I will call him. Mr. August, on the date of April 2nd, you disguised yourself to look like Adam Hudson and you left the hospital through the front doors."

"Yes, I did." Ezra nodded.

"You boarded a carriage and were taken to a nearby hotel. I was with you. What did you see when you stepped out at the hotel?" Robin asked.

"The ground, mostly. Policemen lined the walkway and yet we were shot at. You took me down on the ground," Ezra said.

"When I pulled you up and we ran for the hotel, a man blocked our path and pointed a pistol at you. Is this the pistol?" Robin held up another weapon from the evidence box. "For the record, it's an Aston percussion pistol and it is .50 caliber."

"I remember thinking later how much longer it was than your Colt. That might be the weapon. I can't be sure," Ezra said.

Robin set it down in the box. "You identified a body in the morgue. Was that the man holding the pistol?"

"I believe so, yes," Ezra said.

"How can you be certain in all the chaos of being shot at and running?" Robin questioned.

"All I saw was his chest covered in blood. White shirt. No ascot but a simple black necktie, tied a certain way. And a beard. That's how I identified the body," Ezra admitted.

"Thank you, Mr. August. That is all I have for this witness," Robin said.

The district attorney walked out then. "Mr. August, you identified a body in the morgue by clothing and a beard. You never saw his face."

"That's right," Ezra said.

"That man could have been anybody."

"No, he could not."

"How are we to take your word for it? Are you a tailor? Are you a valet? Have you any special expertise that we are to consider?" the district attorney asked him lightly.

"I'm an artist by trade," Ezra said. "I happen to make a living painting accurate portraits of people."

"So you are saying that the neck tie and beard are unique enough to be unlike any other tie and beard?" the district attorney said.

"That is right."

"Let the record show this is not the DA's time for questions yet," Robin spoked up.

"I'll allow it. I'm interested." The judge sat forward and folded his hands on the desk.

The attorney turned his back to Ezra. "You could draw my portrait then? Right now."

"I object. My witness is not on trial," Robin spoke up.

"I'll allow it. Goes toward the witness's special credibility," the judge said.

Ezra met eyes with Robin.

"What color ascot am I wearing, Mr. August?" the attorney asked.

"Black. Tied in a bow and tucked into your vest," Ezra said.

"Good guess. Most men wear a black ascot to court," the attorney said. "What about my mustache? How would the artist describe it?"

"Old fashioned. Too long. Grey hairs in it," Ezra said.

That made the court room laugh a bit.

"Enough circus, your honor," Robin called out. "Mr. August is correct."

"Nothing further," the district attorney said. "Going for a shave now."

Robin arrived at what was now called the Hudson mansion, just hours following Zoey and Adam's return.

Robin entered the room he was shown to and paused with hat in hand. "You might have asked me to wait until you were done with your bath."

"I might have," Adam responded. "But then how could I assess your character, sir?"

Robin laughed and turned to the dresser to pour himself a glass of brandy. "Can I bring you one?"

"Wouldn't mind it a bit," Adam said.

Robin nodded, his back to the bathing tub. He poured two brandy snifters and then carried one to Adam. Then he pulled up a chair beside the tub, but back far enough not to see anything over the porcelain sides but Adam's bare shoulders. "Keeping your bandages dry, I see?"

"Trying to, anyway." Adam sipped his brandy. "You're here to tell me you are leaving for home. As such, I would make it as uncomfortable as possible. Of course, you conveniently arrived while I was already in the bath."

Robin shook his head. "We will stay on at Elizabeth's for another few weeks as Marie wants to do shopping. Marie just gave me wonderful news. I couldn't wait to tell you. She is expecting again."

"Really? Robin, so is Zoey!" Adam said. "This is wonderful."

"Congratulations, Mr. Hudson," Robin said. "How long have you known? Before you made her sleep on the floor in that attic?"

"Couple weeks before." Adam nodded. "No one else knows. We are not announcing it until she begins showing."

"Wise." Robin agreed. "You two were wonderful with Frida. You'll make fine parents. What will you do about travel then?"

"I am content with shows in New York for now. I can stay home and make more paintings," Adam said. "I'm amazingly terrified. But it was made very clear to me that I would one day have to produce an heir. I will just make certain that whether we ever have a boy or not, that any children will inherit when they come of age, if not before."

"I have those sorts of trusts in place as well," Robin said.

Adam held up his glass. "To our children playing together one day."

"Indeed. To our children playing together." Robin held up his glass. "Is Ezra living here now?"

Friedrich Schneider was called to the witness stand once again. Robin paced out in front of him. "Mr. Schneider, is it a coincidence that you found another pistol in the Rothschild house?"

"Not at all. I had that home turned upside down. I had every maid, every stable hand searching every drawer, every cabinet, and every hay bale," Schneider said. "I was present when this weapon was found behind the barn."

"Where behind the barn?" Robin asked.

"Manure pile, sir."

Robin paused and returned the weapon to the table beside a perfectly patching gun. "Remind me to wash my hands later. Let the record show that this is the missing one of a pair of dueling pistols belonging to Gerard Rothschild. They are both .50 caliber. This other one was fired at Ezra August during our hospital escape. Nothing further for this witness."

"I want to speak!" Bernard Rothschild cried out from the defendant's box.

Robin spun to stare at him.

The judge banged his gavel down. "Quiet in the courthouse. Let the defendant speak quietly with his council."

"Bernard," Robin warned, pointing at him as he crossed the courtroom. Robin laid both hands down on the half wall of the box. He leaned forward and whispered, "Keep your voice down. You'd better tell me first what this is or shut up. You're facing life in jail, sir."

Bernard leaned forward, his forehead almost to Robin's. "How many years for conspiracy?"

"What are you saying?"

"I just wanted money. I never wanted him killed," Bernard whispered. "I'll confess to that."

"And who conspired with you. You will confess that name as well," Robin said.

"You already have him," Bernard said.

"You swear to this?" Robin said.

"Yes, I swear." Bernard broke into tears.

Robin stepped back and paced upright into the center of the courtroom. He held his hand to his mouth.

In the audience, Adam and Ezra actually held hands down out of sight between them.

"How do you wish to proceed?" the judge asked.

Robin took a breath and stood formally. "Your honor, my client seeks a plea deal."

The district attorney shot out of his chair. "What? No. This is going to the jury. You, sir, are dreaming."

"Gentlemen approach my bench," the judge said.

Robin and the DA stepped right up to his desk.

"Gentlemen, you have Mr. Sinclare for stabbing Adam Hudson. You have it that Mr. Bernard Rothschild knows who killed Gerard Rothchild, but did not do it himself. This is all you have right now."

The DA fumed.

"Until one of them confesses, the murder of Gerard Rothschild cannot be decided by a jury. At best, you can convict on conspiracy and you have a remorseful defendant weeping uncontrollably over there like a child. The jury are seeing this. What do you wish to do?" Robin said.

"What is the plea deal?" The DA turned to Robin.

"Pleas guilty to conspiracy to steal money from his father. Gives you who murdered him. Throws himself on the mercy of the court," Robin offered.

"Pleas guilty to conspiracy to murder and gives us the killer's name."

Robin shook his head. "He just told me he made a deal with Sinclare to steal the money. He had no idea his father would be killed."

"Sinclare will say it was conspiracy to murder," the DA said.

"Sinclare is already in jail for life for stabbing Mr. Hudson," Robin countered. "Nothing Sinclare can say will change that. Did Sinclare tell you or his own attorney that it was conspiracy to murder?"

"He did not," The DA said.

"Well. You can't get a murder conviction on my client. Don't you want one? You have a very rich man murdered in his own home. You have a very wealthy banking community in terror out there. You can end that right here," Robin urged. "You take the credit. You have the murderer already."

"The jury decides sentencing for your client? Whatever they decide?" The DA said.

Robin nodded. "Whatever they decide."

"I agree. Conspiracy to steal money and tell us who murdered Rothschild."

The judge tapped his gavel on the desk.

Robin strolled back to his client and whispered to him. Bernard nodded and wiped his eyes on a handkerchief.

The District Attorney announced, "A plea deal has been accepted. Bernard Rothschild has entered a plea of guilty to conspiracy to steal money from Gerard Rothschild. In exchange for this plea, he is prepared to tell us who murdered his father."

After the uproar in the room, the DA continued. "Mr. Rothschild, who did you have an understanding with and what was that understanding?"

"Mr. Sinclair, my father's butler, and I agreed that I would open the safe to take all of the contents. He would stand guard at the door to keep my father out of the room. But Adam Hudson was the surprise. Adam wasn't supposed to be there with me. I told him to stay downstairs. He didn't know I went up to empty the safe." Bernard began to cry again.

"How much money was Sinclare to receive?" the DA asked.

"Half of whatever was in the safe," Bernard said.

"And how much money was that?"

"My father always kept a thousand dollars in the safe."

"When you were opening the safe, you heard the shot fired behind you, who did you expect to enter?" the DA asked.

"Sinclare, of course. Or Adam had shot Sinclare. I never expected Van der Kellen," Bernard said.

"The District of New York accepts your plea. The jury will decide your sentence, sir." The DA stepped away. "Mr. Van der Kellen."

Robin stepped up before the bench. "What else was in the safe, Mr. Rothschild?"

"A trust that my father set up for me to receive $20,000 when I turned eighteen. I had that in my hand when you walked into the room," Bernard said.

"You knew your father lie dead in the hallway and you were still stealing money from him?"

"I wanted to prove to you there was that trust. I wanted to show you, I wasn't lying." Bernard wept. "And I didn't know for sure he was dead."

"You are crying why?" Robin asked.

"I only wanted money from my father. I never wanted him dead," Bernard wept.

Marie whispered to Elizabeth and Zoey, "He looks oddly sincere."

"He does, yes." Elizabeth looked down the line, past Zoey, Adam to Ezra on the end.

"Did you have any concern for Adam Hudson who you knew was down at the front door with Sinclare?"

"I was terrified for him. I was far too scared to go out even to the hall where my father was. It was either Sinclare or Adam to walk into the room with me. If Sinclare, then Adam is safe downstairs. If Adam, then Sinclare has run off after shooting my father."

Robin turned and met eyes with Adam Hudson in the front row of the audience. Then he said, "Gentlemen of the jury, you have heard my client's confession. He was due money from his father and he conspired with the butler to get that money. No one was supposed to be shot. Everything went horribly wrong that day, especially since we could have legally challenged Gerard Rothschild for the trust. In fact, that very admission alone frees my client from conspiracy to commit murder. The $20,000 trust actually existed. There is no murderer running around out there killing bankers. Not again. There is a son who lost his father, didn't get along with his father, has entered into some stupid agreements, but he is remorseful. The murderer, Sinclare, is already in jail for stabbing

Adam Hudson just moments before shooting Gerard Rothschild. His trial for murdering Gerard is yet to happen. Bernard Rothschild is 19 years old. He has never committed a crime before. He has a mother and sister who would lose their fortune and home should you send my client to jail for any great length of time. Their family will actually entrusted the estate management to Sinclare, should anything happen to either male member of the Rothschild family. Sinclare could have done anything he wanted with the fortune. What penalty would you give to my client for conspiracy to steal?"

The members of the jury huddled together whispering. They quickly sent a foreman to stand up.

"Have you a sentence, members of the jury?" The judge asked.

"We do, your honor. The members of this jury do find Bernard Rothschild guilty of conspiracy to steal. Taking in account his remorse, his youth and propensity for ill decisions, we sentence him to five years probation and we order that the management of the Rothschild estate come under the direct control of another Rothschild heir. Adam Hudson is to manage the money for the five years of probation or until such time that Bernard Rothschild has proven that he can manage such an estate."

Robin met eyes with Ezra across the dinner table, and this happened so many times through dinner, that finally Ezra said, "I seem to be an object of some fascination tonight. I am not wearing my red ascot that makes you so angry. I see lots of whispering between you and Marie. What can I do for you, Robin?"

Robin sat back and looked at his wife. "What do you think, Marie?"

Marie smirked. "I think you must ask him. I think he's perfect."

"Ask me what? Do you have another mission where I get to roll all over you, climb up you, duck beneath you all the while dodging bullets again?" Ezra asked.

Adam, Zoey, Lena, and Marie all laughed.

"Similar mission, really," Robin said. "Less bullets."

Marie gave a scolding look to her husband. "We'd best leave this to me. We were going to wait until we were alone to ask you but perhaps it is best with Adam and Zoey here. They know you so well."

"You wish to adopt me? Yes," Ezra said.

"Is he ever serious?" Robin asked.

"Not often," Adam said.

"Ezra, my friend thinks that you are a very great painter and you have a nice gallery, and you ran Adam's art show like showman," Marie began. "I happen to agree. I also think you are funny and you were very brave masquerading as Adam in that gun fight. My very good friend would like you to court her."

Adam shot a look from Marie to Ezra and back. "What? No!"

"Me court a woman?" Ezra thought about it and then had a good drink of his wine. He set the crystal stemware down gently beside his porcelain dinnerware. "She was at Adam's show?"

"He doesn't even realize he sold her a painting!" Adam blurted out.

"I what?" Ezra looked at Adam. "You're joking. Mrs. Miller? Isn't she married? Why do we call her Mrs. Miller?"

"Elizabeth is a widow," Marie said. "She asked me for everything I know about you, which isn't much."

"We're actually serious." Robin leaned forward and set his elbows on the table. "Ezra, you need a wealthy benefactor. She needs a young man her own age and she needs someone bold enough to drag her out of mourning, back into society."

"But this young man fancies men," Lena spoke up. "No offence, Ezra. You are another son to me when you helped my Adam escape from those killers. But there are things that I know."

Ezra sat back, feeling very examined and judged. His face flushed and then he stood up from his chair. "Excuse me. I need a minute." He left the table.

"Nice, mother." Adam rose and hurried after him. He followed Ezra down the hall to the music room.

"Don't make fun of me. Don't." Ezra waved a hand up at him.

"I'm not." Adam strolled into the room and around Ezra to see his face but Ezra turned as he did. Finally, he had to grab his arm. "Ez, you need to think about this. She is rich and beautiful and a widow. Her husband was about sixty years old. She's never had a young man."

"Well I have, Adam. You know that. I kissed you for Christ's sake," Ezra said.

"It's the same thing, kissing a woman," Adam said. "Intimacy though...a little different."

"How different? You know, don't tell me," Ezra warned. "I don't care if your mother knows. Nobody can put shit past your mother anyway. But I really didn't want Robin to be so sure about me. All right?"

"Robin likes you just as you are. Go back in and ask Robin and Marie your questions," Adam said. "She wants you to court her. She's seen you. She knows your lack of fortune. She is so rich she doesn't care. In fact, oh my God, she wanted children so bad that she asked Robin to give her one."

"Who wouldn't?" Ezra said. "Really? Elizabeth Miller asked Robin to make her with child?"

"That's why he left New York so quickly after being shot."

Ezra looked down at himself in one of the two new suits that Adam bought him. "Ah he was tempted."

Adam patted him on the arm. "You're not repulsed by the thought of doing it with a woman are you?"

"No, I've seen naked ladies you know," Ezra said. "I had an erection the entire time I was painting that one Robin had to turn toward the wall. I know why he had to turn it around. Right? I've just never…"

Adam laughed. "I know. You can almost see her…"

"Hmmm. Rich lady wants to court me. I have to think about this. I thought you said she was kind of a bitch?"

"She used to be. She's not anymore."

"But once you are one you always can be again. I know because I'm a seriously royal bitch," Ezra said.

"Yes you are."

Ezra grabbed Adam by the shoulders and kissed his mouth. Then he moved around him.

Adam threw up his hands. "What was that for?"

"Rich beautiful woman wants me, me, not you pretty boy." Ezra started back down the hallway. "Me with my big nose and big mouth and hairy…."

Lena met them halfway and blocked Ezra. "Ezra, look at me, son. Do you want to be poor your whole life? Go meet with Elizabeth. She is lonely and you are very handsome and funny boy. You are good for her. Go on. Try something." Lena kissed him on the cheek, though he had to stoop down for it, and then she started up the stairs. "You are too smart not to."

"Thanks, Mom," Ezra said. "Nice touch. I like the mind trick thing."

Adam moved to kiss his mother's cheek. "Good night, Mother. I'll talk to him."

Ezra returned to the dining room and stood behind his chair. "I beg your pardon for the rapid exit. I had to go rip out my hair. Luckily I have more than an ape. And now I am terrified. So thank you for the wide range of emotions that you...."

"Ezra, sit," Robin said.

Adam patted his friend on the back and sat down at the head of the table. "Ape? What were you going to say was hairy?"

Ezra took his seat again. "My ass. What did you think I was going to say?"

Adam and Robin burst out laughing.

"Ezra..." Marie waited until there was silence, but she was smiling. "Jesus. Elizabeth's husband was elderly and he passed almost a year ago. She needs your humor and your energy. She is 23 years old. How old are you?"

"I am twenty-five," Ezra said. "I am a twenty-five-year-old queer Turk with a hundred dollars to my name, until I sell the gallery anyway. Then, yay, I will have eight hundred dollars to my name. And no prospects for the future."

"She doesn't care about money," Marie told him.

"Because she has plenty of it. She knows what I am?"

"The whole town saw your purple suit," Robin remarked. "I'd worry more about your drunken dancing."

Ezra glared at him. "I don't make fun of your attire. How...how would this go, from here? Marie, if you would please." He mouthed the word help.

"You come out to dinner as her escort. Robin and I will accompany you as your chaperones. Robin will pay for dinner," Marie explained. "Then when you take her out yourself, Jonas will be chaperone and he always pays. You do not have to worry about money. You just need a tuxedo and a few more suits like this one."

"Why would you make fun of my attire?" Robin asked.

Ezra shot Robin an innocent look.

"I will take him," Adam said. "I will make certain he doesn't get a purple tuxedo. Don't worry. I will let him have a hint of color in it. Maybe a purple vest or something. And a dozen white shirts."

"It's all right Robin. You're just older than we are. You can't help it," Ezra said. "I don't have to pretend to be straight, entirely?"

"You can be yourself," Robin said. "Just be very gentlemanly in public, *unlike now*."

Ezra smirked ear to ear.

"You have to be straight in public anyway," Adam remarked. "So what's the difference?"

"You'll be fine. You ate very daintily tonight. You used the correct silverware. You held your wine glass correctly," Marie told him.

"Got lucky on all of that," Ezra admitted. "You must teach me the silverware. I didn't grow up with eighteen pieces of silver around my plate ever. I mean this tiny fork. What the hell is this for?"

"I suppose I have to teach him how to dance too?" Adam said. "It's for oysters."

"Yes, please," Robin said. "He's a public danger, otherwise."

"I'll teach you how to dance but *stop kissing me*." Adam gritted his teeth.

"What?" Robin asked.

"Which one of you will lead?" Marie questioned. "I should teach him."

"But if…if she actually likes me and we do court, as it were, I have never been with a woman," Ezra said. "I would be terrified."

Marie said, "I'll take this one, gentlemen. Ezra, I can't think of anything that would thrill Elizabeth more, than to teach you how."

Adam's mouth just fell open.

Robin held eye contact with Adam across the table and struggled to withhold comments in front of his wife. He eventually made some sort of snort and sunk his mouth to his brandy glass.

"She asked many questions about you," Zoey spoke up. "At the party here after the art show and after the courtroom last night. She likes you, Ezra."

"She did and we didn't know very much to tell her," Marie said.

"Oh my God. All right. I agree. Of course, I agree. I had a great time dancing with her," Ezra said. "Just try not to let me do anything stupid. She is beautiful. She wants to court me?"

"Ezra, yes," Marie said. "She said you were a beautiful creature."

He lowered his dark eyes and just wet his lips.

"And now I can tell her you said she was beautiful," Marie said.

Ezra let out a long breath. "I thought she was married. She wanted to pay me $1,000 for a painting of Robin."

"Damn. You didn't sell her one?" Adam said.

"No. We debated the price on your painting and then she grabbed my hand and folded money into it. I didn't even count it until she left. She smelled so amazing," Ezra said. "There I was sitting there starving and she put two hundred dollars into my hand."

"I have your letter to her. Just sign it." Robin pulled the paper from his inside pocket and laid it on the middle of the table. "This is your letter asking her to dine with you at a French restaurant on Friday night. You will come round with Adam's carriage and driver at six. Marie and I will be joining for dinner, of course as we are her house guests. You would not wish to leave us at home. I figured the French restaurant would be easier on you since you lived in Paris for a time."

"She's not afraid to be seen with me in public?" Ezra asked.

"You are an art dealer and painter. Why shouldn't you accompany her in public?" Marie said. "Adam, get him a black tuxedo, white ruffled shirt, as ruffly as he likes, and a shiny new purple or blue vest with matching ascot. Black top hat. Got it?"

"Yes, ma'am," Adam said. "I will be his valet that night myself. He will be resplendent, clean shaven, and curly haired. And he won't smell like a hookah bar, as he usually does."

"What is old looking about my attire?" Robin finally asked.

Ezra and Adam looked at each other and burst out laughing. Adam put a hand on Robin's arm. "Nothing. He's being obnoxious. He drools over your clothing every time he's behind you."

Robin let out a sigh. "She's gonna eat him alive that first night."

"Ha? What now?"

"What is this?"

"Shisha. It's tobacco mixed with herbs and molasses," Ezra explained. "Shut up and smoke it, Captain."

Robin smoked the pipe first. He shook his head after. His eyebrows rose. "Whew. Been a long time since I was in the East."

Ezra took it next and dragged from it. He passed it to Adam. "You'd better take it easy. Just a puff, New York. I don't know what it's like in India. But this is pure Turkish shisha."

Adam barely took a hit from it. "Oh my God." He passed it back to Robin.

Robin smoked it again. "They would dance while we smoked, removing skirts and wraps and veils…."

Ezra and Adam sat back grinning.

"And then what did you do?" Ezra coaxed.

"Well…took a couple of them back to my bed." Robin sat back and closed his eyes. "Did them both."

Ezra reclined on one side of him, looking at Adam over him. "What's the trick to it?"

"To what?" Robin asked.

"To a woman," Ezra clarified.

"Ah." Robin smiled and sat back. He looked at them both eagerly awaiting him to say anything. "Ahm, women are... A woman will fit perfectly to your own body. Pleasing her will satisfy you better than anything on earth. And…" Robin reached over and laid a hand on Adam's shoulder. "Having children with a woman you love is the greatest emotion. The bond with her, a partner and an equal, is amazing. I'm not going to tell you the graphics of what to do in bed. Your own body is going to tell you that just fine. Right, Adam?"

"I…couldn't have said it better. Not bad poetry for a lawyer," Adam said. "By the way, your hand is still on me." Adam patted Robin on the chest and Robin withdrew his hand. "You'll make Ez jealous."

"Which one of us would you have physical intimacy with, if you had your choice?" Ezra reclined languidly beside Robin, smoking.

Robin's brow furrowed. "I do have my choice. Neither."

They burst out laughing.

Friday night brought Adam's large carriage into the central courtyard of the Miller's wrap around mansion. The driver climbed down to open the carriage door.

Ezra August ducked his top hat out and hopped down. He looked up and around at the mansion, as light snowflakes fluttered down through the lamplight all about him. "Holy Hagia Sophia...."

"Good luck, Ezra."

He saluted the driver as he climbed the steps toward the bronze and glass doors. Jonas opened the doors for him. "Good evening, Mr. August."

"Good evening, Jonas." Ezra entered the home and removed his hat. He held the hat in his left hand, close to his knotted stomach and let out a long hard breath.

"This way. You are expected, sir." Jonas led him down the marble hall toward the parlor.

Some of the house staff stole a glimpse of the young suitor, finding him tall, handsome, exotic-looking and animated. They also found him to be well dressed with an athletic walk. He nearly bounced on his heels. He was young and so smooth of face. Was he younger than most of them? Was he younger than Elizabeth? They knew him to be a friend of Adam Hudson and he had been highly praised by Captain Van der Kellen.

Ezra followed Jonas, afraid to stare at the riches in passing, oriental vases and golden mirrors and the like. But he did pause to fluff up his hair in a mirror. "Hat hair," he remarked.

Jonas gave him a look as if to ask if he was finished.

Ezra raised his eyebrows. He opened his hand, palm up to the butler.

"May I present Mr. August." Jonas led him into the parlor.

Elizabeth rose from a sofa, wearing a new floral silk gown with red velvet bodice and skirt of red and yellow poppies on a white background. Her eyes went to Ezra and she smiled warmly. It was him. Her heart pounded. Her long blonde hair was up in perfect coils and ringlets. Her neck and shoulders were bare. Even her ears were bare. She wore no jewelry.

Behind her was the painting that Ezra had made of Adam. She had reframed it in an ornate golden frame. Of course, Ezra noticed it immediately. It made him smile, as if Adam were there to help him.

Marie and Robin rose also. Marie wore a navy blue silk gown with lacy collar and Robin was in his new tuxedo from Amsterdam.

"Good evening, Elizabeth. I hope you were not waiting long." Ezra held a hand to her, palm up. "You are radiant."

She put her white gloved hand into his hand and watched Ezra kiss the back of her glove. She gripped his fingers. "I was delighted to accept your dinner proposal. And what a wonderful choice of restaurant. I absolutely love it."

"Hello Ezra," Marie said.

"Marie, you look lovely tonight." Ezra moved to kiss Marie's gloved hand as well and to shake hands with Robin. "Robin, lovely also."

That made Elizabeth laugh.

Ezra smiled and gave a bit of a toss to his hair. "But then Robin always is."

"Charming as ever, Mr. August," Robin told him. "We should probably be on our way."

"Furs to keep the ladies warm in the carriage," Jonas reminded. He offered one to Robin and one to Ezra.

Ezra imitated what Robin did, and gently draped the fur cape around Elizabeth's bare shoulders while he inhaled the scent of her hair. "That must feel delightful on your neck. Like a cat."

"Yes, now that you mention it," Elizabeth said. "What a surprise your invitation was."

Ezra flashed her a shy smile as he offered his right arm to her. "To me most of all."

That made her giggle and wrap her gloved hands about his forearm. "I forgot how tall you are. And Marie said you are twenty-five years old. You don't look it."

"I am both, twenty-five and exactly this tall."

That even made Marie laugh.

"Six feet?" Beth looked up at him.

"Just shy of it, I'm afraid. Five eleven with boots on," Ezra replied. "But my hair makes up for it."

"Indeed." Elizabeth could not look up at him for fear of smiling too broadly.

Elizabeth boarded the carriage first, sitting turned forward and slid across to the other side. Marie boarded next and sat across from her. "He has a great voice." "He's so handsome," they said simultaneously.

Robin climbed inside and then Ezra after they exchanged a few comments outside. "How are you?" "Cliff diving. Love it."

As it was odd for Ezra to sit facing forward as the master of the carriage, he fiddled with the hem of his coat. "I'm always amazed at young ladies climbing stairs in your gowns and tiny shoes. I tried it myself in a long coat and I fell on my face."

Robin nodded. "Saw you dancing. Not surprised."

Elizabeth giggled. "You seem graceful enough."

"Oh you perjure yourself. I almost knocked you flat out on the dance floor," Ezra said.

"I never laughed so hard in my life," Elizabeth said. "You're not schooled at all in ballroom dances."

"And yet you are still here, going to dinner with me," he said. "You must want to see if my conduct is any worse at a dinner table."

"Ah Marie, did we ever banter on like that when we were first courting?" Robin asked.

"No, because we had slept together already," Marie said, making everyone laugh. "Too late for flirtation."

At the restaurant, Robin emerged from the carriage first and assisted Marie and then Elizabeth down.

The women whispered to each other. "He smells so good. Adam gave it to him, no doubt. He's nervous. We must make him feel at ease. But how? My hand on his knee beneath the table... Oh God no."

"Ladies, contain yourselves," Robin scolded them. He held an arm out for Marie to latch onto.

Ezra stepped down from the carriage, resisting the urge to jump the step. He placed his top hat back onto hair not really parted in the middle of his head. Then he offered his right arm to Elizabeth to take hold of as they entered the restaurant together. His left hand pushed his hair behind his ears.

Robin handled the introductions at the host podium. They were shown to an elegant round table near the fireplace and windows. The table was set with a white cloth, golden chargers, candlesticks, and a floral arrangement in the center. Their overcoats and hats were taken from them. The gentlemen held cushioned chairs for the ladies and they sat boy-girl, boy-girl around the table.

Menus were offered to them and as Robin had made the reservation, he was asked to order the wine for the table. He chose a red and a white, not knowing what each guest would order for dinner.

Looking at the menu, Ezra donned small gold spectacles, wrapping the temple tips around his ears. He tucked his hair behind his ears again.

Marie said, "I didn't know you read French, Ezra."

"Limited to menu's, I'm afraid," Ezra said.

"Oh you look so studious in those spectacles." Elizabeth sighed.

Ezra looked at her, his dark pupils taking her in over the round lenses. He smiled a closed-lipped grin. "Can't read small letters."

"Do you wear them when you paint? No doubt why your paintings are so amazing. Do wear them," Elizabeth encouraged.

He shook his head. "Canvas is at least arm's length away. I don't need glasses to paint."

Robin ordered boeuf bourguignon, and Marie the bouillabaisse. Elizabeth and Ezra both ordered the coq au vin. As such, they needed red wine for the Van der Kellens and white for the new couple. Appetizers such as oysters and fresh bread were served first. Fresh green peas would be a delicacy in mid-winter.

Ezra returned his spectacles to a narrow box within his inner jacket pocket.

"Marie said that you lived in Paris for a time. How did you find it?" Elizabeth asked.

Ezra was grateful that Adam made him eat a small sandwich before this, so that he could nibble on appetizers and make conversation. "Paris is amazing, even more wonderful than I had imagined. I was sixteen when I arrived there. For three years I studied painting in the most incredible places, in the Louvre, in the palace, in the gardens. I sold paintings in Parc Monceau, and along the Seine. Many times I painted in front of the Notre Dame and sold every piece."

"What else did you paint in those days?" Elizabeth asked.

"Figures, mostly. I've always been mostly figurative."

She held her napkin to her mouth. "What does that mean?"

"Naked ladies. They sold. An artist has to earn a living," Ezra explained. "And landscapes of the city sold as well."

"And what inspires you to paint now?" Marie asked.

"Naked ladies. I saw his studio," Robin said.

They laughed.

"Forgive me, but the human body is a beautiful thing, objectified by artists for hundreds of years. Light and shadow. Tension and softness. Why even the greatest patron of the arts purchased figurative works, that being the Catholic church, of course," Ezra said.

"Spoken like one educated in Protestant Paris," Robin teased.

"I imagine the Catholic priests really enjoyed the naked ladies, even if they were representations of the Virgin Mary and the annunciation," Ezra said.

Elizabeth laughed. "I should warn you, I am Catholic."

"Oh my God," Ezra said.

"No, I'm not. I'm Protestant." Elizabeth laid her bare hand on his arm.

Ezra looked down at her hand and blushed so, as he laughed.

Marie and Robin looked at each other. Robin leaned in and kissed her mouth.

"All right. I deserved that for my mouth running on so," Ezra said.

"Not at all. I enjoy watching your mouth saying anything. Tell me. How did you come to America then?" Elizabeth asked.

"Well, too much artistic competition in Paris. I had this idea that I would come to New York and show how wonderful a painter I am and become famous." Ezra sipped his wine.

Their next course was served to each of them. Wine glasses were refilled.

"And then Adam walked in, made ten portraits of Robin, and achieved everything I dreamed of in one night," Ezra said lightly, however with an underlying tinge of pain. "And I watched."

"No doubt due in some part to your talents as an instructor," Elizabeth said. "You don't regret teaching him, do you?"

"No, of course not. Adam's my best friend. Tomorrow we are going to look for a building to buy. We want to do an art gallery on the bottom floor, studio space above it, and rooms up top to live in," Ezra said.

"Did you say you own that gallery near your attic studio?" Robin asked.

"I do. I have had this guy bugging me to buy it and make tenements out of it. It is a stupid neighborhood for a gallery anyway. The only way I made sales was to bring paintings into wealthy homes for personal showings," Ezra said.

"That's rather brilliant," Elizabeth said. "Wealthy patrons won't come into that neighborhood."

"How did you happen to then?" Ezra asked her.

"Carraige broke down. I told Jonas I would rather walk about than stand there waiting," Elizabeth said.

"All that time I spent digging up cobblestones paid off."

Elizabeth laughed uncontrollably into her napkin.

"I made a couple hundred dollars on a portrait of Adam, of all things," Ezra said.

"Which I put a two-hundred-dollar frame on. I think I owe you, sir."

He winked at her.

"Why did you paint Adam?" Marie questioned.

"We had a deal. I would teach him how to paint and he would let me paint him," Ezra said. "He's pretty as a girl, isn't he?"

The girls giggled while Robin just brought a wine glass to his mouth.

"When you find a building, I would really like to look over the contract for you. Just to be sure," Robin offered.

"Please. It's all on Adam. I'm sure he would welcome you," Ezra said.

"So you're going to buy this building together? As friends it is best that you document who is responsible for what. Don't ever let money come between you," Robin said.

"Very good advice. Actually, Adam is buying the building alone. I am cashing out on the old gallery. I will run the gallery and wine bar. What do you think of that?" Ezra turned to Elizabeth with his wine glass. "Glass of wine, darling, while you peruse the paintings. French or Italian?"

"The wine or the paintings?" She played along.

"The models," Ezra quipped. "Have you always lived in New York?"

"Yes. I was born here. I traveled rather extensively with my parents before they passed. I have no siblings but I do have many cousins," Elizabeth said. "Where are you from, Ezra? Where were you born?"

"Ankara, in the Ottoman Empire, far east side of the Mediterranean Sea. Ankara, as I remember was a wonderful city. Lots of Roman ruins," Ezra said. "I left home about ten years ago because I was being conscripted into the war with Greece. No offence, Robin, but I was a 15-year-old boy who wanted nothing but to draw pictures. I was too gentle to do any fighting or shooting. Took a boat to Rome. Worked in a fish market for a bit. Used to cry for the fish. Took another boat to Nice. Worked my way up to Paris."

"And how did you study painting in Paris with so little...means?" Marie asked.

"Took whatever work I could find. And originally I wasn't formally trained. I set up an easel beside other painters and watched and learned. I became one of them. Got some sponsorship for formal classes from some of my patrons. I was selling paintings right and left. They all sold. I could copy any of the masters works already. We would set up inside the galleries and paint," Ezra said. "Tourists would buy them. Can't tell you how many I painted of the Notre Dame. It's even better than the Basilica in Nice. I could do it in my sleep now. Morning. Evening. Rain. Moonlight. Any lighting you wish. Of course, doesn't hold up compared to the Hagia Sophia in Constantinople."

"I'm fascinated. I've been to the Notre Dame in Paris," Elizabeth said. "Wouldn't it be amazing if we were there at the same time? You must have had to learn to speak some French?"

"Oui, mademoiselle. Je parle un peu francais," Ezra said.

"Tu parles si bien francais," Elizabeth told him.

Ezra smiled. "Merci beaucoup."

"May...may I?" Elizabeth reached to feel one of his ringlet curls. She chose a ringlet just in front of his ear, to pull it straight and let it coil about her finger.

"Nothing would please me more." Ezra lowered his chin.

"He's blushing," Marie said.

"We spent an hour getting mine to do this," Elizabeth said.

"I spent hours trying to make mine stop doing this," Ezra admitted. "Obviously I gave in to it."

"So happy you did."

After a leisurely dinner for over two hours, they boarded the carriage again to ride back to Wall Street in two inches of fresh snow. The narrow carriage wheels pulled through the snow easily. Parked inside the courtyard of Elizabeth Miller's home, she said to the gathering, "May I have a moment alone with Mr. August? If you don't mind."

"Of course," Robin told her.

"We'll be just inside," Marie said. "Good night, Ezra, dear."

"Thank you for coming tonight," Ezra told her. "Thank you, Robin."

"My pleasure, sir." Robin stepped out and helped Marie exit the carriage. They closed the door against the cold and started up the stairs.

Inside the carriage, Elizabeth pulled her fur closer around her and turned to face the artist. "Mr. August?"

"May I call on you again?"

"Really?" A girlish smile spread across her face as she gripped his hands.

He made intense eye contact with her. "Please call me Ezra."

"Come to dinner here tomorrow night, Ezra. I will get Robin and Marie to go to Adam's," she said. "Send me a thank you note for dinner and I will send you the invitation."

Ezra smiled, leaned in and kissed her on the mouth. In the surprise, her mouth was open. His lips were full and soft and his mouth was warm. He kissed her passionately, but briefly, with a touch of his tongue to hers. Then he sat back and slid toward the carriage door and opened it. "Allow me to see you safely through the snow, my dear Elizabeth."

Her heart was pounding such that she didn't think possible. She followed Ezra out, taking his hand firmly. They had shoveled the walk, but her feet still felt the cold snow. She felt his other hand on her back, beneath the fur shawl.

Jonas was standing on the stairs reaching out to her.

She was still gripping Ezra's hand.

His dark eyes met her light blue ones.

"Mrs. Miller," Jonas said.

Then she just released his hand and walked up the stairs, taking Jonas's arm instead.

Ezra saw her get inside the house before he turned and looked up at the falling snow from above, and then at Adam's driver. He boarded the carriage and collapsed inside, holding his heart.

Mrs. Elizabeth Miller,

I thank you for accompanying me to dinner evening last. Might I call on you again sometime?

Ezra

Mr. Ezra August,

There is a painting I wish to discuss with you. Might you join me for dinner at my home at 6:00 tonight? My house guests will be dining out.

Looking forward to your company.

Elizabeth Miller

Chapter Eleven Brandy Alla Van der Kellen

Ezra, Adam, and Robin stood together on the sidewalk, looking up at a brownstone, 3 story building on Pearl Street.

Some ladies walked past and Robin tipped his hat to them. "Good day, ladies." They giggled and lingered as they passed by. Two of them bumped into each other.

Ezra and Adam turned to glare at him. "Again?"

"This is the one, isn't it?" Robin asked.

Ezra hopped in front of the large windows to turn and spread his arms wide. "And opening Friday night to a packed crowd, the combined show of Adam Hudson and Ezra August, complete with dancing girls and fountains of wine…."

"Wealthy patrons do not like dancing girls. Their wives will be with them," Robin said.

"The combined show of Ezra August and Adam Hudson. That sounds better," Ezra said.

"Let's see the papers," Robin said.

"Kill joy. It's always the lawyer," Ezra said.

"Do you want to know what Elizabeth said to Marie this morning?" Robin teased. "Or shall I just let you walk into your evening totally unprepared?"

"What did she say?" Adam urged. They went back inside the building to look around again. "Was he too funny? Was he too feminine?"

"She liked the kiss."

"There was a kiss?"

"Not like the one I gave you," Ezra said. "Very light, open mouth, touch of tongue, left her wanting more."

Robin shuddered. "You kissed Adam?"

"Had your chance, Dutchman." Ezra set his hands on his hips.

"You have never been with a woman and you are about to go into the lair of the she-wolf," Adam said.

"She-wolf?" Robin protested, leaning beside a counter.

"Oh my God. I am going to be eaten alive." Ezra moaned. "Not again."

Robin wiped his eyes. "All right, may we please look at the papers?"

Adam unfolded them onto the counter. He met eyes with Ezra across the counter. "What else did Elizabeth say?"

"I don't know if I can read much English," Ezra said.

Robin flipped a page and continued reading the purchase agreement. "Put on your spectacles."

"Oh I can't believe I did that last night in front of Elizabeth," Ezra said. "I'm so stupid."

"For five minutes to read what you're signing, I think you can bear it," Robin shot back at him. "She liked them."

"What does that say across the street there?" Adam asked.

Ezra folded his arms. "Bakery. I can read across the street. I can smell the pastries from here."

"So can I." Robin was still reading.

"What's the special?" Adam asked him.

"Ah, apple crumb something," Ezra said. "Sounds good actually. You buying?"

Adam took the papers from Robin and held up the front page to him. "Can you read anything on this, even the large letters?"

Robin stood back with a hand on his hip. "I was in the middle of...."

"I can't read much English. I told you that," Ezra said.

Adam stepped back one step. "Can you read anything on this?"

Annoyed, Ezra looked at Adam and then his mouth opened. He said slowly, "Property deed and Purchase Agreement. Twenty-two Pearl Street."

"Where did you learn to read English? It's not even read in the same direction as Turkish," Robin blurted out. "Your family was wealthy."

Adam reached into his pocket and drew out his leather purse. He counted out some coins which he held out to Ezra. "Buy us some of those apple crumb things."

Ezra looked at the coins. "Not wealthy but my father was a doctor. Still is, I suppose. Not everybody paid him in money. I remember him coming home with chickens and baked goods. I was taught English and Turkish as a child. Three apple crumb things coming up."

"Now what did Elizabeth say about him?"

"She liked the kiss," Robin said.

Ezra took Robin by the chin and kissed him on the mouth. When Robin stepped back, Ezra stepped forward to continue kissing him.

Desperately, Robin turned away, laughing.

Adam burst out laughing.

"Lesson learned. Better to beg for forgiveness than ask for permission." Ezra walked out toward the bakery. "Gave me more tongue than you did, New York."

Ezra arrived the following evening, taking Adam's carriage even though it was only a few homes down the same street. There was more snow that night. Although it seemed silly to him being hauled down the street by carriage, his trousers would have gotten wet to the knees if he'd walked.

Jonas opened the door to receive him. "Mr. August."

"Jonas, good evening." Ezra carried with him a black leather-bound portfolio, kept tightly closed at his side, as he climbed the stairs. It was about two by three feet in dimension.

Inside, Jonas said, "May I take your coat and hat, sir? You may wait in the parlor."

"Thank you." Ezra removed his top hat and handed it to him. His overcoat was harder to remove without dropping papers. Jonas helped him. "Don't approve, do you?"

"It is not for me to say. But anyone Mr. Van der Kellen praises is surely welcome," Jonas said.

"Mr. Van der Kellen praised me?" Ezra said.

"Yes, sir. He said you were most brave during the incident at the hospital. And that you fashioned some ingenious escapes for the both of you during the chase," Jonas said. "Pour yourself a drink in the parlor, sir. The lady is always late to dinner."

Ezra carried his binder of drawings down the marble hall. He glanced back to find Jonas handing his coat and hat off to a maid. Inside the parlor, he laid his drawings down on a card table. He looked up at that portrait of Adam. Pour himself a drink. He looked about.

From the doorway, Elizabeth observed him in his black suit, crisp white shirt, and purple vest. His hair was tied loosely with a black ribbon, allowing a couple ringlets to fall out on his right temple. His ascot was paisley with the same purple of his vest.

The bar in the corner had a display of substances that were amazing to him. He picked up some to read them at arm's length. "Scotch almost as old as I am. Wine that is actually older than I am. Brandy alla Van der Kellen. Twelve years old. Works for him. Let's give that a try."

"Always talk to yourself?" Elizabeth asked.

His shoulders went up. "Caught. Yes. Well, I am a man who likes the sound of his own voice."

"Never met a man who didn't. Brandy alla Van der Kellen? Let's both have one before dinner." She sauntered into the room with a smile on rouge-colored lips. "Then we can be cool and confident like him."

"And gorgeous. Don't forget that." He smiled and pulled the cork from the brandy. He poured into two gold rimmed snifters. He brought one to her. "In my defense, I was told you were always late to dinner."

"You should know that he who told you that is likely standing in the hall just out of our sight," Elizabeth said.

"Hint taken. I appreciate that lest I say something inappropriate." Ezra raised his glass to her. "Sagligniza. To your health."

"Sagligniza," Elizabeth did her best to repeat what he had said.

"L'chayim, my dear."

"I've heard that. What does that mean?" She sipped brandy.

"To life. Or the Dutch if you prefer, proost."

"A votre sante," Elizabeth said.

"Yes." Ezra smiled. "Very good."

They both smiled and sipped.

"May I tell you something about this painting you bought?" Ezra asked.

"Don't tell me you didn't paint it."

"No, I painted it all right. We were so excited. We were so into art at the time, talking about colors and composition. Hours passed like seconds. I kissed him," Ezra said.

Elizabeth glanced quickly toward the open doorway. "On...on the mouth?" Then back to Ezra. "What did he do? He didn't shove you?"

"No. He just stood there. Froze. To be honest, I've gotten better responses kissing my own arm."

Beth burst out laughing.

"At least Van der Kellen burst out laughing. That was something." Ezra grinned and sipped the brandy. He paced a bit, taking in her reaction to his revelation with pleasure. "Adam does a fantastic impression of Robin. You have to see it sometime. And Robin doesn't know, but he does it all the time right behind his back. I have one. Want to see it?"

"Yes. I do."

Ezra sat down in the armchair and crossed his legs. He raised his chin and brushed back his hair with his right hand. His lower lip pushed out thoughtfully.

"Yes. That is him." Elizabeth pointed at him.

"Wait. Wait for it," Ezra warned. He brushed his hair back again and said with a Dutch accent and intensity, "I require three recruits for a very dangerous mission and one hero among them. Are you up for it?"

She held a hand to her mouth, laughing so hard.

Jonas was even heard laughing in the doorway.

Ezra sipped his brandy and smiled at Elizabeth. "Who's going to refuse that, right? I ran through bullets after that."

"But you were a hero. You ran through alleys with Robin while you both were shot at. Oh my. You are so brave. What is this? What did you bring?" She pointed at the portfolio.

"Drawings. I thought I would show you some after dinner," Ezra said.

"Show me just one, right now. I insist. I can hardly wait."

"Show you one. All right." Ezra rose and downed more brandy. He opened the portfolio and looked inside. He filed through a few, pretended to reject a few, shaking his head. And then he selected one. On a large sheet of fine art paper, was a drawing of Robin asleep on the sofa. It was drawn with a combination of graphite and charcoal.

She stood up and walked closer. "Ezra, that is beautiful. Did you do that from memory?"

Jonas peeked around the corner, silently, trying to see it.

"Oh no. He fell asleep in my studio. We all descended on him like locusts. Stayed up all night drawing him," Ezra said. "I swear we ran out of paper."

"You would do that? Just stay up all night with inspiration?"

"I do, yes. Because there are plenty of other nights with nothing. No inspiration. No nothing happening. So when it hits, you must let it take you," Ezra said.

Jonas cleared his throat from the doorway. "Excuse me. I am told that dinner is ready."

Ezra extended a hand to Elizabeth.

Instead of taking his arm, she took his hand, and she was not wearing gloves. Her gown was not over the top wealthy, just a pale blue velvet. He escorted her to the hall.

The dining room of the Millers had a long white draped table with flickering candelabras and marble fireplace crackling. The table was set for just two.

Ezra waited for her to choose the chair on the end and he held it for her, pushed it in for her. Then he sat beside her.

"You meant that when you kissed Adam, that Robin burst out laughing?" Elizabeth whispered.

"No. Yesterday at the new building I planted one on Robin and he burst out laughing. It was a joke, really. I wasn't serious. Curious, naturally." Ezra leaned closer to her to tell her this. "I never believe anybody's truly straight."

"Well I...even I've never done that. Perhaps you can transfer this kiss to me later," she quipped.

Ezra smiled warmly. "Happy to. I can't hold it in much longer."

Four staff members, who all knew Adam Hudson, now served Ezra the artist and Elizabeth the widow. Elizabeth paused conversation as long as anyone was in the room with them. Eventually Ezra got the rhythm of it and picking up the conversation began to come easily when they were alone again.

"There is a painting I want to talk to you about but I don't want you to get the wrong impression," she said. "Could you possibly not be offended if I asked you how many drawings of Robin do you have? Is it enough to paint him, now that you know him?"

"I was planning to anyway," Ezra said. "Just to commemorate our adventure together. You can have your choice."

"Oh? You're going to make more than one?"

"What would be the wrong impression you do not want me to get?" Ezra questioned.

"To think that I have anything but admiration for my best friend's husband, of course," Beth said. "Are you ever afraid to show your paintings to people?"

"No. They will love them or hate them. I don't care. It's not me. It's separate from me. It's over there. I just made it. And each viewer will see something different, experience something different within a painting. I can talk about a painting but very often I can't tell you how it got from one stage to another. It is an out of body experience when a work of real art is created," Ezra said. "I can mechanically paint a fruit bowl, a landscape, a person. Sure. And it will be good. But when that higher experience happens, when the magic happens, I'm a conduit. I can neither influence it nor control it. And I have to warn you, I can disappear into it for six or seven hours and suddenly realize I'm about to faint because I haven't eaten or drank water all day. Is that going to be hard to deal with? Just don't let me miss an important occasion."

Elizabeth reached onto the table and laid her hand on his.

Jonas entered.

Ezra did not let her hand go. After two tries, she stopped trying to pull hers back.

"Miss Elizabeth asked me to be a proper chaperone." Jonas took a chair at the far end of the table, sat down at it. "By her own instructions, I am forced to take this position and insist that you refrain from touching her, if you would, sir."

Ezra changed the tilt of his head. His dark dark eyes met Elizabeth's light blue ones. "I think we make him nervous."

She stifled a laugh.

"Did you ask him to not let me hold your hand?" Ezra questioned.

"I just asked him to chaperone," Elizabeth said. "I can ask him to leave."

"Oh no. Don't do that," Ezra said. "This is way more fun."

They both laughed.

Jonas frowned.

"I say we pretend he's your father. Look," Ezra said. "Tell you about myself. I just sold my gallery. I have fifty something paintings that I have to move out in two days, or the new owner threatened to burn them, calling them blasphemous filth. Yes, you heard me. I sleep on the floor. I owe ten dollars to the Hungarian woman on the second floor because I broke her iron on my hair."

"Wait. What?" Elizabeth burst out laughing.

Jonas couldn't help but laugh.

"I tried to iron my hair, burnt the top of my ear, and accidentally threw the iron out the window. The handle broke off when it hit the cobblestones three floors below. I'm lucky I didn't kill somebody."

Jonas and Elizabeth laughed. In fact, several maids in the kitchen were laughing.

"Um, can I offer you one of our carriages and a driver?" Jonas said.

"For?" Ezra said.

"To move your paintings," Jonas said.

"Oh you can store any here that you need to," Elizabeth said. "I saw your gallery. Which ones were blasphemous?"

"Oh the ones in the back facing the walls. The naked lady paintings, otherwise known as the ones that sell," Ezra said.

"Who did you sell one of those to?" Jonas had to ask. "Most recently."

"Strangely enough, a woman bought three of them for her bathing room. I'm not one to judge," Ezra said.

"I like this game. What else would you explain to my father if you had to?" Elizabeth said. "Did you say you sleep on the floor?"

Ezra took a drink of wine. "Well, there is a mattress on the floor. Let's see. What do I imagine a father would grill me about before I court his beautiful daughter? Ask me something, Jonas. Anything."

"I don't wish to participate," Jonas said.

"Ask him something," Elizabeth urged.

"Very well. How old are you, sir?"

"Twenty-five."

"Have you any relatives in New York?"

"No. Everyone's still in Ankara, I believe. Nine younger sisters and brothers. Some of my brothers probably had to serve in the Greek war, unless they left like I did," Ezra said. "I'm an artist, not much of a warrior."

"You should know that Robin praised you very highly about that hospital escape," Elizabeth said. "Said he gave you a medal of some sort."

Ezra smirked and lowered his chin. "Yes, he did."

"He said there was no way Adam could have run or climbed that ladder as you did," Elizabeth told him. "You saved Adam."

"I believe all credit belongs to Robin. It was his brilliant idea to dress me up as Adam and let Adam escape out the back door wearing a gown," Ezra said.

"A dress?" Elizabeth asked.

Jonas laughed. "Adam in a gown?"

"His sister got it, very lovely frock. Too big for her. All Van der Kellen's brilliant mind. Our escape was harrowing. I was quite sore for days. Still possess a few contusions, especially the one on my arm. This old lady was about to strike Robin over the head with a broom stick so I blocked the blow with my arm," Ezra said. "In the presence of your faux father, may I ask you, respectfully, have you courted anyone else since your period of mourning?"

"You may not ask her that," Jonas said.

Ezra slid his hair behind his ear. "So that's um, that's hundreds of men."

Elizabeth burst out laughing.

"Did you court anyone else before your marriage?"

"Not that either," Jonas cautioned.

"Of course not. I was seventeen," Elizabeth asked. "Have you courted any women since coming to America?"

Ezra's eyebrows rose. "No. I have not. Why did you ask for me?"

"You invited her out," Jonas insisted. "With the Van der Kellens."

Ezra looked at Jonas for a moment and then wet his lips. "What do you do for fun?"

"I recently, attended an art opening of a friend of mine. The master of ceremonies was most amusing. I laughed so much that night that he was all I could think about. He expressed himself very well. He was very knowledgeable about art. His voice was... different."

"Different isn't always good," Ezra said.

"In this case it is. A voice loud enough to speak to a room full of people and yet soft enough to converse at the table, with such a vocal range actually...."

"I sang in church, as a boy," Ezra explained. "I sometimes sing while I paint."

"Oh that would give me chills. I'm certain you have a wonderful singing voice. And I was just going to praise you for being bold enough to speak to a crowd. I thought then that you would be bold enough to...court me, if interested."

He lowered his chin and kept his dark eyes on her blue ones. "Being bold is something we have in common. Aside from that, I think opposites attract. Don't you?"

Elizabeth lightly touched the whiskers beneath his chin with the back of one finger.

He moved his knee against hers beneath the table.

"I believe I am going to have to have a word with Mr. August." Jonas stood up.

"We should see your drawings now anyway." Elizabeth rose from the table.

Ezra rose and took her hand, linking fingers with her. "Delighted to show you."

"Mr. August," Jonas said, "I shall have to accompany you."

"You may wait in the hall, Jonas," Elizabeth said. "We will take dessert in the parlor."

"Mr. August, may I have a word with you for a moment?" Jonas asked.

"It's all right. Elizabeth, go ahead and start looking through the drawings. Be careful. You'll get charcoal on your fingers." Ezra lingered in the dining room as Elizabeth left.

Elizabeth walked across to the parlor where the leather portfolio lay on the card table. She touched the handle, thinking of Ezra's hands on it. And when she raised the side to reveal all the loose papers, the aroma of pressed handmade paper and charcoal met her nose. She leaned close to sniff the other scents lingering in the paper and leather, not even knowing them to be turpentine, linseed oil, and even a hint of tobacco. These were the aromas of an art studio and her first time encountering them. They would forever remind her of Ezra.

In the dining room, Jonas came to stand before Ezra while the maids began clearing the table. These maids tried hard not to make eye contact with the suitor, but he was watching them.

"Mr. August, may I implore to your more gentlemanly side, that Mrs. Miller is a widow and a young impressionable woman," Jonas said.

"These things I know. Get to the point, Jonas. Do you wish me to leave?" Ezra asked.

"She takes Mr. Van der Kellen's recommendations very highly," Jonas said.

"So do I," Ezra said.

"Then I implore you to…."

"It is Mr. Van der Kellen's standards that I must live up to on an evening such as this." Ezra glanced at the maids. "It is Elizabeth who must take advantage of me, if she wishes. And if she does, she is in charge here, isn't she?"

Laughter could be heard all the way to the foyer. Robin handed his top hat and overcoat to Jonas while Marie let her fur be taken by a maid.

"Is there anything you can do about the situation, sir?" Jonas whispered to Robin.

"Ezra is still here?" Robin asked.

"They are…"

"Laughing." Marie started right down the hall. And then she blocked Robin beside the door. They listened.

"Robin insisted we turn these to the wall. I actually think they are too arousing for some people. He's obviously one of them. He was protesting so much. I just loved it when Adam told him to get down off his high horse," Ezra was saying.

Ezra's figure drawings were laid out all over the floor. He was on one side of the room with a brandy in his hand, prancing above them. Elizabeth sat on the floor, her skirt spread all around her, looking over the drawings and up at Ezra.

Marie gestured to Robin.

Van der Kellen entered the room. "And I did, didn't I?"

Ezra shook his brandy up into the air when he jolted. It fell on his cuff and his knee.

Elizabeth burst out laughing, pointing at Ezra. "At least you weren't doing your impression of him."

"Is that what you're always doing behind my back?" Robin asked.

"No sir. Admiring your tailoring, is all." Ezra gave him a brief bow.

Marie strolled in, stepping carefully around drawings. "Elizabeth, may I help you up, darling?"

Beth reached a hand up to her and stood up. "Aren't they amazing? Ezra has so much talent. He is an incredible artist, is he not?"

"Yes. Yes he is," Marie said. "Are you all right? Jonas is afraid these are inappropriate drawings."

"They're art. There is no inappropriate art," Elizabeth said.

"Thank you, Elizabeth," Ezra said.

"Gather these up, Ezra. Thank you," Robin said.

"It is late. I should be going." Ezra began picking up his drawings and gathering them into the portfolio. Elizabeth handed him a couple of them. They looked at each other across the table. "May I call again to discuss the painting you wish to commission?"

"Yes. Please."

They both lingered.

"Thank you for a lovely dinner," Ezra said.

"Thank you, sir." Elizabeth found the table was too broad for them to kiss. She would not get that kiss he promised.

"I will walk him to the door," Robin assured.

A maid brought Ezra his hat and over coat.

He put on his hat and leaned in to whisper to Elizabeth, "I've been handed my hat, quite literally. What would you have me do?"

"I would have you stay," Elizabeth whispered.

"You know I can't do that," Ezra told her and then whispered, "Just yet."

"Write to me tomorrow," Elizabeth asked.

"Yes, madam," Ezra said. "I am a painter at your service."

"A painter on his way home," Robin added.

Ezra donned his hat and let the maid help him on with his coat. When he looked at Elizabeth he could not be sad at leaving, but rather smiled at all of the fun they'd had.

Ezra exited with Robin, holding the portfolio under his arm. Robin walked him to the door. And there they looked at each other. Robin patted him on the arm. "Thank you for not taking her up on it tonight."

"You kidding me?"

"Do you have any idea what you're doing?"

"No, I don't have any idea what I'm doing. You got me into this," Ezra said. "You'd better get me through it. I have to drink just to keep my hand from shaking in there."

"Ezra, allow me to tell you. Stress is something you feel when something you care about is at stake."

Ezra looked at him, just breathing for a moment. "So it is. But I can't give her what she wants. Yet."

"You are supposed to marry her first," Robin said.

"You buy a horse without riding it?" Ezra asked.

"The best horse I ever had, as a matter of fact. When you know what you want, you want it, don't you?"

By Susan Eddy

Ezra walked out the door and down the stairs to Adam's awaiting carriage. "Goodnight, Dutchman." He tipped his hat to Robin.

With Elizabeth's open carriage and Adam's open buckboard, Ezra's gallery was emptied but it still took two trips back and forth to Adam's carriage barn. Both carriages came with drivers, so that left Adam, Robin, Ezra, Albert, and Pierre to load and unload all of the canvasses.

"The next thing you have to do is stand the test of her society friends," Robin said to Ezra as they carried either end of a framed canvas.

"What does that mean?"

"It means dinner with old fat rich people looking down their noses at you because you're not five generations rich," Adam said in passing.

"Oh like selling paintings to them, you mean? Yeah, I am not new to that," Ezra shot back.

"It does mean holding your own, being a gentleman, not getting snarky as I've seen you," Robin told him. "Some of them are just going to hate you because you're not five generations rich. But some are going to think you are charming. Try to be charming but not way over the top."

"Charming but not over the top charming. What the hell, Robin?" Ezra's voice split.

"You are worldly. You are knowledgeable about art," Adam added. "Use that."

"You trained in Paris," Albert reminded.

"I still don't like him being courted by a woman," Pierre said. "He's never been with a woman."

People walked past them in the street, paused to look at them.

Ezra set down a large canvas and replied, "Thank you for broadcasting that to the entire district. *Why don't you just paint* virgin on my forehead?"

Even the strangers burst out laughing.

Ezra took a bow. "Thank you very much."

Ezra was pacing in the parlor, back and forth.

"You're going to make me nauseous. Sit down," Adam said to him.

"What time is it?" Ezra asked.

"Five minutes after the last time you asked. You like her," Adam said.

"Is that a carriage?" Ezra bolted toward the windows.

"Don't do that, man. Just sit down. She'll be here." Adam burst out laughing.

"It's her carriage." Ezra let the curtains fall back into place and rushed to the nearest mirror to check his hair, his teeth. Then he raised an arm and smelled himself.

Adam laughed harder. "You're killing me here."

Mr. Hobson went to the front door and opened it.

Ezra checked the buttons of his trousers and sat down across from Adam. Then he stood up again. "I shouldn't seem too eager. I should be upstairs or something."

"Doing what? Ironing your corset?" Adam asked.

"From you that is just wrong, man." Ezra returned to pacing.

Zoey entered from the hall. "She's here. How are you, Ezra?"

Ezra hurried close to Zoey and asked, "What do I smell like?"

Adam laughed.

Zoey patted Ezra on the vest. "You smell like Robin."

"You mean like after he has just had a shave not like after he's been on a horse all day?" Ezra asked. "Right?"

Hobson appeared at the door. "May I present, Mrs. Elizabeth Miller."

Beth stopped in the doorway. "Could we just call me Miss Elizabeth from now on?"

"As you wish, Mrs. Miller," Hobson replied.

She met eyes with Ezra as they all laughed. Ezra went to her, extending both his hands to her. Beth grabbed hands with him and he stole a quick kiss to her cheek. "Sorry I'm late. I couldn't decide what to wear. I didn't want to seem too eager or too..."

"Gorgeous? Well, you failed miserably." Ezra moved his hand around her, low on her back.

"Are you joining us for dinner?" Zoey hinted. "Adam's mother sends her regrets. She is at her bridge game with her ladies."

"Yes. Can we just have a minute?" Elizabeth asked.

"Of course. Come Adam." Zoey pulled Adam with her and down the hall.

Hobson lingered long enough that Ezra briefly glared at him. Hobson shook his head and retreated to the kitchen.

"What is it? Something wrong?" Ezra asked.

Beth laid both hands on his vest and the silk of his lapels. "It's just that I...I can't stop thinking about..." She dropped her voice to a whisper. "That kiss."

"Oh. In the carriage? That kiss?" Ezra teased.

She blushed and withdrew her hands.

Ezra grabbed her by the wrists. "What were you thinking about it? Too much? Too wet?"

"Would you just shut up and kiss me?" Beth blurted out.

He smiled. Then he wet his lips and tilted his head.

She took a deep breath and looked up at him.

Ezra stepped closer until her skirt stopped him, preventing him from pressing his hips to hers. He looked down at it, trying to figure it out. Beneath that silk there must be a lot of structure.

She freed her hands and reached for his waist, forcing her crinoline flat in front and out behind her.

When Ezra said, "Oh…" their mouths met. His kiss started with surprise and then warmth and then something more, passion.

Beth wrapped her arms around his waist inside his jacket, finding him so slender. Ezra folded around her and tilted his head the other way to continue kissing her. She felt him draw in a deep breath.

Beth didn't let go of him but let the kiss end. She looked up and traced his lower lip with her fingertip. Ezra was studying her blue eyes.

"I ah… don't know what to do now," Elizabeth said.

"Are you going to step away from me? Cause I don't think I can step away from you," he whispered.

"Well…I don't think we can eat dinner this way," Beth whispered.

He smiled. "I'll bet we can."

She giggled. She moved her hands onto his lapels again. She toyed with the bow of his ascot, wondering about untying it. His warmth came through his shirt onto her hands.

"May I ask you something?" He said.

"Anything."

"What on earth is under that dress?"

She laughed and took a step back to pull up her skirt just enough to reveal the stiff linen crinoline hoop skirt beneath her dress.

"Wow. Look at that." Ezra stooped down to feel the hoop.

Just then Adam cleared his throat in the hallway. "What in the hell are you doing?"

Elizabeth burst out laughing.

Ezra stood upright. "I haven't seen that anywhere except France. Isn't that amazing?"

"I believe it is from France." Beth shook her skirt back into place over the under garment. "You men aren't supposed to know about such things."

"Well stop showing them to us," Ezra said.

Ezra leaned in and stole a kiss during dinner.

Beth smiled at him.

"Ezra," Adam cautioned.

"What?" Ezra just looked down at his plate and chased some peas with his spoon. He smiled.

"With my mother out, don't do anything to get me and Zoey in trouble," Adam said.

"I'm not doing anything." Ezra smiled.

Elizabeth giggled and laid her hand on his arm on the table. "We need some unchaperoned time just to get to know each other. That's all."

"Oh come on, Adam. You didn't go through this society dating ritual. You did Zoey in the laundry room," Ezra said.

Beth gasped. "Did you really?"

Zoey grabbed onto Beth's other hand. "He was so shy and sweet and so hungry."

"Really? Can't imagine Ezra being shy," Beth replied.

"Not since I was twelve, no," Ezra said.

Ezra was the only one in the parlor, and he was about to rise from the sofa when Beth entered. She gestured for him to remain seated so that she could swoop in beside him, close to him.

He smirked at her and kept his hands in his lap. He brought his knees together and sat up.

Beth turned to smooth her hand down his lapel. She explored his ruffled collar and the way he tied his ascot. "You're warm. Why don't you take off the jacket?"

"I am afraid Hobson will tell Lena," Ezra admitted. "And I'm really afraid of Lena."

"It is warm in here." Adam took his seat across from them on the other sofa. "They really got that fire going. Zoey will be here in a minute."

Ezra took Beth's hand into his and linked their fingers, feeling the electricity of her touch. Her hand was so much smaller and fingers so delicate. He felt every bit of each finger. And she felt every bit of his hand.

Adam sipped a glass of brandy quietly.

Beth examined the stitching on Ezra's cuff, the embroidery around the buttons. "Do you like music, Ezra?"

"Love it. We often have friends play their instruments in the studio while we paint," Ezra said.

"Really?" Beth said. "What style of music?"

Zoey entered and handed a glass of wine to Elizabeth. A maid followed her with a tray to serve glasses of red wine to Ezra and Adam.

"Oh everything. We have two friends who are in the orchestra at the opera. And we have one who plays the violin in a few restaurants at dinner. Oh and we're not opposed to a couple Hungarian folk musicians who live downstairs of the attic studio."

"Yes. The Hungarian woman who's iron you ruined," Beth said.

Ezra nodded. "Her husband and his brother, yes. Mandolin and clarinet, in that order."

"Oh, picture this," Adam told her. "Paintings lining the walls and making up interior walls, a fireplace on either end, mattresses on the floor, tables all full of paints and brushes. Easels everywhere. That was his attic studio."

The front door opened and Lena entered the parlor. She gasped when she saw Ezra and Elizabeth sitting so close together. "Ezra, what are you doing? Come here, boy. You sit over here."

"Ahhh." Ezra stood up slowly. "Didn't the bridge game go well?"

"Don't talk back to me. Sit over here, young man or you won't be able to sit for a very long time." Lena indicated the chair across from Elizabeth. "Adam, you let him share the sofa with Elizabeth. You know better."

"Look, Mrs. Rothschild, I was only..." Ezra tried to explain.

"No. I told you to try something, not try it on my sofa. Sit down."

Ezra sat where he had to. He met eyes with Elizabeth and they both tried not to laugh.

"Why are you still entertaining so late?" Lena asked. "Elizabeth's carriage is outside."

"You told me to sit. I don't dare move now," Ezra said.

Adam burst out laughing, but then added, "Should I get the wooden spoon or lend you my belt?"

Lena smiled but she shook her head. "Mrs. Miller, I apologize. I mistakenly thought my son would be a proper chaperone."

"Adam was a fine chaperone. This is our fourth dinner together, Mrs. Rothschild. I just wanted to get to know him better," Elizabeth said. "We were only holding hands."

Lena stood behind Ezra's chair and put her hands down on his shoulders. "What do you want to know about this boy? You can ask it from there." She looked down and began stroking a hand through Ezra's hair.

Ezra's eyes went wide.

Adam and Zoey tried not to laugh.

Lena continued to stroke Ezra's hair, the curls and how thick it was. "What?" She looked from Elizabeth to Adam and Zoey. Then she moved around the chair to see Ezra quickly blank his expression. "Maledizione. Where do you get such hair?"

"Huh! I know what she said. She just cursed at me," Ezra cried laughing.

Lena laughed. "Oh, I had so much sambuca. So much."

Ezra grabbed Lena's hand and they all laughed together. "Break out the sambuca, Mom."

"How do you know what is maledizione?" Lena took a seat next to Elizabeth.

"Oh I know a lot of Italian curse words. It's like dammit or hell or something like that. I was so bad as a fish monger in Rome, I got called every bad word you have," Ezra said. "I'm sorry. I was afraid of the fish. They were so ugly and the smell, and they weren't dead yet. I cried when I had to cut off their heads and take out the insides. What is coglione?"

"Oh!" Lena put her hand to her mouth. "Don't say that word."

"Do you know what that is?" Ezra asked Adam.

"It does mean idiot but that's not what it is," Adam said.

"I got called that all the time, until I quit one day," Ezra said. "What is it? Really?"

"Don't tell him," Lena warned. "Not in front of the young ladies."

"They called him a dick?" Elizabeth asked.

"No but you're in the right bodily area."

Chapter Twelve   Blizzard

"Ah, Mom, I think you had rather a lot to drink last night." Ezra looked up at Lena as she took her seat at the breakfast table. "You were really funny."

"So were you, Ezra boy."

"I thought you were really going spank me for a while there," Ezra said. "Can I ask you something seriously?"

Coffee was poured for both of them and then the maid left them alone.

"Please, before the others come down," Ezra said.

"Ask me your question," Lena said.

"I don't really know what the custom is for me at this point. What am I not supposed to do with Elizabeth? Because every time we are alone...."

"You're not supposed to be alone with Elizabeth," Lena said.

Ezra lowered his eyes.

"When you are alone with her, what happens?" Lena asked softly.

"She wants to do things. And I... Am I supposed to stop her? I know Robin would say so. But I want her to like me," Ezra said.

Lena poured cream into her coffee and stirred for a moment. "She likes you. Would you like to do things with her?"

"Well see, that's part of the problem. I'm afraid she will find out how much I do really...want her," Ezra said quietly. "My heart won't stop beating so fast. I'm breathing hard. I'm afraid...what if I...what if we are alone together and I belch or something?"

Lena smiled. "Then you both laugh. It happens. She's in a corset. She is more afraid she will belch than you."

Ezra grinned, lowering his chin.

"Ezra, are you thinking about proposing to her?" Lena asked.

"I'm thinking about it."

"Did you sleep with her?"

"No. Of course not," Ezra said. "I'm not ready for that yet. I need time to get used to this. Can you ask her if she can wait for me?"

"You can ask her this question yourself. You still must be the man in the relationship."

"That's just it. I don't know what that means."

"It doesn't mean anything. You ask her to be patient with you. Tell her your feelings. Bring her a present, a gift. Ezra, marry her. Give her a child. You will be safe for life this way."

"A package for you, Elizabeth." Jonas gestured.

She entered the parlor and saw a gift on the table. "Who from?"

Marie hurried beside her. "Read the card."

Elizabeth opened the card and read aloud. "For the next slightly warm sunny day. Please reserve a walk for me, Ezra."

"Wow, what can it be?" Marie looked over her shoulder.

"I have a feeling you already know." Elizabeth began opening the wrapping paper and handed the bow to Marie. Then she opened the wooden box to find a pair of leather boots. She pulled one out curiously, to find a flat heeled leather boot that would come up halfway to her knee.

"Walking shoes, it would seem," Marie told her. "You can't very well take a long walk in February in tiny silk heels, now can you."

"Why didn't you just give them to me?"

"Oh no. It was his idea. But he needed the size from me. I wear your shoes all the time, so I went to the cobbler for you," Marie said.

"I love them!" She enthused. "He wants to take a walk with me. You know what I will send back to him? A very warm fur scarf."

"Not fur. Too wealthy."

"A very warm wool scarf."

"Shall we go shopping for one?"

"Get your coat."

February 4, a Friday, seemed like any other day for a young couple to take a walk right from Elizabeth's front door out onto Wall Street, round the corner and down to Pearl Street to see Ezra's new gallery.

He wore a top hat and black wool overcoat with his new red wool scarf wrapped about his neck.

Elizabeth wore her new walking boots, leggings, a warm dress and winter fur collared hooded overcoat. Her hands were in a fur muff if not inside his coat pocket.

He unlocked the door to the gallery and she entered.

"Have a seat. Hang on. I'll get a fire going."

Ezra knelt at the fireplace to arrange kindling beneath the split logs that were stacked inside the hearth. He used some straw and scrap paper with a flint to get that lit.

"Did you just use that rock to make the fire start?" Elizabeth huddled in her coat, sitting on a wooden crate beside him.

Ezra looked down at the flint in his hand. "It's a flint. You strike it and the sparks start the fire. Paper is a good target."

"Is it hot?"

He had the fire safely started in the kindling and turned to lay the flint into her hand. "It's quite cool. See?"

"So fire just hides in this rock until you need it?" Elizabeth asked.

Ezra smiled. "Yes. I never thought of it that way. You can do it next time."

She handed it back to him and he laid it on the hearth.

From there, he used a piece of kindling to light a whale oil lamp and then a few candles to reveal a surprise picnic lunch on the counter.

"This will be a nice gallery, I think. It's long and narrow, lots of wall space for paintings," Elizabeth said.

"That's what I thought. Albert and Pierre are living upstairs. I don't think they're home right now," Ezra said. "They're still hauling things over."

"And you are living upstairs as well?"

Ezra lowered his chin and shook his head. "Actually, I've been staying with Adam. Albert and Pierre are a bit mad at me right now. I got tired of them ganging up on me." Ezra poured two small glasses with brandy and handed one to Elizabeth. "This will warm you."

"Thank you." Elizabeth took a sip. "I like the red scarf on you. Bold color seems to work well on you, with your black hair and dark eyes."

"I like it very much. Thank you." He sat across from her on another crate. "I like red and purple."

"Am I the reason for the rift? I'm so sorry."

"Well, it's a strange relationship I've had with them from the start. I believe most of the difficulty we are having right now is that I am to manage the gallery. I choose what goes on the walls. They no longer get to put up whatever they make. Not everything they make is good."

"Sounds like a manager. You were schooled in Paris, after all," Elizabeth said.

"They're a little upset with me being with you. They think I'm only doing it for money," Ezra said. "They don't realize I'm also doing it to get my gallery into society."

Elizabeth looked at him.

"Joking. Elizabeth. Please, I'm not with you for money or society. I'm just hoping I can figure out the intimacy part." Ezra's eyebrows waggled. "Should it come to that."

She burst out laughing. "I'm sure you can, one day."

"I'm still trying to navigate strange waters," Ezra said.

"I love the way you say things, however confusing they may be to me. We are finally very alone. I feel safe alone with you, like I can just be my true self. Is there something you wish to talk with me about? You are not...losing interest?"

"Not at all. I wanted to see if you can be at all comfortable in my world. That's why we are here and on foot. Which is about all I can afford, a walk and a lunch," Ezra said.

"Oh Ezra, I have never been so embarrassed by my inheritance as now. I have been raised in a sheltered, spoiled, snobby little world," Elizabeth said. "And it's boring."

He smiled.

"I find this a little bit dangerous. Though I'm not afraid of you. My parents, if still living, would never have allowed me to court you. That made this initially very exciting," she said. "I know that you are a man of your word. You are a talented artist. And you risked your life to help a friend."

He lowered his chin. "Thank you, Beth."

"Ezra, it's all I can do not to buy you so many things, to dress you up in fine suits and the thought of you sleeping on a mattress on the floor or going cold at night...Oh how I want to care for a man."

"I would be very unaccustomed to such care." He let out a long slow breath. "But not opposed to it. I'm preoccupied with my occupation, of course. This fills a man's mind quite a lot. And society requires a certain amount of time to pass before any next steps in a courtship, so Robin tells me. I'm so afraid there are all these wealthy society men calling on you."

"No. There are not. I've met them, sons of Edward's friends, cousins, friends of friends. They don't have any spirit. They are boring. They don't...interest me. Ezra, I never had any fun growing up. Then I got married and never had any fun. I thought at least if I had children I would have fun with them. But with you, we laugh all the time. You show me a world, that I didn't know existed."

"We do have fun. You want to see my world? You want to? Come with me and be done with it." He took her hand and the oil lamp. They climbed to the second floor and looked briefly at the painting studio with easels and a kitchen. Then they climbed to the third floor where there were four small bedrooms.

He opened the door to the room in the front, overlooking Pearl Street. There was a mattress on the floor with pillows and wool blankets. There were a couple duffle bags of clothing on the floor and no furniture save a small table. A small fireplace was dark and cold, with a few items on the mantel, a wooden box and a tobacco pouch.

Elizabeth moved into the room, pausing to touch her fingers to the shaving supplies, mirror, and hairbrush on the table. She was now standing on the opposite side of the mattress from him. When her footsteps were not sounding on the wooden floor, the only sound was the wind.

"I couldn't very well bring you back here, now could I? This is just how poor I have been until I met Adam. This is all I have," Ezra said. "Well and sable brushes from Paris that I cannot live without."

"Ezra, it would be lying down here that you would take me?"

Ezra's mouth came open.

She sat down on the mattress and then laid back to look up at the ceiling. "I just want to imagine it."

Ezra pulled at his ascot to loosen it a bit. He was looking down at her body reclining on his bed, her bust, her tiny waist, down the skirt to tiny ankles. "You have a very romantic view of poverty, my love. Is it not cold in here? And dark in here? And it smells of oil paint and turpentine from downstairs. It's hard to sleep when you're hungry. It's hard to sleep when you are cold."

Elizabeth got up and took a hold of him by his coat in front as he pulled her to her feet. "It is in my room that you will take me, in my canopy bed, beside my fireplace, where it is warm and comforting and you want for nothing because you will have it."

"Elizabeth, my lovers have all been men."

"Will you..." She swallowed hard. "Will you not make an exception for me?"

"I...I want to. I do." He looked down and collected her cold hands into his against his chest. "Can you be patient with me?"

"Yes. Yes, absolutely. And we will continue to court?" Elizabeth said.

"Yes. I would love to." Ezra wrapped arms around her waist. They both needed an embrace and a moment of comfort together. So he held her for a long time and she snuggled up to him. "Are you shivering? Let's get you back downstairs to the fireplace."

"I have told my friends about you. They know Robin and Marie. They know about the hospital escape and that you are an artist. I think you are an amazing painter," Elizabeth rambled on as they walked down the stairs by the light of that one oil lamp. Their shadows danced around the stairway walls. The sound of wind outside echoed through the very empty building.

"That's not just because you wish to bed me?" Ezra asked.

"Well, not only," Elizabeth said.

He turned and smiled at her.

Downstairs they returned to the crates by the fireplace, but their eyes went to the large windows at the front of the gallery. It was a white out in the street. The snow was coming down and blowing very hard.

"Oh no. Look at that," Elizabeth said.

"Um, perhaps it will let up. I'll get you a sandwich."

"Well, let me see if I can help."

They both stood behind the counter and opened the picnic basket, packed by a nearby café. Ham and cheese sandwiches were wrapped in a towel on plates. Silverware for two was included. Muffins and two slices of apple pie were wrapped up in a pie tin. Ezra pulled out a bottle of wine. Wine glasses were wrapped in napkins.

Elizabeth found a bronze corkscrew in the basket and held it up curiously.

Ezra held out a hand for it and began opening the wine bottle. "You know, where I grew up, we don't use all this silverware. Hard bread is often used to sop up soup and to spread a ground paste of beans and spices onto. Coffee is very very strong. It is acceptable to drink the soup from the bowl. I find that I have to eat like someone else in this country and it weighs on my soul a bit. There was a pastry my mother made with dates and raisins in it. Your fingers would get all sticky and sweet."

"Keep telling me about you, Ezra. I have only been to Europe. I longed to travel beyond to exotic parts of the world. You are sensitive for a man. I like that about you." Elizabeth slid some of his curls behind his ear as he looked down at the wine bottle. "I don't want a simple thing like how we dine to cause you harm."

He raised his chin to look into her eyes. His arm was against her shoulder.

"You know, I only ever once had a picnic such as this. It was traveling with Robin from the train station all the way to Canterbury. We stopped along the way to rest the horses." Elizabeth looked up at Ezra beside her. "I ate fried chicken with my fingers."

"Really? How revolutionary."

"I know, right?"

Together they set out the sandwiches and pie onto the plates.

The front of the building creaked with the wind. They both stared at the windows again.

"I'm really worried about that," she admitted.

"Don't think I planned this," Ezra said. "I did not consult a witch regarding the weather."

That made her smile. "How many witches do you know?"

"Well, just Pierre." He shrugged.

They both laughed. They sat down by the fire to eat the sandwiches. They had to set wine glasses down on the hearth.

"There is enough firewood to keep this going all night," he said.

"Is there? They'll be worried about me if I'm not back before dark."

"They know you're with me and I will keep you safe. Can't very well go looking for us in a blizzard. We'll all have to settle down wherever we are," Ezra said. "We can make a new plan. Tell me about yourself, things you cannot say with Jonas overhearing. Why did you marry Edward?"

"It was arranged by my father before he passed."

"Why did you agree to it?"

"Well, I was terrified and alone. I inherited the fortune but as soon as I married it would all pass to my husband. My parents, quite rightly, feared that I would marry some young fool with long black hair and tight trousers." Elizabeth made him smile. "Edward was very kind and caring."

"I'm certain. I do beg your pardon," Ezra said. "How did you lose your parents?"

"We were on the ship coming back from Calais and both came down with the fever. It was spreading so badly through the ship that I was moved to stay with several other young ladies confined to another first class cabin. We all lost someone in our families. I lost both parents. Suddenly in the mid-Atlantic our butler came to me and said that I was now head of the family. And that is how I learned my parents had passed."

Ezra grabbed her hand. "Oh I'm so sorry."

She laid her other hand on his arm. "It's all right. We can talk about that another time. Ezra, I realize was married to an old man."

As he looked at her, his stomach growled and he hoped she could not hear it.

"When I first saw Marie and Robin together I envied so much the passion they had for each other. I felt I missed out on all of that. Maybe I didn't deserve it." She reached out to touch a bit of his ear showing through his curls.

"I had a similar feeling when I saw Adam and Zoey," Ezra admitted. "There are things you can have if you marry that you cannot otherwise."

"Many things." She slid his hair back behind his ear, touching his long sideburns, and the curl of his ear. "Is it terrible that I have been married before?"

"I am terribly sorry for your loss. That is all," Ezra said. "Your touch is so light and delicate. Please do not stop. Making me tingle all over and I suddenly realize how long it's been since I've been touched."

"Oh? Really?" She slid her whole hand into his thick hair, marveling over the texture and fullness of it. "What things can you only have if you marry?"

"Um...someone to care for you. Someone devoted to you. Children," he whispered. He leaned his head toward her hand and closed his eyes.

"Do you like children?"

"Very much so."

"You can't have children if all your lovers are men," Elizabeth said and then looked at him in horror. "I don't believe I said that. I'm so sorry."

"It's true. It is very true. Can't marry him either," Ezra said. "You can say it to me. It is the truth after all."

She touched his long sideburns on one side of his face and then the other. "Your eyes are so dark. Your lashes are longer than a girls."

"They hit my spectacles. My eyes cannot stop looking into yours. You know we are so opposite, from two sides of the world. Your eyes are so light blue and hair so blonde. Look, your skin is lighter than mine. I hear your voice in my head and not my own anymore."

"Not a single line on your face. Not a white hair on your head," she mused.

"Oh that is not true. I have two of them. Here." Ezra showed her the side of his head. "But I've had them all my life and only these two."

Elizabeth smiled. "They're adorable. I shall look for them always."

"Well, there are three more. I can't tell you where," he admitted with a smirk.

Beth giggled. "Our little secret then. Your skin is so firm and I have no doubt, your body is so hard all over."

Ezra set his plate down on the hearth and held out his hand for hers. Half touched sandwiches could wait on the hearth. With coats on and knees touching, they kissed their most delicate and deep kiss. And Elizabeth traced a fingertip across his full upper lip and then his pouty lower lip, as their eyes searched each other's.

"Your kiss is so different," she whispered.

"Is it? What do you mean?" His eyebrows rose. "You can say it."

She looked down and whispered, "With your tongue."

A sudden smile from Ezra made her giggle.

"You've never been kissed like that?" Ezra had to ask.

She shook her head.

He giggled too. "Do you like it?"

"So very much except that..."

Ezra raised her chin with one finger. "Except what? Tell me."

Her cheeks blushed red and she whispered, "It's so arousing."

That made him smile. He sat back and nodded. "Well...that just made my day."

The wind really howled outside.

"I had better take a look about and see to our safety.... or something less arousing anyway." Ezra walked to the windows and wiped his hand on the glass to clear it. "Can't even see the streetlights. They've blown out. I don't hear any carriages either. I think the wind is too bad for travel. Let me take a look out back. See if it's any better in the alley."

"All right." She remained sitting by the fire. She held her cold hands to her cheeks to cool them. The hearth was finally warm enough that she could unbutton her coat.

Ezra disappeared into the rear of the building for a while. A door opened. He called to someone, over the wind. It sounded as if he asked if they needed help. He closed the door and walked back to her. "I'm afraid it is very bad indeed. A carriage overturned in the wind not far from here. People injured inside. They've gotten them all out. The temperature is dropping fast. I'm so sorry, Elizabeth. My plans have failed."

"Not at all, Ezra. It is a fine picnic," she said. "We will spend the night in your room."

"We will spend the night right here," he said. "I'll drop that feather bed down the stairs and make it up here for you, by the fire."

"Well then." She stood up. "Before we drink anymore wine, let's make the bed up."

Ezra shrugged. "Can you take the lamp for me?"

"Of course, dear."

"Don't drop it."

"I won't."

"Don't burn down my gallery."

"I won't." She burst out laughing.

By Susan Eddy

Up, up to the top floor they went into Ezra's room and he just grabbed the whole mattress, blankets, and pillows to drag it to the stairway. "Watch your step. Hold the rail."

"I've got it." Elizabeth followed him down the stairs as he dragged the mattress down and around each landing. He pulled it through the gallery. Then he had to move the crates and set the bed right before the hearth. He stacked more wood into the fire. There was a half cord of wood beside the hearth, more than enough for the night.

Elizabeth replaced the pillows to the head of the bed and glanced again at the windows. All light was about to fade outside. She removed her coat and laid it on the counter. Then she took her piece of pie and went to sit down, cross-legged on his bed.

Ezra smiled. He brought his pie and sat down facing her, sitting cross-legged like she did.

"Save the muffins for breakfast, don't you think?" she said.

"Yes. Good idea."

They would finish their sandwiches and the pie simultaneously. Ezra refilled their wine glasses.

"There is a kitchen upstairs. Is there anything in there?"

"Just dishware. Water. Coffee, I believe. We did make some coffee on the stove the other day." Ezra squirmed out of his coat and laid it beside the bed. He unwrapped the wool scarf. Then he unbuttoned his jacket. When he started untying his ascot she stopped him.

"What are you doing?"

"Huh? I'm choking in this." Ezra removed the ascot and opened a couple buttons at the high neck of his white shirt. There was a gold chain about his bare neck.

"You should try a corset," she said.

Ezra smiled warmly. "Make yourself comfortable. My home is your home, such that it is."

"How do men like you survive without women in the kitchen?"

"Café down the street," Ezra said. "Bakery always had day olds. Pierre always brought home leftovers from the restaurant. Albert can cook. He just can't bake anything."

"Who does your washing?"

"Chinese laundry," Ezra said.

"Who cares for you?"

"No one has cared for me since I was...well I can't count back that far," Ezra said. "I can only imagine that in the evening, in your home, someone stokes up the fireplace in your room, turns down the bed linens, and lays a flower on your pillow. I can't be that person."

"Absolutely not. Someone would do those things for you in my home," Beth said gently. "Are you experiencing anything like that at Adam's home?"

Ezra's eyebrows rose for a moment. "It is very comfortable, very opulent. The pillows are magnificent clouds from heaven. Almost every room is nice and warm. Rather strange that my clothing is ironed and set up for me in the wardrobe and I think Adam keeps slipping new things in, stockings and..."

"So these nice suits are kept at Adam's house?"

"Oh, yes there are just some old painting clothes upstairs. What do you want in your life now?" he asked.

"Am I to never know what it's like to love someone so much that I can't think of anything else? That passion just takes me away... That I just look at him and I see our future children." Elizabeth looked into Ezra's eyes. "Does everyone in your family have dark hair and dark eyes?"

He thought a bit and said, "No. My youngest sisters had light hair. Dare I ask you then, are you over Robin?"

"That was a different Elizabeth." She began removing hair pins. "She doesn't exist anymore. She thought the world revolved around her."

"What are you doing?"

"I can't lie down with these in my hair." She began piling the pins on the hearth. "Are we sleeping together here? Can I count on you to...behave yourself?"

Ezra let out a difficult breath. His eyes rolled toward the fireplace.

"What is it? Ezra, you can tell me anything. May I boldly say that I find you fascinating just as you are? I'm about to spend the night on the floor of a future art gallery, the most exciting night of my life," Elizabeth said. "Where did you get this pie? It is very good."

"Elizabeth, I can give you what you wish but I need some time. I can't tonight. I need to be friends first. Can we do that?"

"Oh Ezra, please let's do that. Is it all right that I want to buy you all sorts of things and dress you up wonderfully. Is that all right?"

He nodded. "Would you have noticed me as I was, before Adam dressed me up as a gentleman?"

"I did notice you. I remembered you from the gallery when I bought the painting from you. I wrote to Marie about you. Ask her. You were sitting in the back, on top of your desk, cross-legged, with a book in your lap. What book?"

"Italian art, probably. Drawings, reproductions of art such as I saw in Rome."

"Were you dreaming of traveling? You've been to Rome."

"Dreaming of painting a masterpiece of my own. I want to paint something that will tear at your soul and change the world."

In the darkness and flickering light, he was exotic and dangerous to her, and yet there was the reassuring endorsement of Robin Van der Kellen. The wind picked up outside and they knew it was impossible for anyone to pass even the few blocks between Wall Street and Pearl.

She watched him go to the counter and light a hand rolled cigarette off the candle. He walked toward the front windows again to listen to the outside as he smoked to calm his nerves.

"You like tobacco do you?" she asked him. "Tobacco?"

"Yes. Does it bother you?"

"Not at all. Edward smoked a pipe after dinner. It smelled different than this," she admitted. "Will you drink a brandy now?"

"I really don't drink much." Ezra tapped his cigarette into the fireplace as he moved back to sit near her. "One of the benefits of not being able to afford liquor." But he smiled at her and his eyes had a mischievous glint. His chin was raised.

"Want to know what my secret pleasure is?" Elizabeth said.

His eyebrows rose. "Yes. Very much so."

"Chocolate. I keep chocolate in the drawer beside my bed," she said. "Very expensive chocolate from Europe."

He puffed on his tobacco. "Doesn't sound like something to keep secret. Unless you don't want to share it."

Then they both laughed.

"Tell me more secrets," Ezra encouraged.

"I've never been drunk. I'd like to see what it is like," she said.

He gestured toward the brandy bottle on the counter.

"Not tonight." She laughed.

"Have you ever kissed...a girl?" Ezra asked.

"Oh. No. Only my cousin when we were eight years old or something, practicing," Elizabeth said. "But then we also practiced curtseying and wearing veils."

His eyebrows rose and he smiled. "So did I."

"You did not."

"Did so. My sisters dressed me up like one of them."

"And your father did not object?" Beth asked.

He shook his head. "My father was a doctor. He was never at home." He rested his elbows on his knees. "Before I left home I already had my first boyfriend. I already knew I was...different."

"Look at how...flexible you are."

"You mean that I can love a boy or a girl?"

"No. Well yes. But look how you're sitting."

Ezra laughed out loud. He looked down at his crossed legs. "You want to see something? All right." He tossed the remainder of his cigarette into the fireplace. He could bring one knee up to his chin with that leg crossed over the other. And then he could switch them. "I'm pretty bendy for a man."

"You are. I don't think I can do that," Elizabeth said. "Let me try."

Elizabeth slid beneath the covers, fully clothed in her gown, corset, underclothing and winter leggings. Her boots she set beyond their pillows on the floor. She watched Ezra remove his jacket and vest, and then pull his shirttails up from his trousers. As he did so, she caught a glimpse of his bare flat stomach above his belt. He slid out of his boots and set them beside hers. He smiled the biggest, shyest smile as he climbed down with her into the bed. She was nearest to the fire.

Between them, their hands met. They linked fingers.

"Are you okay?" He asked.

"Yes. Wonderful. You?"

"Terrified."

"Of me? No one is terrified of me," she declared. "What is it, darling?"

"I'm told I have to be the man in the relationship. I don't know what that means. I'm afraid it might mean...it might mean...making love to you tonight," Ezra whispered.

She got up on her elbow to tell him, "People think I'm very bold and forward but I'm not. I've never been with a young man. You don't have to be a different kind of man. I don't want a man to tell me how to do everything and that I can't do this or I must do that. I've had that. I want whatever we make this relationship to be."

"You know something? I really like that about you."

"What can I do to help get your gallery going?"

He smiled. "You are going to come round and hammer nails in walls and sweep up the place?"

"Wouldn't know what to do with a hammer but I do have tons of wealthy friends to bring round when you have your opening, an opening of mostly your paintings. I've looked very closely at your painting of Adam. I don't know how to describe it but he looks so real that he could talk to me. His skin is luminous."

"Luminous. I like that." Ezra smoothed her blonde hair back from her eyes, finding how silky and very long it was. He got up onto his elbow to look at the shine of her hair across the pillow in the firelight. "Will you let me paint you? Something you could surely hang in your home and think of me always...."

"My heart's beating so fast right now."

"Are you all right?"

Elizabeth kissed his mouth and he responded with a romantic and slow loving kiss of the sort that she never had before. She slid her hand up into his dark curls. She felt his long sideburns and his ear and the back of his neck. She felt him align his body alongside hers.

"May I ask you…."

"Ask me anything."

"Were you in love with Albert and Pierre?" she whispered.

"No, it's more like they're my friends but I have let them…"

"Let them what? I must know to understand you."

"They have done things to me," Ezra said. "They are a couple. They are in love. But they took me into their relationship as sort of a fire starter, like the flint."

"Does that mean using you?"

"No. They care about me. Pierre is not speaking to me right now. But they do care about me," Ezra whispered.

"And before them you had other male lovers?"

"Yes. I have been young. I have been hurt. I've cried for someone I could not have," he whispered. "I had a crush on Adam when I first met him."

"Never a girl?"

"There was a girl in Paris who wanted me to marry her. But I had no money and I wanted to go to America. I couldn't bring her. And I didn't love her," Ezra said. "I never slept with her either. We were friends. She was an artist. I have had a lot of friends who are girls. For some reason, I seem to make friends easily with girls."

"Like Adam and the maids."

"Oh? Yes."

"I thought Adam was like you were. But he married and he is so in love with her." Elizabeth snuggled closer to Ezra. "Maybe you can too."

He wrapped his arms about her and took her head to his shoulder. "Yes he is. Adam came to me so driven to make these paintings of Robin, so driven that I thought he was madly in love with Robin. I think he was at some point, certainly on that ship sailing for Amsterdam when he made all those drawings."

"He made drawings of Robin back then?"

"The drawings he used for the paintings," Ezra said.

"Oh my God, you smell so good," Elizabeth sighed.

He giggled a bit. "You don't want to know."

"Yes I do." She raised her head to look at him. "Why does that make you giggle?"

"Adam gave me Robin's aftershave and hair tonic."

Beth laughed. "So the three of you are using the same?"

Ezra laughed. "He's going to kill us."

"They tell me each perfume smells different on each woman."

"Well, you'll have to sniff the three of us and let me know." He kissed her. "Beth, I'm being very honest with you. Are you frightened by any of this?"

"No. You have really never been with a woman?"

"Never." He used his finger and wrote out the word on his forehead. "Virgin." She couldn't tell he spelled it in Turkish, and wrote it left to right.

That made her burst out laughing.

"And frightened. That's why we must be friends first," Ezra said. "I'm serious."

"You are." Elizabeth pulled the covers up to his chin and warmed her hand on his chest. She aligned her body with his to share in his warmth. He wrapped his arms about her. "There is nothing to be afraid of with me."

"I believe that," he whispered.

They kissed and snuggled and eventually fell away to sleep together. Through the night, whenever one of them moved or rolled over, they met with a kiss and little whispers. Ezra would reach over her to toss more wood into the fireplace. They would embrace and share in each other's warmth. The wind howled through all hours of the night, but they kissed.

Chapter Thirteen   The White Ascot

Adam looked on the mattress beside the fireplace, the empty wine bottle, the plates and then at Pierre and Albert. They all heard the floor creak above their heads. "Shhhh." Adam put a finger to his lips. Then he led the other two quietly up the stairs.

Adam paused on the landing, hearing some giggling, he thought. He signaled below for them to stay put. Slowly he crept up a few more steps until he could see into the artist studio with the kitchen on the right. An oil lamp illuminated the space. The aroma of fresh brewed coffee escaped the kitchen.

Adam climbed the remaining stairs on all fours.

Ezra had Elizabeth backed against the cabinets, kissing her. Her arms were about his shoulders. She arched back, aligning against his body for their passionate kiss.

Adam stood up and put his hands on his hips. "And to think we were worried about you two."

She shrieked and Ezra threw her behind him as he spun. He turned to look on Adam in the doorway.

"And here you are picnicking, drinking wine, and whatever else this is," Adam said.

Albert and Pierre scrambled up beside him.

Elizabeth stayed behind Ezra, quickly buttoning up her dress in front. Her long blonde hair swished behind him.

"Ah, Mr. Hudson, my landlord," Ezra said. "A knock would have been nice."

"Jonas is threatening to kill you," Adam said. "You might want to tuck in your shirt."

"No. No. He sheltered me. He was a perfect gentleman," Elizabeth insisted from behind Ezra, still buttoning.

Ezra looked down and tucked his shirt down into his trousers.

"Relax. Robin is the one you've got to worry about," Adam said. "We told them you were probably trapped here when the blizzard hit. We came to check on you and look what we find."

"Ezra, you are marrying her now?" Albert asked.

"I..."

"You have to now," Albert said.

"Does he?" Pierre asked.

"We didn't do anything," Ezra said.

"Ezra!" Elizabeth gave him a bit of a shove.

He turned to take her into his arms again. "They're teasing. It's all right, Beth."

"Oh, it's Beth now?" Adam strolled into the room. "Any coffee left?"

"Plenty. Help yourself. Taught Beth how to make coffee." Ezra moved Elizabeth back to her seat at the table and to their coffee cups. "It's all right, darling."

"You don't know how to make coffee." Albert moved in and around them.

"I watched. I remembered," Ezra said. "I could make some Turkish coffee that would choke you Americans. You can stand a spoon up in it."

She let out a long breath and picked up her cup. "Don't you give me that look, Adam Hudson. You're the one who has to do up my hair again."

"What did I do?" Adam said.

"You saw us."

"Special circumstances. He did shelter you in a blizzard," Adam said. "I think society can make exceptions. Maybe you should walk into your house just like this."

"Maybe I don't want to," Elizabeth blurted out.

Ezra's eyebrows rose briefly. He slid a hand down her back and leaned in to tell her, "I'm sure between the four of us queer guys we can do up your hair again."

Into the grand foyer of the Miller mansion, holding hands with Elizabeth, Ezra met the glare of Robin Van der Kellen.

"Are you all right, Beth? We worried so." Marie took her from Ezra and pulled her into her arms.

"I'm fine, Marie. Ezra and I had to take shelter in his gallery when the storm picked up. He took most excellent care for me. We're quite hungry now though we had sandwiches for dinner. He had a wonderful picnic supper for us. Jonas, see that Ezra's things are brought over from Adam's house. Adam is expecting this. I want a nice hot bath for each of us. We've been chilled to the bone in that carriage."

Jonas looked to Van der Kellen, however.

"You've compromised her in a most egregious way," Robin scolded.

"What would you have me do? Walk her home in a blizzard and give her frost bite?" Ezra shot back boldly. "I am not responsible for the weather."

"Jonas, did you not hear me?" Elizabeth said.

"Mr. Van der Kellen, was this just a plan all along to...to marry her?" Jonas asked. "He cannot think that we would allow that now. Would we?"

"Gentlemen, I would have taken advantage of her last night if that was the plan. And I did not," Ezra replied. "Take Beth aside and ask her."

"He was a perfect gentleman," Elizabeth insisted. "Fetch his things Jonas and move him into another guest room. Two hot baths and get lunch started. Please."

Robin stepped forward and patted a hand on Ezra's shoulder. "Considering the storm, all right, Ezra." Robin looked to Jonas then and nodded.

Jonas began issuing orders to the staff, hot bath for each of them, lunch to be ready when they emerge, fetch Ezra's clothing from Adam's house. The staff took off in many directions.

Ezra escorted Elizabeth into her home, on his arm. He needed a shave. His beard was coming in pretty good in the form of mustache and on his chin.

The maids had pressed and prepared one of Ezra's fine suits for him and it was Van der Kellen who brought it into the room, where Ezra jolted in the bathing tub. Water and suds splashed about.

"For God's sake don't get up." Robin shut the door hard, and hung the suit over the rack. "Beth told Marie everything that happened. I appreciate you looking after her last night. She might have foolishly tried to walk home if you hadn't kept her there. I had to come in here and make a show of putting you in your place, for the staff."

"In my place?" Ezra looked up from his hot bath. His hair was wet and dripped down onto bare shoulders. "I'm having a heart attack."

"I set you up together. When it comes to it, are you attracted to a woman or not? That's what I want to know," Robin snapped.

"Oh my God."

"She's expecting fireworks from you tonight. Are you able to deliver?"

"I assure you it works, all right?" Ezra said.

"Are you going to do it when she expects you to?"

"Robin, I thought she's supposed to remarry first. Buy the horse without riding it first, right?" Ezra snapped. "Are you whoring me out?"

"Ezra, focus, would you?" Robin moved around the tub and took a seat at a good distance in front of him. "All I want to know is do you go both ways or are you strictly that way?"

"Oh my God. Get out if you said that to me."

Robin put his fist on his hip.

"Don't you ask me that again." Ezra stood up in the tub and reached for a towel.

Van der Kellen looked away and snapped, "Thanks."

"Who's in charge here anyway? Elizabeth or you? I think we'll just find out." Ezra stepped out of the tub, wrapping the towel about his waist. He grabbed another towel for his hair. "And I saved your ass with that ladder and you know it!"

In a moment, Robin started to laugh.

Ezra padded the towel to his hair. He looked at Robin sideways.

Robin outright laughed. "Just making sure you've got the balls to put it to Elizabeth. And if you can stand up to me, I think you do. Is there anything you need to ask me before tonight?"

"Not in a towel," Ezra overly articulated.

"You did a great thing for Adam and you did help save my life a bit," Robin said. "This could be very great for you and for Elizabeth if you are sincere."

"She's a little girl, really. Sheltered. It's that part of her that I really like." Ezra retightened the towel about his waist.

Robin nodded. "You are expected to propose to her. You had opportunity last night. Her reputation can probably withstand this if it is followed with an engagement. There's no out at this point, unless she turns you down. Don't have another heart attack, but I have to slam this door when I leave and I plan to make a good show of it, particularly after I told you not to stand up in the bath."

Ezra August toweled off, put Robin's hair tonic in his hair to calm down his curls, shaved to perfection, and dressed in the tailored black wool suit. He had a brand new white ruffled shirt and tied a polka dot ascot about his collar. Looking at himself in the full-length mirror, he smiled and there was a knock on the door.

He opened it to find Adam. "Hey. Here to yell at me too?"

Adam entered and shut the door. "No. There's no valet here. I came to see if you need any help."

"Why? Doesn't this look resplendent?" Ezra stepped back and opened his arms.

"Yes. Yes. Well done. I'm invited to lunch. Brought all of your stuff over. All of your stuff. You moving in here?" Adam said. "Are you ready for tonight?"

"Ah. I don't know. We were pretty comfortable last night. I think if she wants me to, I will do it," Ezra said. "Did Robin tell you how, the first time?"

"No. Zoey showed me how. We did whatever she wanted," Adam said. "I think that will work for you."

"What was her husband like?"

"Edward was sixty-two years old, a banker, a very smart banker," Adam told him. "I think she's ready to move on. She's never had a young man, virile like you. You ready to be ravaged?"

"Not my first time being ravaged, New York."

"We'll see about that. Go easy on the alcohol. You're going to last about two minutes. Just tell her to wait a half hour and you can do it again."

"Wait. What?"

Elizabeth, Marie, and Zoey arrived at the dining room for lunch, and their gentlemen all rose at the table. Each one pulled out a chair for his lady. And they sat to be served the first course.

"Did the gallery survive the storm?" Robin asked. "I heard there were windows broken out on Waters Street."

"Everything looked fine. Not even a roof leak," Ezra said. "There was a carriage overturned nearby and some people hurt. I offered to help but they were pulled out already. Tomorrow I need to get over to the gallery at first light and paint the walls, I think. Fresh coat of white paint before we start hanging paintings."

"Paint it yourself? Walls, I mean?" Elizabeth asked.

"Were the horses okay?" Robin asked.

"Albert and Pierre will help. We are quite experts at painting after all," Ezra said. "What Robin? Oh. I assume so. They didn't say."

"Of course. You prefer to do it yourself," Elizabeth said.

"Always wanted to paint the old gallery but I never had the funds. And we are putting in a wood shop in a corner of the studio. Albert knows a fellow who can make frames for us in there. Frames just like these. He's an excellent carver and then you just paint gold leaf to get this effect," Ezra said. "Pierre has worked with gold leaf."

"You can leave the paintings at my place as long as you need to. You know that, right?" Adam said.

"Thank you. Appreciate that. I also need to get some fresh canvas prepared, very large," Ezra said. "I have some new portraits to get started on."

"Are you going to paint Beth?" Marie asked.

"Like a princess." Ezra smiled honestly.

Marie and Beth looked at each other in excitement.

"You have to help me choose what to wear for the portrait."

"I think your artist might have something to say about that. You'll have to do a fashion show for him," Marie said.

"I would use some fine strands of gold paint for the highlights in her hair," Ezra said. "I have to pick up some more pigments. You know that shop, Adam, that we like?"

"Yes. What fun you'll have going in there and buying whatever you like," Adam said.

"Yes, whatever you like," Elizabeth told him. "All of it."

"Can I make Jonas carry it?"

"You can make Jonas pay for it."

That afternoon Ezra and Adam both did some drawings. Ezra was focused on drawings of Elizabeth. Adam made drawings of Zoey, Robin, and Marie. He even made one of Ezra drawing Elizabeth.

After dinner that evening, Elizabeth rose and held out a hand to Ezra. "I would like to show you around."

"So I will accompany you both?" Jonas rose also.

"Not this time," Elizabeth told him. "Jonas, see to the Van der Kellens, if you would please."

Ezra nodded to Robin and Marie, and took her hand. He followed her into the hallway and up the winding broad stairway. Elizabeth held his hand and climbed stairs in the very middle, holding up her skirt. "Anything in particular you wish to show me?"

At the top of the stairs, instead of going to the right for guest rooms, they went left.

"Yes. But first, I would have you know that the master bedroom of this estate is empty. Look at this." She opened the doors to what was Edward's room.

"They light lamps even when not in use?" Ezra asked, wandering inside.

"Yes. The lights are seen from the street," Elizabeth said. "One in every window."

Ezra looked at the grand pedestal bed in the center of the room. It was masculine in heavy mahogany and draped in red damask. "What did you...do with his things?"

"Sent some to his sister and her children in Albany and his brother in Boston. I kept a few memories for myself and put them away."

Ezra wandered into the room, feeling studied. "I think it must be very hard to lose someone, even with such an age difference."

"In some ways he replaced my father, except for those occasions that he requested me to come in here," Elizabeth said.

"In here? It is with respect to your loss that I ask you, did you ever enjoy your physical love life?" Ezra asked.

"No. Have you ever been in love?"

"No," Ezra said.

"Have you ever enjoyed your love life?" she asked him.

Ezra smiled a bit as he paced. "Occasionally."

"Which one were you with? Albert or Pierre?" she questioned.

"I was with both together. They both had affection for me until I became friends with Adam. From that moment on I was cut out. Couldn't say if it was because he bought me things or because we became such close friends. Friends only with Adam, I assure you."

"Except for that kiss. He refused you, on grounds that he is married, no doubt." Elizabeth walked forward and opened a door. "Look in here at the dressing room."

Ezra looked inside at empty racks, armoires, ironing equipment, and furniture. "Maybe I'm not his type. I can be rather...effervescent."

Beth smiled. "Just what I need. May I dress you up in nice things? Would that bother you?"

"If you like me for me, no matter what I wear?" Ezra sat down on the sofa and gestured for her to come to him. "What if I wear nothing?"

She stepped closer until Ezra took her by the hips and pulled her toward him. Her knees were between his and he looked up at her, his hands roving over her corset. "Will you show me your room now?"

She closed her eyes and leaned her head back.

Ezra reached up and took hold of her bosom. "Awful lot of fabric here."

That made her laugh.

He stood up taller than her, looking down at her for a moment. His hand reached for her cheek and neck. He kissed her open mouth. Beth unbuttoned his jacket and slid her hands inside, onto his vest at his sides. He moved closer, his body against hers. Beth wrapped her arms about his waist, finding him easy to wrap around. His body was warm. He was breathing heavily. He tilted his head in the other direction and kissed her deeply again. Her hand slid down the silk back of his vest, down onto his firm backside. She felt him with both hands back there.

Stunned, he stopped his kiss.

"Sorry. Is that all right?" Beth looked up at him.

He smiled shyly. "I just didn't expect a girl to touch me. I liked it. I'd like more."

"Come away from here." Beth led him to the hallway.

Ezra opened her bedroom door.

Beth whispered, "I so fear maids entering when morning comes."

"They do that?" Ezra asked.

"Oh yes. To stoke the fireplace and lay out my robe and slippers," Elizabeth said.

"Well, trust me..." He began untying his ascot. It took him a moment as it wrapped around his neck twice. He then fashioned it into a nice bow on her door handle. "They won't tomorrow."

She giggled and held her hand to her mouth. They entered and shut the door with the bow on the outside.

Elizabeth walked with him into her bedroom suite. "Could I offer you a drink Ezra?"

"First I must tell you something."

"Don't tell me something bad," she said. "What is it about?"

"It is about me. Elizabeth, Beth, I don't know how to do this." He looked at her with such doe eyes of dark brown. "It is this I must tell you...you must teach me how. I'll do anything. I do not know what it is you want."

"Oh Ezra, I could not ache for you more."

"Really? Is that a good thing?"

She moved closer to him and slowly unbuttoned his vest. "I don't know if I can talk about such things, now that I need to."

He held onto her waist for a moment and then touched her blonde hair and her bare neck. "You can just move my hand where you want it. You can play with me."

"You're very unusual, Ezra. I do want to play with you. You're so very handsome. Your eyes are so dark. I have to know, do you have much hair?"

"Huh? What?"

She unbuttoned his shirt down from the collar and stroked the hair in the middle of his chest. "Down here?" She unbuttoned the shirt all the way to his belt and looked down for a peek into his trousers. "Are you attracted to a woman?" She stroked where his buttons were in the front of his trousers. "Oh yes you are."

"I cannot hide that. Easy. That feels awfully good." Ezra swooned. "How do I undo this corset?"

"Hmm. I see you have no corset experience. My gown buttons in the back." She spun around for him.

Ezra began undoing her buttons. He kissed the back of her neck. For a moment he pulled her hips to his and ground his body against her.

That made her sigh. She pulled the gown off her shoulders and let it drop to the floor.

Ezra looked into the mirror at her reflection and he pulled the bodice of her corset down in front, revealing her breasts. She was breathing hard. "Are you warm enough?" He began untying her corset in the back.

"So warm. I'm still wearing too much. Remove your shirt." She watched his reflection as well.

"Anything you wish, my love." He pulled back his shirt and vest together and dropped them onto a chair.

"Oh my God. Your skin is so beautiful." She watched his body as he continued untying her corset. "How far have you been with a girl?"

Her corset could be pulled off then. She dropped it and turned to face him, to feel his bare chest with both her hands. He was so hard all over, his muscles were so firm and when she touched his nipples he moaned.

Ezra pulled her pantalets down off her hips. "Not even this far."

"You've seen women?" She smoothed her hands over his abdomen.

"As much as to paint them." Ezra leaned and kissed her breast. He was breathing hard too.

That made her sigh. She took his hand and put it between her thighs. He was free to explore her and that made her press her forehead to his shoulder. She sighed so hard.

"Show me where," he whispered.

Elizabeth sat down on the edge of the bed and took his hand in hers to teach him. And she sighed when he found the right place.

He whispered. "How does it fit?"

"Let us see." She began unbuttoning his trousers. She opened them and dropped his trousers down his legs. Then she opened his underclothing. "Most wonderfully. Trust me." She stroked him and made him moan.

"I didn't know a girl would touch me like that," Ezra said.

"Oh darling, your skin tastes so good."

"Can we...Can we get into bed? I need to lay down. I'm getting too...." Ezra whispered.

"Yes. Too what? Darling?" Elizabeth pulled down the covers and slid into the center of the bed.

Ezra crawled onto the bed with her, sliding his feet down beneath the covers.

Beth leaned down over him. "Too what, darling?"

"Dizzy," Ezra admitted.

She felt his forehead. She laid down along him, touched his cheek and kissed him. "You're all right. We'll just slow down a little. Just breathe, darling."

Ezra closed his eyes and embraced her. They began moving together, the feeling of skin against skin being so good to both of them.

She stroked his locks of black hair back from his face. "You're very aroused. Just wait a while. Are you still frightened?"

"Not of you. Let me hold you. Let me...on top of you," Ezra whispered.

"You're not dizzy?" Beth rolled back with him.

Ezra got onto her and spread her legs with his knees. "I think I have to do it."

She reached down between them and helped him.

Elizabeth lay back in her canopy bed, her head on an eider down pillow. Her long blonde hair pooled about her head. Ezra's chin was against hers and he moaned. She reached up to his bare shoulders, looking at his eyes clenched shut. His hair came forward about his mouth. The gold cross about his neck bounced on her chin a few times.

"Are you all right?" she whispered.

"Oh my God." He thrust into her a few more times and sighed again.

"Oh Ezra, you feel so good. This is for you, darling. Do what your body needs," Beth whispered to his throat.

He kissed her temple and thrust harder, holding her down. He moaned as passion ebbed through him.

Her hands roved over the muscles in his back. The canopy above them rocked. One of the pillows hit the floor. His back went wet and Elizabeth smiled. She clung to him as he lost control. He moaned as quietly as he could into her pillow. And then he collapsed, breathing heavily.

She could freely feel the muscles of his shoulders and the back of his arms. His slender hips weighed on hers as she unwrapped her legs from about him. His body was so warm, that she felt no chill at all with no covers over them. Soon, the only sound in the house was their fireplace crackling.

"Beth," he whispered. "Are you all right?"

"Yes, my love. Are you?"

"I don't know. I didn't know it could feel like that," he whispered. "I never felt that in my life."

She giggled a bit.

Then he laughed. "I love you, Beth. I never felt closer to anyone."

She giggled into his shoulder. "I can't breathe, my darling. You're so heavy and manly."

He rolled off her and began to pull up the covers over them.

"Rest, darling. And then I want on top of you." She touched the hair in the middle of his chest and that small gold pendant Robin had given him. His breathing was already back to normal. "I love you, Ezra, every inch of you."

Ezra in Elizabeth's bed

Elizabeth had Ezra leaning back against the headboard of the bed and
she was on his lap. She held onto the headboard and climaxed hard,

trying not to cry out too loudly. He was breathing hard into her chest and looked up to kiss her.

"Do you wish to be on top?" She asked him.

"Can you...just keep moving as you were? I need to do it again, now." He grabbed onto her hips. "Right now."

"You can do it again? Oh Ezra." She sighed and complied with his wishes.

He arched toward her and moaned again as if he were dying.

Beth watched him do it, and then she smoothed his hair back from his eyes. She touched his dark black eyebrows and his long lashes. "I always dreamed of passion like this. You fulfill my every dream."

He caught his breath and looked up at her. He slid her blond hair aside, to reveal her full breasts. He squeezed them in his hands and then reached up to touch her flushed cheeks. "You're so beautiful, Beth. Like a beautiful model, I can make love to."

Elizabeth awoke in the middle of the night to the sound of wood being added to the fireplace. Ezra, in his underclothes, got up from the hearth to pour himself a glass of brandy. As his undershorts were not quite buttoned all the way up, they hung off his hips, revealing the top of his buttocks and in front, the start of his dark hair. His thighs were muscular. And he walked about the room this way, unabashedly.

Elizabeth sat up to freely look at his body, his bare chest and arms, his taught abdomen, and the light hair on his thighs.

He carried the brandy to the bed, chin down with dark eyes looking at her.

She pulled back covers for him, wearing only a satin negligée.

He slid in and shared his brandy with her. They snuggled together in fine linens and beneath quilts. He asked her, "You look at me?"

"I do. I love to," she whispered.

"I love looking at you. We can look at each other."

"Really?" She kissed his sideburns and his ear. "You're not feeling dizzy anymore?"

"Ah, no. I'm so sorry about that." He lowered his chin shyly. "I don't know what...."

"You were overwhelmed. I was rushing you," Elizabeth said.

"I was overwhelmed with so many sensations and feelings and being afraid," he admitted.

"And then you felt better?" She whispered, stroking her hand over his chest and abdomen. "What were you afraid of? I hope you know you were wonderful."

"I didn't expect so many emotions. Afraid of being terrible at it. Afraid of opening my whole heart and soul to you when you could have anything from me, do anything to me. You could have destroyed me or lifted me on a cloud."

"You have the soul of a poet, my love. You have nothing to fear with me. I had those same fears. Oh my, Ezra. What if you didn't like it with me? What if I couldn't get you to conclude it?"

"What? I was struggling not to from the time I walked into your bedroom." They both laughed together. "I feel pretty stupid for avoiding it."

That made her laugh.

"I guess I needed it to be you."

Robin stared at that white ascot dangling from Elizabeth's door handle and put his hands on his hips.

Marie whispered to him. "Leave them be. She's falling for him. He loves her, doesn't he?"

"He tried to get me into bed with him."

"Maybe they're meant for each other," Marie said. "She said he wanted to be friends first last night."

"We all say that," Robin said. "Guaranteed to get you into bed. He kissed me on the mouth."

"I'm having breakfast delivered to them. Come away." Marie drew him aside. "On the mouth? Really? I'd like to see that."

Chapter Fourteen   A Different Class

She gifted Ezra with a long black velvet robe and brought the cart of breakfast into the room. Ezra stacked more wood into the fire and then took his seat at the little table and chairs between Elizabeth's bed and the white marble fireplace. He smoothed hands down the velvet on his chest, looking down at some sort of black mink on the lapel and cuffs.

She sat down across from him and stared at the coffee pot for a moment.

He laughed. He reached and poured coffee for them both. "Coffee doesn't pour itself, darling."

"You are going to let me buy you wonderful things to dress you up, won't you?"

"Like a doll, my dear. You can dress me like a doll. I love this robe, by the way. You know I cannot buy you much when you already have everything," Ezra said.

"You can make for me what no one else on earth possibly could, a painting from your heart and soul. And don't you forget, that is priceless," she said. "Are you okay with this?"

He smiled warmly. "Are you okay with this?"

Beth giggled. "Your hair is a mess."

"I told you my hair is a mess in the morning." He ran a hand up through his curls shyly.

"You still have some bruises," Beth told him.

"Ah, yeah." Ezra felt his right side. "Robin's knee, I believe. I pulled him through a window. He landed on top of me."

"Weren't you terrified?"

"That's why I ran so fast, yes." He sipped his coffee and then selected a pastry. "What was it like when he got shot? He stayed here after the hospital, didn't he?"

"Yes. In the same room he has now. He was very weak and pale. Adam had to help him up the stairs and get him into bed," Elizabeth said. "You could see the pain on his face. They kept changing his bandages because he kept bleeding."

"You saw him in the hospital?"

"I brought Marie. It was awful. I almost fainted."

He ate his pastry and found other treats on the cart, sausages, eggs, and biscuits. "For some reason I'm starving."

"I can't imagine why," Beth said. "You are thin, Ezra. Please, have your breakfast. Have you had times when you...went hungry really? How did you own that gallery?"

"I...there was a time when I sold some paintings for almost a thousand dollars. I bought the gallery building. I tried to live above the gallery but eventually needed that space for storing paintings as well. Eventually the remaining money ran out. Around that time, I met Pierre and Albert and we sort of banded together to get by."

"Your paintings are worth several hundreds of dollars. You will charge more for them on Pearl Street than you did before?"

He nodded. "I go into other galleries. I see what the value is on this side of town."

"Ezra, how come you haven't... It is morning and you haven't..." Elizabeth saddened. She put a hand to her eyes.

Ezra grabbed her hand across the table. "I'm falling in love with you, Beth. Give me time. I am struggling with being a bought man. I am..."

"Oh, no, you are not bought. I can't help it that I'm rich. I just want to..."

"What do you want?"

"I want a man to care for. I want this great love that I've never had. I want children." She looked at him. "I am so attracted to you I can't stand it."

"Oh?" He held a hand to his heart. "You can have all that you want. Just allow me my occupation. It's my identity. I am an artist first. And I don't know how to walk out that door right now. What they all must be thinking of me."

"No one in my house will even look at you the wrong way. I will not allow it."

"Elizabeth, promise me something? Promise?"

"I promise you, Ezra. Anything," Beth said as they grabbed hands.

"Please don't tell anyone that I almost fainted. Not even Marie."

"I promise and you did not almost faint. You were just overwhelmed. That's all. Completely normal. But private things like that between us, stay between us," Elizabeth vowed. "Robin is going to be angry with you if we are not engaged."

Ezra's eyebrows rose. "Allow me a little liberty with Mr. Van der Kellen, if you will."

"Isn't there something you would say?" Robin asked.

Ezra held the chair for Elizabeth and sat down beside her. "Goedemorgen."

Elizabeth looked at Marie beside her and smiled a bit.

"Ezra?" Robin got up from his place beside Marie and walked slowly the long way around the table. He stopped beside Ezra's chair, looking down at him as he drew something from his pocket. He dropped that white ascot into Ezra's lap. "You and I are going to have a talk."

Ezra held up the ascot. "I thought you hated the red one."

"Ezra, you'd better tell him now," Elizabeth said.

The artist rose and was standing almost nose to nose with Robin, though taller than Robin. And Robin collected the black ascot that Ezra was wearing slowly into his fist. "You'd better tell me what I want to hear, Ezra."

"I do believe," Ezra began. "You and Adam are using the same hair tonic."

"Ezra, you have thirty seconds before I'm taking you outside."

"Robin, as much fun as that sounds, I must decline. You're just going to have to get over me."

"What?" Robin tightened his fist about that necktie.

Elizabeth burst out laughing and collected Marie's hand into hers.

"Ezra, I trusted you to do the right thing. Do not think for one minute that you can disappoint me," Robin told him.

Ezra patted Robin on the upper arm. "It is Elizabeth I didn't disappoint."

"Are you fucking with me, Ezra?"

The slightest grin began in the corner of Ezra's mouth. "I am engaged. I am sorry, Robin. You had your chance."

Marie burst out laughing at that.

"I could still hang you by this." Robin shook him a bit by the ascot.

Ezra grabbed onto him for balance. "Just can't keep your hands off me."

Robin pushed him back a step, against his chair.

Ezra did not let go of Robin by the arms.

Elizabeth leaned over to Marie and whispered into her ear. "I can hardly walk this morning. Can't get my knees together. Just wanted them about him all night."

It made Marie burst out giggling. "How was he last night then?"

Robin let him go to stare at his wife. "Waat?"

"After the first time, wonderful," Elizabeth said.

Ezra winced. He withdrew his hands as if cringing in pain.

"Oh I knew you were fucking with me," Robin snapped. "What did he do the first time?"

"He just was a bit...surprised," Elizabeth said.

Still wincing, Ezra took his seat again.

"How surprised?" Robin sat beside him, studying him with his elbow on the table. "Finished right then, was it?"

Ezra smoothed his black bow into place.

"I let him take the first time as he needed. I imagine it's like that the first time for every young man. But he could do it again less than an hour later," Elizabeth rambled on. "I don't wonder your love of stallions, a fine ride they make."

Ezra could not meet Robin's eyes anymore. His cheeks flushed.

"This is no stallion," Robin declared. "A young buck at best."

They all four burst out laughing.

Marie took Elizabeth into a hug. "You're getting married again. And Ezra is so young and handsome and funny. I'm so happy for you. How did he propose?"

"I told him we are getting married and he said yes we are," Elizabeth said. "You know what? You know those two white hairs on the back of his head? He has three little ones right down beside his...."

"Please leave me a little mystery." Robin reached into his pocket and pulled out a box of tobacco cigarettes. He offered one to Ezra. "Can I have a word with you?"

"Oh. Please." Ezra accepted a cigarette and stood up sniffing it. He followed Robin to the hall and down to the gentleman's parlor.

Robin shut the door for them and they lit their smokes.

"Where did you get this? This is very good," Ezra said.

"Never mind where. You were obviously intimate with Elizabeth. We need to talk," Robin said.

"As a matter of fact, we do. Elizabeth asked you to give her a child?" Ezra said.

"Who told you that?" Robin was taken aback.

"Never mind," Ezra said. "Did she ask you or come on to you?"

"Normally I would say it was none of your business," Robin said. "Did you talk to her about it?"

"No. I only asked her if she was over you," Ezra said. "She said that was a different Elizabeth. Did she come on to you? How?"

Robin puffed on his hand rolled cigarette. "She said to Marie and I that she had been married for years with no child. She said, 'I think you know what desperate thing I would ask'. But I stopped her from saying more."

"She never laid a hand on you?"

"Not like you did," Robin remarked.

Ezra's eyebrows lifted briefly. "Well, how did Adam find out?"

"Adam? I told Edward the next morning that we would be going home as soon as we could get train tickets. He said I looked offended. Then he realized Beth had asked me. He scolded her loudly enough that I believe the kitchen staff overheard."

"Edward yelled at her?"

Robin thought a moment. "You could say that."

"Well, I am never going to yell at her," Ezra said. "You have my word on that."

"I will have your word on more than that," Robin said.

Ezra found an ash tray to tap his cigarette on. "You told me to do what I did last night, to spite all that buy the horse crap. You told me she was expecting fireworks from me and I was not to let her down. I did it. Twice."

"You will not engage in that sort of behavior with Pierre or Albert again. At least, if you do, you had better not get caught by anyone," Robin said. "You don't want to get caught in sodomy with another man. That will get you five years in jail and there is nothing I can do about it."

"Pierre is not speaking to me and when Pierre is not, Albert is not allowed to either. Not going to happen," Ezra said. "Adam on the other hand...."

"I'm not laughing," Robin said sternly.

"Look. I know. We can't let anything disgrace Elizabeth," Ezra said. "Least of all me."

"So you are going to have to resist those urges because you are marrying a woman now," Robin said.

Ezra paced around. "Robin, you get hit on by women all the time, I understand. How do you resist those urges exactly?"

"I go home and make love to my wife," Robin said. "You're lucky. You will have Adam here to talk to once I'm gone. You can look after each other and your families together."

"I will eventually be friends again with Pierre and Albert and Marco and the others. I won't have relations with any of them again. Small price to pay for all that I have with Elizabeth," Ezra said.

"And you remember that. I love it that you are very comfortable with who you are. Believe me. But you need to be very careful in public. Society will be watching you now. With Elizabeth you have security for the first time in your life, financial safety, anything you want to buy, and she loves you," Robin said. "She's a brave and good woman."

"And a little girl who never got to have any fun. So we're going to have fun and I hope my back can take it," Ezra said.

Robin turned away from him. "Wild cat?"

Ezra puffed on his cigarette. "I just prayed my boy parts would still be there when she got off me."

Robin coughed on his cigarette. He turned his back to him completely.

"The first time was... She said that was just for me," Ezra said. "I still can't believe how fast I finished. I've lasted so much longer. I've almost had a hard time finishing with Albert."

Robin remained turned away. "Do I have to hear that?"

"I figure I wasn't that excited about him. I don't think it was his technique."

"Ezra," Robin said. "I can't un-hear things."

Ezra said, "Robin, relax. I am seriously pushing you and you are not laughing. It's a joke. I can't believe I made you that uncomfortable. I'm so impressed with myself."

"You joke around but you are the most feminine man I've ever known." Robin turned and looked at him. "You've also come onto me more than any man I've known. And watch it with Adam. I've seen him throw a man to the ground in a fight after an incident between them."

"Adam?" Ezra said. "Well Adam is a romantic. Adam doesn't just want sex with anybody. I would keep an eye on that man if I were you, if he's still in your life. That man tried to compromise Adam."

Robin's brow furrowed. "I think you're right."

"I know I'm right. I would have engaged in a romantic relationship with him if not for Zoey and Beth," Ezra said. "His broken heart was a beautiful thing that he had to put on canvas. You broke his heart, Robin."

"I could only give him friendship. What else was I to do?" Robin said.

"I know." Ezra nodded. "Why Adam painted you is not why I will."

"Wait. Does Adam still have feelings for me?" Robin asked.

"Did you kiss him on the forehead once?" Ezra said. "He still holds onto some hope there."

Robin rubbed his face in his hand. "There is no hope there. What do I do? I thought I was giving you advice."

Ezra smiled warmly. "Tell him he's still your best friend and don't rush out of town like you did last time."

Robin nodded. "Why are you going to paint me?"

Ezra became enthusiastic again. "Oh to commemorate our adventure. I'll do a couple of them. Elizabeth wants one."

"Would you make one of Marie and myself?"

Ezra patted Robin on the arm. "And Frida. Absolutely. Just for you."

"Don't know how I'll get it back on the train."

"Well, maybe you'll invite Beth and me out for a visit and I will paint it there," Ezra said.

There was a knock on the door.

Robin went to open it and find Beth and Marie in the hall.

"Making sure you're not killing each other," Marie said.

Robin sat down with Ezra and Elizabeth in the office of the Miller mansion. He had papers in front of him on the desk. "Elizabeth asked me to take a look at Edward's will and the trusts that he set up for her financial welfare. I have them here and I have read them all."

"What happens if I remarry?" she asked.

"Elizabeth was a minor when she married Edward. As such, all of her fortune transferred to Edward. He also had money of his own, the bank, this estate, and a chalet in France. During the marriage he purchased the beach home on Long Island."

"You have a beach home?" Ezra looked at her. "Did she get the chalet in France?"

"The bottom line is, when you remarry, three quarters of the combined assets and the three properties belong to Elizabeth. Profits from the bank continue to be distributed to the assets. One quarter of the assets is freed to transfer to your new husband to be used as he sees fit, immediately upon marriage. That one quarter currently is worth two hundred thousand dollars. You will have to purchase her wedding ring of course."

Elizabeth grabbed Ezra's arm. "You see? You can have a wonderful gallery. We can travel. You can paint in Paris and Rome and... wait 'til you see the chalet in France."

Ezra wet his lips and looked down at his hands in his lap.

"Don't you see? Robin and Marie, Adam and Zoey, you and I can do the grand tour together. Wouldn't that be wonderful?" Elizabeth said.

"You can of course contest the will, but given the very short period of courtship and your previous financial status, you're not likely to win," Robin said. "Do not find this embarrassing. No one will know. They're going to assume that you are in charge of her fortune now."

"I don't...I don't want her money. I just wish to live comfortably and have about a dozen children," Ezra said.

"Dozen? Good heavens, darling," Elizabeth snapped. "I'm not a cat."

Robin laughed. "Look, you two are just fine. Together you can do whatever you want with your fortune. It's just that alone, without Elizabeth's signature, it's the two hundred thousand that Ezra can spend without any entanglements. Perhaps you will want to reach out to your family in the Ottoman Empire and help them. Perhaps you have a brother or sister to bring here to live."

"Yes. Oh, Ezra, will you write them?"

"I can try. I can't even be sure after ten years that my letter will find them," Ezra said. "Robin, do I have to change my name the way Adam did?"

"What documentation do you have proving what your name is?" Robin asked.

"Nothing. I have nothing," Ezra said. "I came over on a ship in steerage. I was afraid they wouldn't let me on board so I pretended I couldn't speak English. I made a mark in their logbook. They didn't even take down my name."

"And you will never need to inherit under the name Arikan?"

"Oh hell no," Ezra said. "Nine other brothers and sisters and how many times did my father's patients pay him in chickens?"

"Then I don't see any reason you can't marry with whatever name you choose," Robin told him. "From then on you will have a marriage license with the name Ezra August on it. You will have to sign at the bank with that name. And Elizabeth will be Mrs. Ezra August. Choose a middle name."

"I'll just move Arikan to the middle."

"I will take your name, Ezra, whatever you tell me it is," Elizabeth said. "Why do you not want the name Arikan?"

"Arikan is a very Muslim name. Muslims were considered protected under Ottoman law, back home. Not protected anywhere else, I find. I won't have you endangered by my name. And I'm not a practicing Muslim anyway," Ezra said. "I have nothing against my family name. But it's too dangerous to share."

"Is August really your middle name?" Elizabeth asked.

"Well it's Agustos in Turkish, but it means the eighth month of the year."

"Ezra Agustos Arikan? I should know who I'm marrying," Elizabeth said. "Is that because you were born in August?"

"Yes. August 1st. When is yours?"

"July 8th."

"Elizabeth has family who should be notified of your engagement. A carefully worded letter should also be sent to Edward's sister and brother. I can draft it for you," Robin said. "Do you wish the engagement to last a while before taking these measures? Two or three months is rather customary."

Ezra and Elizabeth looked at each other.

"No. I could be with child right now. No wait is necessary," she said.

Ezra wiped his eyes.

"You all right?" Robin asked.

"Can I do something for Albert and Pierre?" Ezra asked.

"Yes, of course. What would you do?" Elizabeth said.

"Financially?" Robin said. "I would recommend a trust that pays them a monthly sum for X number of years. They are not experienced in managing a large amount sustainably. Neither are you, Ezra. Let the accountants Elizabeth has in place take care of this for you."

"They have been my very good friends. They have shared their food with me when I had nothing and no place to sleep. And I won't be living with them anymore," Ezra said. "Or helping put food on their table."

"Yes, do it," Elizabeth said.

Ezra smiled a bit.

"You know I'm not a counselor but I do feel a bit responsible for bringing you two together. Elizabeth, are you happy?" Robin asked.

"I am thrilled. I love him so." She grabbed onto Ezra's arm enthusiastically.

He smiled at her. He took her hand.

"Ezra?"

"I'm…" He turned toward Elizabeth and took her hands into his. "Am I overwhelmed by everything? Yes. I am happy about everything. And I am falling in love with you, Beth. Please let me take this little by little and…believe in me."

"I do. I do. Your hands are shaking."

They grabbed onto each other and cried.

Robin had to get up. He made his way around the desk. "Happy tears, right? Both of you?"

"Yes, Robin."

"Yes."

"I should have been a Pastor. All I'm doing is marrying people." Robin made his escape from the room.

Ezra's room was established next to Robin and Marie's corner room of the guest wing. Past their rooms were the servants quarters. In the other direction, Ezra walked down the hallway, passing Oriental vases and paintings of flowers when he realized four of the maids were still looking at him. He stopped.

They pretended to be dusting or scattered toward rooms.

"Wait," Ezra said. "Everyone, please wait. Can I talk with you?"

"Yes, sir. Mr. August." The four young ladies gathered before him, four of them between his age and Adam's.

Ezra straightened his posture and held his hands behind his back. "Um. I know you are friends with Adam Hudson. You worked with him for years. You know him well. This must be really weird for you."

They smiled and laughed a bit. "What can we do for you, sir?"

"I wish I knew." He sighed. "Just be kind to Elizabeth. She's been through a lot."

"She's very happy now."

"We've never seen her so happy."

"Really?" Ezra relaxed his arms and then set his hands on his hips. "So tell me, what is the dumbest thing you ever saw Adam do?"

Ezra and Elizabeth entered a haberdashery together. "I would like you to set up Mr. August with everything he wants. An open account. He may stop in here at any time and request anything. Please measure him."

"Yes, Mrs. Miller. I shall be delighted."

That made Ezra wince. And then he selected a top hat and placed it on Elizabeth. That made her laugh.

He smiled. "Looks good on you. Have you ever tried on a suit, Beth?"

"No never. You mean trousers?"

"Well, I won't unless you will."

Jonas folded his arms at the door and frowned.

"Could I have you on the platform, Mr. August?" The tailor prepared his measuring tape. Secretaries gathered around to take down measurements.

Ezra popped up onto the platform and posed with his hands on his hips.

Elizabeth removed the top hat, laughing at him.

"Remove your jacket if you would, sir?"

"Anything else?" Ezra asked.

"Just the jacket, please."

Ezra smiled at Elizabeth as she circled him, to look at him from behind.

"Waist 28. Hips 30. Length of trousers 44. If you would hold the tape please, sir, I can get your inseam."

Ezra held the tape between his thighs, where his current trousers were. Luckily he'd done this before with Adam.

"34. Are you getting this? You're a very tall and slender fellow. Circumference at the knee is…."

Ezra and his friends began moving paintings from the back of the gallery and lining them up on the floor along the walls. "No, take that one out of here." Ezra pointed.

Pierre removed a landscape.

"Is that yours?" Elizabeth asked.

"No, it's his," Pierre said.

"Wait. Let me look at it." Elizabeth sat down by the fireplace to study this landscape of a foggy morning field. The focus of it was on a cluster of asters in the front. And they matched foggy blue skies in the distance. "Asters. The symbol of love, wisdom, and faith."

Ezra looked over at her. He continued sorting paintings, selecting two new ones of Adam's including his portrait of Zoey. Beside that he put Pierre's portrait of Zoey from the same sitting but different angle.

"I love to watch him do this. It's painful but he has such an eye for drama," Albert admitted. "And then we fight like dogs over them. But it's his call."

"I love this. Why would he not want to display this one?" Elizabeth asked Albert.

"He's going for something," Albert explained.

Adam had a lesser-known painting of Robin standing on the deck of a ship. He placed this exactly in line where one's eyes would go upon first entering the gallery. "Where's that framing guy? Wasn't he supposed to be here and get to work?"

"He'll be here. Something about having to fix his window at home before he left. The snow was blowing right in," Pierre said.

"Very well. I can't open until these have proper frames. The painted walls look good. I'm glad we did that," Ezra said. "Take this one to the back and bring me the blue lady. Bring that."

"You're going to put her in the front room?" Pierre asked.

"There's nothing dirty about the blue lady. She's just unclothed and blue because she's sad," Ezra said. "Sad like shadows on the snow."

Pierre took a canvas from the wall and walked past to the very rear of the gallery where at least fifty paintings were stacked and organized.

"Are your rich friends going to be opposed to such things as this?" Albert asked as the blue lady painting passed them.

"Wait. That is beautiful. Amazing even." Elizabeth stood up to see where Ezra was placing her. Then she walked over to stoop before it and read the signature in the bottom right corner. Ezra. The blue lady was reclining in a garden, nude and in blue shadows, as people walked past her with their parasols and top hats. "They don't see her."

Ezra stopped and looked at her. "You're the first person to get that."

"Oh. Oh." Beth stood up.

Pierre said to her, "He's good at painting crowds. Look at that, just suggesting a crowd and you get that."

"What do you think of him in this suit? Do you like those trousers with the stripe down the side?" Albert asked.

"I like them very much," Elizabeth said. "He's so slender, don't you agree?"

"Oh when we first met him he was very skinny. He's put on about ten pounds, I think," Albert said. "All muscle. You should see his back. Did you see his back?"

"Do you think he needs a haircut? I would have Adam do it," Pierre said.

"Before we get married, do you think he should have a haircut?" Elizabeth asked.

"Yes. Have Adam do it," Albert said.

Ezra stopped and looked at them all with his hands on his hips. "Anything else you wish to discuss about me? We did my ass, back, and my hair. What else?"

"Best parts already," Pierre said.

Beth added, "Top five for certain."

The guys laughed.

Albert asked, "How did he perform, to a woman's standards?"

"Oh no. Don't do it. Don't give them any more ammunition against me," Ezra said. "They gang up on me enough."

"But I've never gotten to discuss a man's parts before," Elizabeth said. "Tried once to get Marie to tell me about Robin but she wouldn't."

"You asked the wrong person. You need to ask Adam about that. He told me everything," Ezra said with both of his hands a certain distance apart. He mouthed the words, "Not aroused."

"When did Adam see Robin?" Elizabeth asked through the laughter.

"Robin was really drunk on absinthe in the Dutch king's palace. Adam had to put him to bed. I was told there was a bit of a strip show," Ezra said. "Followed by a whole lot of vomiting."

They laughed.

Ezra looked down at himself. "I think I'm the same length."

"You always say that," Pierre said.

"You're taller, so proportionally, you're not," Albert said.

Elizabeth blushed laughing.

My dear Elizabeth,

Your cousin Josephine informed us of your impeding marriage to an artist, of all horrid things. I absolutely forbid this marriage. I will be arriving on Tuesday to see that this has an end put to it. He is not of a good family. He has no fortune. He is a Muslim. You cannot even consider this. Are you going to raise your children not in a Christian way?

Your aunt Esmeralda will be accompanying me. Prepare our rooms.

Hannah

"Ms. Elizabeth." Jonas held out a silver dish at their dinner table.

She took the letter off the dish. "Baltimore. My cousin received my letter about the engagement." She opened and read it. "Oh no! What day is this?"

"Monday," Marie told her.

"Oh no! They'll be here tomorrow! My horrid two aunts are coming to stop the wedding. My cousin Josephine must have told them I'm marrying a poor Muslim artist."

"That's how you described me?" Ezra's eyebrows rose.

"Why did you tell me he's well endowed?" Marie asked.

Robin's head came forward on his shoulders.

There wasn't a sound except for Adam's fork hitting his plate as he dropped it.

Ezra's eyes slowly turned to meet Adam's.

"Robin," Elizabeth coaxed.

"Um, darling that has nothing to do with money," Robin said.

At which point Ezra pinned his hand over Adam's mouth.

"I'm sorry?" Marie looked around at them.

Adam shook his mouth clear. "I really have to respond to that."

"No you don't," Ezra insisted.

Robin cleared his throat. "So when do the old bats arrive?"

"I'm so sorry, Zoey. How do we explain?" Elizabeth said.

"No need. I saw him without his trousers," Zoey said.

Adam and Ezra started to cry laughing. Robin burst out laughing.

"Oh? Endowed there?" Marie had to laugh at how hard the men were laughing. "How did you see him without his trousers?"

"In the attic, when Ezra was helping Adam get out of bed."

"He walked around the attic in his underclothing?" Marie asked.

"He walks around in less than that in my room," Elizabeth said.

"You are overlooking the heroic qualities of this young man." Even Robin spoke up for him. "As injured as Adam was, he could not have run from gunfire the way Ezra and I did. Adam needed to have a peaceful, quiet escape from the hospital."

"This young man, whatever he has done for you, Mr. Van der Kellen, he is still a different class from Elizabeth. This relationship, whatever it is, has finished," Ezmerelda said. "How do you know he is not in this for financial gain? He has nothing to offer Elizabeth."

After enduring much of this at the dining room table and after that in the parlor, something changed in Ezra. His armor had chipped away and words wounded him now, repeatedly. He'd been peeled away from Elizabeth and was now farther down the parlor, closer to the hall.

"This marriage cannot happen. He is in a far different class than you, Elizabeth. You've had your fun. Now move on. There are plenty of society men your age who will match you appropriately. This man is nothing."

"I'm nothing. Thank you, very much. Let me tell you something, nobody from my class would say anything as rude and as hurtful to you as you have just said to me. You talk about me as if I can't hear you." Ezra walked out, straight down the hall and out the door.

Robin and Adam scrambled after him.

Elizabeth broke into tears and Marie took her into her arms. "They'll talk to him. He'll be back. You'll see."

"You're better off this way, Elizabeth."

Chapter Fifteen   Seduction

"Ez, you can't listen to those old bags. Elizabeth doesn't believe it. She loves you." Adam grabbed his arm on the outside steps.

"Just leave me be."

"We are going back in there to tell those old bags to go the fuck back to the twelfth century where they came from," Adam said.

Ezra tried to shake Adam loose when Robin took hold of his other arm.

"Oh, please, I don't need a talk from the elegant Dutchman right now," Ezra insisted. "You're just as much of an immigrant as I am. I'm quite certain you never had to endure being called nothing right in front of your woman."

"Life isn't fair and there are far worse things in life than being called names," Robin told him. "Or spoken to rudely. When I was about your age, I fell in love with a girl. She was young and blonde. She played the pianoforte and sang with this angelic voice. She was not from a wealthy family and my father opposed to the marriage."

Adam lowered his eyes to the snow on the steps.

"I married her anyway. And seven months later she died in my arms and so did our unborn son," Robin said. "My only point is this, Ezra August, you can't let what life deals you, gnaw on your heart so bad that you lose perspective. You're an artist. Hold your perspective. If you were a soldier, I'd tell you to hold the line."

Ezra let out a breath that was almost a sob. "What? That I am poor. That I have nothing to offer her."

"You offer her love, fun, a life together, and children," Adam blurted out. "Right now she's in there crying because she doesn't know if you are coming back."

Ezra nodded. He braced up a bit.

Robin said, "It's important Elizabeth sees him resilient."

"Is this resilient? Is it?" Ezra said. "You didn't see her begin to listen to them. She wouldn't look at me."

"Embarrassed by what they were saying," Adam insisted.

"I have fallen in love. I've never hurt so in my life," Ezra said. "Standing there hearing her family tell her that I'm nothing? I'm not in her class? Does anybody give a shit that I...."

Adam said, "Say something, Robin."

"We're going to do better than throw out the old bags. We're going to win them over." Robin took Ezra under his arm. "One more moment of incredible courage is all you need to walk back in the door. Just one. And then this is what you do..."

Maids spread word through the house that Ezra had returned. Elizabeth, Marie, and Zoey were all hurrying from the parlor.

Ezra was the first to enter. His jaw was set and mouth pursed. His eyes, dark as coal, were determined.

"Ezra, I was so worried." Elizabeth ran forward into his arms, hugging him tightly about waist.

Ezra embraced her. "Sorry about that. I needed some air."

Robin and Adam entered beside him.

Jonas offered a silver tray of glasses. "Warming brandies for the gentlemen."

Robin accepted the first and gave it to Ezra.

"Are you all right, my darling? I'm so sorry for everything they said. They've gone to bed, the old..." Elizabeth looked up at Ezra. He was staring straight ahead down the hall.

Adam tapped on Ezra's back.

"Think nothing of it, Beth," Ezra said. "We'll take care of everything."

Robin stepped around and tapped his glass to Ezra's. "We are in fact, the three Musketeers now. One for all."

Adam tapped his to Robin's. "All for one."

In the morning, one of Ezra's friends was summoned to sit at the grand piano in the music room and play Chopin softly as the breakfast table was being set.

Adam was up early and tending to Ezra in his room, fixing his hair, dressing him to perfection in everything he loved.

The hallway was adorned with portraits of Elizabeth that Ezra had been drawing.

Rose petals led Elizabeth curiously down from her room to find the portraits and music in the hall below. The room at the far end had become Ezra's temporary studio. She looked in, expecting to find him painting but instead, a large canvas was on the easel with a folding room divider blocking all view of it.

"Elizabeth? Elizabeth what is all this?" Esmerelda was gathering up rose petals on the stairs.

Beth stepped out of the studio.

"What is all this mess?" Esmerelda said. "And music before five o-clock? This just isn't done."

"Apparently it is." Elizabeth looked up at the top of the stairs and there he was.

Ezra August stood at the top, a rose tucked behind his ear. He wore that black/purple suit with black vest and lacy ascot.

Robin Van der Kellen walked around him and down. "Morning, Elizabeth. We have special plans for you today." Van der Kellen passed the elderly woman and held out his hands for her rose petals. "Goedendag, Esmerelda."

"Captain Van der Kellen." The woman dropped the petals into his hands unexpectedly. "Perhaps you can make sense of all this."

"Elizabeth, your fiancée has a portrait to unveil today. He was working all night on it," Robin said.

Adam appeared up beside Ezra. They looked at each other.

Aunt Hannah came up behind them. "Do I hear piano? It's not even nine in the morning. It can't be."

"Yes, Aunt Hannah, it is piano. May I escort you to breakfast?" Adam bowed and extended a hand to her.

"Is that a rose on his head? Does he know it is there?" Hannah took Adam's hand. "You're that valet turned banker's son, aren't you?"

Adam met eyes with Ezra and then he turned on his most charming smile. "Which is why Ezra is so perfectly coiffed today. I can work wonders with hair. Even silver hair. You know a bit of powder can really make it…."

"Hannah, talk some sense into her, will you?" Esmerelda called.

Hannah took in Adam and his porcelain skin and blue eyes. And she smiled at him.

Adam gave a wink to Ezra and started down the stairs with the aunt.

"What can you do with silver hair?"

Marie and Zoey took their places downstairs. Lining the hallway.

Ezra started down the stairs only then, stepping gracefully down the middle. "I have gathered all this morning for the unveiling of my masterpiece. There have been many paintings in my life but none such as this." He strolled into the grand hallway, between the two aunts, between Adam and Zoey, between Robin and Marie. He walked toward Elizabeth and while pausing before her, he removed the lavender rose from his hair and offered it to Elizabeth. "Love at first sight, of course. The lavender rose signifies love at first sight."

Elizabeth kissed the rose.

"If everyone will please enter the studio?" Ezra said. "The masterpiece awaits."

Elizabeth took his arm.

Ezra drew her inside to sit on the central chair before the easel.

Adam quickly took his place on the other side, taking hold of one side of the room divider that hid the painting.

Everyone gathered into the room. The two elderly women were sat on a love seat beside Marie and Zoey.

"Ladies and gentlemen, I give you, my portrait of the goddess Elizabeth." Ezra signaled and Adam dragged the divider to the side.

The painting of Elizabeth sitting in sunlight, not in his studio, but in a sunlit garden of lilacs. The lace about her neck picked up rays of light. Strands of pure gold in her hair shimmered in sunlight. And her lavender and purple gown perfectly complemented her hair and fair skin. Everything was gold and green and lilac around her.

Robin started the applause that everyone else picked up.

Elizabeth stood up to fully examine the life size likeness, and then she jumped into Ezra's arms, lifting her feet right off the floor. "I love it! Oh Ezra!"

"It is rather good," Hannah said.

"Oh, Hannah. She still can't marry this boy," Esmerelda said. "Even if he is an artist."

"Breakfast is waiting. You must be starving," Robin said. "May I escort you to the dining room?"

"He's a good painter." Hannah stood up. "Do you actually own that gown, Elizabeth? I've never seen you in lavender. Not with your eyes."

"It was blue but he painted it lavender," Elizabeth said.

"His vision is..." Adam began.

"Careful," Ezra whispered.

"Perspective," Adam said firmly. "Your treatment of the lace. You should have seen it. At three in the morning, he just climbed up on a chair with a palette knife and swiped it. And there was lace!"

"Ezra, it is wonderful," Zoey said.

"It is the most beautiful image of anyone I've ever seen," Marie added. She hugged Elizabeth.

"Ezra, you are a genius," Robin said.

Ezra embraced Elizabeth warmly and kissed her. "This is my heart on canvas."

"And I couldn't love you more if I sat before it in tears for its beauty, Ezra." Elizabeth hugged him again.

"I mixed paint until we ran out of cobalt violet. And then he mixed the gold powder into the titanium and cadmium to make the light in her hair. There must be a hundred dollars worth of gold on there," Adam went on. "That chromium blue for the bit of sky, an afterthought at four in the morning. And look how it brings out her eyes and the shadow beneath her chin. The whole thing is so wet we dared not move it."

"Adam, let us retreat to the dining room and give them a moment." Robin took Adam by the arm. "Give them a moment."

Marie and Zoey were holding hands in the doorway. The two aunts had gone to the dining room already.

Ezra had Elizabeth in an embrace and rocked her slowly side to side in his arms.

Ezra led her into the dining room and held the chair at the end for her. Then he took his place beside her, across from Marie. Breakfast of waffles, sausages, fruit and jams were served. A choice of coffee and tea was provided. Hot black currant juice was offered. That's what Ezra chose to drink.

"You were up all night, Ezra?" Elizabeth asked.

"Yes. It's ah...starting to hit me now," Ezra said.

"This is inappropriate conversation," Esmerelda said. "You will not discuss sleeping."

"Have something to eat and then get some rest," Elizabeth told him. "Were you up all night also, Adam?"

Adam drank coffee. "Oh yes. Every time I fell asleep he prodded me with a paint brush and bade me make more green or white."

Ezra inhaled a deep breath and sat back in exhaustion.

"Your painting is magnificent, Ezra," Marie said. "It looks just like her and yet it's so magical."

"He is truly the finest artist I have ever seen," Adam said.

Elizabeth took his hand. "I do love it so."

Ezra ate a bit and soon had to kiss Elizabeth on the back of the hand. "I'm sorry, my love, but I must take my leave. I cannot keep my head up any longer. I have to retire to my room for a few hours sleep."

"I shall walk you."

"You will not, young lady," Esmerelda scolded.

"I'll walk him." Robin stood up.

"No need, Robin," Ezra sighed.

"I insist. I need a word with you anyway, briefly." Robin walked him to the door and out, up the stairway.

"What is it?" Ezra asked as they climbed.

"I wish to make certain you are not running out for real. The plan is working. Just give it time. You've got half the old ladies already," Robin said.

Ezra continued to climb and at the top held his head in his hand.

Robin collected him by the elbow. "You are not running out again?"

"Could not run if the house was on fire."

Robin walked him to his room and saw him inside. "Sleep then. You've done well. Sleep soldier."

"Yes, sir."

"Mr. August. You will put on a shirt immediately!"

"Been a hundred years since you saw a young man. Well this is what it looks like." He spread his arms out wide, revealing underarm hair and all. "You walked in on me in my bedroom. You will just have to shut your eyes then."

Esmerelda turned her back to him. "You must vacate this home immediately and let my niece to meet suitable second husbands. This fling of hers is surely over. You are taking advantage of a young widow, sir!"

"I'm in love with her, most ardently. I'm not going anywhere," Ezra said.

"Oh!" Esmerelda stormed out and slammed the door.

Ezra fell back on pillows. His arms above his head on the pillows. "Son of a bitch. I just want to sleep."

Two police officers entered the gallery.

"Can I help you with something, officer?" Albert asked.

Ezra looked up from paperwork he and Adam were going over on the counter.

"We have some business with a Mr. Ezra August," the officer said.

Robin immediately shot from his chair.

Ezra stepped around the counter. "I am Ezra August."

"Mr. Ezra August, you are under arrest. Put out your hands please, sir."

"What?"

Robin stepped forward. "I will see this warrant."

The police officers reached out to grab Ezra by the wrists and began to place hand cuffs on him.

"This can't be happening," Adam said.

"I'm his attorney. I will see this before you touch this man," Robin insisted. "What are the charges?"

"Seduction."

The paper was handed to Robin. He skimmed it quickly. Then Robin put his hand on Ezra's arm. "The warrant is real. Say nothing. You are under arrest. But don't worry, you're not going to jail for this. I'm accompanying my client to the police station."

While one officer held Ezra by the handcuffs, the other started to pat him down roughly and extracting things from his pockets. Ezra's leather purse, his spectacles, his cigarettes were set on the counter. His hair comb and even his handkerchief were all being taken from him.

"Get out of my clothes, man," Ezra protested. "Are you going to bend me over too?"

"Shut that mouth," the officer warned. "Seduced a young girl, did you?"

Adam grabbed up Ezra's belongings for him and hurried with Robin out the door. Adam locked up the gallery.

"What young girl?" Ezra protested. "What the hell are you talking about?"

"Too many to remember, huh? Elizabeth Miller," the officer said.

Ezra and Robin looked at each other.

"Five years? I could get five years for this?" Ezra exclaimed.

Adam reached through the bars to hold onto Ezra by the arm. "No. You are not going to jail for this."

"I am in jail for this!"

"I'm getting this before the judge as soon as possible. Stay calm, Ezra," Robin said. "They've done this late on a Friday on purpose."

"We're going to win over the old bats. That's what you said. That old bat put me in jail!" Ezra exclaimed. "There is no way Elizabeth is going think I'm worth all this."

"I just have to talk to Elizabeth first. Stay calm, Ezra."

"Hold on. I'm going to the nearest café to bring back some decent food for you," Adam said.

"Stay with him for now. I will have a word with the guards." Robin walked away from the cell and back to the gate. "Guards, I have a court order for you. May I speak with you?"

"I don't want your lawyer nonsense," the guard said.

Robin handed a folded piece of paper through the gate. "Read this. It's an order to put Mr. August under suicide watch. He will not be housed with any other inmates. He will be checked at least hourly, if not monitored, especially through the night."

"The little fornicator? You think we believe you? We'd love to put him in with the other inmates. They think he's their new entertainment," the guard said. "Oh yeah. They like him all right."

"This is signed by a judge. Mr. August is officially under suicide watch and as such cannot be housed with any other inmate and cannot be left alone for more than one hour. This is serious, officer Jamison, and officer Reynolds. Don't think I won't press charges against you if this is not adhered to by the letter of the law," Robin said.

Monday morning found Robin standing outside the cell bars with a clean suit wrapped over his arm, waiting for the key.

Inside, Ezra sat back on the cot, against the opposite wall, cross legged. He looked at the elegant Van der Kellen in misery.

The guard opened the cell door.

Robin entered and was locked inside. "Did he eat anything?"

"Doesn't look like it." The guard indicated the tray on the floor with bowl of soup and bread still there from the night before. The bread looked chewed on. "Been there all night."

"Where is his breakfast?" Robin asked.

"He doesn't get that until he eats dinner," The guard said.

Robin reached through the bars, grabbed the guard by the collar. He yanked him forward so hard that the man's face hit the bars. "Bring his breakfast before his trial. He is not a convicted man."

The guard backed off, swatting Robin's fist away. "Kiss my ass, lawyer." He left.

Robin turned to Ezra and laid the suit down beside him on the cot. Then from inside his pocket he produced a napkin with a fresh sandwich inside.

"Oh my God." Ezra sighed, taking the sandwich in both hands and devouring it.

"Shhh. Here, we don't have much time." Robin also began to comb Ezra's hair for him as he was eating. "They didn't allow a blade so I can't let you shave until we get upstairs. But trust me, we will. Let's get you changed into clean clothes."

Ezra unbuttoned his shirt and peeled it back off his shoulders, still eating. "Give me that comb. Let me do it."

Robin held out the clean shirt and noticed bruises on Ezra's side. "What happened?"

"Nothing. Nothing I want to talk about." He stood up to take the new shirt on. "You brought me these?"

"Yes. Just get these on. Did they put you with other inmates?"

"No. Will Beth be there?" Ezra unbuttoned his trousers and pulled them down.

"She will of course, to support you." Robin collected his pants to fold them with the shirt.

Ezra put on fresh underclothing and then clean trousers. "I don't know how you kept me away from the animals in here. They taunted me all night. The things they said…."

"You just focus on this. You will be a gentleman in court. You will be polite and honest," Robin coached.

"If I'm sentenced for five years, I won't survive. They've already said I'm getting attacked on night one if I come back down here." Ezra gripped onto Robin's shoulders. "And you know what I mean. You know what I mean, Robin."

Robin helped him on with the jacket. "You're not coming back here."

Ezra buttoned his trousers up. "I'm so scared I can hardly do buttons."

Robin put the ascot around his neck and began to tie it into a bow. "You need some water?"

Ezra nodded. "The water they gave me had things in it. Wiggling things."

"And the bruises?"

"There was a rat in here," Ezra said. "He was so mean. When I said anything, the guard just…"

Robin brought the two sides of the jacket together and buttoned it. "I forgot a vest. So just keep this buttoned. You're all right."

"Robin, I'm so…."

"Listen to me. I'm taking you up to a water closet near the court room. You wash your face and shave. Drink water. Do what you need to do. You'll have about ten/fifteen minutes. Then I will take you into the courtroom. When it begins, I don't predict it to last long at all. Elizabeth has allowed me to use the fact that she was not a chaste woman."

"What? You can't say that. That's my defense?" Ezra outraged. "I have to insult her?"

"It's the truth and it will end this immediately. I'm sorry I got you into this, Ezra. But I will get you out of it."

Ezra reached for Robin and needed his embrace. "You didn't get me into this."

Robin hugged him hard. "Hang on, Ezra. Let's get you out of here."

Elizabeth, Marie, and Zoey huddled together with Adam Hudson in the courtroom. And Beth began to cry as soon as she saw Ezra.

Ezra August was held by the arm by Robin Van der Kellen and escorted to the defendant's box. Robin then stepped behind the judge's desk to pour a glass of water which he offered to Ezra.

Almost immediately the judge came from his chambers. Seeing this he approached them. Quietly he said, "Van der Kellen, who do you think that water is for exactly?"

"For the judge, of course, your honor. But my client had no water in his cell all night. No decent water," Robin said very quietly, just for the judge and Ezra. "And someone beat him in there. I don't appreciate the conditions of your jail one damn bit."

"Neither do I. I will look into that. Let him have the water." The judge watched Ezra bring the glass to his mouth. "Need a few minutes or shall we begin?"

"I'd like to get this finished quickly." Robin laid a handkerchief on the desk before Ezra.

Ezra drank heavily from the glass and then wiped his mouth and forehead with the RVK handkerchief. Then he looked at the embroidered initials, thinking about the one Adam coveted. His thumb passed slowly over the embroidery. And then again. RVK. He looked at Robin.

Robin walked out in front of the judge's desk and took his place. He gave a look to his ladies and Adam. He gave them a hand signal.

Adam whispered to the ladies not to cry. Robin will win.

"I call the case of Ezra August, charged with seduction. All rise. Let us swear in our prosecutor, defending attorney and the defendant. Then the floor will belong to the prosecutor."

"Ladies and gentlemen, forgive me for you are about to hear a salacious case. We have here a poor young man who used seductive wiles to ensnare a wealthy and vulnerable young woman, who shall not be named. Just look at him. Does he not look bewitching to the young ladies of the court room? He is not even remorseful, has offered no apology statement. And his profession, prepare yourselves, he claims to be an artist. Why we all know them to be an unscrupulous lot, staying up all hours with drinking and painting nakedness on their canvases. Let me ask him just one question and be done with this. Mr. Ezra August, did you sleep with the young lady?"

The room gasped.

"You are under oath, Mr. August." The prosecuting attorney slapped his hand down on the defendant's box. "Did you sleep with this girl?"

Ezra wet his lips and could not look at anyone. "Yes I did."

"There! He does not even deny it. Prosecution rests. Go ahead and try to defend that wicked man!"

Robin waited until the prosecutor took his seat before rising behind his desk and strolling out onto the floor. He turned to look around at the gathering and the judge. And only then would everyone hear his elegant voice.

"Ladies and gentlemen, forgive me for you are about to hear a salacious case, at least that is what the prosecution would have you believe. However, I must inform you that merely a young romance has happened and no crime whatsoever. My client, Mr. Ezra August, is accused of seduction. An innocent man has been arrested and held for 3 nights in jail. This has nothing to do with his profession or her fortune. They're a young couple in love. Seduction is not what you have been led to believe. Seduction, as defined by the law, is the enticement of a chaste woman for a sexual encounter," Robin said. "Prepare yourselves. I am about to reveal the name of the young woman, with her permission. I will have these charges dropped as Mrs. Elizabeth Miller was previously married. She is in fact a widow of one year."

"You would defame a widow just to save your client, sir?" the prosecutor said.

"It is not defamation to say that a married woman was married. Elizabeth Miller was married for four years," Robin said. "By definition in the law, you cannot seduce a previously married woman. There is no law against a previously married woman having sexual encounters with anyone else who is not married to another."

"Scandalous. That's adultery," the prosecutor argued.

"One must be married to commit adultery. Neither of these two are currently married," Robin replied. "This is the jealous act of an overprotective aunt, brought against a young couple, a young *engaged* couple. The goings on in their bedroom are none of her business, or yours for that matter. The aunt wished to prevent their marriage by having Mr. August arrested."

"Forgive me, Mrs. Miller. You are engaged to the defendant, Mr. August?" the judge asked.

Elizabeth stood up. "Yes I am, your honor. My elderly aunt misunderstood. You have my fiancée there. Don't do this. We are to be married."

The judge banged his gavel on the desk. "Charges dismissed. This is not seduction. Release Mr. August and clear his name in the records. And by the way, I will see you two in here at noon tomorrow to be married."

"What?"

"And bring your aunt to witness."

"Your honor, please do not deny them their big church wedding." Robin rushed forward toward the judge. "An innocent man spent three nights in jail. Don't make me declare the conditions he endured, because I am about to."

The judge looked from Ezra in the box to Elizabeth and nodded. "Very well. Take this gentleman home. I will expect to see a wedding invitation."

Robin and Adam helped Ezra up into the carriage. While Marie held out a tin of cookies and Elizabeth offered a canteen of water to Ezra, he could not speak. His head was down in his hands.

"Easy. Elizabeth, give him time and room. He's just come from a terrible ordeal. And it is best that right now, he just focuses on what his body needs to recover. Food, water, and rest," Robin coached. "Catch your breath, Ezra. Take some water when you can."

"Oh my God. Why can't he even drink water yet? What have they done to him in there?" Elizabeth outraged.

"Easy. Elizabeth. Calm your voice for Ezra's sake. Let him catch his breath," Robin said. "Is that what you need right now, Ezra?"

Ezra nodded, still shielding his eyes with his left hand, and holding his stomach with his right.

Adam slid across to sit on Ezra's other side and rested his hand on his shoulder. It made Ezra jolt. "It's just me. You're all right."

At that point Elizabeth put her head to Ezra's and she was crying.

Marie sobbed.

"All right. Listen everyone, it is over. We won. Everyone here is all right," Robin said.

Adam produced a flask of brandy, opened it, and put it into Ezra's hand. "I'd want this, if I were you. And I don't drink."

Ezra looked down at it. "Oh Adam." When he tipped the flask to his mouth, the tears streamed down his face.

"This should never have happened to you. I'm so sorry," Elizabeth told him.

"I'm so sorry." Ezra was rocking back and forth. "I can't take this right now. I don't know how to..."

Beth pulled out her pocket handkerchief and wiped her eyes. She nodded and strengthened. "You don't have to be brave now, darling. We're all here for you."

Marie nodded her approval to Beth.

Ezra drank the brandy and then sat back with a hard breath.

Adam patted him on the knee. "You know, I've been trying to reach Pierre and Albert. I sent one of my stable men to the old attic just in case. No luck yet but I'll keep at it. I know they would have come to see you if they knew what happened."

"Adam." Robin shook his head.

"Do you need to lay down on the seat, Ez?" Adam asked.

"I can sit. I just couldn't eat anything in there."

They arrived at Elizabeth's mansion where Ezra was met by both elderly aunts inside the foyer. Hannah was in tears.

Robin handed a sack containing Ezra's dirty clothing to one of the maids and whispered, "Boil these."

"Excuse me?"

"And burn the sack. Just a precaution. Get Ezra a hot bath and prepare a very good meal," Robin said to the maid and Jonas.

"Right away." Jonas set people into motion.

"I am so sorry, young man," Esmerelda said. "I thought you would just leave her. I had no idea you would actually be arrested."

Elizabeth held Ezra by the arm. "Well he's not leaving. I will contact our church to see what date we can have. Send for the physician. He's badly bruised on one side."

Robin moved in and took Ezra. "I'll bring him to a bath. Send the physician up when he arrives. Beth, just keep away from him until we get the jail house washed off of him. Trust me."

"One moment," Ezra paused. "Robin, how do I ever thank you? And Aunt Esmerelda, I forgive you. You were looking after Elizabeth. That's all that will be said on this matter."

Robin brought Ezra up the stairs and Adam ran after them.

The vanity room between Ezra's and the elderly ladies had a bathing tub that was being quickly filled with hot water by the bucketful. Maids also stoked up the fireplace. Adam took cues and went to Ezra's room for another fresh suit and underclothing.

The maids exited.

Robin poured a couple glasses of brandy and handed one to Ezra.

Once he stepped out of all of his clothes and into the hot bath, Robin gave the clothing to a maid in the hall who promised to boil those as well. But she asked why. Robin politely said, "Vermin from the jailhouse. Just give them a thorough boiling."

Adam carried an armful of clean things for Ezra and entered with Robin again.

"Wash his hair good, I mean really good." Robin paced about angrily. "If you itch anywhere, Ezra, scrub it good with soap."

Ezra collapsed back in the tub with wet hair slicked to his head and eyes closed. His brandy glass was empty. Robin refilled it. The water was so hot that Ezra's skin turned red.

"Hey, Ez, sit forward would you?" Adam poured shampoo into his hands.

Ezra put his face in his hands and sat up, sudsy water was up to his shoulders.

"He's in pain," Robin said.

"You are?" Adam lathered up Ezra's long black hair. "What happened to you in there? They didn't put you with inmates did they?"

"Guards beat me when I complained about the rats," Ezra said softly. "Ow. Watch my ear."

Adam had a good look at his ear and then looked at Robin furiously. "His ear needs stitches. Needed them about two days ago. Behind his ear is black and blue. Hit in the head."

Robin nodded. "And he was kicked in the ribs. Do you have any idea which guards did this?"

Ezra nodded as Adam went back to gently shampooing his hair.

"The two who were there when I saw you?" Robin asked.

Ezra nodded.

"I'll file charges first thing tomorrow," Robin said. "Keep him in that bath a good long time. I'll bring the doctor up when he arrives."

Ezra was dressed in a black suit, plaid vest, brand new ruffled shirt with lace on the collar. Adam had fixed the rushed shave job by perfectly shaving and trimming his long sideburns. And his black curls hid the new stitches on his right ear that Ezra had wept through the whole time they were being administered. He met Elizabeth with a hug and kiss before taking a seat at the dining table. He looked pale and steam rolled.

"What did the doctor say?" Beth asked.

"I'm okay. I'm just exhausted," Ezra said.

"What...what happened to your ear?" Beth slid his hair back to see the stitches across the top of his ear.

"I don't want to talk about it now. Okay? I'm just happy to receive this meal and looking forward to sleep," Ezra said.

Marie suddenly had to run out of the room. That made Robin and Zoey meet eyes. They both stood up.

"Let me go. She's a bit sick." Zoey went after Marie.

"What's happening?" Elizabeth asked. "Marie is sick?"

"She's fine. It's just...I do hope that you can have your wedding soon. I will have to get Marie back home to Connecticut in about a month or so," Robin said.

Adam smiled a bit. "Unfortunately, I mean, you're leaving in a month or so."

"Robin! Why didn't you two tell me?" Elizabeth exclaimed. "Marie is expecting?"

"So is Zoey," Adam whispered.

Ezra looked at his two friends and smiled the first big smile since his arrest. "My two friends are going to be fathers? And Robin for the second time?"

"Ez, are you okay?" Elizabeth asked.

He nodded. "Go."

She patted him on the shoulder and ran out after her friends.

"You gentlemen are not talking about what I think you are?" Hannah asked.

"Not at all," Robin said.

When Elizabeth returned, they finished eating their meals. "Marie went to lay down and then so did Zoey. Apparently Zoey can't watch someone else get sick without getting sick herself. So she is laying down as well."

"I need to check on her." Adam slid his chair back. "Excuse me ladies, and Robin."

"Thank you, Adam," Ezra over enunciated, as Adam left.

"It's the lace. Looks masculine on you though." Robin sat back and sipped his drink.

Ezra smiled. "No, it doesn't."

"What did...what did the doctor say?" Elizabeth asked.

Ezra swallowed a bite of roast beef before answering. "Well, I have a concussion from three days ago but since I didn't sleep, I should be fine. My eyes are fine."

"Ez..." She held onto his arm and worked her way to holding his hand, his slender artist's fingers.

"I'm going to have to go lay down soon like the pregnant ladies," Ezra said.

"You mustn't talk about such things," Hannah scolded.

"I knew that's what they were talking about," Esmerelda said. "Why are those two ladies out in public?"

"They're...they're not out in public. They're only in this house and Adam's house. We will stay for Elizabeth and Ezra's wedding then I'll be taking Marie home for her confinement," Robin explained.

Elizabeth walked Ezra up the stairs and at the top she would not release his arm. "Come and sleep in my room. You'll be more comfortable there and I can look after you."

"Really?" Ezra looked down at her.

She slid her hand up his vest and into the ruffles. "You need to be looked after. This is all my fault. Please, Ezra, my love."

He closed his hand on hers, on his chest. "This is all my fault, because I'm not some great society man who can court you. I'm just some distraction in tight trousers before you meet this man."

"No. We should be married tomorrow. Then Marie, who is pregnant, can go home and rest. My aunts can ride their broomsticks back to Baltimore. We can always plan a big church wedding ourselves later." She walked him to her bedroom.

"I think you should talk to your church first. How do you know a date is not available?" Ezra said. "If you are going to marry me you should at least do it right, get an amazing dress...that I can try on."

She laughed. "You are delirious."

"I am. I couldn't sleep for fear of a big scarry rat in my cell. If I put my foot down he went after my ankles." Ezra peeled off his jacket and laid it on the fainting couch at the foot of her bed. "Got beat up for kicking that rat at the guards."

"Ezra...Oh my God."

"I'm so sorry. Didn't mean to do that to the rat. It bit me and startled me. Robin told me not to tell you anything about being in there. But I was so scared. So scared." He began to sob and Elizabeth took him into her arms.

He pulled her down onto the bed with him and he shook as he cried. Elizabeth cried too, telling him, "I was so worried about you. Afraid you would just decide I'm not worth all this."

"Ow. Ow. Not my right ear. Sorry." He rolled onto his left side, rolling her over him. "I hurt so bad and I just need to sleep so."

"Sleep my darling. I will look after you. Do you need some laudanum? Or brandy?"

"You have laudanum?"

"I have everything."

"Please...please give me some laudanum so I can sleep? Please."

Beth crawled off the other side of the bed and went to her dressing table. She opened a cabinet and poured him a tiny golden demitasse of laudanum.

"Why do you have this?" He accepted and drank it. Then he held up the tiny glass to examine it. "In a magic potion glass of gold? Are those rubies on it?"

Elizabeth took the empty glass from him and refilled it with brandy. "My monthly can be quite painful. My physician gave me a small supply. I always thought pregnancy could fix that. Drink this to get that medicinal taste away."

"I...hope you don't think I can do anything tonight. I am destroyed. I am so desperate for sleep. I am not even human at this point." He rocked in her arms.

"Sleep my love. I will look after you." She held him and rocked him down to the pillows.

"Wake me for supper? Maybe I could eat again later." He laid his head down on the softest pillows of his life and closed down long black lashes letting tears leak beneath them. "I'm sorry I'm not some great soldier. I've held on as long as I can. And I can't anymore. I was so scared."

She pulled a quilt over him. "Sleep my darling. I will be right here, standing guard. You're safe now. Robin is in the house. Anything that you need…. I don't want a soldier. I want you, my artist."

Chapter Sixteen   Broken Hearts

The laudanum put him out for many hours. Elizabeth had maids bring in a cart of supper on heat bricks. They set up plates on the table, just in case he awakened later. She ate there at his side. And they whispered to her, "Mr. Van der Kellen asks how he is."

"Thank Mr. Van der Kellen for us and tell him Ezra is sleeping. I gave him some laudanum. He needed to rest. I think he is quite unaccustomed to laudanum and is deeply sleeping," Elizabeth whispered.

"Madam, ring if you need anything during the night. He's beautiful, madam."

Elizabeth saw them to the door. "Yes he is. I can play with his hair while he sleeps and he doesn't even know."

"And to forgive your aunt for all he's been through? He is a hero."

Ezra slept though supper and all through the night, only waking up in the morning when he heard the cart being exchanged for coffee and pastries. He rolled over, pushing blankets down off his shirtless body. He stretched in fine linens, feeling the fabric glide over his skin.

Elizabeth was in her robe and slippers, as her two maids stocked the fireplace and set up the table. Then the maids left quietly.

Filtered sunlight twinkled on the carpet beside the bed through lace sheers.

Ezra sat up against the pillows, wiping his eyes. He had removed his trousers at some point in the night. He saw those arranged neatly on a chair bedside the bed. The black velvet robe awaited him there as well. He reached gingerly to feel his right ear and winced.

Beth sat down on the edge of the bed, still brushing her long blonde hair. "How do you feel, darling?"

"I'm sorry. I feel like I slept for days," he said softly in his deep and slightly raspy voice. "This must have bled on your pillow a bit."

"Don't you worry about that. The physician called again last evening and said it was good that you took the laudanum and got your rest. He will come by again today." Elizabeth got up and brought a cup of coffee to Ezra.

That made him smile as he accepted it. "Coffee served to me in bed. Never had that before. Never."

"Well, get used to it if you like." She smiled.

"Yes, I could very much get used to it." Ezra smiled a bit and sipped his coffee from a fine china cup, holding the saucer on his lap.

Elizabeth reached forward and smoothed fingertips down the bruised ribs on his left side. "Do you need something for pain?"

"Only hurts when I move," he said. "So I won't move."

"This is soon to ask you, when you're not awake yet. But there are some dates available at my church and I am rather pressured by the fact that my two best friends are with child and should not be seen in public," Elizabeth began. "This Friday or next."

"Yeah but you are one crazy ass American woman if you still want to marry me," Ezra said.

She burst out laughing.

Ezra laughed too. "I don't know how I got so lucky as to meet with you. But I do think you're crazy to marry me. However, before you change your pretty little mind, set whatever date you want. I'll be there. I will say I do. I will take you as my wife. And I will devote my life to making you happy, Beth."

"Oh my goodness. All right. Then I must see how soon they can make my gown. That might determine whether I take this Friday or next," she said. "And I do want you to get a new tuxedo, very fancy."

"Another new tuxedo?"

"Yes. Whatever you like. Very fancy."

"Ha. That's a trick comment. I'm still getting a black one. But I...may surprise you with the vest and ascot," he said.

"You were kidding about trying on my dress."

"I was not. Why do ladies get to wear all the pretty things and men always have to dress as if in mourning. I at least get to try on your veil," Ezra said. "I'll never fit in your dress. My shoulders are too big."

"You would look ridiculous in a veil."

"Without the gown, of course." He nodded. "You should get a tiara."

"I..." Elizabeth looked at him seriously. "You think so?"

"Oh yes. I would see you in the most expensive tiara that would make all of your society friends turn green upon sight of it," Ezra said. "This is our wedding, darling."

"Do you think I should splurge like that? You must go see that tailor I brought you to, today, and see how long it will take to cut you a new tuxedo, very elaborate, once you choose the fabric. Take Adam with you. He has very good taste in such things," Elizabeth said.

"I can do that. What time is it, darling?" He asked.

"You don't have a pocket watch? Do you? I shall get you one as my wedding gift to you," Elizabeth said. "It's only quarter to nine."

"In the morning?" He glanced at the windows.

"Yes, silly," Beth said.

He smiled. "I never know until I see a window."

"I will send word for Adam to come at once. I must get dressed. I have to see if Marie can come with me to the tailors and the dress maker, if she's not feeling ill this morning. Ask Adam about a haircut."

"Sweetheart, wait." Ezra caught her arm. He set his cup and saucer on the bedside table. "I love you."

"Oh Ezra, I love you so," Elizabeth sighed.

"Is there anything you want from me, in all of this?"

"Well. This must be overwhelming for you. I only asked you to court me. And here we are getting married, when you have been a man on your own for all your life since you were very young. I know what marriage is. Perhaps you don't know yet," Elizabeth asked.

"Well I have the benefit of a best friend going through the same thing, if only slightly ahead of me. We'll make good husbands, Adam and I," Ezra said. "And not to each other."

She laughed. "Do you regret any, leaving your old bachelor ways? Of sleeping on the floor with whomever you choose, and more than one?"

"Oh you mean sleeping alone on the floor without anything to eat? No, I don't regret leaving that. I must tell Adam how grateful I was that he bought the gallery building for me and was changing my life as it was. And he's brought me to you, for it was me teaching him to paint that brought us together."

"What will you do, now that you can do anything as an artist?" Elizabeth said.

"I was thinking of discussing buying that building from Adam. The building only cost $900." Then Ezra rolled his eyes. "Did I say that? Only $900?"

Beth laughed. "And we shall take our picnic and walk at the first warm spring day. In fact, let us make it an annual thing, to remind us, that I would have married you on your income and been just as happy."

Ezra sat forward and kissed her mouth. "I love that you said that. Personally, I think we can be even more happy with all this gold and crystal."

She smiled. "You might be right."

"So back to my question, what do you want from me in all this?" Ezra asked.

"Be honest with me. Do you like intimacy with me? Is it all right?"

"You are wonderful in every, every way. And I am making a vow to you, to give up my old ways, as long as I can still be me. I'm always going to dress a little too feminine. I'm always going to comment to you quietly that Robin is beautiful or that Adam is so cute I could just hug him. And I might. But, having said that, you are marrying a man who can turn either way."

"You do realize that when we marry, I do not want to share you with anyone."

"And you are to be my wife. No other man will have you. I can get better at this love making," Ezra said.

Beth blushed. "I am certain that everything you have tried to learn, you have done well at."

"Hmmm, polite way of saying I need some training." Ezra grinned.

Beth laid her hand on his wrist and looked down at it. "I am going to say something to you that you may never say to anyone except one person. You may... I said I would not share you. I mean that I do not want you having relations or feelings for anyone else with one exception. And this is someone you already have feelings for. He is your friend. He may be just as afraid as you are. You may have him as long as you never get caught."

Ezra watched her stand up and fuss with the coffee cups. She was returning them to the table and about to try to pour herself more. He quickly scrambled from the bed to block her from the hot coffee pot. "Let me get that for you. Beth."

She looked at him with wet eyes.

Ezra, in just his under shorts, turned her to look at him. "You do not have to let me have Adam."

"I will not be the one to deny you, entirely, that which is your nature," Beth said. "Just to serve my own selfishness."

Ezra kissed her forehead. "He's more terrified of getting caught than I am. You may as well have given me to Robin."

Adam entered the artist's studio to find Ezra stretching new a new canvas and hammering tacks into the back. He joined Ezra at the table and helped hold the canvas down on the opposite side. "This is a nice size one. What are you painting on this?"

"I wanted to talk to you about that. I don't know how you are going to feel about it." Ezra set down his hammer and put his hands on his hips. He looked at Adam across the table.

"What?" Adam shrugged. "Is this just for you or do you have a commission?"

"Both. Well technically two different commissions. You see, ah…"

Adam insisted, "What already?"

"Robin. Elizabeth wants her own painting of Robin and I wanted to commemorate our mission together with a portrait," Ezra admitted. "And well, Robin also asked me to paint a family portrait of him, Marie, and Frida. I can't wait too long on that or I'll forget what Marie looks like. I have done some drawings. On the other hand, I told him maybe Beth and I can visit Canterbury and I'll paint it there. I'm sorry."

"There's nothing to be sorry for. I don't own Robin. And after the masterpiece you made of Elizabeth, I can see why anyone would want you to paint them," Adam said. "Rather glad I was your first."

"I'm so sorry, Adam."

"Make the paintings, Ezra. If we all make paintings of Robin not one of them will be the same. The world needs all of them, I think," Adam said.

"Thank you." Ezra nodded.

"Hey, I came to see if you had lunch."

"Ah, I don't even know what time it is, so no," Ezra said.

"Let's finish tacking this and get gesso on it. Then I can take you to lunch," Adam said. "It's just after one o-clock."

"All right, yeah."

As they worked together on the large canvas stretched on boards at a 4 foot by 6 foot in dimension. Adam said, "Robin said he would write up the property transfer of title for us."

"You don't mind? After the wedding, Robin said I could pay you for it." Ezra hammered the rest of the tacks in, going around the canvas.

"I don't mind. It makes perfect sense," Adam said. "Where are Albert and Pierre?"

"I don't know. If they keep this up I don't give a shit either."

"They didn't come to see you since you got out?"

"No!" Ezra almost shouted.

"I sure don't understand why," Adam said. "Are their things here?"

"Why wouldn't they be?"

"Get the white gesso going. I'll be right back." Adam turned and bounded up the stairs to top floor.

Ezra stood the canvas up on his brand new very large oak easel. He got out the pail of white gesso and a large house painting brush. He started painting it onto the bare cloth. He had to keep applying paint to various parts of the canvas or else it would shrink unevenly. So he painted quickly. And the longer it took for Adam to return, the more angrily he painted. At the sound of Adam's boots on the stairs, Ezra set the brush down on the edge of the pail and wiped his hands off on a towel.

Adam had a paper in his hand. "Did you have the money from the sale of your old gallery upstairs in the..."

"Wooden box on my mantel upstairs," Ezra finished the sentence. "Why?"

Ezra,

We know you will understand. You're rich now and won't miss this. We'll pay you back some day. But we are leaving for Boston. We didn't have any choice. You just left us for her. You broke our hearts and you didn't even ask if we were all right with it. It was good to see you happy. But we suffer so. Goodbye.

Albert and Pierre

Ezra looked up from the paper and started for the stairway. Adam grabbed his arm. "Don't bother. All their things are gone and so is your money, I assume."

"They took everything? Adam, it was only three hundred dollars in there. The rest I had at Elizabeth's. They can't survive on that, not for long," Ezra said. "Not with a train ticket to Boston and nobody to stay with there."

"I know," Adam said.

"But..." Ezra read the note again.

"So they didn't know you were arrested. They were gone already," Adam said. "Do they know anybody in Boston? Maybe they just went back to your old neighborhood."

"I can ask Marco if he's seen them," Ezra said. "They never mentioned Boston to me before." Ezra almost wept. "I'm such an ass."

Adam let out a hard breath. "I don't know what to tell you. This wasn't your fault. They could have lived here and been safe here. So what the hell, they just couldn't bear to see you happy with somebody else?"

"With a woman," Ezra said. "That's what pissed them off. You and I both left for women."

"Finish painting that canvas and let's go. We'll stop at your place, tell Elizabeth where we're going, and we'll take my carriage," Adam said.

"Thank you, Adam." Ezra did sob. "I don't know how to thank you."

"Marco! Marco, hang on a minute." Ezra hopped out of his carriage and hurried to catch a young man on the street.

"Oh you've got a lot of nerve coming here like this," Marco said. "Fancy carriage and a driver and all!"

Adam had the carriage wait and he stepped out.

"What are you talking about? Have you seen Albert or Pierre in a few days?" Ezra asked.

"I saw them when they were moving out of the attic," Marco said. "Nice job."

"What are you talking about?" Ezra asked.

"Got yourself a rich woman, and man for that matter." Marco indicated Adam Hudson. "They were thrown out of the attic and then left to do what?"

"We bought them a building to live in," Ezra said. "They were set for a place to live and work. Where did they go?"

"I don't know where they went. I know where you went." Marco even pushed him back a step.

"Hey," Adam spoke up. "He really did buy a building for a gallery and rooms above. Albert and Pierre stole his money and took off on him."

"Oh that's why you're here to look for them. You think they stole from you," Marco said.

"I don't give a shit about that. I give a shit that they took off on me. I don't know where they went. I don't know how they will survive," Ezra said.

"The same way they did before they took you in, I guess," Marco said. "Nice suit. Nice carriage. All you had to do was fuck a rich woman."

Ezra swung back to punch him but Adam grabbed him by the arms.

"Let's go, Ezra. We're done here," Adam urged. "We'll look somewhere else."

"I can't believe this. I did nothing to you but put your paintings up in my gallery," Ezra said to Marco. "And I still could today. But you know what? You crossed a line, buddy."

"You can put on those silk lined suits and marry a woman but you know what you still are." Marco walked away.

Ezra moaned and struggled against Adam's restraint.

"Come on. Focus. Let's go check at the restaurant Pierre used to work at," Adam said.

"What can I do for you?"

"Man, it's Ezra. Are you drunk or something?" Ezra said.

"Oh my God. I didn't recognize you in the fancy suit and hair pulled back like that. What is this about?" the owner of the restaurant said.

"I just want to know if you've seen Pierre or Albert lately," Ezra said.

"No. Not in a while. Haven't seen you in a long time either," the man said. "What's with the fancy suit anyway?"

Ezra shook his head. "Listen, just if you see one of them please tell them I'm looking for them."

"Ezra." Adam moved up beside him. "We never did have lunch. It's nearly 3. Why don't we have a seat and think about this?"

Ezra stared at him and finally nodded.

"Do you have money to pay for this?" the owner said.

"I have money to buy this place out from under you. Yes. Tell Alex not to spit in my soup or I'll break his arm for real this time," Ezra said. "Thank you very much."

The owner raised his eyebrows. "Right this way then, gentlemen."

They were shown to the same table where they had their first meal together, only weeks before. This time, Ezra sat and flicked the napkin into his lap. He looked over his shoulder as the water glasses were filled and coffee cups were set down between him and Adam.

"Alisha, have you seen Pierre or Albert in the last week?" Ezra asked.

"No. Haven't seen them since he quit a couple weeks ago," she said. "Pierre that is. He said they were moving with you uptown. What are you doing here?"

"Looking for them. They took everything and moved out."

"I heard you were getting married to a rich lady," Alisha said. "You look the part."

"Could we order lunch?" Adam asked.

The woman shifted from one foot to the other. "You clean up nice, Ezra. You're very handsome and lucky."

"Sorry." Adam shrugged.

"No, it's all right. Alisha, can you bring us some lunch? Whatever is best back there," Ezra said. "And some for yourself."

Someone brought her a basket of fresh bread and she set it on the table. "I will bring you the pork loin."

Adam reached for the bread and took a slice. He buttered it and smiled.

"What?" Ezra asked.

"I was just reminded of our first lunch here when you were the one hungry," Adam said. "Now it's me."

Ezra nodded. "Well. Meeting you was a world wind."

"Ezra, some people will always hold that against you. You can't do anything about it," Adam said. "I wanted to talk to you about something, if you don't mind."

"Please. I'm not accomplishing anything else today."

"It's just that I know the house you are moving into. I have some advice for you and you can take it or leave it," Adam said. "Make friends with Jonas. He can really make life easier for you there. He likes cigars. Hint."

"Oh." Ezra nodded. "I know a nice shop around the corner. We'll go there next."

"When you marry Elizabeth, even though she owns the house, you are going to become the master of the household," Adam said. "Suddenly you are dealing with things you never imagined. You might have to fire someone. You may have to handle questions such as, Elizabeth wants a party of twenty people but the table only seats 12. What should they do? The coal delivery is late. There is a vase missing from the kitchen."

Ezra sipped his coffee. "Sounds like your house."

Adam nodded. "Yeah, all of it last week. Don't get caught alone with any of the maids. They all talk."

"Yeah they do. I heard about the time you spilled an entire carafe of ice-cold water on yourself," Ezra said. "And then you slipped on the wet floor and went sliding on your ass."

"What?"

"Yeah, those maids do talk." Ezra grinned.

"Yes, I have heard some talk about you sleeping there in her bed with nothing on but a blanket," Adam said.

"Be glad Beth put a blanket over me. As you know, I'm not shy."

Robin and Ezra peeked into the master bedroom to find Elizabeth and Marie inside. "We're back, ladies."

"Oh. Come in." Elizabeth had baby Frida in her arms.

The men entered the room.

"We were just discussing renovations to this room. Of course, it depends on what Ezra would like. I'm thinking the whole room is too dark and..." Elizabeth started.

"I still don't know if I could ever sleep in here," Ezra admitted. "With respect. It just doesn't seem right."

Robin strolled inside and looked about as he made his way to wrapping his arms about Marie from behind her. He affectionately kissed her cheek.

"After next Friday, this is your home and this is your room," Elizabeth reminded. "So is the beach house."

"Oh! Let's all go there after your wedding!" Marie blurted out. "You offered it to us and we never got to see it."

"You want to go on their honeymoon?" Robin pulled her to him.

Ezra laughed. "She can't get any more pregnant. Right?"

They all laughed.

"What do you want to do for a honeymoon?" Elizabeth questioned.

Ezra's eyebrows rose. "What I want is not for public discussion, my love."

"Good answer." Robin laughed.

"Let's go to the beach house and bring our best friends, Robin and Marie," Elizabeth suggested. "And Adam and Zoey too!"

"And how would that be different than here?" Robin asked.

"It's on the beach, you fool!" Elizabeth said. "We'll drink and lie about...."

"And fornicate," Ezra added.

"With our legal and respective wives," Robin added.

"Especially you." Ezra pointed at Robin.

"Yeah especially you." Marie looked up at him.

"I love it," Elizabeth declared. "All of my best friends secluded together in a beach house, to celebrate our wedding. Maybe it will help me get one of these of my own." She hugged the child.

"The only thing that can help you with that is..." Robin pointed at Ezra.

Then Ezra went to Elizabeth and reached out to take the baby.

"What are you doing? Do you know how to hold a one-year-old?" Beth asked him.

"Of course I do." Ezra took Frida into his arms and cradled her up against his shoulder. She immediately grabbed onto his long black hair. "I had 9 younger brothers and sisters, didn't I?"

Marie stepped forward and placed a cloth on Ezra's shoulder. "She may spit up on you. She's been doing that lately."

"Won't be my first time." Ezra spun around slowly and began to sing a lullaby to the baby, softly, in Turkish.

Marie smiled up at Robin, over her shoulder.

Elizabeth folded her arms in front of her, watching and listening to Ezra and his beautiful voice. She whispered to Marie, "What a lovely song. I wonder what it is."

Ezra carried the baby closer to them and said softly, "We used to sing it in my home. My mother taught us. We sing it to keep the demon away from the children."

Dear Mother and Father,

I hope this letter finds you well. I hope my brothers and sisters are well. I deeply regret how many years it has been since I left home. As the eldest son, I have set a bad example. I regret not writing. I miss you all so much.

I have traveled across Europe to find myself now in New York, America. I am writing because I am to be married this Friday. I am an artist and through a friend of mine, I met my fiancée Elizabeth Miller. No she is not Muslim like us. But we plan to start a family of our own.

I have enclosed some money. I will send you more when I hear back from you. Would perhaps any of my siblings want to visit me in America. I will send money for the passage.

Please know that I am well and I love you all. Seni seviyorum.

Ezra Agustos Arikan

Ezra and Elizabeth emerged from a hat shop, each of them carrying two hat boxes, with Jonas behind them and two more hat boxes.

"Elizabeth, I haven't seen you in so long," A woman said.

"Helena, oh and Violet." Elizabeth turned and looked at the two women. The women were about ten years older than her. "I'm delighted to run into you."

"I would hug you but I see your hands are full of hats," Violet said.

"We received your wedding invitation just yesterday," Helena said. "Is this your finance?"

"Yes. Ezra." Elizabeth drew him closer.

Ezra could gather two hat boxes into his left hand and reached out his right to each of the ladies. "Ezra August, ladies. At your service." He kissed the back of each of their hands.

"Ezra, this is Violet Asby and Helena Carter," Elizabeth said. "Bankers wives."

"Pleased to meet you, Mr. August. Will you both join us for lunch? We were just about to enter this café," Violet said.

Elizabeth looked to Ezra who only smiled at her a bit. So she said, "We would be delighted. Jonas, can you take these boxes to the carriage?"

"Yes, ma'am." Jonas stepped forward and in the passing of hat boxes from Ezra to him, he slipped paper money into Ezra's hand. He whispered into Ezra's ear, "Take the check for lunch. There's more than enough."

"Thanks Jonas. Appreciate it," Ezra said.

"Can you handle these?" Elizabeth asked him.

"They're not heavy," Jonas said. "I'll manage, ma'am."

Ezra held the door to the café for all three women to enter. The women stood at the host podium and said nothing. As soon as Ezra stood with them the host spoke to him. "And how many dining with us, sir?"

"Table for four, if you would please," Ezra said.

"Of course. Let me see. Yes. Right this way." The host directed them toward a nice table for four, set with a floral arrangement in the center and candlesticks.

While Ezra held a chair for Elizabeth, the host did so for Violet and Helena. Then Ezra took his seat. Menus were handed to each guest and the wine list to Ezra. Before he took out his spectacles, he asked, "Would the ladies like some wine?"

"Oh yes, that would be lovely Ezra. You remember my favorite?" Elizabeth asked.

"I do. Of course." He put on his gold spectacles to look over the wine list. "Your French one and your Italian one."

Their server arrived, telling them the special was Zuppa al pomodoro and gnocchi alla romana.

Elizabeth looked at Ezra, fearful for him as it was Italian.

"Tomato soup and gnocchi alla romana is little cheese filled dumplings in a tomato, artichoke, garlic mixture," Ezra explained.

"Exactly correct, sir," the server agreed.

"Do you speak Italian, Mr. August?" Violet asked.

"Not exactly. But I lived in Rome for a time," Ezra said.

"I think that sounds delicious. I'm planning to have the special," Elizabeth said.

"Can I answer any questions about the menu?" the server asked. "Before I bring the wine."

Ezra requested the Italian white wine that Elizabeth liked.

Then the servers brought fresh bread, olive oil, and the wine to the table.

"How long were you in Rome, Mr. August?" Helena asked.

"About three months. I was only sixteen then and working my way to Paris where I would live for three years to study painting," Ezra explained.

"You may have heard that Mr. August is an artist and good friends with Robin Van der Kellen," Elizabeth said.

The wine was given to Ezra to taste and he approved. Then it was poured for the ladies. Then the server took their orders.

"Is it through Robin Van der Kellen that you met? I remember the art show of Adam Hudson's," Violet said.

"Ezra was in charge of that very art show. You would have seen him there. Yes, Robin properly introduced us," Elizabeth said. "Jonas, my butler, was chaperoning us until we joined with you today."

"And we are delighted," Helena said. "Mr. August is so young and handsome, Elizabeth. Is he younger than you, pray tell?"

Ezra smiled.

"He is two years my elder, in fact," Elizabeth said.

"And how do you find it, being friends with Mr. Van der Kellen?" Violet asked. "Have you known him long?"

"He is very admirable and a most loyal friend," Ezra said. "I met him the night of Adam's art show, actually. Then Adam was stabbed and hospitalized. I feel Robin and I achieved a bond equal to years of friendship, as we ran through gunfire together. It was his idea to have me masquerade as Adam leaving the hospital, and let Adam escape peacefully out the back."

"Doesn't he say that so casually? When all of that was so terribly heroic?" Elizabeth said.

"Yes. We heard about the incident, all related to the Rothschild shooting, of course," Violet said. "How terrible."

"So you are the hero Van der Kellen spoke of?" Helena said.

"He is that very man," Elizabeth said.

Ezra smoothed a hand down his ascot and vest, modestly. "For my part, I followed his orders. But twice we were trapped and while he was occupied with defending us, I found a way out for us. It would not have done us any good for me to stand there and panic. Anyway, I am under his orders not to frighten any ladies with harrowing details of our adventure."

"Have you spoken with Sophia?" Elizabeth asked.

"She is still away with relatives in Baltimore, in mourning of course. Her daughter is with her. I understand the son is still in the city," Helena said.

"Berard? Yes he has visited Adam a few times," Ezra said.

"Has he?" Elizabeth asked. "I'm shocked Adam would receive him."

"Berard is remorseful," Ezra nodded. "Adam is more gracious than I would be."

"How telling. What would you have Adam Hudson do in this situation?" Violet asked.

Ezra felt he'd crossed a line. He gave it a thought before saying, "Whatever Van der Kellen advises."

"That would be best, of course," Violet walked it back.

"I beg your pardon." Ezra tapped a hand to his heart. "I'm protective of Adam. Can't help it after being shot at in his stead."

Elizabeth drew a deep breath. "Thank you, Ezra. Let us speak of something lighthearted now."

"Tell us of your wedding plans," Helena suggested. "Does Mr. August have a bit of an accent? Where do you hail from originally?"

Ezra nodded. "I am from far eastern Europe. Southern, far eastern Europe. I have failed at completely losing the accent."

"I love to listen to his voice," Elizabeth admitted. "We will be a little scandalous in our wedding plans. We are having two couples stand up for us. With Marie Van der Kellen as my maid of honor, and Adam Hudson as his best man, we couldn't very well leave Robin Van der Kellen and Zoey Hudson alone in the audience, now could we?"

"Oh I think that is a fine idea. Besides we will get to lay our eyes upon Robin Van der Kellen up in the front for the ceremony," Helena said.

That made Ezra grin.

"Were you buying six new hats for yourself? When we met you out there, didn't you have six hat boxes?" Violet remarked.

That made Elizabeth laugh. "Oh no. Three were Ezra's. He's fond of hats too."

"We both tried on nearly every hat in the shop," Ezra added. "It was great fun."

"You did not try on women's hats, did you sir?" Helena asked.

"Absolutely I did. What do you think, Beth? The giant purple one was exquisite. Wasn't it?" Ezra said.

"That's why I bought it, for me to wear though," Elizabeth said. "You found a hat something like Robin's, didn't you?"

"His leather one? Yes. Love that wide brim."

At the end of dinner, Ezra took care of the check as if he'd done it a hundred times. Internally, it weighed on him, and he would have to make amends.

Chapter Seventeen Super Double Insanely Secret

Ezra walked purposely past his guest room in the Miller mansion, toward the servants' wing. He passed two maids exiting, gave them a nod, and then met Jonas.

"Sir, what may I do for you? No need to come all the way down here. Just pull the cord," Jonas said.

"It is you I want to talk to," Ezra said casually. "Where is your room, Jonas?" Ezra had a small wooden box beneath his arm.

"If you wish. This way." Jonas took him to a small room on the far end. It had a small pot belly stove and windows overlooking the stable.

Ezra looked down at the box and offered it to Jonas. "I want to thank you for all you have done for me. I want to do more than this, but it is a start."

Jonas accepted a wooden cigar box and opened it to sniff and admire a fine cigar. "Sir, this is far too generous."

"Nonsense. I've seen you smoking. You'll enjoy these," Ezra said. "I have talked with Beth about this. I think you should move into the guest room I will be leaving when we marry. You'll have a nice fireplace and comfortable room, after all of your years of loyalty to this house."

"I...I don't know what to say. It seems inappropriate," Jonas said.

"Who's going to know? We'd like you to have a more comfortable room," Ezra said. "Look, Jonas, I'm not used to all these stations. I'm a poor guy. Right? I know it. I'm no better than you or any maid here or the guy who shovels horse shit out there."

Jonas laughed.

Ezra smirked. "If there is any change I would make in this house, it's that we treat everyone who works here better. Pay you all more. Give everyone one day off every week. Can't give everybody Saturday off but maybe a rotation," Ezra said. "I want to thank you so much for allowing me the dignity of paying for that dinner with Beth's friends. Without you, that would have been embarrassing for me and for Elizabeth."

Jonas nodded. "Thank you, sir. Those are the exact reasons I work very hard to avoid any such situation. If I may be of any help to you in that way, just tell me. Of course, I strive to provide it before being asked."

"Thank you, Jonas. I was never told your last name."

"It is very insignificant. Smith. Jonas Smith," Jonas said.

"Not insignificant to me, Mr. Smith." Ezra shook hands with him. "In very few days when I move out of that room, you will move in."

"What...may I ask, what will you do with the master bedroom? We are moving your things there after the wedding, are we not?" Jonas asked.

"I have a real hard time with that room. I do." Ezra strolled closer to the window to look out. He wiped his hand on the frost to clear the view.

"Perhaps it will ease your mind to know that Mr. Edward Miller did not pass in that room. I found him on the floor in another room, and I will not ever tell anyone what room it was," Jonas said.

Ezra's brow furrowed. "Why is that?" He turned from the window to study Jonas.

"There are some secrets I keep for the gentleman I serve," Jonas said.

"With respect, does Elizabeth know?"

"She does not, sir."

Ezra changed the tilt of his head. "The vanity closet?"

"No, sir." Jonas let out a long hard breath. "I don't wish to get off to a poor start with you. I am compelled to tell you, but telling you will serve two purposes. One, I will find out if you can keep a secret and a trust when the secrecy is meant to protect the woman we both care for very much, from the hurt it can only cause."

"Understood. And the second?" Ezra asked.

"It will show you, prove to you rather, that I can be just as loyal to you as I am only breaking this trust after his passing," Jonas said. "You see, there was a maid who quit and left soon after Edward's passing. She had served the house for forty years. I think you might be seeing what room I found him on the floor in."

Ezra's mouth fell open. "Oh my God. Oh...my God. You mean to tell me he yelled at her for wanting a child with Van der Kellen all the while he had a forty-year affair with another woman?"

"You knew about Van der Kellen?" Jonas folded his arms. "Do you see? Elizabeth does not know. This can never leave this room. Do you understand, sir?"

"I do and it won't leave this room. It won't ever be spoke of again. Jonas, the age difference was just too much for them. Is the woman all right? Do you know where she is?" Ezra ran a hand up through his black locks. "Jesus. All right. I hate the furniture in the master room. I want white French Rococo. Do you understand? It comes out of my money, after the wedding. I'm not sleeping in that dark mausoleum. Reminds me of the room a Catholic Pope dies in. No way."

Jonas laughed. "I don't know where she went."

"So. We understand each other and a fuck of a lot more about this house." Ezra spun about. "Until the new furniture, I will live in Beth's room. Everyone can just get over it. Besides, we are taking a honeymoon to the beach house. And if she does not have children it won't be for my lack of trying. I'm just starting to get good at it."

Jonas Smith cried laughing.

"The closest thing to my culture would be this Turkish restaurant. I hope none of this will be uncomfortable for you. Will you try this once for me?" Ezra asked as he was about to step out of their carriage.

"Yes, my love. My eyes and my heart are open," Elizabeth said.

"It will be strange to you. But picture my family table like this one, with children and grandparents and strangers alike all sitting together, on the floor around a short table. Can you do this?" Ezra asked.

"Yes. How exciting. And the food? You will not let me eat anything too spicy?" Elizabeth said.

"I won't let you. I promise." Ezra stepped out of the carriage and held his hand up for her.

Beth stepped out into his world, or closest thing to it, in the shadow of a Syrian church on the Hudson River side of Manhattan. Some wore traditional clothing here. She pulled her scarf up over her blonde hair, just as Ezra had told her to do. She was also wearing one of her plain travel dresses and no jewelry. Then she walked with him into a dining establishment. It was dimly lit inside by oil lamps and candles. The smell of spices and roasted lamb filled the air.

And she heard Ezra speaking Turkish for the first time, as he spoke to the host inside for a rather lengthy exchange. Ezra was always animated when he spoke, with hands and gestures. It was certainly more than asking for a table for two. He must have been explaining where he was born, perhaps.

They were shown to a large round table where they were to join several other couples of all ages. Ezra held onto her arm to assist Beth in sitting down on a cushion on the floor. "They know we are to be married." He took his place, sitting cross legged on the cushion beside hers. "And obviously we are from different sides of the world."

From a large bowl in the center of the table, a smaller bowl of broth was ladled for the couple to share. There were two spoons and napkins laid before them.

Pure white bread was passed about the table and Ezra broke off portions for himself and Elizabeth. As he passed it on, and gave Beth her portion, their eyes met. She was smiling.

She watched him dip his bread in their shared soup bowl and then take a bite. So she did the same. The soup had an egg swirled around in a vegetable stock.

Bowls of beans, potatoes, and corn were passed around the table and each time, Ezra served portions onto a plate that he and Beth shared. They ate with their spoon or another torn off heel of bread.

"Oh watch out for this one. Very spicy. Try only a tiny bit if you will." But Ezra dunked his bread into the paste generously and ate this.

"You can eat such spicy food?"

Ezra drank water after this bite. "Love it. I crave it, actually."

She took a tiny amount on her bread and sniffed it first. There was some laughter about the table.

Ezra spoke to them in Turkish.

More laughter.

She tasted curry, smoked paprika, garlic, and peppers in the bean paste. But it did burn her lip a bit.

Ezra handed her the water glass.

"It smells wonderful. But how do you tolerate the peppers?" she asked him.

"Love it. I don't know. I like my mouth on fire, I guess."

That made her laugh and then everyone at the table around them laughed.

She noticed most of the people were passing the big bowl around and spooning into it or dipping their bread into it, sharing the bowl together. "Why do we have our own bowl?"

"English ways would not approve of eating like this. I thought this would be easier on you," Ezra said.

"All right. Do they think less of me because I need our own bowl and plates?" Elizabeth asked.

"Not less. Only different. There is no judgment here. Only sharing," Ezra explained. "Be careful if you try the coffee. It is very strong." He drank his and went back to eating the spicy curry paste with a heal of bread.

A big bowl of spicy lamb was brought to the table as well as a small, much less spicy bowl for Elizabeth.

"Do not be embarrassed. This is an acquired taste. You know Robin tells me he came to love curry when he was in India," Ezra said. "Curry is actually a mixture of spices."

"He can eat what you are eating?" Elizabeth asked.

"Oh yes. Told me he loves it so hot that it makes you sweat," Ezra said. "We should bring him and Marie here, if the thought of returning to this table doesn't horrify you."

"I find this fascinating. I had no idea. You write a language in the opposite direction, left to right. You dine on the floor and share dishes. You eat everything with a spoon or with bread. We must bring them here," Elizabeth said with excitement.

He was told something in Turkish that made the table laugh again.

"You're blushing. That must have been good," Beth said. "What did they say?"

"The spicy curry will help us make babies," Ezra said.

She pushed the bowl toward him. "Well, keep eating it. Go on."

Everyone laughed.

"Have this cheese after. It takes down the fire," Ezra offered. "It's goat cheese."

"Goat cheese? Goats have milk?"

"Of course they do. What else do baby goats feed on?"

That made her laugh. "I never thought of it that way. Why do they not eat beef or chicken?"

"Can't afford beef. Cattle don't survive in the arid climate where I come from. The chickens are eaten in the summer. They're used up by this time of year," Ezra explained.

"Nothing is salty. They do not like salt?"

"There is the belief that salt has poison or toxins in it," Ezra said. "Because in Turkey it just might. Oh and it is considered a sin not to eat everything on your plate. It is wasteful. So I'm going to help you with our plate."

They smiled at each other. "Wouldn't want to sin before our wedding."

"Wouldn't dream of it."

"What are the Turkish wedding traditions?" Beth asked.

"Well, we are doing one of them already. Gifting each other with gold, to start off with prosperity. Usually it's just a gold coin. But I gave you a gold painting and you are giving me a watch, right? And another tradition, the first one to step on the other's foot after the wedding vows will have the say in the marriage," Ezra explained.

"You're going to step on my foot at our wedding?" Beth asked.

He laughed and translated for the table, shaking his head. "Of course not. I don't want the say in our marriage."

"What else?"

"The bride wears red to symbolize purity," Ezra said. "Hence my red ascot."

"There's nothing pure about you," Elizabeth teased. "Red? How did that come to be the scarlet letter in western culture?"

Ezra laughed.

Before the end of the meal, a set of prayer beads was given to Ezra. It was a strand of dark seed beads and he put it on over his head, letting it come to rest among his western ascot and lapels. Another smaller set of red beads was given to Elizabeth. Ezra wrapped these about her left wrist. "These are red coral, probably from the coast of Greece," he explained. "Purity."

Elisabeth beamed with happiness. "Will you thank them for me? How do you say thank you in your language?"

"Tesekkur ederim. Or Sagol," Ezra said. "Thank you or Thanks. You can say it. Sagol."

"Sagol," Elizabeth said.

Their companions at the table enjoyed that very much.

They all enjoyed dessert of baklava and rice pudding with their Turkish coffee.

Before leaving the restaurant, Ezra paid for the entire table in a demonstration of missing his family and homeland. He and Elizabeth strolled casually back to their waiting carriage. She climbed inside and when Ezra joined her she blurted out, "Oh I do hope your family will come to visit. Or we must take a diversion from Europe to visit them in Ankara."

He shook his head. "We can't visit there. There is war with Greece. Greece lays in between Europe and Turkey. With that blonde hair you wouldn't be safe. Kind of like why we don't take the name Arikan. But don't worry, if my letter reaches my family, I will send money for passage to America for whoever wants to come."

"Wait. Wait. What?" Ezra followed Jonas into the kitchen and there he found most of the maids and cooks gathered. "How many of you do not want to work here after the wedding?"

Few of them met eyes with him while others had their heads down.

"I can't tell you how much this hurts me," Ezra said. "Why don't you want to work for me? I...I don't want to change anything here. Except, except that I did tell Jonas that I want all of you to be paid more and get a day off every week. Is that so terrible?"

"Sir, what you overheard was...taken out of context," the chef said.

"What are you afraid of?" Ezra held onto the back of a chair.

When no one responded, Jonas explained, "I have heard some discussion around how things may change, that there are some concerns regarding what they have heard about artists."

The tilt of Ezra's head changed. "What about artists? Jonas, whatever it is tell me and I will fix it."

Jonas shook his head.

The chef finally spoke up, "Artists have a reputation for being very libertine, sir."

"Libertine?" Ezra repeated. "You don't like it that I'm queer?"

Some of them gasped.

"Hey, it is what it is. Elizabeth doesn't seem to mind. And I'm giving that up when I marry her," Ezra explained. "So you have no reason to fear libertine activities in this house. I paint pictures in that room and that's all. Mostly I will paint at the gallery anyway."

"And there...there will not be drunken behaviors in the house from other artist friends? Sir?" The chef questioned. "Or other behaviors?"

"You don't want my friends here?" Ezra asked. "Or many of you are planning to quit?"

"I...I don't think we were taking it that far," the baker spoke up.

"Well it should please you to learn that two of my good friends were very angry with me for marrying Elizabeth. They stole $300 from me and split to Boston. Or to anywhere and just told me Boston so that I can't ever find them." Ezra lowered his eyes. "Soon Robin will return to Canterbury and the only friend I will have left will be Adam. You know Adam. You can't have a problem with him, can you? So that should please you."

The chef and the baker lowered their eyes.

"You know," Ezra began and paused to wipe his eyes. "I am not rich. I am a poor painter from Ottoman Turkey. I have cut fish for a living. I have cleaned chimneys. I have repaired fences. I laid cobblestones until my hands bled and my back ached. I have had every sickness you can get between Turkey and here. I have enough trouble facing Beth's wealthy friends without feeling looked down on like an insect. I never imagined this from you."

That had two of the younger maids in tears.

"Do you wish us to go after the wedding? We are needed until then," the chef said.

"You are needed after then," Ezra said. "I don't want any of you to go because of me."

"Sorry, sir," the baker said.

Ezra nodded sadly. "How many of you still want to leave?"

Jonas stepped around the table, toward him. "None of them, Mr. August. You have changed their opinions. I am terribly sorry that you overheard any of that."

"Have a seat. Cup of tea, sir?" One of the older maids suggested. She pulled out a chair for him.

"Everybody just sit down. Would you? What are you afraid of? I'm friendly enough," Ezra said.

"We need someone to taste the pastries," the baker added. "Would you mind, sir? I tried to make this for the first time. I don't know if it can pass for it or not. Tried to make baklava."

"You made baklava for my wedding?"

The baker moved a tray of the pastry onto the table. "Tried to, sir."

Ezra sat down. He reached forward and selected a piece of baklava, already seeing that it was the Greek version and not Turkish. But he tasted it.

"What do you think? How may I improve on the next batch?" the baker asked.

"Pistachios. It's very good. The nuts that should be inside are pistachios, if you can find them. The honey in this is really good though," Ezra said.

"Pistachios? I didn't think of that. Thank you, sir," the baker said. "What do you think of almonds?"

"Better than walnuts," Ezra told him.

"Thank you."

"Jonas knows a market where you can find pistachios. Right Jonas? Near that Middle Eastern restaurant we went to yesterday?" Ezra said.

"Oh yes. I can find my way back there," Jonas said. "Just follow the spire of that church."

"But you don't have to worry about that for the wedding. This is wonderful," Ezra said. "Very thoughtful. I appreciate it."

"I understand you are not moving into the master suite after the wedding." The older maid sat down across from Ezra at the table and selected a piece of baklava for herself. "Why is that?"

"Do not ask him that," Jonas scolded.

"Just trying to understand where we are to bring his belongings," she said.

"No offence to those of you who are cleaning and caring for rooms of this house, but what did I tell you Jonas the room reminds me of?" Ezra said. "Mausoleum for the Pope?"

"To die in, yes," Jonas added, to much laughter.

"You want to know the truth? There is more to my problem with that room," Ezra said. "I am a second husband in that room."

"Technically you are a second husband in every room," Jonas told him.

"Yeah but how many rooms do you think they did it in?" Ezra asked.

The staff burst out laughing.

"Come on. I'm sure a young man like yourself can hold up to the comparison," the older maid said with a smirk. "Or keep it up, as it were."

Ezra laughed then. "I will do my best. But not in that room. Not just yet."

"I found the French furniture you are wanting for that room. Adam's butler Hobson told me where to find it. He went looking for new furniture when he moved into his estate," Jonas said.

"Great. I'll go there with Adam to pick it out." Ezra ate another piece of dessert. "No more questioning my virility."

"What?" Elizabeth pushed the kitchen door open.

The staff burst out laughing and hurried away to get back to their work.

Ezra blushed and looked up at her. "Baklava, darling?"

Ezra held hands with Elizabeth and walked into the chambers of her church.

"Come in. Come in, my bride and groom," he said. "Reverend Astor. Mrs. Elizabeth Miller I have known since she was a little girl. And you, young man, I have not met before."

"Ezra August, Reverend." Ezra shook his hand.

"Please both of you sit down. We will have a talk," the elderly reverend said. "Mrs. Miller, how long was your period of mourning? It was a year was it not?"

"Yes. A year already," Elizabeth said.

"And so you are to be married again. I am pleased that you have chosen a man closer to your own age. Mr. August, you are not offended at all that your bride was married once before?"

"Ah, no, sir. I am only sorry for her loss," Ezra said.

"How did you find your bride then?"

"Oh. Um, she bought one of my paintings. I'm an artist. And it turned out that she knew my best friend very well," Ezra explained. "She's the most beautiful thing I ever saw."

"And through this best friend, you courted?" he asked.

"You could say that, yes," Ezra said.

"And what makes you want to marry this young man?"

"Well, he is very brave. He's an amazing artist. He is wonderful with children," Elizabeth said.

"Children? Are you planning to have children in this marriage?"

"If we are so fortunate, yes," Ezra said.

"These best friends, will they stand up for you?"

"Yes. Adam will stand up for me and his wife Marie will be her maid of honor," Ezra said. "In fact, we would like to as a favor. Could we have Adam's wife and Marie's husband also stand up for us?"

"We have all been through so much together and are such great friends. It would not seem right to have Robin and Zoey sit in the pews," Elizabeth said.

"Very well. Very well then." The reverend looked seriously at Elizabeth. "Elizabeth, are you prepared to honor and obey a new husband now?"

"I am, yes. I do honor him," she said.

"And you will obey him?"

"I'm not big on the whole obey me part," Ezra said.

"Well as the husband you must be the authority, young man. She is expecting that. You must cherish and protect your wife. You must care for her. And you must be faithful to her."

"I will, yes." Ezra nodded.

"Very well. Do you have any questions for me? I am a married man myself. There is nothing you cannot ask me," the reverend said. "I just want to be certain, young man, that you understand your bride has been married once before. I would have you be prepared for your wedding night."

Elizabeth gripped Ezra's hand.

Ezra inhaled deeply. "I am very aware that Elizabeth was a widow when I met her."

"And as such, in her previous marriage there were no children. Are you prepared that there is the possibility that there will be no children in this marriage either, and you must still keep your vows to honor and cherish her always?"

Elizabeth nearly dug her nails into Ezra's palm.

He winced. "Yes sir. I will love her no matter what, until we are two old oak trees with intertwined roots and branches."

She looked at him.

"Very lovely, young man. All right then. Bring your two couples to stand up for you and I will marry you tomorrow."

Ezra and Elizabeth walked out of the chambers behind the altar and wandered out into the chapel, holding hands. They went out among the pews and looked back toward where they would be married the next day. She whispered to him, "Two old oak trees?"

"Would you rather I assured him that I have already been banging your headboard into the wall?"

"Don't you speak like that. Not in here." Elizabeth grabbed onto his lapels and whispered up to him. "Are you certain you are not disappointed that I was not a virgin?"

"Are you certain you were not disappointed that I was?" Ezra grinned. "I almost fainted...."

She laughed. "Let's go tell Robin and Zoey that they're in the wedding too."

Elizabeth's house was a frenzy of preparations for festivities of the following day. The ballroom was being decorated. Ezra's musician friends were practicing on the piano and violins. The cooks and bakers were working frantically here and at Adam's house to prepare a banquet. The dining room and the parlors were being set with tables and chairs all in preparation for fifty guests.

That night Ezra went home with Adam and they sat down alone in the sitting area of Ezra's room upstairs.

"The reverend made her promise to obey me, made me promise to be faithful," Ezra was telling him. "I thought she'd dig her nails clean through my hand when the reverend tried to explain to me not to be disappointed on our wedding night that she was deflowered already."

"Seriously?" Adam gasped.

Ezra showed his hand to him, and the marks of her nails were still there. "Kept me from blurting out that I was deflowered by a boy in my father's attic."

"I've never been more grateful to have been married in Dutch, then. I didn't get that counsel. Did you tell him you're Muslim?"

"No. You think I'd tell him I was raised that all Christians and Jews are out to kill us?" Ezra sat back and closed his eyes. "It's just that I'm finally happy with Beth and you and Robin. But all my artist friends are lost to me."

"Maybe they will come around," Adam said softly.

"I hope so," Ezra whispered.

"I think Albert and Pierre left because you came between them. Not because of Elizabeth."

Ezra nodded "In part."

Adam put a hand on his shoulder and rubbed his jacket beneath the collar. "Don't be sad. You can be so happy tomorrow and for the rest of your life. You'll be all right now. You'll be safe and Elizabeth will have the children she always wanted."

Ezra nodded, but he still so rarely was not smiling.

Adam leaned up against him, shoulder to shoulder with him. "You want a drink?"

Ezra shook his head.

"Do you mind if I do?"

"Go ahead."

Adam got up and went to the bottle of brandy on the nightstand. He poured two snifters of it. "When I'm feeling sad or unsure at all, I like to drink what he would. It feels something like…being closer to him." He took his seat again close beside Ezra on the sofa.

Ezra accepted the brandy. "You know he's very sorry that he couldn't be with you like you wanted."

Adam considered that, as he sipped Robin's brand of brandy. "Are you afraid of never being with a boy again?"

"A little," Ezra whispered. "We both know there is no chance with Robin. And it's all right. He's straight. That's all." He brightened enough to almost smile. "His only flaw."

"Nobody's perfect." Adam set his hand down on Ezra's thigh.

After a while, Ezra put his hand down on Adam's. They didn't look at each other as they sipped their brandy. Ezra linked fingers with him.

"Can I ask you something?" Adam whispered.

"Sure. Anything."

"Do you think that at some point in the future if one of us..." Adam's voice trailed away. The hand with the brandy snifter tried to wipe his eyes. He tried to pull his hand back from Ezra's.

Ezra let his hand go and turned to face him, laying his arm around him on the back of the sofa. "I love you, Adam. I will never turn you down. We just have to keep it...very secret."

"Insanely secret," Adam said.

"Super double insanely secret. So secret even we aren't sure it happened," Ezra said.

That made Adam laugh out loud.

Ezra lowered his chin, smiling. "You're a good friend, Adam."

"You're the best, Ezra."

"Why are you crying? Everything all right with Zoey?" Ezra whispered.

Adam nodded. "I'm just scared about this baby coming. I'm just scared. And I can't let on with her that I am. I have to be so confident for her. You know?"

"She'll be all right. There's nothing to babies. They're easy," Ezra said. "I dropped my little brother Elijah. He was just fine. Practically bounced."

Adam laughed. "That's not funny."

"I gave all this cough tonic to Caleb because he would not stop screaming. About a half hour later, he went to sleep just fine," Ezra went on. "So did the whole family."

Adam lowered his chin, smiling.

Ezra reclined back, stretching his legs out toward the fireplace. "Thank you for everything. I can't tell you what a relief it was just to have the new gallery and know where I'm sleeping every night."

"I think with your talent you would have gotten there on your own anyway," Adam said.

"What are you going to paint now?" Ezra asked him.

"I don't know. I had to paint Robin and I did," Adam said. "I might be done with it."

"I hope not. You are great at it."

"But you are incredible. You have to keep painting," Adam said. "I can't wait to see your Robin paintings."

Adam had given Ezra a haircut, layering all of his black locks to curl and come down to just the top of his shoulders in the front and a little bit longer in the back. He was shaven very neatly with trimmed sideburns down to his jaw and he kept that little touch of facial hair beneath his chin.

Ezra's tuxedo was black with shiny satin lapels. His white shirt had crisp high collars with pearl buttons. His vest and ascot matched in an iridescent material reminiscent of peacock feathers. It had an essence of purple, green and red to it. And yet without sunlight on it, from a distance, it would look almost black.

Beneath the shirt was Adam's gift to him, a silk undershirt and underwear, luminous and with pearl buttons, incredibly comfortable.

And he wore Robin's cross about his neck, beneath it all.

Ezra, Adam, and Robin arrived at the cathedral together and looked inside to see the guests arriving. The chapel was highly decorated with floral arrangements on the end of each pew, candlesticks everywhere, a white drape down the aisle leading up to the altar where huge floral arrangements surrounded.

Adam drew the groom and Robin back into a side hall and shut the door. "I have a surprise for you, Ez. Many of your friends are here, just not Pierre and Albert. I'm sorry about them. But I did find Marco and he brought a whole bunch of your artist friends today. He also brought your musician friends. They've been practicing with the orchestra Elizabeth hired for the whole week. They'll all be playing tonight at the party."

"Adam, that's all fantastic. How did you pull all that off?" Ezra said. "Guys, I'm so nervous."

"Nothing to be nervous about. You look great," Adam told him. "You say I will."

"I brought you this." Robin pulled a flask from his inside pocket. "A present for you."

Ezra looked at the beautiful silver VOC flask. "I love it. Thank you, Robin."

"It's full, Ezra," Robin added. "Hint. Hint."

"Oh shit." Ezra unscrewed the cap and drank a gulp of Robin's brandy.

"Good thinking," Adam said.

Ezra coughed after and before taking another gulp said, "You do know everything." He passed it to Adam next.

Adam downed a shot. He passed it to Robin.

"Of course." Robin drank also. "I've been married three times and twice to Marie. Drunk every time."

There was a knock on the door and then it opened. Zoey looked in. "Oh Robin. Come quick. Marie got sick."

Robin passed the flask back to Ezra and hurried to the door. Zoey drew him away.

That left Ezra and Adam to wait, and pace, and wait. Someone from the church informed them that it was almost time. And Robin returned just in time to join them.

"Marie's fine. She had some cold water and laid down in the back some place for a bit. She should make it through the ceremony," Robin reported. "How about you, kid? You look like a good vomit would suit you as well."

Ezra let out a long breath and just stared up at the ceiling.

"He's fine. You're fine." Adam patted Ezra on the chest.

"Don't mention vomit. I haven't vomited in almost ten years and I'm really going for the record," Ezra said.

Robin smiled and affirmed a hand on Ezra's shoulder. "Change your first diaper, my friend."

Elizabeth wrapped her hands about Ezra's forearm, "Darling, I think you should come with me."

Ezra slid a hand onto the lower back of her wedding gown. "What is it? Something wrong?"

"No. I have a wonderful gift for you." Beth drew Ezra along the side of the ballroom, greeting guests as they went. Robin was dancing with Adam's sister. Adam was dancing with his cousin Erika.

"Are Zoey and Marie all right?" Ezra asked as he hurried beside her.

"Yes. They are having more dessert, I believe. Over there. See?" Beth drew him into the hallway.

And there Ezra saw Albert and Pierre at the entry hall, waiting with Jonas. Pierre was weeping.

Ezra went to them immediately.

Beth hurried beside him.

Albert stepped forward to give Ezra a quick hug and pat on the back.

"You're here. I'm so glad you're all right," Ezra said. "Pierre, what happened? Are you okay?"

"We saw your wedding. It was so beautiful," Pierre said. "I'm so sorry, Ezra. We were in the back."

"It's all right. Everything's fine." Ezra hugged Pierre as well.

Albert joined hands with Elizabeth. "Congratulations Mrs. August. That's what he's using, isn't it? August?"

"Yes. I'm so glad you came. Please do come in," Elizabeth told him.

Pierre tried to put a sack of coins and money into Ezra's hands. "I'm so sorry. It's not all of it."

"No. Keep it. Keep it, Pierre." Ezra tucked the sack back into Pierre's pocket. "I don't care about that. I just want to know you two will be okay."

"It's just so hard to see you get married," Pierre admitted. "I'm so sorry, Mrs. August. It's just so hard."

Elizabeth grabbed Pierre's hand. "Come and have a seat in the dining room. Have some supper and drinks. Stay on in one of the guest rooms."

"Adam gave us a room," Albert said. "We're staying there, but thank you. We don't want to impose on your family."

"Ezra? Elizabeth? You're wanted in the ball room," Adam called.

"Stay? Are you staying?" Ezra asked his friends. "Marco is in there I think."

"We will go join Marco. Then, let us see you dance with your wife," Albert said.

Elizabeth grabbed hands with Jonas and told him, "Thank you, Mr. Smith. You found them!"

Pierre looked so much like he needed to be consoled. He just walked toward the dining room with Albert, at arm's length from him. Arm's length and yet miles apart.

Ezra wiped his eyes. He kissed Elizabeth on the forehead. "Thank you. I know it is not easy for you either."

"You're my husband now. Having your friends here means everything to us, like having my cousins here and my best friends. Let us dance some more." Elizabeth looked up at him. "Unless I hurt your foot when I stomped on it."

Ezra found on his side of the bed a luxurious red satin oriental robe. He held it up to examine embroidered birds and flowers. The inside lining of the collar was black fur. The inside lining of the whole robe was black satin. And there was gold thread in the cuffs and buttonholes.

"Do you like it?" Elizabeth asked.

"This is magnificent. This is for me? I absolutely love it," Ezra enthused.

"Yes, my husband. I have many gifts for you, if you don't mind," Elizabeth said. "I can't wait to show you this one. What do you think of this?" She set a hat box down on the bed.

Ezra gently laid the robe down on a chair and then reached for the hat box.

"You don't mind?" she asked.

"No. You wish to give me things? Dress me up like a doll? I'm all for it."
He undid the ribbon and raised the top off. Inside it looked like a fur
animal curled up. But he pulled out instead, a fur hat. And he smiled
broadly. He turned it and decided which way to wear it, and placed it on
top of his head, with a slight tilt.

"Oh I love it!" Elizabeth exclaimed.

He laughed and set down the hat. "I love it too. I look like a Russian or
an Armenian. I have something for you. Hold on." He pulled the cord for
the bell in the kitchen to ring. "Just wait a minute."

When there was a knock at the door, Ezra opened it and brought in a
box of similar size to the hat box. He closed the door and carried the box
toward Elizabeth when the box made a little whimper.

"Wait. What is that?" She bounced with delight.

"Shhhh," Ezra said to the box. And then it yipped.

"Ezra?"

He held out the box. "Open it but be really careful it doesn't fly out."

"What?" She withdrew her hands.

He laughed.

"There's something alive in there," she said.

"There had better be. Or else I have serious complaints about the
kitchen staff right now," Ezra said.

Beth stepped closer and lifted the lid of the box. Inside was a small King
Charles Spaniel puppy. "Ohhh. Oh the darling thing." She reached in and
picked up the puppy, taking it up beneath her chin to cuddle.

"I'm told this is a boy. What will you name him?" Ezra glanced into and
then set down the box. "He didn't pee in there."

"Oh, Ezra. Is he really mine?"

"All yours, darling. The gift of unconditional love," he said.

"Oh he is a boy puppy. Oh I don't know what to name him yet."

"Same way you checked my sex, to be honest."

Elizabeth brought the puppy to him and kissed him on the mouth. "I love you. And I love this baby."

"You can practice mothering, I thought. And I guess I will practice house breaking a dog," Ezra said. "I wanted a great big dog but I figured you would like a little guy you can carry around in a basket."

"I do. I really do!"

"All right." Ezra looked out into the hall again and pulled in the basket with the dog bed in it. There were several dog toys in there as well.

"Where do we keep him?"

"Where do we keep him? He's a puppy," Ezra said. "He can sleep with you or put him in this big basket he can't get out of yet. And I'll have to take him outside to, you know, do what dogs do outside, several times a day. Although I do think there are several maids who would love to take turns walking him, and cuddling him."

"You gave me a pre-cuddled dog?" Elizabeth said.

Ezra looked at her.

"Joke, Ezra. Breathe." Elizabeth laughed.

Ezra held his hand to his heart. "Sorry. A lot of pressure on me today. My two jobs, and I only had two. One job was to stand up there and say I will. The other job was to find you the perfect gift…."

"And you did. You absolutely did. I love you and I really love this baby puppy." Elizabeth hugged him.

"I love you so."

Ezra August with long hair

363 The Dutchman 3, Three Musketeers   By Susan Eddy

Chapter Eighteen   Canterbury

Just over a year had passed and the warmth of mid-May brought a shiny black brougham to a stop in front of the country store. The driver climbed down and opened the carriage door. "I need some directions. I believe we are in Canterbury. I'm not exactly sure though."

"Let me look." A gentleman stepped out, carrying a small blonde dog. He set the small dog down on the ground and retained a leash in his hand as he lit a cigarette from a lantern on the side of the carriage.

A man crossed the street toward them.

"An officer of the law. How lucky I am to find you, sir. I am on my way to find a Mr. Robin Van der Kellen. He lives not far from here, I believe," the driver Aaron said. "Are we in Canterbury?"

Poole was noticing the black-haired gentleman with the tiny fluffy dog. The suit was masculine enough, but the shirt he wore had lace collar and cuffs. The vest was paisley and the ascot was purple silk. There was a gold chain about his ascot and gold pocket watch chained to his gold buttons. The hand holding the cigarette had a diamond ring on it, like a woman's wedding ring. "What is your business with Van der Kellen?"

The carriage door opened and a blonde woman stepped out, assisted out by the man. "Michael, it's Elizabeth."

"Ohhhh." Poole recognized her immediately, but he was still trying to understand the man with the dog. "You're her driver. And who is..."

"Yes. Could you be so kind as to point me toward the right road?"

"I'll do better than that. I'll get my horse and lead you there. You don't even know where you are." Poole walked toward Elizabeth.

She wrapped her arm about the gentleman's.

Poole observed the little dog relieving itself beside the carriage wheel. "Pull that little one out of there. If that carriage moves, it's dead meat."

Ezra turned and drew the dog beside him. He handed the leash to Elizabeth and extended that hand to the constable. "Ezra August, constable. I've heard all about you." He smirked mischievously.

Poole shook his hand. "Michael Poole. How are you, Elizabeth Miller?"

"It's Elizabeth August now, Michael. This is my husband, Ezra." She beamed.

"So this is Canterbury? I presume?" Ezra glanced about. "What? Ten buildings?"

Poole set eyes on Ezra, looking him up and down. His shirt had ruffles of lace at the collar. "So you're the queer artist who married the rich widow."

Ezra smirked. "Whoa, I can see Robin almost strangling you when he first met you. I can see it now."

The sound of a baby crying inside the carriage distracted them all.

Elizabeth turned toward the open door. "Catherine, is she all right?"

"Yes, mum. Just hungry I think."

"Excuse me. I'd better get inside. You'll lead us toward Robin and Marie's?" She looked at Michael.

"I'll get my horse. Don't forget your mutt, sir. Pick it up before something eats it and wait right there."

"With bated breath, constable." Ezra puffed on his cigarette. The breeze tossed his long black locks and his purple silk scarf.

"Hand me Prince Andrew." Elizabeth climbed back into the carriage.

Ezra picked up the golden King Charles Spaniel and set him inside the carriage. "Darling, I've got to see this town."

"What for?" Elizabeth asked from inside. "There's nothing to see."

"Robin's hometown. Seriously." Ezra smoked. "What a sight for sore eyes he would be walking down this street."

Aaron climbed up into the driver's seat.

Ezra looked down the road at the blacksmith, the livery, the tavern, and the market right beside him. There was the small chapel Robin and Marie got married. He very casually puffed on his tobacco cigarette. He pictured Robin walking into this small tavern.

When Poole rode up, he circled and pulled in beside the driver. "Let's have all the ladies inside, shall we?"

Ezra put his hand on his hip and opened the carriage door. "I'm going to ride up top, darling. I want to see the landscape at sunset." Ezra put out his smoke and climbed up beside the driver.

"Move out. Move out now. Good boys," Aaron called out.

Ezra held on and watched Constable Poole riding ahead of them as they rolled out of town, going North.

Aaron whispered to Ezra, "You hate him, right?"

"I don't give him a thought, really." Ezra shrugged. "You just don't let on that you're anything but straight and keep an eye out for a man named Jasper. Don't get involved with him. Remember I said he was cruel to Adam."

"I remember. I can still apprentice with your painting, can't I?"

"Of course. I have to paint Robin and his family so I will need a canvas prepared after we settle in." Ezra lit another cigarette off the carriage lamp. "I never saw the American countryside. Bucolic, isn't it? Imagine the magnificent Van der Kellen chopping wood, tending horses, stacking hay. And still he was no doubt the most elegant man around."

"Bucolic… I can't wait to meet your Robin."

"Adam's Robin."

The Van der Kellen's home with the stone arch that read "Lodewijk" opened up with a red wooden home on the right, and a stone mansion on the left. A series of barns lined the hilltop behind them.

Poole brought them past a fountain and garden of tulips toward the grand entrance of the stone mansion. The front double doors burst open and Marie stood there. She had one baby on her hip and a small three-year-old clinging to her skirt. She hurried down to the carriage level.

Behind her came Marta to collect the children and Robin Van der Kellen himself in a plain black riding pants and jacket. It was the plainest Ezra had ever seen him.

Ezra looked down on him from the top of the carriage, leaned his elbows on his knees and just grinned.

"Welcome to Canterbury, D'Artagnan," Robin called.

"Good to see you again, Aramis. Living rustically, I see," Ezra replied.

"How is Athos?" Robin asked.

"He's doing well. His son is a year already." Ezra began to climb down.

Aaron climbed down to open the door for Elizabeth.

All of Robin's staff arrived to help with babies and baggage alike. Luke, the stockman came from the barn to tend the horses.

Elizabeth stepped out to embrace Marie warmly. "Your son looks just like Robin. And little Frida just like you, darling."

"Oh let me see your child. What did you have?" Marie asked her. "You didn't say in your letter. I've been dying to know."

"I couldn't decide so I had one of each. You see? A boy just like Ezra and a girl just like Ezra." Elizabeth laughed. "Nobody with blonde hair but the dog."

Ezra shook hands and embraced Robin. He gave Robin a kiss on both cheeks and Robin did the same to him in the Dutch tradition, something that made Ezra smile broadly, but made the stockmen stand there in shock.

"Safe travels, I hope?" Robin asked.

"Uneventful until meeting the constable," Ezra remarked. "I expected no less from him of course."

"Well good then. Wouldn't want to disappoint you." Robin patted him hard on the back.

Ezra laughed. He went to pick up his son while the nanny carried the baby girl out of the carriage. And Elizabeth carried the dog.

They were all shown inside the mansion and to the parlor. Marta gushed over the twin babies. June organized the bringing in of all the luggage.

"That one, keep that trunk downstairs. It's painting supplies," Ezra pointed out.

"Painting supplies?" June stammered.

"He's an artist. He's going to paint our portraits. Right, Ezra?" Robin explained.

"Absolutely. My driver, Aaron, is also an apprentice of mine. He's going to help me. Just give him a room in the servants' quarters," Ezra said. "And the same for Catherine, our nanny."

"Elizabeth, you remember Miles Champagne and Jasper Schaffer," Robin introduced. "Miles and Jasper, this is Ezra August."

"Mr. August." Miles extended a hand to him.

"Mr. Champagne. A pleasure." Ezra shook hands. "And Jasper. Heard all about you fellows from Adam Hudson."

Jasper shook his hand too. "How is Adam? A father too, I heard."

"Yes. He's got a son. Cutest little thing," Ezra said. "Has Adam's perfect little nose."

"I can't believe you traveled with twins. And you only just had them," Marie drew Elizabeth off to sit down with her in the parlor.

"Imagine our reverend's shock when he had to baptize two of them, after warning Ezra that there were no children in my first marriage," Elizabeth laughed. "Here we are, two for the price of one."

"Do twins run in your family?"

"No and not in his either," Elizabeth said. "Just lucky I guess. Although feeding them both is killing me."

Marie leaned in and whispered to her, "Perhaps I can help. I have more than enough."

"Is that possible?"

"Yes, and it's quite proper I hear. Wait until you meet Mrs. Poole. She's a midwife. I learn things from her," Marie whispered. "How is Ezra holding up?"

"Horny as hell. Like any man," Elizabeth complained.

Marie burst out laughing.

"I haven't let him yet but it's only been a month. I was told to wait," Beth whispered.

"To wait how long?" Marie asked.

"Until I'm ready," she whispered.

"Oh. Oh my. He is having trouble with patience."

"No. He's just hard all the time," Elizabeth said. "As if breathing alone does it."

"Oh my goodness. Well, he is young," Marie said. "He's not now, is he?"

"Not after Poole called him queer. No."

Trunks were being brought into the building and taken to guest rooms upstairs. Ezra would be established in a room beside Elizabeth and across the hall from Miles and Jasper's rooms.

Ezra was escorted onto the terrace where Miles offered him a lit candle and a cigarette. Ezra accepted and puffed as he lit the cigarette. Then Miles lit his own. "Marie does not want any smoking inside the new home. So outside, if you don't mind it."

"Thank you." Ezra puffed on the cigarette. "Whatever the lady wants."

Robin put a hand on Ezra's back as he joined them. "How are you holding up, daddy?"

"Ah, fine if you don't mind not sleeping at all in the last month." Ezra closed his eyes as he smoked.

"You've got two babies. You need help, Ezra. Plenty of women in this house to care for the children. We are going to get you some sleep while you're here," Robin said.

"You're going to convince my wife to let me sleep in the carriage?" Ezra droned in his raspy deep voice.

"I can give you a room in the old house." Robin pointed at the red wooden home across the roundabout drive. "Try your room upstairs but if that is not quiet enough we'll give you a room in the old house. One night. You will be amazed how much better you feel after just one solid night's sleep."

"Right now, I can't even remember what a solid night's sleep is."

"I will have Marie talk to Elizabeth. How much are they crying?" Robin said.

Ezra laughed. "You're about to find out. As soon as one stops the other starts. She can't nurse two at the same time."

"Get that midwife of Poole's out here. Maybe she can help. Or we'll have to house all men in the old house," Miles suggested.

"Poole, come here," Robin called. "We need your wife's help with all these babies."

"Oh, nothing would please her more." Michael paused in front of the men, looking at Ezra from head to toe. "So I can see why Elizabeth married this one. He looks like her type."

"He does, yes," Robin agreed.

"I'm so tired, I don't give a fuck what that means," Ezra said.

The men laughed.

"All right. We're going to fix you up." Robin patted Ezra on the back. "What do you need? They're putting supper on the table. What else?"

"A good stiff…" Ezra puffed on his cigarette. "Drink."

"Good Lord. Didn't know where he was going with that," Poole remarked.

Even Ezra burst out laughing. "You go ahead and worry."

"Oh trust me, Ezra does tend to say whatever is on his mind," Robin said.

They sat down all about Robin and Marie's grand dining table in the new marble dining room. "This is Aaron Hayes. He drives my carriage but he's also an apprentice artist. He's going to help me get some portraits started," Ezra announced.

"Welcome Aaron. I am Robin. This is my wife, Marie. That is Constable Poole. He led you from town of course. This is Miles Champagne and Jasper Schaffer. They run my horse business. And then we have June, house manager. Marta and Louise house maids. The chef out there is Sandy. Outside there are also some stockmen, Luke, Henry, and Ted."

The first course was served by Louise and Sandy.

Across the dinner table, Michael Poole questioned, "Do you carry a gun at all when you travel, Ezra?"

"No. Don't own any guns," Ezra said.

"You may want to rethink that. Your wife wears a lot of gold. And so do you," Poole said.

Ezra looked down at his gold necklace and gold pocket watch.

"He has never traveled wealthy before," Robin spoke up. "Before they return home, we can have a talk with them about traveling safely. You remember, Elizabeth, that you and I had a talk about that on the train."

"I remember you telling me to keep jewels in my trunk," Elizabeth said. "I don't recall you telling me not to wear gold."

Ezra looked at her beside him. "All right. I will talk to Robin and Michael about that later."

"You taught Adam how to shoot. Are you planning to teach Ezra?" Michael asked.

"Not necessarily. Anyway, we will take that subject up on another day. Not when our guests are so tired and have just arrived," Robin said. "All right, Michael?"

"Yes, sure," Poole agreed. "I'll bring Alice out here tomorrow to stay over for a bit."

"Thank you, Michael," Marie said.

"After my confinement for so long I just couldn't wait to get out of the house. The travel wasn't that bad. We just were not expecting twins until about a month before they were born," Elizabeth said. "Thank goodness I brought Catherine along. She was so helpful on the train. We had her in one cabin or else her and I in one and Ezra beside us in the next cabin. I'm pretty used to not sleeping more than a couple hours at a time as I have been that way for months now. I'm afraid for Ezra, this is so difficult." She laid her hand on her husband's arm.

"All part of being a new father. It will pass though," Robin said.

"Ezra, how is Adam handling it?" Marie asked. "How is Zoey?"

"Zoey is great. Adam is better than I thought. I mean, I love children, always have. Probably because I never grew up myself," Ezra said. "I don't think Adam was ever around babies or children though. It was a whole thing just to teach him how to pick up a baby. And his right arm is still weak, so he has to keep that in mind."

Elizabeth and Marie talked mostly. Ezra was observed by the men and the women for that matter. The delicate way he held his wine glass was offset by the fact that he used the same spoon for everything. He even spread butter on his biscuit with the spoon. The rest of the silverware went ignored beside his plate. It wasn't that he wasn't neat and delicate when he ate, because he was. He just used that spoon and a piece of biscuit to gather peas or mashed potatoes.

After dinner, Ezra presented Robin with a crate of fine scotch. Robin pulled out a bottle to marvel over it. "Where did you find this? You can't purchase this in New York."

"I have my connections in the lesser-known sectors of New York city, my friend," Ezra said. "That came by way of a Canadian importer to a Turkish grocer I happened to meet at dinner one night when I took Beth to dine on middle Eastern food. Imports from Scotland or England here are not exactly legal but when they come by way of Newfoundland, nobody checks every case."

"Well, mind if we open one of these?" Robin said.

"They're yours now," Ezra said. "Don't ask me."

The gentlemen all moved out to the terrace again, on a warm May evening, to pour glasses of scotch and smoke outside away from the women and children.

"Was Elizabeth completely shocked by that dinner?" Robin handed the first scotch to Ezra. "The middle Eastern food?"

"Ahh, she hid it well enough. I mean, we all sat on cushions on the floor around a big table and passed dishes around. I explained to the host what the situation was. So Beth and I shared a plate and a bowl. But the rest of the table shared all together. I just warned her about food that was too spicy for her."

"A lot of it, I'd imagine." Robin handed glasses to Miles, Jasper, and Michael. He poured the last for himself. "Ezra hails from Ottoman Turkey, on the far east end of the Mediterranean Sea. Where he comes from they don't use silverware. They use bread to spoon up their meal. They sit on cushions on the floor like that. As I recall, fabrics were very bright colors, fabrics on the table and the clothing."

"Yes. It's all so black and white here," Ezra said.

"How long have you been in America?" Miles questioned.

"Ahhh, about six years now. I studied art in Paris for three years before coming to New York," Ezra said. "I'm actually finding the light out here in the country to be so amazing. I mean, look at the sunset over these fields. The air is clearer. Look at the colors in the mist out there."

"Something only an artist would notice," Jasper remarked.

"What does an artist do? You make portraits and such?" Miles asked.

"He did an amazing one of Elizabeth, absolutely astounding likeness," Robin said. "He taught Adam how to paint."

"I did a few preliminary paintings of you, for Beth mostly. I couldn't bring any with me. Doesn't matter. I brought all the supplies to make the portrait of Robin and Marie and their family," Ezra said. "You just need to give me a place where I can make a bit of a mess and there is good light."

"Maybe the ballroom. Nobody's using it. I'll take you to have a look at it," Robin said. "You can use any room you want."

"Any room June agrees to," Miles remarked, just as a baby started to cry inside the house.

"That sounds like mine, actually," Robin said.

"I know," Miles said.

"Miles is a confirmed bachelor," Robin remarked.

"Or at the very least he's infertile," Jasper said, making them all laugh heartily. "But we know Ezra's got some fire power there. Twins."

"Excuse me," Marie said from the doorway.

The men laughed all the harder.

"I believe Elizabeth had the babies. Anyway, I came to see if Ezra was being looked after," Marie said.

"And you're sorry you did," Miles quipped.

"I am a bit. Yes," Marie admitted. "Ezra, darling, are you needing anything? Are they keeping you awake when you should be resting? Elizabeth has gone upstairs to lay down."

"I am well looked after, Marie. Merci beaucoup," Ezra said. "Thank you for looking after Beth. She has to be exhausted if I am. Did she want me to come right up?"

"No. Not that I know of," Marie said.

"Off the hook." Miles met eyes with Ezra across the porch.

"Barely. My leash is short. Oh damn. Where is Prince Andrew?" Ezra asked.

"Who?" Marie said.

"That dog of hers. That's his name," Ezra said.

"The dog went with her," Marie said.

The men laughed again.

"Thought that impressive breed of canine was yours," Poole said.

No one laughed harder than Ezra. He almost cried laughing. He had to wipe his eyes and say, "I gave that puppy to her as a wedding gift. Wanted to see if she could keep that alive before we had children."

"Well, you certainly can count on that dog for protection," Robin told him.

"Don't make fun of my dog. You have no idea what that little hand muff cost me." Ezra laughed.

"Your manhood," Miles suggested.

"Not when as he has twins," Jasper said.

"Hey, my manhood doesn't suffer at all when I'm holding that dog. It's if I lose it, my wife will castrate me. She has a boy and a girl from me. I've already been told my balls are just ornamentation at this point."

Robin walked Michael Poole out as he planned to ride home for the night. He looked back at the guys on the porch. Ezra was sprawled back with a scotch glass on his chest. Miles was refilling their glasses.

"I'll bring Alice out in the morning. You got a room she can stay in?"

"Oh sure. I could put you up in it tonight if you want," Robin said.

"Thanks. I'm all right to ride home. Plenty of moon light tonight. Anyway, you've got your hands full with three babies and a three-year-old in the house," Michael said. "So, Robin, he really did all that you said? Ran with you through the alleys and led you up ladders? Bullets flying. Hudson could escape out of the hospital safely?"

"Ezra? He's the one. Yes," Robin said. "What do you think of him?"

"Funny. Queer as hell. I didn't think I would say this, but I like him." Poole mounted his horse and reined it in beside Robin. "Let's see if he can really paint your picture."

Ezra went upstairs to find Elizabeth in tears, holding their daughter while Marie sat down with Ezra's son. Marie's back was to the door. She sat in Elizabeth's bedroom.

Beth held up her hand to Ezra. "Just wait right there. Shhh."

Ezra stood in the doorway. "What is wrong?" he whispered.

"Just stay there. Marie is nursing him," Beth whispered.

"He was just hungry," Marie whispered. "He's okay. Aren't you? You're a good baby."

Ezra leaned his forehead to the frame of the doorway and shut his eyes.

"You think I'm just not making enough?" Beth asked.

"We'll ask Alice tomorrow. I have more than enough for Liam. Let me try helping you for a while," Marie told her.

Ezra slid down the door frame to sit cross legged in the hallway, his back to the room. And he dropped his forehead into his hands.

When Robin came up the stairs, he stopped in his tracks. This is the way he found Ezra, weeping into his hands.

Elizabeth got up, her baby girl in her arms and she went to the door. "Ezra, it's okay. He's nursing now."

"What's wrong?" Robin asked softly, moving closer to them. He stooped down beside Ezra.

"It's so beautiful. I can't believe what Marie is doing for us," Ezra whispered.

"What is she doing?" Robin asked.

Elizabeth indicated for Robin to look inside. He could see Marie with a baby nursing from her. Clearly from the black hair on the baby, this was not Liam.

Robin smiled. He nodded and then tapped Ezra on the shoulder. "You should get some sleep. C'mon. Your room is right next door. The women have this under control." He helped Ezra to his feet and walked him to the next room.

Ezra sat down on the edge of an ebony four poster bed. He wiped his eyes while Robin moved an oil lamp from the table over to the nightstand beside the bed.

"It's warm enough, right? We can light the fireplace if you need it," Robin told him.

"It's warm enough. It's really wonderful. Thank you, Robin." Ezra wiped his eyes. He looked down at white linens on the bed and four down pillows just for him. "How many of us sleepin in here?"

That made Robin smile a bit, warmly. "You'll find everything you need in here. Your trunk is over there. They probably hung up your suits in the armoire. Pitcher and bowl on the stand. Get some sleep."

Ezra stood up and closed his hand around Robin's arm. "Hold on a minute." He turned his shoulder to Robin's so that he was facing behind the Dutchman. "Tell me. Is this taking food away from your own baby Liam?"

Robin turned and warmly laid his hand on Ezra's back. "I don't think so. Marie knows what she's doing. And Liam is starting to eat real food already. It's probably actually a really good thing that you came here now. Marie can help Beth with these twins of yours. Good night, Ezra."

Ezra nodded and sat down on the bed to pull off his boots.

Robin left him and closed the door. The whole house went quiet.

Chapter Nineteen   Marie's Gift

In the morning, Robin knocked on the same door. He knocked again and then opened it a bit. "Ezra, you okay buddy?" He looked in.

Behind him in the hallway, Jasper folded his arms.

Robin walked in.

Jasper could see around him, that Ezra rolled over in the bed, shirtless.

"Come on down to breakfast in a bit," Robin told him.

"What happened? Are the babies all right?" Ezra asked.

"Everybody's fine. Beth sent me to check on you." Robin turned back toward the door. "See you downstairs or keep sleeping if you need to."

"No, I'm coming. Thanks."

Robin walked out and shut the door. "Jasper, how are those two mares doing?"

"I'll check on them."

"Check on them now. Breakfast after," Robin said.

Ezra burst into the dining room, in simple black trousers, still pulling on a jacket over a white shirt. He found Elizabeth sitting with one baby in her arms. Beside her, Marta was holding the other baby. Pink blanket on one and blue on the other. Marie and Robin were sitting across from them with their children.

Ezra went straight to Elizabeth and embraced her from behind her chair, around her neck. "Are you okay? What happened last night? I'm so sorry."

"Everything is fine. They slept halfway through the night," Beth said, taking his kiss on the cheek. "Half the night."

"What?" Ezra stammered.

And just then Michael and Alice Poole entered. Michael set down a bag of hers. June met them to help with coats and the baggage.

Alice made her way to stand between Marta and Elizabeth. "Oh look at these darling twin babies. They're so sweet. Let me look at these angels."

Marta stood and handed the baby gently to Alice. She stepped aside then, toward June near the hallway.

"Oh they don't look like their father at all, do they?" Alice said. "Dark curly hair already."

Elizabeth grinned. "If I wasn't there, I wouldn't believe they were mine."

"Michael said you are having some troubles, they are crying every two hours," Alice said.

"Should I fetch the doctor?" Michael asked.

Ezra looked with worry from Michael to the midwife. He gripped and leaned on the back of Beth's chair, standing up behind her, rocking.

Alice was examining the baby girl, unwrapping her a bit. "They are small. But twins don't happen all that often. I've only seen one other set of twins born around here. Baby seems content now. What is happening?"

"I helped with the nursing last night and this morning," Marie said. "They finally slept well."

"Can we have a bit of privacy here? Except for the father. Except for both fathers. Everyone else, leave us for a few moments, please," Alice said.

Michael just nodded. "I'll take her bag upstairs. Show me which room."

"We'll take you up. Come along Marta," June said.

Alice looked up at Ezra. "Have a seat, daddy. You look like you're about to drop."

Ezra pulled out the other chair beside Beth, near Robin.

"You are blessed with twins. But feeding twins is not easy. I think you need help, Elizabeth. You need rest and more food yourself. And this is a case where we would bring in what we call a wet nurse. You are lucky to have a best friend right here, with more than enough to feed her own baby."

"It went really well, both times. I fed the boy last night and she fed the girl. We switched it this morning," Marie said. "She's tried cows' milk but they didn't tolerate it."

"No. They're too young for cows' milk," Alice said.

"But what about Liam?" Ezra asked in a shaky voice.

"Liam is fat and happy," Robin blurted out. "He's not missing out on any milk."

Marie and Alice laughed at that.

"Liam is starting to eat regular food. Marie is still able to nurse. It makes perfect sense for Marie to help with feeding these newborns," Alice said gently. "It is natural but not spoken about. This is why you have never heard of this. We do it behind the curtains. And this is how it has been done since time began."

Elizabeth teared up and then Ezra held onto her and put his head down behind her.

"Now, new father, Ezra, stop blaming yourself for giving her twins. New mother Elizabeth, stop blaming yourself for not making enough to nurse two babies. Two don't happen very often," Alice said gently. "You were very smart coming here. We can help you. Things are going to be a lot better now. These babies can put on some weight and they will start sleeping better. Elizabeth needs to rest and eat. Ezra, you need to sleep so that you can support your wife. You've been up all night worrying for far too long. Now, did you have breakfast?"

"We just all came down," Marie spoke up.

"Okay. Get everybody back in here and get some breakfast going. The new mom and dad need to eat a good meal. Then mom should go get some rest upstairs. We will take care of these little ones. What are their names?" Alice said.

Robin pushed his chair back. "I'll tell everyone to come back in and let the men come in for breakfast."

"Thank you, Robin," Marie said.

"Robin." Ezra bolted up and followed Robin from the room. He stood before him, unable to even stand up straight for the knot in his stomach.

Robin took him by the arm. "I know what you're going through. It's not that bad. Alice and Marie will help. So you just relax now and be strong for your wife."

Ezra folded into Robin's arms.

"Hey. It's all right." Robin embraced him. "You get something to eat. Get some coffee in you. See that your wife eats. She will feel more like eating if you are there being normal. Okay?"

Ezra backed off, nodding. He wiped his eyes.

Miles, Jasper, and Michael were observing this from the hallway.

Robin waved them over. "We can take our breakfast now. Come on back in."

Ezra turned his back to the men, wiping his eyes and collecting himself. He was the last to retake his seat the table.

"So what are these baby names?" Alice asked.

"This one, the boy, is named Adem," Elizabeth said. "That's Adam but with an e. It's the Turkish spelling."

"Adam with an e?" Miles asked.

"Adem," Ezra spelled it out.

"And this is Arabella. But we can call her Bella," Elizabeth said.

"I love them," Alice said. "Wonderful names. Adem and Bella."

Louise and June served a breakfast of bacon, potatoes, biscuits, and fresh coffee. Sandy began bringing out additional bowls and plates of food.

After breakfast, Ezra and Aaron walked with Robin across to the old red house. They entered through the kitchen door.

Ezra looked up at baskets of herbs hanging from the ceiling, and down at the wide wood plank flooring. He laid his hand on the kitchen table.

"What is it?" Aaron asked him.

"Adam told me all about this room. He had drawings of it. Looked just like this. I can see Robin and Marie falling in love right here," Ezra said.

Robin's eyebrows rose. "Artists..."

Ezra's fingertips slid along the top of the table as he walked toward Robin and toward the hallway.

"This was my father's home. The dining room and library are down there. Parlor here. Through this door..." Robin opened the double doors.

"You will find the old ballroom. Can you use this room? We can bring in tables for you."

"I need a couple big tables but I don't care if they are just boards laid out on sawhorses or regular tables. If they're tables, I'll ask Louise or someone for some really old and ragged tablecloths that I can ruin." Ezra walked in and paused before a big mirror to adjust his hair and opened a few buttons on his shirt collar.

"We need some lumber to begin making canvas stretchers and to fashion a big easel for him," Aaron asked.

"Oh you can find all manner of wood and lumber out in the barns. I'll have Jasper or Luke show you," Robin said. "Have anything you want."

"I would hate to ruin your floor. Would you have an old rug maybe, one that can get paint on it?" Ezra asked.

"June would know. She'll find you one or two."

"Can I pull a sofa or chair in here? I'll need you and Marie to sit for me for a bit," Ezra said.

"Take whatever you want from the parlor."

"All right. All right." Ezra turned around in the room, looking at tall windows. "It will be good to be working again."

"I'll get Luke to bring your trunk of art supplies over," Robin said.

"Aaron and I can do it. No need." Ezra shrugged. "This is a perfect room."

"Well, what's first? Lumber?" Robin said. "Let's walk out to the barns."

"Would you look at that," Luke remarked. "That's one of you, isn't he?"

Jasper walked over to look out the barn door. "That's not offensive at all."

"Well what do you call that?" Luke asked.

Ezra walked between Van der Kellen and the young blonde Aaron, a boy of about 16 years of age.

"I just wonder if the young one is his girlfriend, you know?" Jasper remarked.

Luke set down his shovel, watching the men walking toward them. "I thought the young one was normal."

"Shhh," Jasper warned. "Robin, what can we do for you?"

Robin brought Ezra and Aaron into the main barn. "I need you to set Ezra and Aaron up with lumber to make some easels and art supplies with. And can you make them a really large temporary table out of some of it. Nothing pretty. He's going to ruin it with oil paint anyway."

"Make a table?" Luke looked at the stack of lumber in the corner. "I suppose I could. Four legs. Frame around the top. Planking laid across the frame. How big do you want it?"

"Four by eight," Ezra said.

"Feet? Four by eight feet? I can come up with that," Luke agreed. "How tall?"

Ezra held his hand down. "Average table height. I'm not fussy."

"Since when?" Robin remarked.

Ezra laughed.

"Do I have to finish it?" Luke asked.

"No. Just plain wood," Ezra said. "You'll probably make firewood out of it when I leave here. And the easels."

"Use whatever you want," Robin told him. "Will this kind of stuff work for your paintings?"

Aaron picked up some boards, two inches by three inches thick and eight feet long. "This is perfect. Hey, Ez, how big were you going to make this painting of Robin and Marie?"

"Well, after seeing the house and the size of the walls," Ezra pondered aloud. "I would say it needs to be eight by ten foot."

"Really? You would do that? Your Elizabeth portrait was that big, wasn't it?" Robin said.

"Yes. I have to figure out how to get you a frame like the one she dressed hers with," Ezra said. "I'll have one shipped out here. You'll love it. Look great in your stairway."

"I need to borrow a hammer and nails too," Aaron said.

"Come right over here and take your pick." Luke directed him to a work bench on the side. "Bring it back when you're done, is all."

"Oh perfect." Aaron selected a hammer. He started looking through glass jars of nails. "If I use all of these, I won't interfere with the work around here?"

"Left over from building the barn, I think. Roofing nails. Take them," Luke said.

"Look Ezra. We can nail the canvas on with these."

"Those will work," Ezra agreed. "So let's get set up in the ballroom. Start on the table, if you would, Luke. Grab those nails. I'll carry these." Ezra selected the boards to hold the new painting.

"Need any of them cut to size, you'd best have me do it," Luke said, looking at Ezra's hands. "Doesn't look like you do much work."

"Oh sawing these to size, I can do just fine. But thank you. Anything more involved than that and I will look for your help," Ezra said.

Luke handed him a saw that could be used to cut those boards.

"How will you cut your canvas to size? Do you need any...." Robin asked.

"I have a knife for that," Ezra said.

Miles was bringing a horse in from the yard. He paused in the barn doorway, holding the reins. "Whoa. Whoa. Step aside, gentlemen. Working barn here."

Ezra and Aaron stepped to the side with Luke and Robin.

"The foal and mare still out there?" Jasper asked.

"Yeah, leave 'em out a bit more. The little one's getting some exercise." Miles led the horse inside and down the row of stalls to let it enter the right one.

"You have baby horses?" Ezra asked.

"Oh yes. How many do we have now?" Robin asked.

"Five and one on the way," Jasper answered. "C'mon over here. Have a look." He gestured for Ezra and Aaron to follow him down the row of stalls. "Here's our youngest foal."

Ezra looked in through the opening. "Oh my God. I've never seen a horse that small."

"You haven't?" Jasper said. "I'll bring him out so you can pet him."

"I don't want to be any trouble," Ezra said.

"I can't let you in a stall in those shiny boots. You wait right here."

While Jasper went inside to fetch the baby horse, Robin walked off with Miles and Luke to discuss the workings of the farm.

Ezra suddenly jerked back from the opening. "Holy... I didn't realize mom was in there."

"Of course the mare is in here. Can't take the little one away from her for too long." Jasper led the baby horse out of the stall door and held onto him. "This one is just about four weeks old. You can pet him. He's really clumsy. He might knock you over if he can. Brace yourself."

Ezra put both hands on the horse to pet him, and the biggest smile spread across his face. "Same age as my own babies."

"Only this one can run almost as fast as his mother," Jasper said. "That's why I'm holding onto him."

Meanwhile, Miles quietly asked Robin, "What's the story on those two twins? Are they going to make it?"

"Yeah. Marie is helping her. I didn't want to say anything, but I couldn't believe how small they were at a month old. Alice says they'll be fine," Robin whispered to him. Luke could overhear.

"Is that because he's...you know?" Luke whispered.

"No." Robin almost spat. "It's because there are 2 babies. What happens when you get twin foals?"

"One or both dies," Miles said.

"Yeah. Luckily humans don't have to succumb to nature. Luke, look at me. Give Ezra a break. He's suffering right now. Nobody understands that better than I do." Robin walked away.

"What's he mean by that?" Luke whispered to Miles.

"Robin's first-born son died, by his first wife."

June walked into the ballroom and looked for a place on the makeshift table to set down the tray of refreshments.

Ezra hadn't noticed her yet. He was staring at the blank canvas as Aaron was painting white paint on it with a big brush.

"Ez, hey Ezra?"

Ezra August met eyes with Aaron and then turned to see June.

She was standing there holding a silver tray.

"Oh." Ezra went to her and moved some jars of pigment over, to make room. "Thank you. Just move something and put it down. It's okay."

"I was told you might be hungry," June said.

She set down the tray and Ezra immediately grabbed a biscuit.

Between bites he said, "You look confused."

"I never saw an artist before." June looked at him.

Ezra lifted the lid off something and found sausages. He put one between halves of his biscuit then.

"So um, are you comfortable in Robin's room?" June asked.

"I'm in Robin's room?"

"Yeah. Well, he usually stays with Marie in the master suite. But when Liam was born, he used that other room."

Ezra murmured, "Robin gave me his room."

"You are good friends with Adam?"

"Best friends with Adam. And Aaron of course." Ezra nodded toward the apprentice.

"How is he doing with married life, baby, being filthy rich?" June folded her arms and finally smiled.

"He is happy, I can tell you that," Ezra said. "How was he here? When he lived here as Robin's valet?"

"Adam was…" June considered these two young men. Obviously there was no one else around. The stockmen and maids were all working elsewhere.

"He was in love with Robin then, wasn't he?" Ezra asked. "He was just starting his drawings. Was he sad about it?"

"No. I wouldn't say sad. They were good friends. They would ride off to town together. Robin taught him how to shoot down by the river. They spent a lot of time together," June said. "Is he sad about it now?"

"I guess. Sure. Robin's gone." Ezra assembled another biscuit sandwich. "But when I go back home, I'll be there for him. Tell me about Jasper."

"What about him?" June was surprised.

"Well, I know him and Adam didn't get along," Ezra said.

"Really?"

"I know they had a big fight up in Halifax. I have my ideas about it," Ezra said. "I know Jasper knows that I know this."

"Well, that's getting really confusing," Aaron spoke up.

"Get your painting done. And eat something of course," Ezra told him. "Does Robin have any trouble with Jasper?"

June shook her head. "None that I know of. Luke, on the other hand."

"You letting Marie nurse that queer's babies?" Luke said.

Robin lunged at him such that Miles swooped in between, holding Robin back.

Luke stepped back. "Sorry. I didn't mean nothing about Marie."

"Don't you say that about Ezra or anybody like him," Robin scolded. "Or you will be out of a job."

"I don't want to fire him. You have to give him this one. His past with Marie and all," Miles said. "His concern is for her."

"I didn't mean nothing. It's just that Ezra is so...." Luke said.

"You are to refer to him as Mr. August or not at all," Robin insisted. "And you follow his orders as if they are mine. Is that clear?"

"Yes, sir."

Ezra made his way down to the river that hot May evening, alone. He wandered the trail, taking in fragrances, rays of light, and dragon flies flicking about. He set a basket down on a big rock and made a neat pile of clean clothing beside it. He stooped beside the water's edge to feel the temperature with his hand, then both hands. It was warm.

From there, he could not see the barns or the roof tops. There was a thicket of trees between river and hillside. Across the river lay only acres and acres of cultivated hay fields broken up by narrow lines of trees.

Ezra unbuttoned his shirt down from the neck. He opened his cuffs. He pulled the shirt tails up from his trousers and unbuttoned the last few shell buttons. He pulled the shirt back off his bare chest and shoulders, off his arms. He laid that on another large rock.

Bird song was all that he heard, and then frogs. These were the last songs of the day before the sun would set below the distant hills to the west.

Ezra removed his boots and stockings. He unbuttoned trousers and dropped them. He removed his under shorts and laid them all in a nice pile together. At twenty-six years of age, his body was lean, muscular, and toned as he stepped into the river. His bare feet found their way around rocks and onto the sandy riverbed.

The water had a lazy current as he ducked his head beneath the surface. As he rose, his thick curly black hair lay wet against his neck and down onto strong shoulders. He reached for his shampoo from the basket and lathered up his hair when he heard a twig snap not far away. He paused in the water, standing waist deep. He didn't hear anything again, and so went back to rinsing soap from his hair.

He dunked completely beneath the surface and stood back up, looking around as he wiped water from his eyes. His body shimmered wet and lean.

391 The Dutchman 3, Three Musketeers   By Susan Eddy

When he turned around, Jasper was standing on the bank with a rifle in his hands.

Startled, Ezra stood up.

"Shouldn't be down here alone at sunset, unless you want to meet up with coyotes," Jasper said. "No gun on you, that I can see."

Ezra stepped into deeper water that went up to his rib cage. "Don't sneak up on me."

"I'm not sneaking. Mind if I join you?"

"Yes. I do mind. I came down here for solitude," Ezra said. "Toss me that towel."

"Come and get it."

"Fuck you, man," Ezra said quietly.

"Easy now. I thought you were so comfortable being queer. You mean, you're not?" Jasper asked.

"Who I am with is my choice. Not yours." Ezra wrapped his arms over his chest as if feeling exposed. "Get out of here."

"I'm afraid I can't. I was told to bring a gun down here and see you up to the house, when you finish of course." Jasper stooped to examine the contents of Ezra's basket. He sniffed the soap and the hair tonic. "Nice. Why does this smell just like Robin's? Using the same stuff, are we?"

"You bother the girls down here like this?"

"Of course not."

"Then why am I any different?" Ezra said. "Toss me that towel."

"I'm not a good throw," Jasper said. "You probably can't catch it."

"Fine. Look at what you'll never have." Ezra boldly walked out of the river, nude, and picked up his own towel. He wrapped it about his waist.

Jasper handed him the hair tonic, looking at Ezra's wet and perfect body, his abs, his muscled arms. How exotic he was, being of this Turkish decent. His skin color was almost golden in the evening light. His cheeks were blushed as if he wore a woman's rouge.

Ezra took the tonic and stepped away to smooth some of the liquid into his wet hair.

"I can smell it from here. So can every coyote that way." Jasper pointed down wind. "This isn't the city. You probably don't even know about rattlesnakes. Did you check around these rocks?"

"Well, I'll just let you walk first up the hill," Ezra remarked. "You fuck with me again, you'll be sorry."

"You are comfortable with being what you are."

"I sure as fuck am. And you're not my type. I can tell you that," Ezra said.

"We're the only ones of this type around," Jasper said. "Unless your boy Aaron is."

"You lay a hand on Aaron and I'll kick your ass. He's sixteen-years-old. He's never been with anybody." Ezra picked up his clean underclothing and stepped into it. He pulled it up and buttoned, pulling the towel up around his neck. "I wasn't raised a gentleman and I don't fight nice."

"I don't mean anything violent," Jasper said. "I see why you're arrogant though."

"Adam told me everything you did to him." Ezra picked up his trousers and stepped into them. "So by the time I get my boots on, your ass better be going up that hill, or you're going to pay for what you did."

Jasper held his hands up. "Have it your way, princess." He stepped back and picked up his rifle.

Ezra buttoned his trousers. He used the towel to dry off his chest and under arms. Then he dabbed his hair with it.

Jasper stepped back another few paces. "Why am I not your type?"

"Because you're mean."

"You don't know what I intended with Adam. It went bad. But it wasn't what I meant to happen," Jasper said. "He took it wrong."

"If you cared for him at all you wouldn't have compromised him like that," Ezra said.

"Compromise? All I did was touch him," Jasper said.

"Against his will. You do that to a woman and they call it rape," Ezra said. "You think Adam wanted his dick touched by you, with his wife and Robin right beside him?"

Jasper lowered his chin. "That's what Adam told you?"

Ezra pulled on a clean shirt and started to button it.

They heard some distant coyotes hooting and yipping.

"Get your boots on," Jasper told him.

"Those aren't close." Ezra put stockings on and stepped into his boots.

"I didn't know Adam thought I was mean," Jasper said. "He was just so young and beautiful. I just wanted him to know that."

Ezra picked up his basket and dirty clothes and started to walk up the hill. "You are tragically awful at this."

Jasper followed him with the rifle. "Watch where you step, would you?"

They walked silently up the hill toward Robin's home in the distance.

"You know? No. I am going to have this out with you." Ezra stopped and turned to face him.

Jasper stopped, holding the gun with barrel down.

"You think that you can just follow me down here and have me? I'm sick of men thinking that," Ezra said hotly. His brow was furrowed and his lips made a snarl. "I won't be passed around like some kind of doll. I'm sick of it."

"That many men have done that?" Jasper asked. "How many men have you had?"

"There aren't enough of us for us to go around being mean to one another. You oughta learn how to make friends first instead of just trying to get your fix," Ezra told him.

"There is never enough time for that," Jasper said.

"There's always time," Ezra said. "Time is all we've been given. Loving and caring for one another is the best we can make of ourselves."

Jasper stared him in the eyes for a minute. Finally, he laughed and pointed up the hill. "Easy for you to say, a gentleman of leisure. You don't have a job. You married a rich woman. You paint pictures."

"I paint really good portraits, amazing portraits," Ezra corrected.

Jasper laughed. "All right. So you do."

"I'm bored with this." Ezra started walking again, the handle of his basket over his arm the way a woman would carry it. His other clothing was in a bundle under his other arm.

"What is your type? Robin?" Jasper followed him.

Ezra laughed. "He's everybody's type. In the city, he tips his hat and carriages collide, women walk into each other. Saw one lady walk into a lamp post once."

"What about Luke?" Jasper moved up beside him. "Is he your type?"

"Luke? That guy in the barn? Robin's horse would have a better chance with me," Ezra said.

Jasper laughed. "Robin's horse is male. It might at that. How did you like doing it with a woman?"

"Don't ask me that. We just had 2 babies. I haven't been laid in so long I can't talk about it without getting hard," Ezra remarked casually. "You thought you could help me out til my wife is ready again? You thought wrong."

"Thought crossed my mind. Obviously, it just crossed yours as well."

"Well forget it. Talk about something else. Talk about hay or whatever this is," Ezra said.

"This is alfalfa," Jasper said. "City boy."

"And what is that?"

"That? Lilac. Can't you smell it?" Jasper said.

Ezra moved off the path to smell the purple bunches of tiny flowers. Then he started breaking off bunches of them, dark purple, light purple, even white. "Carry these for me. Make yourself useful, prick."

"All right, princess. Gather your flowers while ye may."

Ezra sat in the parlor with a baby in his arms and up against his neck, swaddled in a little blue blanket.

Robin set a glass of scotch down beside him, next to a vase of lilacs. "Here you go, Ez. Which one do you have there?"

"Adem. Can't you tell by the blanket?" Ezra reached for the glass and brought it to his mouth.

"Adem with an e. Got it." Robin took a seat beside him. "You know I named Liam after my first best friend also."

"Oh? Don't worry. Next son I'll name after you," Ezra said. "Or daughter for that matter."

Miles and Elizabeth burst out laughing.

Ezra began to sing his lullaby to his son when Frida wandered over to him. He kept singing, softly. Frida looked up at him, holding onto his knee. "C'mon up here, darling. We've got room. Lots of room on Uncle Ezra's lap, baby." She held up her hands.

Ezra held one baby in left arm and drew Frida up into his lap also. Robin reached over to push her up.

Ezra kept on singing even as Frida lay her head down beside Adem's and held hands with the baby.

Elizabeth looked over at Marie and grinned. "He's got room for two or three more children, right?"

"Huh?" Ezra said.

"Sing sing," Frida told him.

Everyone laughed.

"I'll keep singing, darling. Let me have a drink first."

Robin handed the glass to him.

"We'll teach your daddy to sing to you," Ezra remarked.

"Mommy sings to her," Robin said.

"Yeah? Does mommy sing to you? What does she sing?" Ezra put a little kiss on Frida's head.

"Mommy sings this. Do you know this one?" Marie sang her lullaby to the children.

Ezra sang with her, a surprising impromptu harmony.

Then they both laughed.

"Well isn't that just wonderful." Robin rolled his eyes.

"Where did you learn to sing so well?" Marie asked him. "So professionally"

"I sang in the church chorus until my voice changed," Ezra said.

That made the men laugh.

"It is about time for the children to get to bed," Marie said. "Beth, are you coming up stairs?"

"Yes. I'm so tired," Elizabeth said.

"Ezra, have a smoke on the porch?" Robin asked.

"Love to." Ezra sat forward and handed Frida to Marie with a kiss for the little girl. Then he stood to transfer Adem to their nanny Catherine and gave a kiss to Elizabeth on the mouth.

Marta collected Liam and Elizabeth took Bella upstairs.

Jasper, Aaron, Luke and the other two stockmen were already sitting out on the porch, smoking, and having a few drinks.

The gentlemen joined them, passing out glasses of scotch or whiskey around.

Ezra lit a cigarette off a lamp that Aaron offered. He sat between Aaron and Robin.

Conversation went on for a while and then they heard coyotes in the distance.

"There's your friends," Jasper remarked.

"Oh yeah. They like you, boy," Miles added.

Ezra let out a loud and lengthy howl that made the coyotes go silent.

The men on the porch burst out laughing.

June appeared at the door. "What on earth was that?"

Ezra entered Elizabeth's room, checking into each crib for his sleeping little ones, before approaching her bedside. The fragrance of lilacs filled the room. He sat on the edge of the bed and leaned to kiss her forehead.

"I love the lilacs, darling," Elizabeth whispered.

"Can I sleep with you? Just for a while?" Ezra asked.

"Well, what if Marta or Catherine have to come in?" Beth said. "They can't find you here."

"I know but..." Ezra frowned. He leaned down against her and nuzzled her. "Beth, I'm so alone."

"You're not alone. We're right here. I love you, Ezra." Beth kissed him.

"I love you too but I...I can't go much longer without comfort from you," Ezra whispered. "I just need to hold you for a while. Beth, please. I have confidences I must tell you."

"Sleep here then. If we get yelled at, we get yelled at."

Ezra kissed her forehead and happily moved around the bed. He undid his trousers and sat. He pulled off pants and boots at once. Then he unbuttoned his shirt. He dropped that all on the floor and slid beneath the linens with his wife. He kissed her and aligned his body behind hers. He wrapped his arms around her.

Chapter Twenty   The Rift

The evening in May never really cooled off, even with windows open and breezes dancing through sheer curtains.

Two tiny babies began to cry and Elizabeth sat up in bed.

Marie picked up Adem and brought him to Beth in bed, just as a shirtless and uncovered Ezra rolled away from her in his slumber. Marie laid the baby into Beth's arms. "I'll take Bella."

"Thank you, Marie. Please don't wake him. He cried last night."

"Adem?"

"Ezra," Beth whispered.

"Oh." Marie just collected baby Bella and carried her out of the room, closing the door behind her.

Marie met eyes with Ezra across the breakfast table. His face was soft. The whites of his eyes were in honest contrast to the brownish black iris. Black curled lashes seemed a waste on a man. There was a great distance between his eyelid and brows. But the crease of his eyelid was very close to his lashes. He didn't look away, even as he sipped coffee from gold rimmed china.

The men were talking about the horses, planning their day of tasks.

Aaron was telling Ezra that he would get a second canvas stretched and prepared for him. He would get paints mixed.

Ezra blinked and glanced over the plate before him. Waffles with syrup and sausages. Early blueberries topped the waffles. "I need to start some preliminary drawings. I'll need the big sketchbook and graphites first."

"I'll bring them over right after breakfast. Unless you want to start over there," Aaron said.

Ezra looked at Marie again. A spoonful of waffle and blueberries rose to his mouth.

Robin pushed out his chair and left with Miles and Jasper.

"Bring the sketchbook here," Ezra told Aaron.

"Will do." Aaron rose and exited.

Marie sat down on the porch with one of Robin's shirts to mend. She sat down with a sewing basket and scissors. Elizabeth sat in a rocker beside her with Bella in her arms.

Ezra strolled out onto the porch, large sketchbook and small wooden box in his hands. "Where are the other children?"

"Inside, having naps," Elizabeth said. "Catherine's with them."

Ezra was looking at reflected light beneath the west facing porch. He sat down on the shiny oak floor and opened his sketchbook of papers. He selected a piece of graphite from the box and used a knife to sharpen the tip, letting bits fall off into the flowerbed below. "Am I expected to apologize for last night?"

Elizabeth looked at Marie beside her.

Ezra and Marie were looking at each other. He began to draw Marie's face, in the reflected light. Finding his position wrong, he slid off the porch to stand between flowers and the wall, to draw with the papers laying on the floor at his waist height.

"Are you asking me?" Marie said. "I was surprised, is all."

The scrutiny in his face came from his careful observation of features defined by light and shadow. Marie felt intense scrutiny, however. She went back to her sewing.

"Ez, I'm sorry it's all about the babies all the time," Elizabeth said softly.

"It has to be. I get it," Ezra said. "I just need to get on with my work."

"I thought you were going to paint in the ballroom," Elizabeth said.

"I will. I can't paint from nothing. And unless Marie and Robin want to go sit over there for hours on end, I have to begin with my drawings," Ezra said plainly, in a breathy hushed voice.

"I'm sorry. I can sit over there doing this," Marie said.

"Well, you can for a while. You can choose the gown you want to be painted in. Robin, however, is on a horse all day. I don't know how I am to work with that," Ezra said.

"I will talk to him. He'll give you time and sit for you," Marie said. "Especially on a rainy day."

Ezra continued to draw Marie, blending with the side of his pinky.

"Were you upset about us, last night?" Elizabeth whispered.

After looking to see who she was talking to, Ezra said, "No, darling. I'm fine now."

"Is it because we don't…"

"No," Ezra said. "I just needed your comfort for a while. I'm fine now."

"Alice said the babies are doing much better. I think you two can stop worrying so badly," Marie said gently.

Ezra stood upright. He turned the page. "Jasper followed me down to the river to watch me bathing."

Marie let out a breath.

"I just want you to know, if he does something to me again, I am going to kick his ass. Kick it seriously." He stopped drawing and stood back.

"Did you tell Robin?" Marie asked.

"No. It has nothing to do with his work here. It wouldn't have happened if I was not here," Ezra said. "It's just that he did that kind of thing to Adam and that pisses me off. I think I'm going to have a discussion with Jasper right now." He stormed off along the porch.

"Ezra, wait. Just talk to me first." Marie went after him, on the porch.

Ezra stopped and turned to her. "You know, Marie, I respect your opinion more than anybody on earth. You and Robin. You know that right? But how would you feel if Luke went down there to watch you bathe? I feel violated."

Marie stopped in her tracks. "What do you mean, Luke?"

"Nothing. Just an example."

"What happened with Luke?"

Elizabeth was listening from her rocker. "Ezra?"

"I know Miles had to hold Robin back from decking him yesterday. Now why would that be?" Ezra said.

"Luke had an interest in me long ago, before Robin even came here," Marie said. "That was years ago. Surely he doesn't think of me that way anymore. I'm a mother."

"You're gorgeous, Marie. Don't you think like that. You watch it around Luke," Ezra said.

"Ezra, what if Jasper is just lonely? He doesn't have anybody here, if he is that way. He certainly hasn't shown any interest in any of the girls," Marie said. "Can you give him a break?"

"Would you, if he did this to you?" Ezra looked around and then at his wife. "Beth already knows. I told her last night. He wouldn't throw me my towel. He made me walk out of the water and get it myself."

"In your shorts?"

"No." Ezra shook his head. "You know, unfortunately, before he showed up I was having a bonding with nature sort of experience. I was one with nature. I was totally naked out there in the river, just feeling the current, the warm water over my body."

Marie looked at Elizabeth and tried to hide a smile.

Beth burst out laughing though.

"Oh you two don't get it." Ezra threw up his arms and paced back toward his drawings. "All right. What?"

"It has been a long time since I communed with nature with you, my husband. The next time you're doing that why don't I come and watch?" Elizabeth said.

Ezra's mouth twisted into an eventual reluctant smile. "My wife is welcome to look at me whenever she wishes."

"Please warn us first to watch the children for you." Marie returned to her chair and her sewing.

"Think he should let this go with Jasper, don't you?" Elizabeth said.

"Well, I don't have all the evidence. Maybe if I saw what Jasper did," Marie said.

Finally Ezra and Elizabeth both burst out laughing.

And Marie laughed. "I was really afraid I was going to see it this morning."

"Are you doing it with Robin?" Ezra asked seriously, as he picked up his drawing materials. He met eyes with her.

"Wha...ah, well yes," Marie said. "But Beth needs to take some time. She had two babies. Be patient with her a little longer."

"Not too much longer," Beth agreed. "Ezra, darling."

"I'm being a dick again?" Ezra asked.

"Well no. I don't think anyone has the right to intrude on someone's communing with nature," Marie said.

Ezra eventually smirked with his chin down.

"Somebody finds you attractive and wants to look at you. Is that so bad?" Marie said. "Men always want to fight over these things."

"Wow. Never really been lumped in with most men before."

"You're as red blooded as any other man," Elizabeth spoke up. "Maybe more endowed than some."

Ezra posed with a hand on his hip. "Can't deny it, ladies."

Ezra's painting of Robin

Luke carried more lumber into the ballroom and looking around, he chose to set it down in a corner away from the artists. Ezra was laying out drawings on the floor all along one wall. Aaron was mixing potions on the other table. "You want this table the same size, Mr. August?"

Ezra looked over at him. "Yes. If you would. I'll be right back." Ezra walked out past Luke and went into the old kitchen.

June watched Ezra pour himself a cup of cool water. "Get you anything?"

"No. Thanks. Just suffering a bit in the heat. Honestly, given where I was born this is ridiculous. I should revel in the heat." Ezra drank his water.

"Where are you from?" June asked.

"Ottoman Turkey. Ankara to be exact. Do you know where Europe is?"

"Yes."

"Picture it in between Europe and India. It is part of the caravan route to the East. Troy? You know Helen of Troy? *The Illiad and the Odessey*?" Ezra said. "Maybe Robin has a copy, or a map even. I grew up near some Roman ruins. I used to draw pictures there."

"That's why you are so unusual," June said.

He raised his cup to her. "You have no idea." He refilled his cup and carried it with him back to the ballroom.

There he found Luke looking at his drawings, standing over drawings of Marie.

Ezra drank his water, staring at Luke.

Luke suddenly saw him there and stepped back. "Beg your pardon. I never saw such a thing."

"Meaning?" Ezra said.

"How do you sketch it to look just like her?" Luke asked. "I never saw such a thing."

"Well. Wait 'til I make the painting then. Drawing is easy," Ezra said. "I need that table and I need a sort of a tripod to pin a drawing to. I need the drawing at my eye level beside the canvas. Either that or I have to pin things to Robin's wall. I don't think he'd be okay with that."

"What do you mean by tripod?" Luke questioned.

"You take three of these and attach them together at the top. The three legs spread out. I can tack a paper to the top of it," Ezra said.

"Oh. That's easy. Table first or that?"

"Table, if you would," Ezra said. "Aaron, do we have enough linseed oil? Don't smoke in here, Luke. You probably wouldn't anyway. But my turpentine will burn the house down."

"Oh. No, we don't smoke in the house," Luke said. "What are all these potions?"

"Oil paint. Pigments to make the colors. Oil and binders. Turpentine is to clean my sable brushes," Ezra said. "You can look, man. Just don't touch."

Luke ventured closer to the art table and Aaron's jars of mixed paints. "Well they sure are pretty colors. When you paint, do you mind people watching?" Luke leaned down very close to an open jar of cobalt.

"Don't sniff that," Ezra warned. "Breathe that in it will probably kill you."

"Really?" Luke stood up and backed off. "Seriously?"

"Yes, seriously," Ezra shot back.

"Didn't know artists did anything dangerous," Luke said.

"Well I wouldn't eat it either," Ezra said. "As long as the feeling is positive, I don't mind being watched. I've painted on the street, in parks, in galleries. People always watch. Criticism, now that pisses me off. Unless it's from an instructor. Actually, that pisses me off too."

Luke laughed and moved back to his corner to make another table. "Never saw such a thing."

"Yeah, well, I need Robin to sit his ass in here and let me draw him. That's what I need."

"He would for you, I'm sure." Luke began measuring boards with a string that he used for the first table. He marked it with a scrape of his saw. "He's working on a jumping course out in the field. You should see that."

"Jumping course? You mean for his horse?" Ezra stopped what he was doing and looked at the stockman.

"They have competitions at it, I hear." Luke turned so that he bent over with his back side to the wall as he worked on the table legs.

Ezra went to him, stooped and held the board for him to cut it.

After cutting the first one, Luke said, "Not afraid to be too close to me with this saw, are you?"

"Is your aim that bad?" Ezra shot back, seriously.

After a moment, Luke started to laugh.

Ezra stood up and set his hands on his hips. "Well line up the next one."

Jasper was surprised to see Ezra walking out to the jumper course with Luke that afternoon. Robin turned his horse around on the course and rode toward them, taking a couple jumps along the way. He joined them just about at the same time that the three men converged at the edge of the field.

"Something wrong?" Robin questioned.

"Are you out of your fucking mind?" Ezra waved his arm at the course. "Robin, that's fucking insane."

Luke burst out laughing. "I knew he'd say that. Can't believe he said it to you though."

Robin held a hand down to Ezra. "C'mon. I'll take you for a ride."

"No way in hell, man," Ezra said.

They all laughed.

Robin swung down from his horse and let it start grazing where it stood. "Never saw me ride before, did you?"

"How does Marie sleep at night with you doing this?" Ezra asked. "She knows you are riding like this?"

"She has ridden with me," Robin said. "What did you need me for?"

"Well I need you to sit for me when you have time," Ezra said. "Luke was kind enough to make me another table. Canvas is ready. I have a dozen drawings of Marie and she's choosing a gown to wear for the portrait. What do I do about you?"

"You're not doing anything important out here," Jasper said.

The guys laughed.

"Well, have the men work on those gates out there to make sure they fall when kicked down." Robin pointed into the field. "And add the moat that I wanted on number twelve, after the gate. So the horse comes around and sees the gate and moat, and the horse not only has to jump over but also clear the moat with all four hooves."

"Twelve. Yeah we'll have Tom and Henry start digging," Jasper said. "Not too deep. Just enough to keep water in it."

"No cliff on the far side or the horse will catch back hooves on it," Robin reminded. "I'll take Jumper back to the barn and then meet with you for your drawings. How about that?"

"I didn't mean now. But sure." Ezra tucked his hair behind his ear against the breeze.

"Is Miles back from town yet?" Robin asked.

"Not yet," Jasper said.

Robin remounted his horse.

"I still think you should ride back with him." Jasper tapped Ezra on the back.

Robin looked down at them. "No. Not his first time on a horse. Not without a saddle and stirrups. I was only joking."

"I didn't come out here to learn riding and shooting and whatever other manly things you do in the country," Ezra remarked. "I came to make pretty pictures."

"Well I wouldn't want to keep you from your work." Robin rode off toward the barn on his black gelding.

Ezra pointed at the horse. "Is that the one he bought without riding first?"

"That's the story I was told," Jasper said as the three of them walked up the trail.

"And that's highly unusual, right?" Ezra said.

"We don't buy a horse without aging it, riding it, and haggling over the price," Jasper said. "As a rule."

"So I'm guessing he didn't just get lucky. He knew what he was doing," Ezra said. "What I'm getting at is how great of a horseman is he?"

"He's the best most of us in the business have ever seen. He can ride it, jump it, doctor it, and knows what horses are thinking. Don't you know what a cavalryman is? He can also shoot off the back of a horse," Jasper said. "Not to mention that he grew up on a horse farm and did competition jumping as a teen-age boy. Miles competed with him."

"Is that so? I knew Robin was a war hero. I could tell that well enough as we ran through an alley together dodging bullets," Ezra said. "Miles competed with him? Have to ask him about that some time."

"You and Robin got shot at?" Luke questioned.

"You didn't hear that story? That's a good one," Jasper said. "Tell us how you pretended to be Adam leaving the hospital with Robin."

Robin sat down on the arm of the sofa that Luke had pulled into the ballroom. "You know, traditional portraits are done standing up."

"Do I look like a traditionalist?" Ezra stood behind the table Luke had just built, drawing on a stack of fine pressed white paper. "I don't know if this is the pose I want. But I could see Marie sitting beside you with the baby on her lap and Frida seated next to her. I also want to paint you on horseback, really dynamic."

"Horseback?" Robin said. "There's one at my brother's house. That artist went out and painted the horse, painted a generic guy in a uniform, and then had me come and stand there while he painted my face."

"Really?" Ezra looked at him. "That's lame."

"How is that lame? You're not going to have me for days on end, here," Robin said.

"I don't really need that. I just need to draw you in person for a while. Then let's say you go back to your jumping course and I just sit back and draw while you work. I also need to just get used to drawing horses. I never have before," Ezra said. "I need to learn their anatomy."

"Well, you made up Elizabeth for her painting and look how wonderful that turned out." Robin shrugged. "I don't mean to tell you how to do your business."

"Trust me, you don't want a painting of you and Marie standing there in black like you're at a funeral. You'll have to look at that on the wall every time you go upstairs." Ezra picked up his paper and walked around to kneel on the floor and draw Robin from a different angle. "I'm an instinctive painter and I paint a lot from memory. Once I get it in my hand how to draw you, I can invent the pose or even the lighting."

"While I have you on the subject of business," Robin thoughtfully said. "I wish you wouldn't interfere with mine."

"What?" Ezra stopped drawing.

"You told Marie that I had a problem with Luke," Robin said.

Ezra stood up, leaving the paper at his feet.

"I don't have a problem with Luke. Now I think you've just been under horrific stress for a long time. We should just drop all this, right?" Robin asked.

Ezra wet his lips and the tilt of his head changed. "I hate to be the one to tell you but two of my drawings of Marie have gone missing."

"Don't invent who you think took them. Maybe Marie borrowed them," Robin said.

"I know who was staring at them in here when I walked in this morning." Ezra put his hands on his hips. "Marie saw them all yesterday, she and Beth both. She'd say something if she borrowed them. Now, I don't need them to make my painting. But I'll ask him if he has them."

"No, you won't. Don't interfere with my stockmen," Robin said. "They do very difficult and dangerous work and I need them do what I say."

Ezra shrugged. "I'd see if he has Marie pinned up in his bedroom."

Robin lowered his chin. "I'll get your drawings back. Just drop it. Are you sure they're missing?"

Ezra stepped aside and pointed at the line of drawings along the wall and the distinctly empty two positions. "Aaron hasn't moved them. You know what, you question whether I know my own work? Forget it. Don't ask Luke anything."

Robin stood up. "I didn't say that."

"So why did Miles have to hold you off him yesterday?" Ezra asked.

Robin stepped toward Ezra and leaned close to his face to say angrily, "Because he insulted you. All right? And you didn't even need to know that because you were getting along just fine with him out in the field. Now how do you feel? Like someone running his mouth when he didn't know what he was talking about?"

Ezra backed off and lowered his chin. His mouth was a pout. "Called me a queer? I am. So what?" He turned away and began picking up his drawings of Robin and stacking them on the table. Then he began picking up the Marie papers.

"I think until you know where the drawings went, we shouldn't make assumptions," Robin said more gently.

"No. You're right." Ezra began cleaning the charcoal off his fingers with a rag and some linseed oil.

"Are you saying you want me to go? You're done for the day?" Robin pointed at the drawings.

"I can't draw someone I can't look at right now."

After a few moments Robin said in a more gentler tone, "Let's step away for a while. We'll take this back up after dinner." As he went past Ezra, he patted him on the back. That was the only thing that made Ezra lift his head.

"Mr. August? What can I do for you?" June found Ezra in the old kitchen.

"You don't mind if I make some tea?" He was putting water to boil over the hearth.

"I can do that for you. Have a seat," June said.

"It's just boiling water." Ezra sat down at the kitchen table, his back to the kitchen, where June had moved into.

June put some bread to bake in the hearth oven. "You know, we still do some cooking over here to help out the main kitchen. I'm baking some bread over here. I'll have to get it out of there when that sand timer says so. I can't really get to anything else until it's done."

"You want me to take it out for you?" Ezra asked.

"I was actually thinking maybe I could sit here with you until then," June said. "Unless you'd rather I didn't. You look like a man avoiding... people."

Ezra's chin was down. "I do, huh?"

"You know what else I have over here? Wait til you see this." June went into the pantry for a bit and came out two pieces of blueberry pie and two glasses of whiskey.

She set them down on the table and only then saw the young man was in tears. She just sat across from Ezra and slid one plate of pie with a fork in front of him and one glass of whiskey. She started eating her own treat.

Ezra sipped some of his whiskey and wiped his eyes.

June drank some of hers. "I saw those sweet babies of yours over there in the kitchen. Marta and Catherine are doting on them. The babies look the happiest they have been since you arrived."

He wet his lips. "Thank you."

"One or two nights of good sleep doesn't make up for a long time without," June said. "You were missed at lunch over there. They thought you were working."

He tried the pie.

June quietly ate her pie. She checked the sand timer again. "This is going to be a long thirty minutes if I'm talking to myself."

He smiled a bit. "Sorry." After another drink he said softly, "I confided something in someone and she told her husband. Maybe I was tired and shouldn't have said it."

"Husband and wife shouldn't keep secrets, right?" June asked.

He nodded. "That's why I told my wife."

"So you forgot that another husband and wife tell each other everything?"

"If he knows everything then he should not have completely dismissed what happened to me. I told her something happened to me. And all he did was yell at me for the other thing I told her," Ezra said softly. "And tell me to stay out of his business."

"Sounds like he doesn't know everything after all."

Ezra shot a look at her. "She didn't tell him my part."

"This would be a lot easier if I knew what we were not talking about," June said.

"Hmmm. Sorry, I've already learned my lesson about talking too much," Ezra admitted. "And to be told so by him...son of a bitch. I can't say another word."

She reached forward. "I'm sorry. I will have to take the pie back then."

That made Ezra burst out laughing.

June sat back laughing and sipped her whiskey.

He looked down at his half-eaten pie and his half-drank whiskey, with a big warm smirk. "Tell me something then, so that I don't think I'm crazy. There is a certain stockman here who has had a thing for Marie since before Robin ever arrived, and... he still does? Is he dangerous for her?"

Ezra arrived at dinner with Aaron. He gave Elizabeth a kiss before taking the seat beside her. Aaron sat beside Ezra.

"You were working? You missed lunch darling," Beth said to him.

"Sorry. You know how I am," Ezra said. "June brought me some blueberry pie. How are the babies?"

"Much better. They are so much better," Elizabeth said, gleaming at Marie across the table from her.

Miles and Jasper took their seats, deep in conversation about horses.

Robin sat at the head of the table and unfolded a napkin into his lap.

Ezra lifted a glass of red wine to his mouth.

"Alice will be back tomorrow, and Michael," Marie said.

"Oh good. I think she will be amazed at how much more peaceful Adem and Bella are now," Elizabeth said.

"That reminds me. I ran into the doctor in town," Miles said. "He said he would come by tomorrow to see the twin babies. Said he doesn't see that happen much. You don't mind that I told him?"

"Oh no. I welcome a visit by your local physician," Elizabeth said. "Thank you, Miles."

"You look a little less tired," Ezra told his wife. "Noticeably."

"I feel better yes. You must feel better after some sleep for a change." She leaned over and kissed Ezra on the mouth.

And he happily took this kiss, with a tilt to his head and a smirk for her. Beth gave him a big smile. She was oblivious when he lowered his chin after and kept his eyes either on Marie or anywhere to her left down the table.

Of course on Marie's right was Robin seated at the head of the table.

Ezra again ate his entire meal with the same spoon, regardless of which course was served to him. And he had three glasses of wine throughout the dinner, drinking from one of Marie's favorite blue goblets.

When the gentlemen retreated to the porch again at the end of the evening, Aaron returned to the red house to bed, and Ezra went upstairs pausing only to stare at the wall where he intended his painting to reside one day.

Baby Frida was put to bed and then it took the four women to care for and get the three babies to bed, including two nannies Marta and Catherine.

Ezra closed the door to his room and sat cross legged in the middle of Robin's bed, drinking brandy. He reached out to close his hand around the ebony bed post. That's when he got up, got dressed again and bounded down the stairs.

Chapter Twenty-One   Echoes

Aaron took his seat at breakfast, beside the empty one left for Ezra.

Elizabeth looked at him. "Where's Ezra?"

Aaron shrugged. "I figured upstairs. Isn't he?"

"No. His bed was made. Isn't he painting?" Elizabeth said.

"I didn't even look in there. The door was closed," Aaron said.

"You don't know where he is?" Robin questioned.

June set some biscuits down on the table. "Who are you looking for? Ezra?"

"Yes." Elizabeth looked up at her.

"He's asleep on the sofa in the ballroom," June said. "I shut the door over there. He said he was up all night painting. And you should see it. Amazing it is."

"Oh. He does that all the time," Elizabeth said. "Let him sleep where he is."

"Odd he didn't ask me to help him," Aaron remarked. "He's supposed to be teaching me to paint, you know. But he does this all the time. I don't know how he sees what color he's using half the time. He's just got a lamp or two to go by. I think he could do it with a blindfold on."

"I think he just about could. When he gets it in his head that he needs to make a painting, he can't do any other thing," Elizabeth said. "I just let him be. He's an artist."

"What did he paint?" Marie asked.

"I don't think I should spoil it," June replied. "And I don't think he's completed it yet."

Miles and Jasper looked at each other. "Must be why he didn't come out on the porch last night."

Robin, Aaron, Miles, Marie, and Jasper walked over to the ballroom to look on the new painting, and the artist asleep on the couch.

There was a horse rearing up as if about to trample the viewer of the painting. Robin was leaning forward in the saddle from above you, in a blue uniform wielding a sword overhead.

They all stood there in silence.

Beside the canvas, Ezra was sleeping on the sofa, curled up on his side. His arms were wrapped around a pillow beneath his head.

Marie whispered, "Has he ever seen your uniform?"

"No. It's in a trunk in the closet," Robin stammered.

"That's not your horse," Miles remarked.

"Well, that's the strangest thing about it. That is my horse," Robin said. "The white socks, higher on the right. The white mane. That was my horse in India. I dream about that horse all the time."

"Are you saying he got your uniform and horse right without ever seeing them?" Miles asked.

At that Ezra stirred a bit. His hand went to rub his eyes.

"That's not creepy at all." Jasper shook his head.

"Exactly right." Robin stepped closer to the canvas and pointed toward the red sky in the background. "Karmul was on fire. I was leading a retreat when we came under attack again. We won a great victory that day. I think these are the bodies I rode over. See the red coats?"

Marie held her hand to her mouth.

"How did he do red in the foreground and the background and make it work? He told me never to do that," Aaron whispered. "Red comes forward and blue recedes. I don't get it."

"He might not know those are bodies. It looks implied really. But that's what was here, along the lower portion beneath the front hooves," Robin said.

"Well, I hear it's bad luck to wake a sleeping witch." Miles retreated out of the room toward the old kitchen.

Jasper followed him.

Marie and Robin lingered to look at the painting some more.

Miles poured himself a cup of coffee and offered one to Jasper.

"Do you think he reads minds?" Jasper asked.

"How else do you explain that?" Miles said. "He sleeps in the bed where Robin had those dreams, doesn't he?"

Jasper and Miles tapped coffee cups together.

"It's unnatural."

It rained that day. Alice and Michael arrived later than usual, with their covered carriage. Everyone had gone over to the ballroom to take a quiet look at the painting. Afternoon thunder finally awoke the artist and he sat up to stare at his own work.

Ezra walked over to the big house with his jacket up over his head. He pulled that down as he entered the dining room where everyone was gathered.

It thundered again.

Frida ran right to Ezra and he stooped to pick up the little girl, setting her on his hip.

"Are you hungry, Mr. August? May I bring you some lunch?" Sandy asked.

"That would be wonderful. Thank you," Ezra said.

Frida was wiping wet rain drops off Ezra's shoulder and lapel.

Aaron stood up and went to him. "Why didn't you wake me? I would have helped you paint last night. Amazing. Amazing work."

"That painting?" Ezra looked a bit dazed.

Marie stepped around the table and took Frida from him. "Let uncle Ezra have something to eat. Come on darling."

Elizabeth went to Ezra and hugged him. "Are you okay, sweetheart?"

"I'm fine. Why? What's that look for?" Ezra hugged her.

"We've all seen the painting," Jasper said.

Ezra was invited to sit down in his usual chair. Finally, he made eye contact with Robin, who slid his elbows forward on the table and said to him, "Ezra, I know that battle scene you just painted. That's my horse. You got my uniform exactly right."

"I what?" Ezra said.

"You should hear Robin recognizing things in that painting," Miles remarked. "The fire in the background. The bodies in the foreground."

"Bodies?" Ezra said. "Maybe. I'm not sure I interpret it that way. But you can see what you will in it." He drank from a glass of water.

"How did you do that?" Robin asked.

"Ahhh, I started seeing it when I was out by the jumping course with you. It didn't really become clear until last night when I had to paint it," Ezra said. "It was in color so I couldn't just draw it."

Elizabeth smiled. "Isn't he amazing? He paints something amazing and acts as if it's just what he sees."

Chapter Twenty-Two   Strange Alliances

"Jesus Christ! Mr. August!" Luke dashed forward down the row of stalls toward the young man lying on the barn floor. "Mr. August."

Ezra sat up. "What, man?"

"Are you all right?" Luke stooped beside him.

"I'm fine. I'm not in your way, am I?" Ezra asked.

"What are you talking about? Were you passed out there? Are you hurt?"

"No. I had to see a horse from that angle. Why?"

Luke pulled him up by the arm and brushed straw off Ezra's jacket. "You scared the hell out of me. I thought you were dead there."

Ezra burst out laughing.

Luke pushed him back a step. "Crazy son of a bitch."

Ezra wiped more straw off his backside and strolled along the stalls. "Luke, I want my drawings back."

"What are you talking about?"

"You know what I'm talking about."

"You want to draw some horses?"

Ezra spun on his heel and looked at Luke.

"I have need to brush out and clip a couple horses. I could put them on ties out there in the sunlight."

"Really?"

"Facing the sun or back to it?"

"Facing the sun."

"Go get your papers."

Miles walked around behind Ezra, who was kneeling on the ground, drawing the horse before him.

Luke was clipping the horse and letting the hair drift away in the breeze.

"Get your shadow off my paper," Ezra said.

"Oh. Damn. Those are good." Miles stepped aside.

Ezra was doing a study of the animal, drawing hooves, head, face, fore limbs, and some of the entire horse.

"Would you look at that?" Miles stammered. "Plain white paper and then he just makes a horse right on it."

"I know, right?" Luke said as he kept clipping.

"I heard of people who can do that."

"Heard of? What do you think Adam was doing on that ship?" Ezra said. "Adam taught himself how to draw."

"Yeah. I never got to see his drawings of Robin. He kept those hidden. I guess Robin saw them once," Miles said.

"I've seen them. They are incredible," Ezra said. "Here. You want this drawing of Luke?"

Miles chuckled. "No, I do not. I suppose you might."

"Not my type," Ezra said.

"What type is your type?" Miles questioned. "How about you draw some of those colts we have in the barn. I wouldn't mind a couple of those up and around the house."

"Really? I'll think about it after I get my Robin paintings done," Ezra said.

"What do you make from your drawings?" Luke asked. "Money wise?"

"More than you want to know," Ezra said.

"Seriously? What's the most you ever sold a painting for?" Miles questioned.

"Six hundred dollars."

"Six hundred? Jesus," Miles said. "Naked ladies or what?"

"Fully clothed ladies who bought one of my Robin paintings." Ezra got up off the ground to stretch.

Miles and Luke laughed.

"Your wife let you part with one of those?" Miles asked.

"We kept the good ones. That was a practice one," Ezra said.

"Practice one made $600." Luke continued working on the horse.

"What's the least amount of money you ever sold one of your art works for?" Miles folded his arms, amused.

"Hmm. Gave a drawing away for half a sandwich once," Ezra said. "Wasn't in Paris very long. I was running out of money."

"I hear that. Paris is expensive," Miles said. "How did you and Elizabeth get together? She was just out of mourning. She must have taken one look at a pretty boy like you and..."

"And what exactly?" Ezra turned to look at Miles.

"Knocked you flat on a bed." Miles looked him in the eyes.

Ezra's eyebrows rose. "I guess I'm supposed to give you a black eye for something like that. Is that what you men do? Ha." Ezra laughed. "Straight men. Yeah. You're right. She took my virginity. Took it. Road it. Owned it. Just like my heart. She can have anything she wants from me. My last drop of blood if that's what it takes."

"Damn. Is that all?" Miles said.

Ezra picked up his papers. "Thanks for the horse, Luke." He walked back toward the red house.

"Told you, didn't he?" Luke remarked.

"Lucky bastard. That's all I can say. Elizabeth never gave me even the time of day."

Ezra sat down on that ebony four poster bed, and slid one hand along the headboard. The only light came from one oil lamp on his table. The house was quiet and dark. His windows were open and he listened to frogs and crickets.

He heard Robin's sighs in his mind. A lock of his own hair smelled like Robin, and he held it to his nose. Robin took Marie in this bed. Why was it in this room? It was here. Did he have other women in this bed?

Ezra scooted his back up against the headboard and he sipped a glass of brandy.

There was a knock on his door.

"C'mon in, darlin," Ezra said, expecting Beth.

Robin looked inside.

"Oh." Ezra quickly pulled a sheet up over his bare legs and under shorts.

"Sorry, sweetheart. I could see a light on," Robin entered. "Could I have a word with you?"

"Please."

Robin quietly shut the door and revealed a scotch bottle and glasses behind his back.

Ezra downed the last of his brandy and held his glass out for a refill.

Robin set down the extra glass on the table. He poured for Ezra and then poured his own.

"Marie got a new bed for her room?" Ezra asked.

"Yes. Bigger." Robin reached to pull over a chair.

"Huh uh. Right there. Sit." Ezra pointed to the end of the bed.

Robin let out a long breath. "Look Ezra...."

"Sit down. It's my room you're invading. I'm in charge here," Ezra said.

"Very well, my guest." Robin sat down on the foot of the bed. "If I must oblige my guest."

"You brought this bed from Boston, I heard. Why? Liked it that much?" Ezra asked.

"Didn't want to sleep in my father's bed," Robin said.

"Oh. I heard that," Ezra said.

"Ezra..." Robin lowered his eyes. "I can't sleep with us angry at each other. You and I went to war together, basically. I can't live with us having this problem."

"I...am to blame for this. I realize," Ezra said. "Marie told you about what I said about Luke but did she tell you what Jasper did to me. Oh, and Luke totally has my drawings."

"What?"

"Ah hah. I thought she told you and you didn't give a shit what happened to me," Ezra said. "So I was mad at you for nothing. You don't know."

"Ezra, what happened with Jasper?"

Ezra sipped beautiful smokey scotch. He savored its smoothness compared to the brandy fire. "Jasper is lonely. He tried his usual suck ass approach with me and I...well...that is not the way I should tell you the story. I should be a better storyteller, use my Ottoman caravan story telling heritage..."

"What did Jasper do, you crazy son of a bitch?"

They both burst out laughing.

"Jasper came down to the river to have sex with me. He saw me naked," Ezra said.

"No."

"Saw all the majesty yes," Ezra said. "Interrupted my communing with nature."

"Miles sent him down there with a gun to look after you," Robin said. "You don't carry one. That's all."

"I couldn't have a gun in the river if I did own one," Ezra said. "What do you wear when you go bathing?"

"I know what you don't wear when you bathe, thank you very much," Robin replied.

"That's right. You've seen me naked too," Ezra said. "Why am I not seeing anybody naked?"

"I didn't come here to play games. I came to make sure we are still friends," Robin said.

"Of course we are. Don't be ridiculous," Ezra said.

Robin lowered his chin and smiled. "Very well then. Good night, Ezra."

Ezra patted the other side of the bed. "You don't have to go."

Robin stood up and refilled Ezra's glass again. "Don't do *anything* in that bed."

"Nothing you haven't done in it."

Ezra followed Robin out toward the barn, pleading for time to draw him.

"Ezra, pace yourself. You're going to be here all summer," Robin said to him.

Ezra shrugged. "What?"

"You'll have plenty of time to draw or paint me. I promise," Robin said.

"We're only here a few weeks," Ezra said.

Robin crossed the barn to take Ezra under his arm. And he tried to turn him away from the stock men. "Ez, you can't take those babies more than two hours away from Marie. You're here all summer. And it is all right."

"Oh...when was I going to be told that?"

"It's an assumption I made. But then I know Alice and I hear things from Marie. So, you're all right. And you are going to be here probably until summer ends," Robin said gently.

The anguish on Ezra's face was a surprise to them all. And Robin kept an arm around his shoulders even when he tried to pull away.

"Walk with me. Let's talk. What's the problem?" Robin walked Ezra out of the barn, toward the hilltop.

"It just seems like a very long time to impose on you," Ezra said.

"It's no imposition."

"I mean, we are four people, and two babies, and those two fucking horses I don't even need except to get back to New Haven." Ezra shook his head.

"Hey. We can work everything out. What else is…"

"I feel like I need to compensate you, room and board and…."

"No." Robin walked with him out of ear shot of the stockmen. They stopped on the hilltop at the end of the barns. "I stayed in your house for two months. I ate all your food. I drank all your brandy. You have to stay here at least two months before we have that conversation. Besides, you're forgetting the obvious fact that you and I are extremely wealthy men. Right?"

Ezra let out a breath. He was nearly in tears.

"Money is no object between us. What are you stressed about? The team you brought and that beautiful brougham?" Robin said. "I can sell off your horses and take that carriage off your hands. I'm quiet jealous of it. Mine is too small now that I have a family. You only need a horse and carriage to get back to New Haven and we can bring you."

Ezra ran a hand up through his hair and finally nodded.

"You're here for at least two months, probably four. And it's all for your children. It's okay, Ezra."

"You're right of course. I don't know why I didn't understand that it would take that long." Ezra shook his head.

"You and Beth don't talk about these things?" Robin asked.

"I'm not sure she knows the time this will take. She hasn't said a thing to me about it," Ezra said.

"Let's have Marie and Alice talk to her about it. We don't want her to feel stress. And she is going to pick this up from you if you go in there like you are right now," Robin said. "It is better if you and I are completely together on this. You are staying as long as your children and Beth need Marie's help. There is nothing financially you need to do here."

"Robin, don't know how I can ever thank you for this and for Marie. What she's doing...I know... is saving my babies lives."

Robin took that and paused. He looked out over the river valley. "I couldn't love her more. I like your cavalry painting. We won that battle. Why don't you finish it?"

"Oh I will. Then I will start the family portrait," Ezra said.

"About that carriage," Robin said. "I want to buy it from you."

"Don't be ridiculous. Take it," Ezra said. "For all the troubles I cause you."

Robin laughed. "That carriage isn't worth all your trouble. You make me laugh. Now those old nags you brought here..."

"What would you do with them? If when we do leave you take us to New Haven with your new bigger carriage and your own giant Friesians?" Ezra asked.

"All they're going to do is eat and shit up their stalls until you have some need for them. I can have the boys bring them to town and sell them off the next time they go," Robin said. "Do you need them?"

"No. I don't even like them. When do they go to town again? I'll need to post a letter to Adam. He'll need to know I'll be gone longer than anticipated," Ezra said. "And to Jonas."

"I thought you were terrible at writing. I mean, you learned to write left to right in your language."

"I am terrible at English. But Aaron writes for me."

"Are you getting along with Jonas now?"

"Oh yes. I moved him into the guest room I stayed in before the wedding and gifted him with a box of fine cigars. He's been my humble assistant ever since."

"And Jasper?" Robin asked.

Ezra's eyebrows rose. "I am trying to make friends with him. Trying."

"I do believe Frida fancies you," Marie remarked.

Ezra looked up, sitting cross-legged in the armchair with Frida sleeping in his arms. "I believe my singing puts her to sleep because I'm boring."

"When are you ever boring?" Marie shot back.

"A soothing reason, my love," Elizabeth said. "Your voice is soothing."

"Thank you, Beth," he said softly.

"Want me to move her to her bed?" Marie asked.

"No, she's fine. I have nothing better to do," Ezra said.

"Mind her kicking in her sleep or she'll make a soprano of you," Marie warned. "Robin learned that the hard way."

Ezra almost burst out laughing. The toddler did awaken enough to wrap her arms around his neck, and that made him smile. "I was a soprano when I sang in the children's chorus. Then overnight, suddenly this voice on an eleven-year-old."

"I like your voice very much," Marie told him.

"How does one not love a man who is so good with children?" Beth beamed at him.

"I can't take credit for that as men never really do grow up," Ezra replied. "I wish I could read to her, but I really only read well in Turkish."

"Except for menus," Elizabeth told him.

"I would like very much to see what your written language is like," Marie admitted. "I can't imagine writing backwards across the paper."

Ezra smiled warmly. "I will show you tomorrow. And maybe you two can help me with my English letters."

"Well Beth will have to help you with that. I only read and write in French," Marie said.

"Beth can't teach me anything. She has no patience," Ezra said.

That made the women laugh.

"He learns very slowly," Beth teased.

They all laughed until Ezra caught on. "Oh. Oh, you're evil if you mean in bed." But then he smiled. "When you're that beautiful, you've got to forgive a guy."

"C'mon. Boys' day trip into Norwich." Robin waved Ezra over.

"What?"

"You're dressed just fine. Let's go. Get out of here for a change," Robin said.

Ezra followed him out toward the barn.

"Marie told Elizabeth we were kidnapping you for a day. We have a list of supplies to shop for in Norwich and we are selling off your horses," Robin said.

"If you say so," Ezra said.

Just then, Jasper drove Ezra's brougham out of the barn, pulled by Robin's two Friesians. He set the brake there in the roundabout. "Climb aboard, gentlemen."

"I'd better get my hat," Ezra said.

"Got it." Jasper handed it down to him.

"Oh. Thank you." Ezra then realized Jasper had gotten it from his bedroom.

Miles led the first of Ezra's two draught horses out and tied it to the back of the carriage. Then he returned to the barn for the other one.

Robin opened the carriage door and climbed up inside. He scooted over on velvet seating to make room.

Ezra climbed in with him.

"You'll take money for this right? What did you pay for it?" Robin began counting out Connecticut paper money.

"No. You can have it. It wasn't that much." Ezra sat beside him.

"What did you pay for it?" Robin had already counted out two hundred dollars.

"Ah, two twenty-five, I believe."

Robin added the twenty-five to it and handed it to Ezra. "I love this thing. You have to let me buy it off you."

Ezra's eyebrows rose. "Sold. If you insist."

"I insist."

Ezra accepted the money and took out his leather purse to put this in it and then repocketed it inside his jacket.

Miles spoke to Jasper outside and then climbed in, to sit facing Robin and Ezra. "Off we go, gentlemen. This is a Clarence, isn't it?"

"What?"

"Yes, it is. I'm sure of it," Robin said. "It's a Clarence carriage. Named after the Duke of Clarence, in England."

"I'm sorry those horses are such a problem," Ezra said.

"No problem if you like shoveling," Miles remarked.

"Simple fact is, if you don't need them, we'll get them sold off for you. You'll get a better price in Norwich," Robin said.

"They won't sell in Canterbury. They're too old to work a field," Miles said.

"You're saying they sold me old horses?" Ezra asked. "Well to be honest, I only needed them to get me from New Haven to your house and back. I was going to sell horse and carriage back when we got to the train."

"We'll save you the trouble," Robin said.

"What did you pay for them?" Miles asked.

"Forty dollars each," Ezra said.

Miles met eyes with Robin. His blank expression said more to Ezra than if he'd teased him outright.

"Oh. It's all right. I never bought a horse before. I guess they knew that, huh?" Ezra said.

"I can probably get you thirty each. Livery in Norwich owes us, after all the business we do there," Miles said.

"If you hold a gun to his head," Robin said.

"I can get thirty-five for those. You watch," Miles said.

"You won't get more than thirty for a fifteen-year-old horse," Robin said.

"Don't worry about it guys. I don't care about the money," Ezra told them. "So what is Norwich famous for?"

"Dancing girls slapping Miles in the face."

Ezra laughed as he looked down at his hat.

Ezra was perusing a white lace shawl as Miles entered the shop and met Robin at the door. Ezra held the lace up to the light and let it smooth over his hands appreciatively.

"He's looking at that for his wife, isn't he?" Miles whispered.

"God, I hope so."

"Got $35 a horse for him," Miles said. "I had to twist some arms to get that. But I got it. Told them we vastly overpaid for that last mare."

"Thank you. I don't know why, but I sensed some shortness of money on his part. He's here longer than expected. He's worried about that for some reason," Robin said.

"That why you bought his carriage?"

"No, I really wanted that carriage. You know what? Tell him you got his $40 back. I'll make up the difference." Robin watched Ezra buying that white shawl and the young lady behind the counter was flirting with him to no avail, reaching to touch his curly black hair. "Do you have the extra ten dollars? I don't want him to see me handing you money."

"I've got it." Miles looked down into his own pocketbook and counted out the paper money.

Ezra met them at the door, putting his top hat back on his head, and the box containing the shawl under his arm.

Miles put the money into Ezra's hand. "Got your $40 a horse back." He patted Ezra on the arm at the same time. "See? You didn't do so badly buying those animals after all."

"Oh? Thank you, Miles." Ezra didn't stop to count it but put it away into his inner coat pocket and his leather purse. "I know that had to be your skill as a salesman."

"You got that right." Miles nodded with a smile.

"Anybody hungry?" Robin asked.

"Always," Ezra said.

"Not the café." Miles pointed across the street to the very same tavern where Robin and Michael Poole had seen the dancing girls, years before. "Jasper said he'd meet us there."

Ezra followed Miles and Robin into the tavern, immediately happy to hear the music but grinning and shaking his head over the dancing girls on the stage. They were shown to a table away from the stage and the loud piano.

A woman server with quite a plunging neckline came to take their drink orders. It was a bottle of whiskey and four glasses.

Ezra was looking up at the girls with an elbow on the table and a hand over his mouth.

Miles sat back, looking up at them as well. "First time, Ezra?"

"Ah, no. I've been to establishments like this before. Besides…" Ezra laid his hands down on the table. "Miles, I've paid women to take off their clothes for me to paint them."

"And you just painted them?" Miles questioned.

Ezra looked at him. "That's right."

The server brought their drinks to them, observing the gentlemen. Her eyes lingered on Robin and then Ezra. "Hmmm. I never saw this one around before. How old are you, young man? You're not out for your first are you?"

Miles and Robin burst out laughing.

Ezra looked up into her eyes and smirked.

"Because we have a few things off the menu for any young man as handsome as you." She leaned in to tell Ezra.

Ezra gestured for her to lean closer. "Sorry, darling but I'm married."

After a moment the woman sighed. "Lucky woman. We have boys too but you didn't hear it from me, hon." She walked away.

The guys burst out laughing.

Ezra looked down to roll up a cigarette. "Please tell me that's where Jasper went."

"Where?" Robin said.

Ezra eyed him and then licked the cigarette paper.

Miles got up from the table. "Wait right here. I'll be back." He left them.

Robin sat back with his drink and a grin.

"He's going too?" Ezra said.

"What do you think?" Robin looked at him.

Ezra's eyebrows rose for a bit. "Well. He's not asking for a boy. Now I know where Jasper went. You ever paid for it?"

"I never had to pay for it," Robin said. "If I went back there with him today, I still wouldn't have to pay for it. Pretend I don't speak English so well. Be charming."

That made Ezra smile. "Just exactly how many notches are on the bedpost I'm sleeping under?"

"Oh that one? No. My adventures were all in Europe and India," Robin said.

"Don't take away my fantasies in that bed."

"Here comes Jasper." Robin waved a hand up to get Jasper's attention across the room of tables.

Ezra looked up as Jasper took his seat with them.

Ezra lit his cigarette for a couple puffs and offered it to Robin then.

"Where's Miles?" Jasper said.

Ezra just burst out laughing at that.

"What?" Jasper patted a hand on Ezra's upper arm.

Ezra pushed his hand off. "What were you doing?"

"Picking up some tailoring," Jasper said. "Why?"

"Where is it?" Ezra said.

"In the carriage. Why?"

"You need to get laid and not with me," Ezra remarked.

"I don't want to get caught here. No way," Jasper said.

"Get a woman," Ezra said.

"Shut up, princess," Jasper snapped.

"Hey." Robin banged his hand on the table. "No fighting or they'll throw us out of here."

"You're not actually looking at those dancing girls are you?" Ezra asked.

"No harm in looking."

Chapter Twenty-Three   Three Musketeers Again

It was quite late when the gentlemen arrived back at Robin's home. The ladies had gone to bed but Ezra stopped in Beth's room for a good night kiss. Their two babies were sleeping. Beth sat up in bed in tears.

"What is it?" Ezra sat on the edge of her bed and took her hands.

"You were gone so long. Ezzy, oh, did they take you to a prostitute?"

"No. What? No, darling. It's a long ride to Norwich and back," Ezra told her softly. "That's all. I brought you something. Look." He offered her a box.

"You really didn't?" Elizabeth asked.

"Of course not. I don't want any woman except you. I love you," Ezra told her. "Besides, you know I'm too shy to be with any other woman. I almost fainted when we did it."

"But I've heard they have those women in Norwich. Why else did they take you there?"

"Just to sell those horses."

"For hours?"

"Really? Want to know? Miles got hooked up," Ezra said. "I think Robin took me to see if I needed to do any shopping and Miles needed to get laid."

"Oh? Oh my." Beth brought her hand to her mouth. "Oh my. Miles is that sort?"

"He's a dick. Can't you tell?"

Beth suddenly smiled. She almost laughed. Then she opened the box he brought to find the beautiful lace shawl. "Oh Ezzy, I love it. It's the lace shawl from your painting."

"And look, darling. Chocolates from Switzerland."

"Come here. I want to show you something." Marie gestured to Ezra to enter the master bedroom.

Reluctantly, Ezra entered, looking around. "Really? I might burst into flames in here."

"You better not." Marie disappeared into her walk-in closet for a moment.

Ezra stood at the seating area near the foot of their bed, looking at the place where Robin and would sleep with her.

Marie came out with a blue uniform jacket and trousers.

Ezra's mouth fell open.

She laid the jacket out on the sofa and then the trousers beside them. And then she pointed toward the two crossed swords over the fireplace. "One of those goes with this uniform."

He glanced quickly at the swords but then back to the uniform. "Thank you, Marie. Do you think I could borrow these for a little while?"

"Of course. Don't get any paint on them," Marie said.

"Does Robin know you are loaning them to me?"

"He said it's all right, yes."

Ezra ran a hand over the lapel of the jacket. "He actually wore this ten years ago? This is beautiful."

"Try it on if you like," Marie encouraged.

"I...oh my God." Ezra quickly stripped off his own jacket and dropped it over a chair. Then he picked up the blue Cavalry coat. He slid his arm down into it and Marie helped him get his other arm in. She lifted it up onto his shoulders. "Careful. I think your shoulders are broader."

He looked down at himself wearing Robin's uniform. He inspected pockets and buttons. "Well and Robin was much younger then. Look at how slim he was. I could hardly button it.

"I don't know how you got it so right without ever seeing it." Marie stepped back to look at him. "You look good in that."

"Me in uniform. I must see this." Ezra moved toward a mirror to look at the jacket. "Thanks for this. I will paint in the details of the jacket and return this to you." Ezra turned his back to her and removed the cavalry jacket. In just his shirt and vest, he carried the jacket to the sofa and picked up his own blazer. "Did Luke ever... attack you?"

"No. Never." Marie saw the way his eyes studied her. He was very serious.

"In the kitchen?" Ezra asked.

"Oh my God." Marie jumped back a step. "It wasn't Luke. It was one of the bank robbers. Why do you ask that?"

"There is still an echo of it, in the old kitchen. I believe," Ezra said softly. "You were on the floor. You run into Robin's arms. Robin took you upstairs and...took you in that bed."

Marie wrapped her arms tightly in front of her. "That was the following night. Adam couldn't have told you that. How did you know that?"

"Luke has never laid a hand on you?"

"No. Not ever. It was the bank robber. Stuart. He tried to attack me, was attacking me, but Robin came in."

"Robin shot him," Ezra said.

"Yes. But that was days later. Do you ever see things that haven't happened yet?" Marie asked him.

"N...no. I pick up echoes of what has happened, I think," Ezra said. "I fear I may have thought ill of Luke when it was this bank robber instead. Sleeping in the old house has me picking up many strange things. Robin's father used to yell at you."

"Yes, but he yelled at everybody," Marie said. "He wasn't well."

"That's kind of you," Ezra said. "I was raised that you never yell at girls."

Marie made eye contact with him and slowly smiled.

Ezra picked up the uniform jacket, folding it respectfully over his arm. "I won't get any paint on this. I promise. I will have Aaron model it for me. It will be big on him. Merci beaucoup." He gave her a kiss on the cheek.

"A letter from Adam." Robin sat down at the table and unsealed the paper. Inside he found it written on the back but containing another letter. "Ezra. This is for you."

He passed another letter in brown paper addressed to Ezra August, 12 Wall Street, New York City, America.

"Oh my God." Ezra broke the seal on that and opened it.

Elizabeth leaned over to see strange writing that made no sense at all to her.

Ezra let out a howl that made Prince Andrew cower beneath Elizabeth's chair. "Whooo oooh! It's from my brother Demir!" His eyes scanned the page quickly, reading the Turkish writing.

"That's astounding. And what does Adam say?" Marie asked her husband.

"He's fine. Zoey sends her love. Jonas brought this letter down to him to see if he could get it to Ezra at our house," Robin read.

"Is everything all right. What does your brother say?" Elizabeth asked.

Ezra was tearing up as he read. He sniffled. "Demir is back from the army. My brother Ozan died in the war. My father has passed. Mother and everyone else is fine. My sister Banou has married and has two children. Mother lives with her. I'm an uncle. Little sister Haleh is to be married soon. They thank me for the money I sent. If I send more, Demir and Aydin would like to come to America. Two of my brothers want to come to see me. Oh my God. I'm the eldest son. I should be looking after my mother. I ran away from home like an asshole."

Elizabeth kissed his mouth. "Do whatever you may for them. Now you have a place to reach them. And look at this wonderful writing in Turkish."

Ezra wiped his eyes and read his letter again.

"How old are these brothers?" Jasper asked. "Are any of them like you?"

"Nobody's like me." Ezra counted on his fingers. "Demir must be 22 now. Aydin would be 19. I'll write a really long letter to them."

Ezra was painting detail into the forelimbs of the horse in his painting, the results of his study of horses in the yard and his numerous drawings. Finally, he could bring out the muscle tone and apply the shading that he needed. He stepped back to take it in from a proper viewing distance, paintbrush in one hand and palette in the other.

"How long have you been there?" he said aloud.

From the doorway, Jasper entered. "A while."

"What do you think, horse man?"

"Amazing," Jasper said. "I've never seen anyone do what you do."

Ezra walked to set down his palette and the brush. He picked up a glass of water only to find a paint brush in it. His brow furrowed. He picked up another glass and poured water from the pitcher into it, for a drink.

Jasper wandered into the room, looking at drawings along the wall and the potions on the tables. "Are you a chemist?" He picked up a jar of blue powder and started to open the lid.

"Don't do that. Put down the pretty powder." Ezra began replenishing his palette with oil colors. He used a palette knife to load dollops of paint from the jars that Aaron had prepared. "Where is Aaron? He's supposed to be doing this for me."

"I saw him drawing the colts out in the pen," Jasper said. "Do you need me to get him for you?"

"Always said one day when I'm rich I will pay someone to do this for me." Ezra delved into a jar of cobalt blue. "That powder makes this color paint but in the powder form, breathing it in can kill you, or so I was told."

"Ezra...can I ask you a question?"

Ezra went for a jar of titanium white next. He wiped off his knife on a towel. "June gave me a bunch of these. Thank goodness. I'm ruining one or two a day. What?"

"Are...are we friends now?"

Ezra stopped and looked at him.

"I...I've tried very hard to be nice to you, since the thing at the river," Jasper said, looking down at the floor.

"Jasper. Jasper. Jasper." Ezra put his hands on his hips. "If there is one thing to come from my being here, besides magnificent paintings, it will be that you finally learn how to hit on a man. And that wasn't it."

"I..."

Ezra waited.

Jasper looked at him and finally let out a long breath. "It's just that...it's not easy. You don't make it easy. You treated me different ever since the river."

"What do you mean? That was my second day here. I only just got here," Ezra said.

Jasper walked around to the other side of the table, across from him. He could speak more quietly being closer to Ezra. But closer to Ezra he could see the colors of his lips and a swipe of white paint on his cheek. "You have paint on your face."

Ezra's eyebrows flicked and he just picked up that towel. He handed it across the table and waited.

Jasper accepted the towel and folded it to give him a clean spot. He then reached across the table to gently wipe the paint off Ezra's cheek and a bit on his nose. But then he tried to touch the back of his hand to the tuft of facial hair beneath Ezra's chin.

Ezra grabbed the towel. "Thank you." He collected his palette and a clean brush before returning to his cavalry painting.

Jasper stayed behind the table, holding onto the edge of it.

Ezra returned to painting the horse, mixing on his palette the shades of brown that he needed.

"You are beautiful," Jasper finally said softly.

Ezra kept painting.

Jasper made his way slowly toward the door, having received no indication of acceptance from Ezra. "I'll let you get your work done."

"Jasper."

He stopped at the doorway.

"Better."

At dinner that night, Ezra met his wife at the table with a hug and kiss on the mouth. Elizabeth wrapped her arms about his vest as he wore no jacket. Her hand even stole a quick feel of the back side of his trousers.

Ezra smiled as he held the chair for Elizabeth and then took his seat beside her. Then he found Jasper watching him from down the table. He just reached for the pitcher of water on the table and poured for himself and his wife.

"We're thinking about moving to Norwich. There's a house we've been looking at and the children can attend school there," Constable Poole was saying.

"Surprised you stayed so long in the old house," Robin said. "Not much need for you in Canterbury, is there?"

"Well, you don't have stockmen breaking up the tavern anymore, so no," Poole said.

That drew some laughter about the table.

"We try to behave ourselves," one of them said.

Ezra looked down at Beth's hand on his thigh.

A basket of biscuits, bowl of potatoes, and bowl of beans were passed about the table.

"The girls went down to the river this afternoon. It was lovely on hot days such as this," Marie said.

"It was wonderful. I never did such a thing in my life," Elizabeth said enthusiastically. She patted Ezra on the thigh and then picked up her fork to select some potatoes.

"You never swam in a river before?" Ezra asked.

"Never outdoors at all. I can't swim, of course. But to wade out into a moving river was so thrilling," Elizabeth said.

"Who went with you?" Ezra asked.

"June and Marie," Beth said. "June insisted on bringing a musket just in case of snakes. She checked all the rocks on the shoreline before we settled down with our baskets. Don't worry. She was most protective."

"I'm certain." Ezra sat back but still met eyes with Jasper. He blinked and looked away from him.

After the dinner of fried chicken and dessert of white cake, the ladies went upstairs with the babies while the gentlemen retreated to the porch out back for scotch and smoking.

Ezra strolled out along the porch, tapping his cigarette ashes out over the flower bed below the porch. He was watching the colors change over the fields as the sun went down. Standing there in black trousers and vest, with white linen shirt unbuttoned at the neck and cuffs, he looked very warm. He pushed his hair back from his forehead but it just fell again as it may.

The warmth of a hot early summer day meant that none of the gentlemen wore jackets to dinner. Most were not wearing vests either. Only Ezra and Robin were wearing vests and did not roll up their sleeves.

"The sun sets here every night, but I never noticed it until he did," Jasper remarked, indicating Ezra.

"He sees it with different eyes," Robin said.

Aaron got up and went to Ezra. "Are you painting tonight?"

"No, in the morning," Ezra said. "You can sleep."

"Whatever you say," Aaron said.

"Where are your drawings of the little horses? You must show them to me," Ezra told him.

"I will. I made quite a lot of them this afternoon," Aaron said.

"He's pretty good," Miles spoke up. "I saw them. He's learning."

"I'm struggling with the perspective. To be honest," Aaron said.

Ezra nodded. "I'll help you in the morning."

Ezra left his bedroom door open just enough to get a breeze through his windows and down the hallway. But inside, with the light of one oil lamp, he unbuttoned his vest. He stepped out of his shoes. Then he laid the vest on the chair and unbuttoned his shirt down from the top. He pulled out the tails and pulled it back off his shoulders when he heard the door creek.

"You are out of your mind if you think…." Ezra spun.

Elizabeth slipped into his room and closed the door. "What?"

He doubled over for a second. "Darling, you startled me." He stood up with his hand to his heart.

"I know." She giggled. "I love to watch you undress. Why don't you keep going?"

"Uh." Ezra paused to pull down the covers on Robin's bed. He moved the pillows to flatten them. "All right."

Beth walked toward the other side of the bed and opened her robe to reveal her nude and slender body beneath it.

Ezra smirked a bit. He opened his belt and trousers. "How do you look that great already?"

Beth slid into the bed, dropping her robe over the foot of the bed. "I don't know. No time to eat anything for myself."

He turned around, dropped his trousers, and sat down. "What, um, you're feeling okay? What do you have in mind?"

"Just kiss me."

He laid down with her and their mouths met. Elizabeth knew to let it start soft with her husband, and let him come around.

Jasper adjusted the stirrup height on one side and moved around the front of the horse to adjust the other. He held onto the reins. "This is Marie's horse. She's very mild mannered and calm."

"I know that, but it's the horse I'm worried about." Ezra looked down at Jasper.

"Funny." Jasper pushed Ezra's boot fully into the stirrup. He began tugging on saddle straps. "The only thing is she likes to take a deep breath when you saddle her. So every time, every time, you have to tighten straps later."

"Cleaver." Ezra accepted the reins from Jasper.

"Don't do anything." Jasper walked over to mount his own horse and pull it up beside Ezra in the barn. "You sure you want to do this?"

"Well, what's the trick to it? It has a mind of its own right? How do I tell it what to go do with itself, without getting myself killed?" Ezra asked.

"Very simple. Pull on the right rein to turn right. Left to turn left. Pull back on both to stop. Whoa means stop." Jasper reached over and patted Ezra on the thigh. "I'll take you around the circle a bit before we ride out to the field. Click your heels into the horse's ribs."

Both horses exited the barn side by side. They walked toward the circle drive.

"A horse has three speeds: walk, trot, and gallop. You are only allowed to walk it until you learn how to stay on," Jasper said.

"And what do you call that shit Robin does on his horse?" Ezra said.

"Insanity." Jasper watched Ezra turn his animal into the circle. "I'm going to stay right beside you. Horses are calmer if they are together. My window of opportunity is over, isn't it?"

"What are you talking about?" Ezra rose up in saddle and adjusted his trousers. "Feel like my balls are being squashed."

"That is why, when riding in a gallop, it is best to get your ass up off the saddle and stand in the stirrups. That's what Robin does when he jumps," Jasper said. "Better now? Your balls need a pillow?" Jasper laughed.

Ezra glared at him. "I'm fine. I reckon. Isn't that what cowboys say?"

"You're back with your wife, aren't you?" Jasper asked.

"That's none of your business," Ezra said. "Is this Marie's saddle?"

"No, of course not. Women have a pommel to wrap their right knee around. They ride side saddle, both feet on the left side." Jasper took them around the circle again. "Don't imagine that's the way your wife rides you."

"Hey!" Ezra's voice deepened.

Jasper stopped their horses. "Don't yell. Your horse might take off thinking you're in trouble." He grabbed Ezra's reins.

"Take me to Robin. He'll teach me to ride," Ezra said. "Or I will try to get this animal there myself."

Jasper moved their horses close together until he hit boots with Ezra. Then he grabbed onto Ezra's stirrup leather. "Ezra, how on earth do I tell you how much I want you? You just won't allow anything, will you?"

Ezra looked away, toward the path that led to Robin's jumping course.

"You are so much fun, and such a great painter. Your body is so fucking beautiful," Jasper whispered to him. "I just want to tell you that."

"I appreciate that very much. But I am not going to be with anyone but my wife," Ezra said softly. "And I'm happy for once in my life. I will not fuck it up."

"You're going to miss it with a man someday," Jasper said. "What then? Or...oh, I see. I see what you did. Adam."

"What do you mean?"

"You and Adam. That's why you almost fought with me down at the river. You didn't want me touching Adam," Jasper said.

"I don't want you touching Adam but not because he's my back up." Ezra adjusted his hat, to shade his dark eyes better. He looked at Jasper. "Now teach me to ride this animal or I won't be friends with you."

Jasper released Ezra's saddle and moved apart from him. "Well that's childish. C'mon."

Both horses started onto the trail then. Jasper held his alongside Ezra's.

"I'll be down at the river after work," Jasper said.

"Take me to Robin and do not say such things to me again or I will have to ask him to intervene."

"You're kidding me right?" Jasper said.

Ezra just held onto his reins and bristled. "I can't even get off this thing, man. Do this or I'm telling you, you do not want to see what he will do to you. Take me to Robin."

Jasper just grabbed the reins from him and drew his horse along slightly behind his down the trail. "You shouldn't be on a horse if you can't get off it."

"You didn't teach me how yet, you dick," Ezra said.

"That horse sees a rattlesnake and you'll get off it fast enough. It's called gravity," Jasper said. "I don't want you to get hurt out here. Horseback riding is dangerous."

Ezra looked down at his European saddle. He held onto the pommel in between his thighs. The two horses walked along casually.

Jasper reached over and patted his thigh again. "Relax. You're all right there."

"Get your hand off my leg, man."

The field with Robin's jumper course was ahead of them. Robin was riding the black gelding in the far side of it. Miles was riding on this side and instructing the two stockmen on how to dig out a moat at one of the jumps.

"How many men have you been with?" Jasper asked. "I'll bet you never have to ask for it. I'll bet you always had a partner."

"You're starting to get on my nerves." Ezra bristled.

"You were so pretty there in the river," Jasper said.

Ezra wet his lips and looked away toward Robin.

Miles heard the two horses approaching and when he turned, seeing Ezra on a horse made him ride over quickly to them. He drew alongside Ezra. "What the are you doing, Jasper? He's never ridden before."

"He wanted to learn," Jasper said. "He panicked a bit."

"Give me those reins." Miles reached out to Ezra. "Give them to me!"

Jasper released the leather and turned his horse away.

"You get back to the barn and that mare, now," Miles ordered.

Jasper galloped away and Ezra shuddered in the saddle, weeping such that Miles reined in his horse and grabbed onto Ezra's stirrup leather. Miles quickly glanced at Robin in the distance. "Mr. August, we've got seconds before Robin is here. What the fuck happened?"

"I don't want to say. I just got scared on the horse." Ezra wiped his eyes quickly.

"That's what I'm supposed to tell him? Then get off the horse," Miles said.

"Tell me the fuck how." Ezra cried and wiped his eyes.

"Jesus. Stay right where you are." Miles reached higher up and grabbed Ezra by the forearm. "You are all right. This horse is not going to hurt you. Wipe your eyes and here, drink this." Miles passed a canteen to him.

Ezra saw Robin riding toward them. He accepted the canteen.

"Sit still. You're fine. Focus on the canteen. Take some water," Miles instructed.

Robin rode to a stop and circled round to take position on Ezra's other side. "What are you doing on a horse?"

"Panicking," Miles said for him.

Ezra turned dark eyes on Miles.

"Drink the water, Mr. August. It will help," Miles said.

Ezra opened the cap and drank from Miles's water.

"I don't understand. What are you doing on a horse?" Robin grabbed Ezra's horse's bridle from his side.

"He asked Jasper to train him but he quickly became panicked. Jasper could not help him," Miles said.

"I don't believe that for a second. Ezra doesn't panic," Robin said. "Take it easy. Breathe. Are you okay?"

"I'm better. Yes," Ezra admitted. "Thank you, Miles. So much." He passed the canteen back.

"I saw you ride in. You looked fine from a distance," Robin said. "If you take a turn around the field with me, you might get past this. What do you want to do, my friend?"

"I want to ride with you," Ezra said.

"Miles, stay on his right if you would." Robin took Ezra's reins and brough them all into a walk forward into his field. "Ezra, look ahead and think where you want your horse to go. She understands you. Relax your knees. Relax your thighs. Set your hands on the horse's neck."

"What? Let go of the saddle?"

"You can do it, boy," Miles encouraged. "That horse likes women."

"Miles!"

Ezra looked over at Miles with a bit of a smirk.

Robin led Ezra's horse. "Take it easy. Take a deep breath. Just sit the horse."

They slowly circled the jumper field with encouraging words for Ezra. Eventually Ezra could take his own reins and ride between the two other horses.

"What happened with Jasper?" Robin asked.

"He just won't take no for an answer." Ezra began to weep again. "I kept telling him I won't do it. This time he kept putting his hand on my leg. I know what comes next. I don't want to go through that ever again."

"Whoa. Whoa, now." Robin stopped their horses. "Ezra?"

"I don't think he would force me. But he kept putting his hand on my leg," Ezra said. "Can you just make him leave me alone?"

"I can. And I could make him go away and cool off for a while," Robin said.

"Just...I don't want to be touched. I don't want to be forced. I will fight like a dog if I am forced." Ezra looked away and wiped his eyes.

Miles and Robin met eyes.

When Ezra didn't continue, Robin watched him collecting himself on the other horse. Ezra wiped his eyes and raised his hat to fix his hair.

"You getting tired of that saddle?" Robin asked.

"I thought you'd never ask. My balls are killing me, man."

When Ezra walked out onto the porch that night, he lit a cigarette and after a few puffs handed it to Robin. He then poured himself a scotch and took his seat by sliding a rocker closer to Robin.

Ezra rocked slowly and sipped his scotch.

Robin passed the cigarette back to him. "Little quiet here tonight. Is Aaron coming out?"

"No he has work to finish up," Ezra said. "This would make Adam very jealous, right here. I have you to myself."

Robin smiled. "You and I have something in common that I never realized before."

"Yeah? What?"

"Tell me this isn't true. You attract men the way women are always attracted to me," Robin said.

"Figured that all by yourself? It only took you a year," Ezra said.

Robin laughed.

"Oh and by the way, I had women hitting on me too," Ezra said.

"Yeah, well, subject change," Robin said. "How is it being wealthy now?"

"Oh that is strange. All of a sudden it's 'what can I do for you sir?' instead of all the 'get away from my window. You're scaring all my customers away'."

"And those old painter friends. Are they still coming to your gallery?" Robin asked.

"Yes. Marco moved in upstairs with Albert and Pierre. They sell some paintings," Ezra said. "Adam has quit painting though."

"Why? He's so good."

"He's very good. I just can't get him to paint again. I keep telling him to just come down to the studio, get in the habit again."

"Where are the girls?" Robin asked in the kitchen.

Catherine and Marta were there with the four children.

"They went to pick strawberries," June said.

Robin met eyes with Ezra. "Come on. Dark clouds are coming."

Ezra shot out of his chair. "Where are these berries?"

"Robin knows. Out that way." June pointed.

Ezra followed Robin out of the house and looked up at a black sky to the west. "Jesus."

"Come on." Robin took off at a good trot and soon turned that into a full out run. Ezra was right on his tail.

It began to rain already.

They dashed out along the vegetable garden, past the clothesline, behind the barns, toward the drop off. And then the hail started.

The girls were below and quickly held hands up to shield their heads.

"Come on!" Robin yelled to them. "Leave the baskets and run!"

Ezra ran right past Robin and skidded down the embankment to gather his wife.

Robin was right after him and yelling, "Over there! Run for the cliff."

They grabbed hands with their wives and ran for the cover of nearby cliffs. Hail was coming down in pea sized pellets but some of them were larger. Beneath the cliff there was just enough room for the four of them to huddle down together and escape the deluge.

The men put their wives between them and they all grabbed onto each other.

"Didn't you see they sky darken?" Robin asked.

"Couldn't see it with the cliff over us," Marie explained. "All of sudden we had hail. I would have brought us here."

"Very good then. We wait it out," Robin said. "Everybody all right?"

"Yes," Elizabeth said. "Ezzy?"

"Fine. Yes." He held her close to him and wrapped around her. Ezra's hair was wet down on his head and neck, as if he'd been bathing.

"Robin, what if this is all night?" Marie asked.

"The worst will blow over. We're already wet through. We'll walk back when the hail and wind stops," Robin said.

"We have to. The babies," Marie reminded.

"Marta and Catherine have them," Robin said.

"The twins will need to nurse," Marie insisted. "We only slipped away to pick some strawberries for pies."

Ezra met eyes with Robin over the girl's heads.

"Don't worry. Let this pass and we'll go," Robin said.

Hail was coming down in marble sized pieces, bouncing on the ground before them.

"That would hurt," Ezra remarked. "The sky's so green."

"Oh no," Elizabeth said. "I've heard that means cyclones. You don't get those here, do you?"

"I've only heard of one or two," Marie said. "In all my life."

Ezra reached down and pulled up the end of Elizabeth's skirt to find her walking boots. "Will they take cover in the house?"

"June will see to it," Robin said. "Miles will get all the horses into the barn. We are the problem. We sit tight for a while."

"Robin, you got a gun on you?" Ezra asked.

"No. Why?"

"We've got a problem," Ezra said.

"What, darling?" Elizabeth asked.

Then they all heard the rattle.

"Ezra…" Robin said.

Before they knew what happened, Ezra stomped on it, hard.

Robin lunged over and grabbed the snake by the tail and swung it out away from them.

Marie pulled Robin back in from the hail.

Ezra sat back down and embraced his wife. "No way that just happened." He looked at his boot.

Robin reached over Elizabeth and grabbed Ezra by the arm. "Don't touch that boot. Let the rain wash it off. That venom is still deadly."

Ezra looked up at him, mouth open.

"You stomped on a rattle snake? Are you out of your mind?" Robin scolded.

"I didn't have any choice! It looked at you for one second and I had to act," Ezra said.

Between them, Elizabeth held onto Ezra's arm and Robin's. "It's safe now? It's dead?"

"Blood everywhere. I think he flattened its head." Robin released his grip on Ezra and took his seat again beside Marie. "Son of a bitch."

"Well, we have all the heros right here," Marie said. "Where did it go?"

"Out that way. I threw it that way," Robin pointed. "It was bleeding from the head. It probably won't make it. Ezra got it good."

"Son of a bitch," Ezra said. "That was a rattle snake."

"Son of a bitch," Marie repeated. "We would have been here alone with that if not for you guys. I love you guys."

"We love you too," Ezra said. "I only feel bad about that strawberry pie."

They laughed and Elizabeth clung to her husband.

Robin checked his watch.

Marie met eyes with him.

The four of them huddled together. The hail passed. Wind increased. Something crashed hard above them. But they remained sheltered from wind and rain where they sat.

"Robin? Could we bring horses down here and pick up the girls?" Ezra questioned.

"Give it an hour. If it comes to that, I will bring back horses for them," Robin said. "You've had one ride."

"I know that. But I need to get my wife to the house within another hour or so," Ezra said. "And I will."

"I know you will. If it is just raining, we can walk back," Robin said. "Remain calm everyone. Ezra, don't ever do that again."

"What?"

"Step on a goddamn deadly snake."

"Shit. We've got scorpions in Turkey. You shut up."

They emerged from the shelter of the cliff when the sky lightened and it was only raining.

"Robin. I want my strawberries." Marie tugged on his arm.

"Really?"

"We worked hard for those berries. Strawberry pie," Marie insisted.

"Wait here." Robin and Ezra dashed off to collect the two baskets of berries.

When the four of them reached the porch, Robin stopped Ezra. He passed the baskets to Marie and Elizabeth who stood out of the rain.

"Get that boot off and let's have it washed off," Robin said.

Miles and Aaron joined them on the porch. "What'd he step in? Need I ask?"

"Rattlesnake venom," Robin said. "Miles, take that boot out to the barn and wash it off good. Scrub it. And be careful."

"What? Why?" Miles said, holding out an arm to steady Ezra as he pulled off his left boot.

"Ezra killed a rattlesnake out there."

"Out where?"

"Near the cliff. Not far from the strawberry patch. I threw it into the long grass," Robin said.

"I have to go find it and bury the thing. It's still lethal, even dead," Miles said.

"I know that, but I had to fling it away from us," Robin said. "He killed it."

Miles turned to Ezra and took him by the lapel. "Did you step on a rattlesnake? You bad ass, crazy son of a bitch."

Everyone broke up laughing.

"Listen, hero, just don't ever do that again," Robin said.

"It looks like the Lee's carriage," June announced.

Marie and Robin hurried down to the front door, just in time as a carriage arrived.

"Mr. Lee. What brings you out here today?" Robin called.

"Well, I was in town and came across something that needed delivery to you, Robin," Mr. Lee called down from his carriage.

"I'm not expecting anything," Robin said.

Ezra came out beside him, just as Adam opened the back door of the carriage.

"This young man needed delivery to you," Lee said.

"Hey!" Ezra ran forward with his arms out.

Adam put hands on his shoulders and laughed as he was pulled over Ezra's shoulder. Ezra spun around, twirling Adam above him. Adam's top hat hit the ground.

Robin hurried in and rescued Adam, getting him down to the ground anyway, for a big hug.

"Where is Zoey?" Marie asked.

"She had to stay home. Expecting again. She said I could visit for awhile and get out of her hair," Adam said. "She sends her regrets, Marie."

"I knew you couldn't stand me here with Robin to myself," Ezra said.

"Excuse me?" Marie picked up Adam's hat.

Robin walked up the steps with an arm around Adam and Ezra.

"The three Musketeers. Together again!"

By Susan Eddy

Made in the USA
Monee, IL
03 July 2024

61182196R00252